Dear Reader,

No doubt you are on the verge of your annual summer
vacation. Don't forget to pack the essentials – suntan
lotion, sunglasses and the two latest sizzling novels from
Scarlet!

Cody Aguillar, in the exciting sequel to Tina Leonard's
novel *It Takes Two*, never does anything he doesn't want to
do! Lavender-haired Stormy Nixon is also used to getting
her own way, so when the two meet in *Desperado*, something's gotta give! Also this month, you are invited, by
Clare Benedict, to *Sophie's Wedding*. Three women gather
for their best friend's wedding, and while Alison wonders
if she'll ever find true happiness, Francine must decide
between an old love and a new opportunity, and Carol asks
herself if her own marriage is worth saving.

Next month sees the start of our exciting *Scarlet* hardback
series. Watch out for our very special launch title and let
me know what you think! Also, don't forget to complete
our questionnaire this month – you could win a sassy
Scarlet T-shirt!

Till next month,

Sally Cooper

SALLY COOPER,
Editor-in-Chief – *Scarlet*

PS: To reserve your copy of *Dark Desire*, our first *Scarlet*
hardback, send us your details NOW!

About the Author

Tina Leonard has a college degree, is married and has two children. She's been to Bermuda, Mexico and the West Indies, and has travelled around the United States.

Tina hails from Texas and her native land is obviously a great source of inspiration to her. We think Tina's writing has exactly the right blend of warmth and passion for *Scarlet* and your very positive reaction to her first three titles for the list, *It Takes Two*, *Never Say Never* and *Secret Sins*, proved that we were right.

Other *Scarlet* title available this month:

SOPHIE'S WEDDING – Clare Benedict

TINA LEONARD

DESPERADO

SCARLET

Enquiries to:
Robinson Publishing Ltd
7 Kensington Church Court
London W8 4SP

First published in the UK by Scarlet, 1998

A copy of the British Library Cataloguing in
Publication data is available from the British Library

ISBN 1-85487-881-6

Printed and bound in the EC

10 9 8 7 6 5 4 3 2 1

Dear Reader,

In a place in Texas there is a small town my family and I love to visit. Nowhere else could Desperado have been set, and I instinctively knew this the first time I passed through. Rattlesnake Annie told her story in **It Takes Two**, but with my imagination and my heart firmly captured by the area, I had to let Crazy Cody tell his. Whether there will be another book set there remains to be seen, but I do know this. There is magic in the place I call Desperado, and when my family and I pass by, we always have to stop for a visit.

Many thanks and hugs of appreciation to my family: Tim, Lisa, and Dean. You make my life special.

Many more thanks to my agent, Paige Wheeler, for keeping me working and lending an ear.

This book would not be possible without the sharp eyes and appreciative critiquing of Leesa Whitson and Georgia Haynes. Your time and effort is invaluable to me. Thank you.

CHAPTER 1

'Crazy Cody ain't gonna do it. You fellows are wasting your time.' In Desperado, Texas, Sheriff Sloan McCallister crossed his boots on the desk and grinned at the two men hunched in chairs in front of him.

'He's gotta! He's got the best and biggest piece of land in Desperado, damn fool snakefighter. Those movie folks are gonna go elsewhere if they can't make their picture here.' Curvy Watkins glared at Sloan for stating the fact that had them wrestled to the ground. Nobody could get Cody Aguillar to do a damn thing he didn't want to do. To a man, nobody wanted to be the one to approach him about using his land for filming a movie. Cody was a loner. He was also crazier than a coot, with his rattlesnake-skinning and his damn guitar. Some nights, when it was late enough to see a good harvest moon, a body could hear him playing that Spanish music. The sound was haunting, and the specter of the lonely man strumming that soulful music, with nobody but his old ma and

1

some barn owls for company, could rattle the bones of a corpse.

'He ain't gonna do it for any of us, that's a fact.' Pick Jenkins picked his teeth in the fashion which had earned him his nickname, and spat. 'That damn brother-in-law of his has made him too wealthy with his fancy schemes. Between him and Zach Rayez, they got enough money to interest the President. I say it's 'bout time they contributed something to Desperado.'

'You say it, Pick, but I don't see you suggesting how.' Sloan grinned at the two older men. Cody and Sloan had built up a healthy heap of respect for each other. If these two old fools thought they were going to elect him to go railroad Cody, they could take themselves back to the post office and sit back down on their self-appointed benches.

'Well,' Pick said, shooting a glance at the closed door of Sloan's office, 'I says we send *her*.'

All three men stared at the door. On the other side sat Stormy Nixon, a movie scout from Los Angeles. She had approached Curvy about the project, since he was the mayor of the town. Immediately, he had commandeered Pick, and together they'd brought Stormy to Sloan's office in order to draw him into the scheme. She'd said her fantastic piece, which brought to mind a vision of tourist dollars floating through Desperado. Pick and Curvy were drooling, but Sloan held back his enthusiasm. It was all well and good for them to think he had some sway with Cody, but it wasn't

2

true. Respect wasn't the same thing as leverage, and, while he had one with Cody, he didn't have the other.

Stormy Nixon, he hated to tell them, wasn't going to have any leverage, either.

'I think you boys are off your horses if you send her out to Cody's house,' Sloan said. 'It's a bad thing, sending a woman to do your dirty work.'

'Ah, hell! It's her job, Sloan. She's the one hunting for a place to film. Let her go ask him.' Pick tried to look innocent, as if the suggestion were perfectly reasonable. Sloan knew better. Neither of the two cowards wanted to be the one to have Cody's boot planted firmly in his butt as he kicked them off his property.

'I'm throwing in my lot with Curvy. You ain't got a better idea, and we can't lose the opportunity of at least letting Cody mull over her proposition. It could mean the difference between putting Desperado on the map, and us always sitting in nowhere.' Pick puffed up his chest to impress Sloan with the importance of his decision.

'Nowhere feels great to me.' Sloan leveled both men with a stare. 'If you want city life, go live in Dallas. Or New York.'

'I ain't saying that's what I want. I'm saying it ain't gonna hurt nothing for Desperado to have a little bit of outside revenue. We could use it.'

Curvy's tone was defensive, but unfortunately, he spoke the truth. The wide highway that had been built through Desperado, basically dividing

3

farmland that had been in families for generations, hadn't brought the business to the town that they had hoped. The Stagecoach Inn didn't see many customers. The local shops the townspeople had opened along the creek hadn't seen as much business as they needed – though they'd managed to turn the creek into a small attraction for road-weary travelers. But that was mostly in the summer. A movie set would give Desperado some luster and bragging rights for certain, all year round.

'Unless you just want our town to be a place where strangers stop to take a piss, we need to at least give this a shot,' Pick added belligerently.

Sloan sighed. 'All right. She wouldn't be in the movie industry if she couldn't handle a character like Cody. We'll send her.'

Pick and Curvy grinned at Sloan's begrudging consent.

'But,' he added, before either man could celebrate too much, 'you pay her lodging at the Stagecoach for as long as she cares to stay in Desperado.' He held up his hand at the sputtering expressions in front of him. 'I'm serious about this. I wash my hands of the whole mess, but I don't want this Nixon gal completely thrown, Mayor. You send her out to beard Cody, and by golly, you can at least reach into the city funds to pay for her room and board while she's here. The city can afford the food one little bitty lady can eat.' His tone left no room for argument.

4

'One of us ought to at least go with her.' Pick didn't look enthused by the prospect.

'Yeah.' Sloan got to his feet. 'You tell Miss Nixon you've thought of the perfect place for her film, and then one of *you* will escort her to the Aguillar Ranch.'

It was half-past five on a humid July evening. Cody had been riding fence checking on his steers, a prospect which was depressing in this heat. Everything that required water to live was suffering. Surely the drought of five years ago had been a stunt Mother Nature wouldn't repeat this soon? No matter how hardy his steers were, he hated to think of the beef market bottoming out again. He knew several members of the farming community just might not be able to hang on to their livelihood for one more round of life-parching summer.

He sat down in the kitchen, reaching for a glass of tea, when someone knocked at the front door. Waiting a moment to see if his mother or his niece, Mary, would answer, Cody got up heavily and went to do it himself.

The woman on his front porch took his breath away in a startling way. 'Yes?' he demanded brusquely.

She shifted, her gray eyes large in her face as she met his stare. 'I'm looking for Cody Aguillar.'

'I'm Cody.' He had never seen hair so wild, so purple. It was stuffed up under something made of

5

a flowery velvet that might once have been a hat of sorts, but which now resembled a rag. He wondered why she wore such a creation in this heat.

'My name's Stormy Nixon. I have something I'd like to talk to you about.' She seemed uncertain as to whether that was still the case. 'Did Sloan . . . I mean, Sheriff McCallister call you to say that I was coming?'

Cody shrugged. 'Not that I know of. I've been out all day.'

'Oh. Well, I just left his office about thirty minutes ago. I got a little lost, or I would have been here sooner.'

Cody didn't know what to say to that. He looked over her head, which wasn't hard since she had to be all of about five-foot-two, and saw a compact rental car.

'Your friends, Pick and Curvy, offered to bring me out here, but I wanted to come alone. Maybe I should have let them show me the way.'

'They're not my friends.' At her perplexed expression, he said, 'What can I do for you?'

'I want to talk to you about a movie we're interested in doing here in Desperado.'

'I don't go to movies.' Though her unusual appearance had caught his attention at first – particularly those wide-legged, flowing pants with the wildflower pattern – there was no reason for her to linger on his porch. He had more work to be done, and no time for movies. 'I'm sorry. If you'll excuse me –'

'Mr Aguillar,' she said quickly, 'perhaps I didn't make myself clear. Sheriff McCallister, and, um, Pick and Curvy – I do have that right, don't I?'

He shrugged, promising himself to lecture Pick and Curvy sternly for sending a strange woman to his house. Those old men had nothing better to do than mind other folks' business.

'Well,' she said, exasperated now, 'the sheriff, the mayor and one other man seemed to think that you might be interested in letting Global Studios make a movie on your land. You *have* heard of Global Studios, haven't –?'

'Lady –'

'Stormy Nixon,' she inserted swiftly. 'How do you do?'

'I was doing just fine until you came along. Your time has been wasted, in a no doubt well-meaning way. I would not be interested in discussing any movie, even if it was being filmed on the moon, but I sure as hell am not remotely dumb enough to let my land be used for such a thing. You've been sent on a wild-goose chase, and if I were you, I would head back down to see Curvy and Pick and tell them to think of someone else for you to play this little joke on.'

She drew herself up in astonished indignation. 'I assure you, Mr Aguillar, this is no joke.' Reaching into an enormous flowered handbag which looked more like a gypsy travel sack, she pulled out a business card and handed it to him. 'We would offer you a substantial amount of money for the use

7

of your land. It would be for a short time, only a few months –'

'I'm sorry.' He handed the business card back. When she wouldn't take it, he slid it into the open mouth of the gypsy carpetbag. 'I don't have a few months to spare. I have a ranch to run. Now, if you'll excuse me –'

'Mr Aguillar. Please. Won't you just hear me out?' Big, gray-iris eyes gazed at him earnestly.

The phone rang, cutting off any chance she might have to plead her case. 'I'm sorry. Good-night, ma'am.' Silently, he closed the door and went to answer the phone.

'Hello?'

'Cody?'

'Sloan. Tell me you did not send that woman to my house.'

'Oh, damn. Has she already been there?'

'Hell, yes, and I just sent her on her way.'

'I got tied up with a – never mind. I meant to warn you she was coming.'

'Warn is right. Where the *hell* did she come from?' He'd never seen anyone quite like her. Sure, he was mighty used to blue jeans and boots on a woman, but he could go for a pair of decent pants or a church dress. What that tiny woman had been wearing, as she tottered on ridiculously high, purple-sandaled feet, was so incongruous on his farm he'd had to work hard not to stare.

It didn't bear remembering that her waist had been so small he could have wrapped one palm

8

around her and carried her off. She'd had delicate face bones, and beautiful full lips.

'Hollywood.' Sloan's voice was dry as it sounded like he was trying not to laugh. 'I hope you didn't scare her, Cody.'

'Scare her? She scared *me*.'

'A little bitty ol' lady like that scared you?' Sloan didn't bother to hide his laughter now. 'What is it your brother-in-law calls you? A cigar-store Indian?'

'Very damn funny.' Cody didn't appreciate Sloan's insinuation that Stormy might have had reason to be startled by his own appearance. 'Don't send any more strange females out my way, Sloan. Especially strange ones with stupid ideas.'

'Well, now, wait a minute, Cody. What's so stupid about her proposition?'

'It's stupid because it's my land they're thinking they're going to use, and if I find out you sicced them on me –'

'No, it was Pick and Curvy. But then I started thinking maybe you just might be interested.'

Cody's jaw dropped. 'Why would I be interested in a bunch of city yahoos squatting on my land, throwing trash and scaring my steers?'

'I meant, *interested in the woman*.'

For a second, Cody was so stunned he couldn't reply. 'Have you lost your damn mind, Sloan?'

'Don't think so, last I checked. It was just a thought, and I guess it was a bad one, so never mind.'

9

'What was just a thought?'

'That you might find her interesting. She's kinda cute, if you like nutty.'

'When have I ever been attracted to nutty?' Cody demanded.

'When was the last time you were attracted to anyone?' Sloan countered.

'I – well, I – that's none of your damn business! You stick to gunslinging, and I'll stick to ranching, and we just might stay friends.' It was outrageous that Sloan, one of maybe a handful of people he trusted, would pull this on him. 'While we're on the subject, why not you, my friend? Since you obviously thought she was worth eyeballing.'

'Because I'm not the one who's still in love with my dead brother's wife,' Sloan said softly. 'Annie's been married to Zach now for years, Cody. It's time to move on.'

Despair and hatred erupted inside Cody at the same time. Despair for the truth, and hatred for the unfortunate soul who would speak it aloud to him. 'Sloan, next time I see you, you're a dead man.'

'I know. From any other man, I could call that threatening an officer of the peace. With you, it's a promise.' Sloan hung up the phone.

'Damn right,' Cody muttered, slamming the receiver down. He was not in love with Annie. She was a remarkable woman, and he had offered to marry her to care for her and Mary had she needed him to do it, to honor his brother's memory. But Annie was a strong woman, and would only marry again the same way she'd married the first time: for deep, abiding love. She had found that with Zach Rayez, and he was happy for them. Cody fiercely loved his mother and Annie and Mary. But it would take a woman so special to get him to the altar that he couldn't envision it happening. He was thirty-five, and not easy to get along with. There was no reason to change at this point. Still, his heart thundered in his chest, uncomfortably loud in the quiet house. Where was Ma, anyway, and Mary? He needed something to keep his mind off what Sloan had said. Air. He needed air to clear his head.

Thoroughly disgruntled, he jerked the front door open. Stormy looked at him sheepishly.

'I locked the keys in my car.'

'You locked your keys in your car,' he repeated, glancing over her head. 'It's running.'

'I know. I was backing out when I decided to leave a business card in your door. Just in case.' She took a deep breath. 'So I hopped out and –'

'Locked your keys in your car while it was running.'

'Yes.' Her voice was breathy, somehow soft but not helpless. 'Do you know anyone who could help me?'

Irritation flowed through Cody as he briefly wondered if she'd done this on purpose. The sweet, questioning look in her eyes kept him from telling her she'd have to call a locksmith to help her. The tilt in her straight dainty nose as she stared up at him made the anger flow out of his tensed muscles. Sloan was a fool if he thought Cody needed a woman, but he could squarely say he was particularly safe from this one.

'Believe it or not, Miss Nixon, if you had to lock yourself out of your car,' he said, 'you came to the right place.'

Men who were good with their hands were a species Stormy found extremely attractive. This one, with his strong facial features and swarthiness, was more attractive than most. The last thing she'd expected to find on her quest for the perfect location was a man whose handsome good looks belonged on the wide screen. Of course, he wouldn't fit there; he'd be out of his element. But damn, oh, damn, Cody Aguillar was a man to make a woman's pulse kick her heart into high gear. And when he went to work on her car with his large, capable hands, Stormy melted.

'There. All set.'

In a second, Cody had the door open, holding it for her like a gentleman. Stormy had seen a lot of fake chivalry in Hollywood, where a man might open a door once, especially if it might lead to her bedroom. Once they found out her bedroom was firmly off limits, they never seemed to remember to treat her like a lady. More like an oddball.

With this man, the chivalry appeared to be firmly in character.

'Thank you so much,' she said, getting into the small rental car. 'I'm sorry to have troubled you.'

'It wasn't much,' he said.

She caught a wry note in his voice, though he didn't smile. Nor did he linger as he shut the car door for her. Swiftly, she jammed the button to let down the window. 'Call me if you change your mind.'

'I won't.'

He nodded at her brusquely, and she had no choice but to nod with a stiff smile and let the window slide back up. Slowly, she reversed the car, conscious of the tall man with the long black braided hair and one feather earring who watched her like a hawk.

In two words, he'd managed to say more than she wanted to hear. He wouldn't change his mind, and he wouldn't call her.

Damn.

13

CHAPTER 2

'Stormy Nixon's holed up at the Stagecoach,' Pick said, throwing the matchbook he'd been picking his teeth with on to Sloan's desk. 'Cody didn't give her the time of day.'

'I could say I told you so.' Sloan sighed deeply. 'But it's too late in the day for me to get in an argument. You'd best take an ad out in the paper and see if anyone jumps at the chance to lease out their land.'

'But Stormy said they'd need several acres to do the project,' Curvy protested. 'Most of the sodbusters have corn well into the growing season now, or crops they ain't gonna want disturbed. Cody's the only one with twenty-five-hunnerd acres. Damn it, he'd never know them movie folks was there!'

The bent–over little man was becoming agitated. He'd had a spinal condition since his youth, making him shaped a bit like a curved bow. Right now, his indignation had him standing the straightest Sloan had ever seen him.

'I've done what I can to help you, and Miss

Nixon. If we don't have the land, she'll just have to hit the next town and see if they'd be willing.' Sloan rose and reached for his hat.

'An ad might be the way to go.' Pick was thoughtful as he glanced at Curvy. 'Stormy said they were offering good money. Could be one of the farmers might be willing to plow their crops under. It's an opportunity to go with a sure thing, especially when we're heading into another long, dry summer.'

They stared at each other for a second. 'Annie Aguillar Rayez,' Pick and Curvy said at once.

'She's got a hunnerd acres,' Pick finished, 'plus she got the farm next to hers where she put her daddy and Gert when they got hitched. There's plenty of room out there, and her farm's right off the highway where the Hollywood folks could get their equipment out easily.'

'You can send Stormy to Annie's to see if the location would be right but,' Sloan fixed the elderly gentlemen with a stern eye, 'don't you dare try to figure out a way to rope Annie into it.'

'Oh, no,' Pick shook his head quickly. Too innocently.

'We wouldn't, Sloan,' Curvy seconded too eagerly.

They hurried from the office. Sloan looked out of the window, watching them head across to the Stagecoach and an unsuspecting Stormy. He frowned as he saw the two men put their heads together. They were up to no good.

15

Just to keep the playing field even, Sloan thought, I'd best put another call in to Cody.

Mary stared at her mother, antagonism stiffening every limb in her body. It hurt Cody to see the two of them at such odds. Mary had once been Annie's lifeline, her only happiness after his brother – her husband – had died in a farm accident.

'I'm thirteen. Stop treating me like a baby.'

'I'm not, sweetheart. I don't want you going to the country fair alone. All I'm asking is for you to go with someone whose parents are going to be there, too. But I can't leave right now. I can go tomorrow, but not tonight. A lady's on her way over to talk to Zach and me.'

Annie's expression was stern but loving. Cody thought she handled the situation well, but it had an explosive fuse to it. Mary was at an awkward stage, wanting to be grown-up and resenting her mother's control over her. She didn't realize how much she still resembled – and sometimes acted like – a child.

'Fine.' Mary flung herself into the window seat. 'If you're going to treat me like a baby, I'll just sit here and suck my thumb.'

Annie sighed. 'That's your choice.'

When the doorbell rang, she went to answer it, and Cody noticed Mary quickly dropped her babyish attitude and tried to appear adult. A Hollywood scout coming to call was a big deal to her. She was too young to know better than to be

16

impressed by people who made their living pretending. Resentment slid through him at Stormy's intrusion in their lives. When she walked into the room, he stared, feeling unwelcome attraction pull at him despite today's even more outlandish get-up. Where in the *hell* did that woman shop?

'You've met Cody, I believe,' Annie said, showing Stormy to a comfortable chair.

Cody barely returned her nod. Hell, yes, he'd met her. And as soon as Sloan had called to tell him Pick and Curvy were sending Stormy this way, he'd hurried over to listen in. Annie was good-hearted and sometimes innocent of the ways of the world. Stormy appeared extremely cosmopolitan – and determined.

Annie introduced Stormy to Zach, who shook her hand courteously. Last, she introduced her to Mary, and Cody saw Stormy's eyes widen as she looked at the teenager.

'You're very beautiful,' she told Mary.

'So are you,' Mary returned shyly.

Shock replaced the resentment inside Cody. Mary wasn't beautiful; she was a child, for heaven's sake! And Mary needed a trip to the eye doctor. Stormy wasn't beautiful; she was exotic like a peacock in a chicken coop.

He had to correct himself, though, as he frowned at Stormy while she began to talk to Annie about the movie project. She *might* be beautiful, if she took off those damn voluminous pants – today a black pair, at least – and that filmy blouse which

17

revealed curves he didn't want to think about.

Mary stared at Stormy, her eyes drinking in every inch of the woman. Cody supposed Mary would think Stormy was glamorous. Thank heaven Annie had the good sense not to allow her daughter to dress like a gypsy.

'Don't you think, Cody?'

Annie's voice snapped him away from his perusal of Stormy's slender feet, which he could see through the straps of black high heels.

She had a tiny rose tattoo on her ankle.

Cody leaned back, crossing his arms. 'Think what?'

'Think that it would be okay for Mary to try out for a bit part in Stormy's movie if it gets made in Desperado?'

'I – hell, no, I don't! I thought this was a discussion about location. Since when did this turn into a casting call?'

'Haven't you been listening, Cody?' Annie frowned at him slightly. 'Stormy thinks Mary would be just right for the part of the awkward teenager in the movie. She'd have to try out, of course –'

He stood abruptly. 'I'm going into the kitchen to help myself to a glass of tea.'

'Oh, good. Will you please bring Stormy one, too, while you're in there, Cody?' Annie sent a pleased smile his way. 'I made some special, just for her visit. It has mint in it from my own garden. Do you like mint?'

Stormy nodded happily. Cody could tell she was delighted at being treated to Annie's brand of warmth, just as many a time he had enjoyed it, too. There was no better woman than Annie. Stormy might be from La-La Land, but obviously she recognized a good heart when she met one.

However, he would not allow her to take advantage of Annie. Stormy's trick of pretending interest in a role for Mary was calculated and underhanded. Cody stomped into the kitchen, pulling out a glass for himself and one for the purple-haired woman. 'Do you like mint?' he mimicked, his mood turning more foul.

'Yes, I do, thanks.' Zach slapped him on the back. 'What's got your braid in a twist, Cody?'

'I don't like any of this.' He threw ice into the beautiful green glasses so hard that ice-chips flew. 'I don't like movie business.'

'And what else?' Zach leaned against the counter.

'Nothing else. It just feels fishy to me.'

'You don't like her, do you?'

Cody half-turned. 'Who?'

'The movie scout.'

'This has nothing to do with her, although I must confess her hair makes me . . . nervous.' Purple, by damn. It could only be called purple.

'I like her hair.' Zach seemed surprised. 'She's a very attractive woman.'

Cody's jaw sagged. He turned to completely face Zach. 'You're pulling my leg.'

19

Zach laughed heartily. 'Relax, Cody. Your secret's safe with me.'

'What secret?' He glowered at Zach to let him know he was trespassing on his business.

'I remember feeling the same way the first time I laid eyes on Annie. She had me turned so inside out I was walking backwards on my hands.'

Cody poured the tea. 'Slick, you've misjudged the situation. I don't like her, don't trust her, don't like the way any of this smells.'

'Yeah, well, you didn't like me, trust me, when you met me, either.'

'There's something wrong when one little weird-looking female can turn this whole town on its ear over some film and people playing make-believe. I've never seen so many folks get in line so fast to be made fools of.'

'Easy, Cody.' Zach thumped him on the back as Cody picked up the glasses. 'You might find yourself next in line.'

'Damn well won't.' He returned to the living room, and handed a glass to Stormy. She glanced up at him gratefully and smiled. Her forearm brushed against his jeans as she reached to take the glass.

Sexual response hit him in the region of his zipper, and he wished Annie had air-conditioning. It was time for Zach to get his wife an air-conditioner; they had plenty of money, he thought sharply.

Stormy looked cool and completely comfortable

in her loose clothes. She went back to animatedly discussing her plans, obviously not struck by the same pull he'd just felt. Disgusted with himself, he sat back in a well-out-of-sight chair, but where he could hear the discussion. Taking a long sip of tea, he allowed his gaze to wander along her face and down her neck. She had tiny freckles on her chest showing above V-neck buttons. She had nicely mounded breasts he tried not to look at a third time, a dainty little waist, and sweetly shaped hips.

She had three tiny, gold loop earrings hanging from one ear, he noticed when she moved her long hair, and only one in the other. Damn lopsided female, he told himself. Couldn't she make up her mind? It was either one earring or three, but she had to sit on the fence.

He downed all the tea in his glass and still felt dry in his throat. Zach was wrong. Stormy Nixon's hair was purple. And she was *not* attractive.

'I appreciate your having me over.' Stormy stood, giving Annie Rayez a heartfelt smile. Words could not express how much she had enjoyed the last hour here. Annie treated her with respect, giving her proposal the attention of a businesswoman to another businesswoman. 'I enjoyed meeting all of you. And you, too,' she told Mary.

The teenage girl had sat beside her inscrutable uncle all evening, never saying a word, though Stormy could feel her excitement. Every once in a while, Cody would reach over to tug teasingly at

21

Mary's long hair, and she would turn and scowl playfully at her uncle. Stormy had a feeling Cody teased the girl on purpose as his way of showing her affection.

If Stormy had been born into a family that had as much love to share as this one, her life might have turned out very differently. Mary reminded her so much of herself at that age. Maybe it was the awkward gawkiness she remembered so well.

'We'll give your movie project consideration.' Annie showed her to the door with a pleasant smile.

'Call me if you decide to take me up on it. I'll be at the Stagecoach. And if Mary should be interested in auditioning for the role, I'd be happy to give her name to the casting director.'

'Well, I'm not sure about that –' Annie began.

'I'd love it. I know I would!' Mary's face lit with happiness.

'We have a while to decide about that, Mary.' She gave her daughter a patient smile. 'Don't we, Stormy?'

'Actually, they'll probably start auditioning in the next couple of weeks. They're hoping to start filming as soon as we have a location.'

'My goodness! I thought this was a future project?' Annie said.

'We had a location which fell through. Since the big name actors have already been signed on, we need to find another location quickly so that they don't move on to other projects. That puts the pressure on me.' Stormy smiled but it was hard with Cody standing in the background, his legs spread, his arms crossed, and his face unwelcoming.

'I see. What happens if we decide not to accept your offer?'

'I think everything will turn out okay. I took a drive up the road today and happened upon Shiloh. Their mayor seemed plenty interested, and completely certain that they had an excellent location for me.'

'He would.' Cody shot her a sarcastic nod. 'Tate Higgins isn't called Wrong-Way for nothing.'

'What does that mean?'

Annie shook her head as she gently steered Stormy out the door. 'Don't listen to Cody. You don't want to hear the tale of two towns while you're here. We want you to go back to Hollywood with a good impression of our little world.'

'I have a good impression.' Nothing could change her mind, but her curiosity was roused. 'I do want to hear a tale of two towns.'

'It's silly, really.' Annie shot Cody a frown. 'Desperado is named for all the desperados and *huaqueros*, or looters, who hid in this area in farmhouses and such. Shiloh is named for the famous General Shiloh, who courageously fought battles down south of here with Karankawa Indians. Headhunters.' Annie grimaced, and glanced over her shoulder at Mary, who was listening with huge eyes. 'Anyway, since the two towns are one

23

right after another on the map, we compete some-what for tourist business. As you might guess, having a famous general puts Shiloh ahead of us in the advertising area. Tate Higgins took advantage of that by posting billboards along the highway telling folks to drop in to the "honorable city where folks have been down-home good for hundreds of years". Naturally, that got folks around here mad, and ever since, they've said that Higgins would send a lost man the wrong way just so he could stick him in the back.'

Zach laughed. 'It could also have something to do with the fact that, late one night when he'd had too much to drink, he had a run-in on a deserted country road with a parked tractor on the opposite side. He was driving in the wrong lane that night, for certain.'

'Goodness,' Stormy murmured. 'I hope no one was hurt.'

'No. But Cody would have liked to hurt him. It was his tractor.' Annie grinned at Cody.

'What was he doing in Desperado?' Stormy's eyes were on Cody as she drank in this small-town lore.

He shrugged his shoulders. 'He's always in Desperado stirring up trouble.'

'Don't you worry, Stormy.' Annie patted her arm. 'Tate Higgins is just fine. If you need to make your movie in Shiloh, you'll be just fine. Cody's just trying to scare you.' She gave Cody a stern eyeing. 'Or impress you with his storytelling.

Cody, did you come over here just to give this poor woman something to take back to the scriptwriters in Hollywood?'

'No.'

Stormy stared at him. Why did she feel that he disliked her so much? Was it the heat in his darkest brown eyes, or his unyielding, stiff posture?

'What are you doing tonight, Cody?' Annie asked.

'Going to hang around here for a while,' he answered, not taking his eyes from Stormy. She felt hot electricity tightening her heart, and wished he would look somewhere else.

'What are you going to do now, Stormy?'

'I'm going back to my hotel room and probably watch TV.'

'Well, then. Cody, I want you to take Stormy to the county fair. She needs to see something more of Desperado besides my house, your house and Sloan's office. It's the proper thing to do,' she said pointedly, when Cody jerked his gaze from Stormy to glare at Annie. 'Stormy, I have a comfortable pair of walking shoes if you'd like to borrow them. We appear to be close to the same size.'

Stormy didn't think so. Annie topped her by a good six inches. However, she would love to see a real county fair . . . maybe she could go back to her room to change and then head over there herself. She started to shake her head, but Annie took her arm.

'I know I've got a pair of white tennis shoes that

25

would fit you. And if I don't, Mary does.'

That was more of a possibility, Stormy thought, as Annie dragged her past Cody's simmering gaze. Stormy didn't even try to smile as they went by him – she couldn't. His black braid seemed stiff with disapproval, his lips carved into forbidding granite.

'I don't think he likes me,' she whispered to Annie once they were in her room. 'Maybe this isn't a good idea.'

'Oh, never mind him.' Annie's focus was on her closet. 'Cody doesn't like anybody.'

'Um – that doesn't sound very conducive to our spending an evening together.'

Annie pulled out a pair of blue jean shorts and a white eyelet top. She threw white ankle-length socks on the bed. 'Put those on. The shorts you can roll a cuff on if necessary. The blouse will be fine. We appear to definitely be the same there.'

She gave Stormy a wicked grin, which she had to return. Annie's enthusiasm was fun, and if she wasn't worried about Cody, Stormy wasn't going to, either.

Annie returned with a pair of Mary's white canvas tennis shoes a moment later. 'The two of you wear close to the same shoe size, thank goodness. Oh. Don't you look nice?'

Country sweet was more the description, Stormy thought. If anyone but Annie had suggested she wear this unfashionable get-up, she'd be certain they were trying to make her look bad.

26

'Now. Your hair. You're going to roast with all that hair on your back.' Annie stared at her thoughtfully. 'Put it up in a ponytail. You'll feel better.'

'A ponytail?' Stormy couldn't even imagine it.

'Yes, a ponytail. Or some other top-do. You're not used to the heat here, Stormy. I know it gets hot in LA, but the sun here is hard even on folks who have lived in Texas forever and are somewhat immune to it. Trust me. You don't want to get heat exhaustion. And I may even send Cody by the store to get you some sunblock.' Annie eyed Stormy's white skin disapprovingly.

'I'll be okay.' Stormy hurriedly pulled her hair into a loose ponytail. 'I won't stay out long.'

Annie nodded. 'Come on, then. Cody's not too patient, and now that I've given him an assignment, he'll be anxious to get on with it.'

Stormy winced at being considered an assignment to Cody, but that was what she was, of course. Though when his eyes widened at the sight of her legs, she felt a secret little thrill of happiness inside. An assignment I don't think he minds as much as he pretends, she thought.

'I want to go, too,' Mary begged excitedly. 'Please, Uncle Cody?'

'Not this time, ladybug.'

Mary's face fell. Stormy couldn't bear her disappointment. 'I don't mind if she comes along.'

'You don't?' He stared at her as if he couldn't believe she had good manners.

'Of course I don't! It'll be much more fun that way.'

A sudden quiet fell over the room. Stormy realized she had just implied that Cody wasn't her ideal choice for an early evening outing. His gaze stayed tight on hers, half-lidded and thoughtful. 'The more the merrier,' she finished lamely.

'Okay, ladybug. Into the truck.' Cody waved Mary toward the door.

'I'll follow in my car.' Stormy grabbed up her flowered carpetbag.

'We'll meet you at the Stagecoach, and then you can ride with us.' Cody waited for her to precede him out the door.

'Okay.' Stormy's heart lifted with anticipation. 'Thank you, Annie! I'll send your clothes back with Mary tonight.' She hurried out to her car, excitement running through her as she followed Cody's truck down the bumpy drive.

Going to a fair with Cody Aguillar. It might not be the most exciting thing she'd ever done, but for some reason she was awfully glad Annie had asked him to take her.

'Hold still so I can put this on you.'

Cody frowned as he slicked some sunblock over Stormy's arms and on her back where the white eyelet blouse didn't cover her neck and shoulders.

'I can do that!' Stormy protested.

'You're making a mess, Uncle Cody,' Mary commented.

28

'And you're getting it in my hair. Cody, give me that!'

Stormy reached to swipe the tube but Cody held it up high so she couldn't reach it. He was trying to be as quick about this as possible, because he sure as hell didn't want to be touching Hollywood any longer than necessary. Lord, she felt soft. And delicate. 'Both of you quit yammering. Annie told me to be sure you had sunblock on and that's why I bought this. You'll be mighty uncomfortable if you fry.'

'It's almost seven o'clock!' Stormy leaned away from him, but Cody deliberately ran one gooey finger down her nose.

'It doesn't matter what time it is. Sun's still dangerous to skin like yours. Now.' He relinquished the bottle to her. 'Be sure to put some . . . there.' Gruffly, he pointed to the exposed skin of her chest that the blouse didn't cover.

'Well, thank you for that! I'm surprised you don't want to put sunblock there yourself!'

Stormy snapped the lid off the tube, glowering at him, but Cody raised his eyebrows at her. 'If you'd like –'

'No, I wouldn't!' Stormy closed the tube and slapped it back in his hand. 'Are you going to put some on Mary or is it just me you want looking like greased pie-dough?'

Cody gave her his most patient stare. 'Stormy, what color is our skin?' He hugged his niece to him, and she grinned up at him.

29

'Dark brown,' Stormy answered begrudgingly.

'That's right. We have Indian and Mexican heritages. You appear to be spawned by a milkman and maybe an Irishwoman. So quit complaining and see what Desperado has to offer.'

'Hopefully men who aren't so damn pigheaded,' Stormy couldn't resist. 'Maybe some who appreciate alabaster skin.'

'Are you hoping to find a man while you're here?'

She blew out a breath of exasperation. 'No! Just a place to film, okay?'

'Man, you guys are way on each other's nerves.' Mary waved at a group of her friends standing around a concession stand. 'Can I go with them for a while, Uncle Cody? You and Stormy aren't much fun.'

'I – yeah. Meet us back here in exactly one hour.'

Cody watched as his niece darted off. Stormy stared at him.

'Guess it's just the two of us for sixty minutes,' he told her.

'What fun.' She rolled her eyes.

He took her by the arm and steered her over to the cow patty bingo game. 'I didn't say this was going to be fun. I got roped into bringing you. Nobody's ever going to elect me for fun tour-guide of Desperado.'

'You got that right,' Stormy murmured.

But he heard her and gave her a light pinch behind her elbow.

30

'Ow!'

The game attendant looked up at her screech. 'I have one last bingo square, and the little lady's called her marker! One dollar, please!'

Stormy gasped. 'What is he talking about?'

'When you made that unattractive noise, he thought you were buying the last number in the bingo game.'

'I'm not!' she cried. 'I'm not going in there!'

'You don't have to.' Cody reached out and handed the attendant a dollar on Stormy's behalf. 'All the squares are bought, and now they'll let the cow in there. The cow drops a patty on a number, and whoever bought that number wins the jackpot.' He grinned at the comical shock on her face.

'It's amazing how some people entertain themselves.' Stormy watched as a young cowboy walked a cow into the roped-off game. The cow meandered contentedly, completely uninterested in the fluorescent colored numbers beneath her hooves. 'I hope she knows her business,' Stormy remarked.

'Of course she does. It's my cow, and I told her to make a square hit.'

She laughed at him. 'You're out of your mind.'

He shook his head. 'You'll see.'

'Number fifty!' the game attendant called as the cow immediately landed a patty. The onlookers burst into laughter.

'Oh, my gosh!' Stormy shrieked in delight. 'That's my number!'

Cody gave her his wisest look.

'Quit! You didn't have anything to do with that.' Stormy glanced up as the game attendant tried to hand her the jackpot. 'How much is it?'

'Two hundred dollars,' he told her.

She looked around at all the excited faces watching her. 'It's not fair for me to take the money since I'm not from here,' she said. 'Let's allow the cow to choose another winner.'

'Don't go away, ladies and gents!' the attendant called out. 'We've got a game again, thanks to Cody's lady-friend!'

People craned to look at Stormy. She looked mighty pleased with herself, and though he didn't want to be, Cody was proud of her quick thinking. It was smart public relations, he reminded himself, and made her look good in the townspeople's eyes. He dragged her away from the game.

'Cody, was it really your cow?'

'Yes. I can be persuaded to do some things for the good of the community.' He spoke harshly to remind her that movie making didn't fall under the same heading as sparing a cow for a county fair.

'Can your cow perform again?'

Stubborn woman was going to ignore his meaning. 'She'll do whatever she's called upon to do.' He wouldn't allow himself to grin when she laughed. 'I should buy you an ice-cream on behalf of Desperado for your spirit of fair play in cow patty bingo.'

Her eyebrows lifted. 'I should buy *you* an ice-cream as I'm supposed to wine and dine you into letting me use your land.'

'It ain't gonna happen.'

'Hmm. How can I get you to be as agreeable as your cow?'

'You can't.' He watched her mull that over. 'Don't try to out-think me, Hollywood. I've seen a lot of city slicks in my time, but none of them has ever bested me.'

'I see,' she said thoughtfully. 'What kind of ice-cream do you want?'

'Rocky road,' he replied, 'like you're gonna find if you try me.'

'Then I'll have the same.' Her smile was sweet. 'I've always loved a challenge.'

Tate Higgins, better known as Wrong-Way Higgins to the folks in Desperado, watched in disgust as Cody Aguillar handed the movie scout an ice-cream cone. Tate had moseyed up to Desperado, ostensibly to check out the county fair, but mostly to see if he might meet up with Stormy Nixon. It was just damn typical that Cody would have the female with him. Where there was a buck to be made, Cody Aguillar and Zach Rayez were never far away.

Tate intended to see that the L.A. folks realized Desperado couldn't hold a candle to Shiloh. Obviously, he had his work cut out for him, as he watched Stormy tug on Cody's arm so that he had to lower his hand. Before the big rancher figured out what she wanted, she nipped a bite off his ice-cream. Startled, Cody laughed out loud at her audacity.

Tate wasn't sure he'd ever heard the grim-faced rancher laugh before. Well, maybe the night Tate had run into Cody's parked tractor. Cody hadn't laughed about that, of course. He'd laughed watching Tate fall out of his car into cow muck. Sanctimonious son-of-a-bitch had told Tate it served him right for drinking and driving.

He didn't figure Cody would laugh if someone helped Stormy see what Shiloh had going for it that Desperado lacked. The two of them walked toward the rides, and Tate cursed meanly.

Way too cozy, he told himself. Gotta do something about that.

CHAPTER 3

'I had a good time. Thanks, Cody, and Mary, for taking me to the fair.'

Cody nodded at her.

'Bye, Stormy,' Mary said.

Stormy got out of the truck and closed the door. Cody watched her walk into the Stagecoach Inn lobby before pulling out of the small parking lot.

'I wish I was like her,' Mary said on a sigh.

'What for?' Cody glanced at his niece sharply.

'Well, she's fun, for one thing.' Mary stared at him with big eyes. 'You and Mom and Zach work so hard that you're not –'

'Much fun?' He turned his attention to the road.

'Yeah. I mean I know you have to work hard, but sometimes I wish everyone wasn't so serious.' She sighed deeply, with all the drama of a wistful teenager. 'Mom and Zach have been extra busy lately planning for the restaurant Mom wants to open.'

'There's a difference between playing and working, Mary. Life can't be all play.'

'Stormy's having fun doing her work.'

He stopped himself from saying that he didn't consider making pictures to be work. Not honest, hard work, anyway. Then he gritted his teeth, realizing that he hadn't known he'd felt that way. Whether he liked what Stormy did for a living or not, she was working, and it didn't matter whether it measured up to his standards.

'It's different, Mary. I like what I do, your mom likes what she does, and Stormy, I guess, likes what she does.'

'I want to be like her when I grow up,' Mary repeated. 'I'm going to dress like her, too.'

'That'll please your mother.' Cody couldn't help the sarcasm in his tone.

'You don't sound like you like Stormy very much, Uncle Cody.'

He sort of did, he sort of didn't. How was that for sitting on the fence? 'She's fine.'

'Well, you think she's nice.'

He glanced at Mary for a second. 'Nice enough.'

'And you think she's funny.'

'Funny ha-ha and funny strange.' That he knew for sure.

'You sure were laughing a lot with her.' Mary peered at him. 'You have to like her. How can somebody you don't like make you laugh that much?'

'I don't want to talk about it any more,' he informed his inquisitive niece grumpily.

'Gosh.' Mary sighed. 'That's what adults always

36

say.' She suddenly gave him an impish smile. 'Did you know you open your mouth real wide when you laugh hard, kind of like a puppet?'

'No, damn it, I didn't,' Cody replied, not catching the swear word before it popped out.

'Well, you do.' Mary looked out the window. 'I wish I was all grown up, Uncle Cody.'

'Ah . . . ahem.' He cleared his throat and wondered what to say to his brother's daughter. She wanted guidance and steering on the shifting sands of pre-adulthood. No light of intuition struck him. 'It'll happen soon enough, ladybug.'

'I guess so.' She sighed heavily. 'My friends were mean to me tonight. They said I dress like a child.'

He looked at her in surprise. 'I think you look nice.' She did, to his mind. She was wearing shorts, bobby socks, and a cap-sleeve top. Her waist-length black hair was in a braid, tied with a pink bow.

'You think that because you're my uncle. You don't understand.'

Her voice was so despondent that Cody felt he had to try again. 'Explain it to me slowly, so maybe I can catch on.'

'Well, for one thing, I have no reason to wear a bra. I have nothing to put in one, which is really a drag.'

Cody could feel heat creeping along the back of his neck. 'I . . . can understand you feeling that way.'

'I'm the only girl in my class who doesn't. And I'm not allowed to stay out past ten, like the other kids. Tonight, they're all going over to Livvy's after the fair closes.'

And I have to go home with my uncle, like a baby. Cody clearly caught the underlying message now. No doubt Mary was experiencing the same struggle most of her friends were, but his heart ached for her. Would nothing in life be simple for this child who was so close to his heart?

'You know,' he said after a moment, 'I was the smallest kid in the class. Your father used to have to whip up on kids who were being mean to me.'

'Really?'

He had her full attention. 'I was ugly, you know.'

'Oh, no, Uncle Cody. You're the most handsome man in the world.'

Grinning at Mary's innocent reverence, Cody laughed. 'Next time you come over, ask Grandma to dig out some of my old school pictures. Check out the size of my ears.'

'You had big ears?'

'Yep. It's a sign of greatness,' he told her, 'but try telling that to a schoolroom full of kids using your ears for spitball targets.'

'Oh, Uncle Cody! I'm so sorry!'

He pulled into Annie's driveway and shut off the truck. 'Life isn't all fun and games, ladybug. I got over it.'

'How come you don't have big ears now?'

38

'I grew into 'em.' He pointed at her to get out of the truck. 'And you'll grow out of your awkward stage, too.'

Sooner rather than later, he hoped. In the meantime, he wondered if Annie needed to know that her daughter was suffering the pangs of adolescence a mite heavily. Didn't have anything to put in a bra, indeed. He was out in left field with that one. 'You know, Mary, your mom will talk to you about all this stuff that's got you twisted up.'

'Oh, no, Uncle Cody.' She shook her head adamantly. 'I couldn't. Mom's always busy with Zach.' A guilty expression crossed her face. 'I mean, I'm glad they're married. I love Zach. But I do have to share Mom now, and it's just different.' She looked at her shoes sadly for a moment. 'She's been crying a lot lately, when she thinks I don't know.'

'Crying?' Cody couldn't help the feeling of alarm that raced through him.

'Well, her and Zach don't think I know, but Mom cries at the drop of a hat these days. One time, he said he didn't think it was gonna rain, and Mom fell all to pieces. Took him about fifteen minutes to make her feel better.' Mary met his worried gaze. ' "Course, it didn't need to rain after that. Mom damn near washed out the house with her tears.'

'Don't say damn, Mary. Your mom'll think I've been cussing around you.'

'You have, Uncle Cody.'

39

'I know.' He pushed the door open. 'I try real hard not to, though. So keep your mouth clean so she doesn't cry, okay?'

'Good idea.'

They walked into the house together. Zach and Annie sat in the kitchen, eating a late-night snack.

'Have a good time?' Annie asked, kissing her daughter on the cheek.

'Yes. Thanks for letting me go with you, Uncle Cody.' Mary turned to leave the kitchen, but Annie gently caught her arm.

'There's something Zach and I want to tell you. Both of you.'

Annie's eyes glowed with happiness. No tears there now. Relief filled Cody. Whatever Mary had witnessed, it had passed, and he was glad for that. He couldn't bear the thought that Annie was unhappy.

'Zach and I are going to have a baby!'

Cody's jaw dropped. Mary stared at her mother in dismay. 'How can you do that?'

'Well, we . . . we love each other, and these things happen,' Annie replied, perplexed by her daughter's response.

'Oh.'

'Congratulations!' Cody said too heartily to cover Mary's reaction. He gave Annie a quick kiss, then shook Zach's hand. 'You old city slicker!'

Mary turned to leave again.

'Mary, aren't you happy?' Annie asked.

'Thrilled,' she said over her shoulder. Half-turning, Mary looked at her mother. 'Are you going to let me audition for the movie?'

'Well, I haven't really given it much thought, Mary. We haven't talked about it. I think your uncle had some reservations about it, though, and I'd like to discuss it with him and Zach more thoroughly. For right now, I wouldn't get my hopes up.'

Mary shot Cody a look filled with resentment – or maybe betrayal. 'Goodnight,' she said, before quietly leaving the room.

Annie's face fell. Zach squeezed her shoulders. They both looked at Cody. *As if I have the damn answers.*

'I think she's having a tough time,' was all he could offer. 'But I know once she realizes she's going to be a big sister, she'll be delighted.'

Tears welled in Annie's eyes. 'Maybe I didn't present it right. I just thought she'd be happy.'

'I'm sure it's a shock.' Zach stood, reaching into the refrigerator for a beer. 'I'm still in shock myself. Cody's right. She probably needs some time.'

They all looked at each other awkwardly. From down the hall, water turned on in the shower.

'Difficult teen years,' Cody said lamely. 'Gotta go. Great news, though.' Once again, he kissed Annie, slapped Zach on the back, and left the kitchen. In his truck, he remembered Mary's pinched, baby-round face.

I have to share Mom now, and it's just different.

41

Mary was going to do a lot more sharing than she'd ever imagined once the baby arrived.

The phone rang at two o'clock in the morning, rousing Cody from a deep sleep. 'Hello?'

'Cody! Mary's gone!'

He tried to make himself wake up. 'Annie?'

'Mary's gone! She's not in her room!' Annie's voice was frantic, terrified, and Cody came clean awake.

'Maybe she's outside sitting on the porch.'

'We've checked everywhere, even at Pop's and Gert's. She's not here, and her bed wasn't slept in at all!'

He sat up. 'Try to keep calm, Annie, and let me think this through for a second.' Rapidly, he ran through the possibilities. His land was across the state highway from Annie's, which made his stomach tighten at the thought of Mary trying to cross it at night.

An impossible thought occurred to him, which he rejected instantly, then forced himself to consider. 'I have a hunch. I'll call you in half an hour. In the meantime, I'll take my cellphone with me. Call me if she turns up.'

Annie wept in earnest now but she agreed to his plan. Cody jumped out of bed, pulling on the nearest pair of jeans. If Mary was where he thought she was, he was going to thrash her himself.

If she wasn't, he didn't know what he'd do.

* * *

'So what's the problem?' Stormy's boss had irritation in his voice that even this late hour couldn't disguise. Of course, it was two hours earlier in California, so he was wide awake. She was getting tired, and extremely tired of listening to him gripe.

'I need a little more time to convince these people that making a movie here is a good idea,' Stormy explained. 'Things move more . . . slowly in small towns, I think.'

'I just can't take a chance on you, Stormy. If this falls through and we have to let the stars we've signed go on to other projects, it's going to cost us big time. The producer doesn't want this movie to run over budget.'

'I know, I know. I'm working as fast as I can.' She sat up straighter and massaged the back of her neck.

'Hey, Stormy. Listen. I love you, you know that. You're my girl. But if you get into the head candy again –'

'I'm not, damn it! I haven't touched a pill since . . . then.' Last year's winter had been long and cold. There was nothing colder than a white room in the winter where people in white coats tried to drain your brain and talk you through your own labyrinth of anxiety. She had a handle on it now.

Everything that was in the past was staying in the past. Her parents, her prescription pills. Opening the window so some of the Texas heat would blow in and counteract the hotel's air-conditioning, she said, 'I've got two good possibilities. Let me call you tomorrow night.'

'Okay,' he said reluctantly, 'but Stormy, this is absolutely, positively your last chance. I gotta have someone who can deliver.'

'Everything's fine. I need to get some sleep. It's two in the morning. These folks get up early around here.'

'Call me.'

'I will.' Slowly, she hung up, rubbing her bare arms to take away the painful memories chilling her soul. Pills had been a common thing in her home. Growing up, she'd assumed all parents downed drugs the way hers did. There were all kinds of vices, and while her teenage buddies were getting drunk and acting stupid, she was managing her teenage angst with a colorful array of little pharmaceutical friends. It was more convenient to tuck a few pills into the zippered pocket in her purse than to sneak around bottles of Strawberry Fields.

Pills had nearly ruined her life. Stormy sighed, looking out the window. She was well now. It was time to move past it, and the best thing to do was make certain she nailed down a location for the production manager. Then she could be on top again – and eventually everyone would forget about the job she'd screwed up by getting whacked out.

Sudden light knocking at her door startled her. It was two-fifteen in the morning, for crying out loud! She wasn't about to open it. 'Who's there?'

'Stormy, it's me, Mary. Are you awake?'

'Mary!' Stormy flung the door open. 'Honey, what are you doing here?' She knew Cody would have taken Mary right home after he'd dropped Stormy off at the hotel.

'I've run away,' she said, before bursting into tears. 'Can I stay here?'

'Run away?' Stormy put her hands on Mary's shoulders, giving her a light squeeze before pushing her into a chair. 'Why?'

'Because . . . I don't know why!' Tears streamed down Mary's cheeks. Stormy turned to get her a glass of water. 'Everything's all wrong!'

'Oh, dear.' Stormy watched Mary wipe at her nose and then try to stop crying. She hiccuped once, and it was a pathetic sound.

'I just need someone to talk to,' Mary said miserably.

Well, that summed up about three-quarters of the population. Stormy reached for the phone. 'I have to call your mother, hon. She's going to be worried sick. How did you get here, anyway?'

'I walked. Then I hitched a ride.'

'Oh, my God.' Stormy's blood ran cold. 'Mary, you could have been –' She broke off her words, thinking that a lecture probably wasn't timely right now. 'Look, I'm going to call your mother, and see if you can spend the night with me, okay? But you have to promise me you won't ever do anything like this again.'

45

Mary nodded. 'Do you have to call my mother?'

'Yes.' Stormy was resolute. 'I don't mind having you here, but it isn't fair to scare your mother and father out of their wits.'

'They're having a baby. They won't care where I am.' Mary's eyes pleaded for pity.

'That's not what I saw when I was over there today. They care very much about you. Tell me your phone number.'

Mary did, and Stormy dialed it swiftly. Her heart was hammering; her palms felt clammy. Of all things she didn't need right now! Surely Annie wouldn't think Stormy somehow had instigated this situation? What if she got mad at Stormy and decided not to consider her offer?

A frantic female voice answered at the Rayez house. 'Hello?'

'Annie, it's Stormy Nixon.'

'Stormy! Why are you calling at this hour?'

She closed her eyes, fighting against the panic rising inside her. 'I've got Mary here.'

'Whatever for? You bring her back right now!'

Stormy could feel Annie's fear and anger crackling through the line. 'She just got here, Annie. She's been crying . . . and says she's –' Running away had been on the tip of her tongue, but one look at Mary's desperate eyes made Stormy amend the truth. 'She says she'd like to stay the night with me.'

'Absolutely not. I'll send Zach for her immediately.'

46

Annie's tone brooked no argument. Stormy sighed, wishing terribly that Mary hadn't involved her in this. 'Annie, Mary told me she was running away.'

'Running away!'

'Yes. So, even though I don't know you very well, I'm kind of glad she came to me. Maybe your husband could come get her in the morning.' As Annie hesitated, she said, 'It's only another four or five hours, anyway.'

'I'm not sure this is a good idea.' Iciness enveloped Annie's voice. 'It isn't easy for me to completely trust someone I've just met. It would be better if Cody came to get her. He has his cellphone, and I can call him.'

'I think Mary's had enough for tonight. I promise to take good care of your daughter, Annie.'

It seemed forever passed before Annie spoke again. 'I will be there in the morning myself.'

'All right.' Stormy hung up, shooting a worried glance at Mary. 'Your mother's not happy, but she says you can stay.'

'Thank you.' Mary slumped in the chair. 'I just need someone to talk to.'

Stormy sighed. It was going to be a long night, and she really needed sleep so she could beat the bushes for a movie location tomorrow. 'Oh, heck. Why don't we go for a dip in the pool? You're all hot and sweaty from walking over here, and quite frankly, I feel cooped up.' Nervous was more like it, from everything closing in on her. A swim would do her good.

'That would be nice. I can just wear my shorts in the pool.'

'Okay. I only have one suit, or I'd loan you one. Let's take a soda –' she took two from the mini-fridge, 'and grab a couple of towels.'

'This is kind of exciting.' The tears had dried up, and Mary's eyes were shining.

At least Mary seemed to have perked up. Stormy slipped into her emerald-green one-piece and headed out the door, with Mary close behind.

They tossed the towels on to chaise-longues, and set the drinks on the ground. Stormy slid into the water gratefully. 'Oh, this is heaven.'

Mary dove off the board and swam to a place about three feet away from Stormy. 'This is great!' Her eyes held gratitude. 'Thanks for letting me stay with you.'

'It's fine.' She reached to grab one of the cans and opened it. 'Now, why don't you tell me what's on your mind?'

Mary looked away guiltily. 'I really feel stupid talking about it.'

Ah. Counseling 101. She'd been here before. 'Talking's not stupid if it'll make you feel better.'

'It won't change anything.'

Mary looked so confused that Stormy felt sorry for her. 'No. It probably won't. But maybe it will help you put some things in perspective.'

'Okay. Well, I really want to try out for that

48

movie part. But my folks don't think it's a good idea.'

'Oh.' Embarrassment flooded Stormy. If she'd stirred up trouble in the Rayez household, she'd feel responsible for Mary's late-night visit to her. 'They know what's best for you.'

'That's just it. They don't know what's best for me! Not anymore. I'm growing up, and they just don't get it.'

'I see.' Stormy cringed, realizing the problem went far deeper than a swim could cure. 'Have you talked to them about the way you feel?'

'I can't.' Mary sighed despondently. 'Mom's about worn out picking out stuff for the new restaurant. And they're so happy about this stupid baby and everything. They don't have time for me right now.'

'Why is the baby stupid?'

'It just is. I mean, how mortifying! When my friends find out my mom and Zach have been –' she hesitated with a strained look at Stormy '– well, *doing* it, they're going to freak. I'll never hear the end of it. I mean, it's so gross!'

'What's so gross?'

'That my mom and Zach have been doing it!'

Oh, lord. Stormy closed her eyes wearily, wondering what she should say in this situation. 'It's pretty normal stuff when you're married, Mary.'

'Yeah, but not when you're old.'

Stormy tried not to laugh at Mary's indignant tone.

'It's not funny, Stormy.'

She jumped at Mary's perception of her reaction.

'It's humiliating to have your mother get pregnant when she's nearly forty years old. And a baby's just going to be more work. That's all they ever do anyway is work. And now there will be more.' Mary gazed at Stormy with rapt admiration. 'I want to be like you. I want to have fun.'

'Stormy!'

She bit back a yelp at Cody's sudden furious shout.

'What the hell do you think you're doing?' He strode into the pool area, dark and tall and overwhelming.

Stormy stared up at him. 'Swimming?'

He chose to ignore that for the moment. 'Young lady, you are in big trouble.' He pointed at Mary. 'Get out of the pool.' His anger directed his attention back to Stormy. 'I had a hunch this was where she'd be, and by damn if I wasn't right.'

Stormy hauled herself out of the pool to pit all five-foot two-and-a-half inches of herself against Cody's wrath. 'Cool off, Cowboy. You don't talk to me like that. Maybe to some cow-eyed female who thinks you're tough stuff here in Desperado, but not me.' She put her hands on her hips. 'We're not finished swimming.'

His jaw dropped for an instant. 'Listen, Trouble, I don't want any lip from you. I knew you'd be a bad influence around here, and sure-as-shooting if I'm not right.'

'Of course you are!' Stormy was building righteous anger of her own. Cody's eyes snapped at her, but blaming her was outrageous. 'You're always right, aren't you, because you're the life authority. Cody Aguillar has everything figured out, down to the last curtain call.'

'I don't do curtain calls, I don't do damn make-believe, but you've got this poor kid convinced that La-La-Land is someplace to look up to. Get out of the pool, Mary.'

'Not so fast.' Stormy put out a hand to keep Cody from pulling his niece out of the water. 'First of all, I'd like to know what's so damn admirable about chasing slobbery cows around a pasture, before poking them with a cattle prod to get them in a truck where they'll shortly end up garnished by wilted lettuce and a radish.'

'Mind your own business,' he growled. 'Mary, come on.'

'I am minding my own business. I don't eat red meat, you know. So what you do for a living seems strange to me. You don't watch movies, so what I do for a living seems worthless to you. But you keep taking potshots at me, and maligning my lifestyle, and you don't know a damn thing about me.' Stormy took a deep breath. 'All I'm asking, Cowboy, is that you slow down a minute, and don't come rushing in here yelling at me before I even have a chance to tell you what happened.'

51

'I know what's happening.' His gaze roved her swimsuit, then returned to her face. 'You've scared the tar out of Mary's mother with your irresponsible behavior –'

'Uncle Cody,' Mary interrupted. 'Stormy didn't know I was running away. She didn't know I was coming over to the hotel.'

'Running away? What are you talking about?' He stared at her.

'I needed to get away for a while. I shouldn't have done it, but I . . . need someone to talk to. You all treat me like a baby, like you are now. Stormy at least listens to me.' Mary met Stormy's eyes gratefully.

Cody shot an eyeful of flame at Stormy, which she returned. 'I don't like men who bellow,' she enunciated clearly. 'I don't like men who have bad tempers.'

'I don't have a bad temper!'

'You do!' Stormy pecked him with one finger on the chest. 'Take a deep breath, count to ten, and be glad I don't throw you in the pool to cool you off.'

'Listen, little lady, I've had plenty of people wish they could –'

'Sh. You're making me crazy,' Stormy told him. 'I can't stand men who are full of themselves. I'm no little lady, and Mary says she's not a little girl any more. And I called Annie and got permission from her for Mary to spend the night with me. We're sorry you had to get out of bed, because obviously you're a person who needs all your rest.

But go away. You're spoiling this girls'-night-out we're having.'

His mouth flattened into a grim line. 'Everything was fine until you came along.'

'Obviously not!' she shot back. 'You're lucky I'm here. So stick that under your cowboy hat, and come back when it's had a chance to soak in.'

She put her hands back on her hips and drew herself up. Once again, his eyes swept her in an assessing glare.

'Fine. I'll be back for Mary at eight o'clock in the morning, sharp. You'd better be ready.' He looked at both of them one more time with disgust. 'No wonder she thinks all you do is have fun.' He stalked off, and Stormy's heart sank.

'Boy, I've never seen anyone holler at my uncle, Stormy. You're so brave.'

'I'm not brave.' She forced herself to take deep breaths. I'm a coward, and I hate confrontation. And I need – no, I don't. I'm just fine.

'Did you know his nickname is Crazy Cody?'

Stormy sank on to a chaise, her blood thundering as adrenalin dissipated throughout her. 'Why?'

'They just say he is,' Mary said simply. 'Nobody gets into it with Uncle Cody.' She dove underwater, swimming contentedly.

'I believe it.' He just happened to hit all my hot buttons, she thought unhappily. 'Oh, dear,' she said out loud. Panic surged into the adrenalin edginess, making her hands shake. 'I've gotten myself in big trouble.'

There goes one location site. And possibly two, if Annie feels I'm trouble the way Cody does.

Then she realized she hadn't heard a vehicle leave the parking lot. Squinting toward the hotel, she saw Cody's truck, well outlined by the street lights. Inside, she could make out his shape in the driver's seat.

Surely he didn't intend to sleep in his truck! The headlights flashed on low and then off again, signaling that he was aware of her perusal. And that he was keeping an eye on her.

CHAPTER 4

Stormy turned and dove into the pool, and Cody knew he'd been dismissed. That was fine. She'd gotten his message loud and clear.

Of course, she'd gotten hers across pretty well, too. 'Such a big mouth for such a little lady,' he murmured. Fire had darn near been shooting out of that purple hair of hers. She'd been plenty riled. And determined. The only other woman he'd ever faced with that kind of determination was Annie.

Cody tipped his hat down over his eyes. He couldn't sit here for the next few hours and watch her running around in that teeny little swimsuit, that was for damn sure, or *he'd* be needing a dip in the pool to cool off. The silly thing had the center cut out of it, which showed her flat little belly, and it rode so high on the sides it was damn near just an excuse for a woman to parade around nude. The day he'd met her, he'd observed she was put together pretty well, but seeing her in that tight piece of material clarified his powers of concentration.

He had never been so struck by the urge to toss a

woman over his shoulder and carry her off to a hidden canyon. 'Damn female,' he cursed. And Mary looked up to her. Trouble was brewing, and he could only hope Stormy would finish conducting her business and head out. Otherwise, he had the feeling he might be suffering a lot of sleepless nights like this one.

Strong, hard banging on the side of his truck shot Cody upright in his seat. His hat fell into his lap. Stormy peered in at him. Their eyes locked, hers lit with saucy laughter, then she sauntered off.

'You're falling asleep on the job, Cowboy!' she called over her shoulder.

He gulped a deep breath to ease the hammering in his chest. 'Damn female,' he muttered, hearing Mary giggle as she approached the truck.

'Are you all right, Uncle Cody?'

'Never been better. You ready to go home?' he asked hopefully.

'You said eight o'clock, and I'm staying till then. Goodnight.' She leaned in and gave him a quick kiss on the cheek, which he scowled at though he didn't mean it. His niece was in big trouble, and she was with Trouble, and this whole mission he was on was a big pain in the ass. He watched Mary scamper off, then glanced at the dashboard clock. *Four o'clock in the morning.*

It was turning out to be the longest night of his life.

★ ★ ★

In the end, his revenge was too obvious. Gleefully, Cody banged on Stormy's hotel room door.

'Room Service!' he hollered.

Rustling on the other side of the door told him that there were two sleepyheads inside.

'We didn't order room service,' Mary called.

'Open up, Mary. It's Cody.'

She did a second later. He happily observed Stormy still partially asleep and looking somewhat disoriented in the queen-size bed. Setting down the tray he was carrying, completely without mercy, he jerked the bedspread off her.

He was proud of his restraint. He'd really wanted to jerk *all* the covers away to see what was underneath.

She sat up with a yelp, snatching the sheets to her chin. 'What are you doing?'

Her gray eyes demanded an answer. He grinned at her disheveled appearance and decided to give her one. 'Bringing you ladies a picker-upper. Got orange juice, some toast, and for the lady who doesn't eat red meat, a vegetable omelet.'

'Thanks, Uncle Cody. I'm hungry.'

Mary sat down and took one of the plates for herself. He was glad to see she was decently attired in a big sleep-shirt that said 'Life's a beach'. But at least she was covered. He'd wondered what Stormy had that was appropriate for a young girl to wear to bed. The first thing that had come to mind was nothing, but that had been a scalding thought, one that conjured up visions of Stormy's perky

57

little butt and bosom with no covering on them. He'd dismissed that thought as fast as he could, deciding that even a woman as outlandish as her would bring something to wear to bed in a strange city.

'Nice of you to loan my niece a T-shirt,' he told Stormy, 'even if I'm not sure I like what it says.' Her easy Los Angeles personality and that beach attitude wasn't something he wanted rubbing off on his niece.

Stormy shrugged and reached for a glass of orange juice. 'It isn't mine. She brought it with her when she came.'

Cody's heart shrank two sizes. He felt a pain in his chest, as if he'd been working too long baling hay and had pulled a muscle. 'You packed a sleep shirt, Mary?' he demanded.

'Yes, Uncle Cody.' She gestured toward a bag in the corner. He recognized her school backpack, which bulged with clothes.

'You really were running away!'

Both women looked at him as if he'd lost his mind.

'Did you not take her seriously, Cody?' Stormy gestured at him to turn around so she could get out of bed. 'I sure didn't think she was taking a midnight stroll for nothing.'

He turned to stare at Mary, not seeing Stormy as she fled from his view. 'Why?' Pain spread through him that he hadn't felt since his brother had died. This child he adored, this flesh and blood of his brother's, was unhappy and Cody had no way of dealing with it.

She shook her head at him. 'I tried to make you understand.'

Rapid knocking at the door startled both of them. Cody pulled it open, never taking his eyes off Mary's slightly guilty, distressed expression.

'Mary!' Annie hurried into the room, enveloping her daughter in a fierce hug. 'What on earth were you thinking of?' She started crying even as she held her daughter.

'Mom. Don't cry.' Mary pulled away, unable to face her mother's angst. 'I don't know.'

'You'd better have something to say to me other than "I don't know"!'

Mary shrugged. 'I'm just . . . I'm just not always happy.'

Cody handed Annie a tissue. 'You know you're grounded,' Annie said, 'at least a week for crossing the highway.'

'Yes, Mother.' Mary's eyelashes swept down.

Stormy came out of the bathroom, fully dressed now. Cody had been so preoccupied with his niece that he hadn't glimpsed what the lunatic woman wore to bed. *Damn*.

'You're looking grizzly this morning, Cody.' Annie rubbed a hand over his beard stubble. 'Chasing a teenager wore you out worse than chasing cattle?'

'Hell, yeah. And these two think they're owls, staying up all night. But they weren't soaring this morning.' He jerked his head toward the tray. 'I brought you breakfast for babysi – uh – for your troubles last night, Stormy.'

Mary shot him a dark look. 'I don't need a babysitter.'

He held up his hands in surrender. 'I'm trying to change my thinking, ladybug.'

Annie looked at Stormy, directness in her gaze. 'I should thank you for taking care of Mary last night. And I do.'

Stormy didn't know what to say. She merely met Annie's gaze.

'However, I can't help wondering if you aren't part of the problem.'

'How do you figure that?' Stormy was outraged.

'Maybe not you exactly, but your presence in Desperado. It's putting thoughts in my daughter's head that weren't there before.'

'Mom –'

Annie ignored Mary.

'Oh, sure, shoot the messenger.' Stormy stuffed some things into the flowered carpetbag. 'Sorry. I'm not buying that. You can try to put the blame on me, and ignore the problems that are obviously surfacing in your family.' She gave Annie a sympathetic look. 'Or you can sit down and take the time to really listen to each other.' Sighing, she went to hug Mary. 'I've got to go. I have an appointment. Don't do that again. You scared us all to death.'

With a malevolent glare Cody's way, she sailed past him. 'You *do* need a shave, Cowboy.'

Then she was gone.

Annie's mouth opened. 'My. She is energetic, isn't she?'

A whirlwind. 'Yep,' he replied stonily. 'Let's get out of here.' He could smell perfume that was distinctly Stormy, and her hair had been pulled into a sophisticated crown of curls, which made him think of elegant old-movie stars. Heck, he'd had no idea a woman could get dressed that fast. Surely there was more of a process involved to looking that damn good.

Whoa! Since when did Stormy Nixon look damn good to me?

'Cody, are you all right?'

Annie peered at him. Mary held a piece of toast between her fingers, which had gotten halfway to her mouth but hadn't made it as she stared at him curiously.

'You look kind of . . . confused, Uncle Cody. Hornswoggled.'

He *felt* hornswoggled. Annie was right. Stormy's presence in Desperado was putting thoughts in at least one head – *his*.

In the Stagecoach Inn lobby, Mayor Curvy Watkins of Desperado and Mayor Tate Wrong-Way Higgins of Shiloh had squared off in a shouting match. Trouble stood firmly in the middle, trying to settle the two men. Cody sighed to himself and went over to see what the hubbub was about. Annie and Mary followed.

61

'You got no business bringing your sneaky-snake self into Desperado and trying to run off with a guest this city is paying room and board to impress, Tate!' Curvy's face was red with exertion. 'Go find your own damn movie scout!'

'Wait, please –' Stormy began.

Neither man batted an eye her way.

'She agreed to meet me this morning,' Tate said, his stance aggressive. 'Can I help it if she can't find what she needs in this two-bit smuggling town?'

'Hold on, please!' Stormy stepped in between the two arguing men. 'I have talked to people in Desperado, and now I have an appointment to talk to people about land in Shiloh. But I must have a location for this movie by tomorrow – no later. Or I will have to move to some of our other choices for the shoot.' Seeing that she had the attention of everyone in the room, which had filled considerably due to the ruckus, Stormy took a deep breath. 'Now. If you will excuse me –'

'Miss Nixon! Miss Nixon!'

She paused, hearing about ten people call her name at once. Cody watched her, telling himself he had chores to see to, but he was fascinated by one tiny woman controlling an entire room of anxious people. She's good at what she does, he thought begrudgingly.

'Can you tell us what kind of film you're doing?'

'Certainly.' She gave the room her brightest smile. 'We're making a horror film called *The Devil's Sun*.

Excitement erupted in the room. 'A horror film!' Annie whispered behind him. 'I didn't know that.'

'Now I know I won't get to audition,' Mary griped.

'You sure as shooting won't.' Cody stepped forward. 'How come you never mentioned before that it was a horror film?' he called to Stormy.

She frowned at him. 'I'm sure I said it was. Anyway, what difference does it make?'

Apparently, lots of other folks agreed with her assessment, because several surged forward to ask more questions, and to beg for auditions.

'Oh, no,' Mary moaned. 'Now everyone's heard about the movie, and they're all going to want to try out.'

'It doesn't matter, ladybug.' Cody steered Annie and Mary from the crowded lobby.

'But I want to be an actress!' she cried.

'Maybe. But horror films are not for thirteen-year-old eyes.' He was adamant.

Sulking, Mary went and got into her mother's car, slamming the door.

'Do you really think that's a problem?' Annie eyed Cody pensively. 'I don't think a horror film would be that bad. She'd have a bit part – if she got it. And I'm of a mind to let her see that trying out for something isn't easy.'

'What if she got the part?'

Annie shrugged. 'So let her see that making a movie is hard work.'

'Hard work?' He stared at the woman he held

above all others. 'Cattle-driving is hard work. Seeding a field and praying that bugs, birds, and the bad side of Mother Nature don't destroy your livelihood is hard work. Pretending is not.'

Annie looked at him. 'Well, you're working awfully hard at it.'

He squinted at her. 'What's your meaning?'

'You know exactly.' She got in the car. 'Thanks for looking out for Mary last night.'

'My pleasure.' He couldn't help the sarcasm. 'Be more of a pleasure if she'd be a good girl for her Uncle Cody from now on.'

Mary stuck out her tongue at him. Annie gave him a sage nod. 'We'll see how good Mary is for you next week when Zach and I go on our second honeymoon.'

'Oh . . . I forgot.' Cody grimaced. 'I did say Ma and me would be happy to take care of ladybug, didn't I?'

'Yes, you did.' Annie smiled at him sweetly. 'And it's too late to back out on your offer.'

'Speaking of offers, what are you going to do about Stormy's?'

Annie shrugged. 'Zach and I haven't decided.'

'Oh, Mom!'

'Sh, Mary. There's a lot we'd have to change to be able to do it. And I'm not sure what all's entailed in a horror film. I was picturing something cute.'

'We have to talk about it, Annie.' Cody's tone was flat and serious. 'You and Zach have to talk about it. In a horror film, there's likely going to be . . .'

'Blood. I've already thought about that, Uncle Cody.' Mary looked at him, and then her mother. 'It's not the same as when Dad died. I'd know it was pretend.'

Maybe. Cody met Annie's eyes in a moment where both clearly remembered the past. As Annie had pointed out, pretending was difficult. She knew it; he knew it. Mary, caught between wistful childhood and teenage drama, thought make-believe could always be separated from reality.

There had been nothing make-believe about Carlos's bloody tractor death. It was the root of many of the problems Mary was having now. And blood stained everything it touched.

CHAPTER 5

Stormy felt that something was wrong the instant Cody took his disapproving glare out of the Stagecoach Inn. But people crowded around her, pressing against her with voices that demanded she stay and answer their questions. No matter how much she wanted to, she couldn't follow Cody and find out if her instincts were right.

Reluctantly, she turned her attention to Mayor Higgins. 'Thank you for coming by to pick me up.' She wasn't fond of the tall man with the well-tended handlebar mustache. Cowboys were cowboys, she supposed, and she needed a location to film fast, but she sure wished Cody left more room to negotiate with than a flat 'no'. As difficult as he was, she still felt she could trust him. And Annie.

It was harder to trust a man with the nickname of Wrong-Way.

'It's a pleasure, Miss Nixon,' Tate said with a charming grin. 'Let the lady by, folks. We've got important places to be.'

Sighing, Stormy got in the truck when he

opened the door for her, hoping that Shiloh, the honorable city where folks had been down-home good for hundreds of years, had a reason to put its trust in this too-agreeable mayor. He got in the truck and grinned at her to make her feel at ease, but Stormy suddenly had a sense of being the egg the weasel dragged off.

Cody ignored the jealousy and anger at seeing Stormy get into Tate's truck. He wouldn't allow his worst enemy to go anywhere with Wrong-Way. But he didn't have any say where Stormy was concerned, and it was her right to look for a location wherever she could, so he'd just have to mind his own business.

And try not to think about what methods that sidewinder would employ to get the cards dealt his way.

It would be better if she did take her business to Shiloh. They sure as hell weren't going to use his prime land, and Annie was going to think twice now that she knew a horror movie was in the works. *The Devil's Own*, he snorted to himself. Stormy was the devil's own and any man ought to think twice before getting himself twisted up with her.

'That sum'bitch Higgins done dragged off our golden goose.' Curvy slumped on the bench outside the post office, confiding his woes to Pick. 'Sure as shooting he'll find her the place she wants. Wham! There goes our place on the map.'

'Did Annie say no?' Pick asked.

'Not yet. But she will, 'cause she knows Cody ain't fond of the idea. Soon as that Nixon gal said horror movie, Cody took his boots outta there. You'da thought she was suggesting we begin ritual sacrifices and start with his heart.'

'Well, hell.' Pick pulled out a matchbook and inserted it between his teeth. 'Gotta apply some other kind of pressure.'

'Like what?' He was so put out he wasn't sure he could think. Tate had been grinning like a possum and it had Curvy's brain short-circuited. He hated to be beat at anything.

'I dunno. Cody's hard to wrestle down. Better focus on Annie. Or someone else who might do it. Anybody reply to your ad?'

'Hell, no,' Curvy said glumly. 'They all want parts letting Tom Cruise suck on their necks, but they don't want their land tore up.'

'Well, then. It's gotta be Annie. But she's having a baby, and it ain't right to pick on an expectin' woman.'

'No.' Curvy sighed. 'Maybe it'll all come out in the wash. Annie's got that restaurant she's gonna open up here in Desperado, and we'll just lure all the Shiloh folks up this way to eat her delicious cooking. They'll leave their money in this town, and we'll have the last laugh on Tate. They might think they're the only honest folk around, but they lie like dogs when they say they can cook.'

'Garbage so foul I wouldn't feed it to my pigs.'

Pick furrowed his brow. 'Did Annie ever get her permit for the restaurant?'

'Don't think so. Think the city is still looking it over.' Curvy looked at him. 'Why?'

'You're the mayor. Seems to me you could hold something up if you didn't think it was for the good of the city.'

'That's blackmail, Pick.'

'It's business, Curvy. She who wants to receive from the town oughta give to the town.'

'Wait just a minute.' He shook his head. 'Annie's damn generous with her time and her resources. We wouldn't have half of what we got if it wasn't for Annie Aguillar Rayez.' He waved Pick's idea off. 'Remember when lumber was so scarce, and she let us cut trees off her property to make desks for the elementary school? Nope. Can't hurt a woman who's done so much for Desperado.'

'Then Desperado stays a place where folks stop to pee on the way to Shiloh to see the statue of the general, eat that stuff they call food, and pay to see the places where the famous actors stayed. Yep.' Pick leaned back against the bench, sighing as if satisfied with the outcome. 'That's what we are. A pee stop.'

'Pick, we'd be putting ourselves on a par with that dishonest Higgins if we stooped to such trickery.'

'I ain't arguing with ya. You're the mayor, and I'm proud to be a citizen of the town with the finest potty stops in Texas.'

69

'All right!' Curvy jumped to his feet and glared down at Pick. 'I'll do it.'

'Better a man's pride than his conscience.' Pick grinned up at him. 'I'll walk over with ya.'

'I hope to hell I'm never the parent of a teenager.' Cody examined the heel of his boot. He sat in Sloan's sheriff's office, hot and airless except for the small fan in the corner, but his mood was already foul and air-conditioning wouldn't have made any difference.

'Me, neither. Heck, I hope I'm never a parent at all.' Sloan nodded his empathy. 'Bachelorhood is nearly as good as sainthood, if you think about it.'

Cody gave him a thin look. 'Why?'

'Either way, you get respect. Any man who gets to our age without getting tied down deserves respect.'

'All I know is that Stormy Nixon needs to finish up her business and get out of here. She's causing trouble.'

'Well.' Sloan leaned back, and the chair squeaked loudly. 'Reckon she couldn't stir up anything that wasn't already a problem.'

'My Mary isn't a problem, Sloan, and I don't like to hear you insinuating it.'

The sheriff gave him a thorough stare. 'Hate to differ with you, friend, but the only reason little Mary hasn't spent a night in lock-up is because I let her off easy – one time only. Just as a gesture to the respect I have for you, friend, but not to be abused.'

Cody's jaw dropped at the warning. '*What in hell are you talking about*?

'Well, this is confidential between me and you. 'Cause Mary made me a promise she was gonna stay outta trouble from then on. I believe she's kept her word.'

Cody nodded abruptly.

Sloan took a hunting knife out of his drawer and began shaving the corner of the desk. 'I found her and three little buddies punch-drunk one day down on my property.'

'When?' Cody's eyes narrowed. Annie kept a good eye on Mary. The child wasn't allowed to run wild.

'One day when they were cutting school. They'd gotten ahold of some disgusting mint liquor – and to this day they won't tell me where they got it – and they were throwing rocks through the apple trees at my horses. Too drunk to hit 'em, but still, I don't know that would have continued to be the case if I hadn't discovered what they were up to.'

'Damn it! I'll thrash her myself!' Cody jumped to his feet, his temper soaring to the red line.

'Hold on, man. Take your seat back.' Sloan stood to shove him back down in his chair, something Cody wouldn't have tolerated if he wasn't practically blind in one eye from rage and quite aware that this man had done him and his family a hell of a favor. 'You ain't thrashing no one, because this is between me and those little ladies. To be honest, I believe they were more than sorry once

71

they started puking their guts.' Sloan pointed the wide-edged knife at him for emphasis. 'You don't know sorry until you've sat with four wailing little girls whose stomachs won't stay down. Gawd-almighty. If I hadn't served in the military, I mighta been throwing up with 'em.'

Cody sat stone-still, though his hands trembled. 'You shouldn't have let her off.'

'It's my business, Cody, not yours.'

'Still. I owe you.'

Sloan sent him a sardonic look. 'Shut the hell up, Cody, and get your ass off that chair. Some-body else needs to bend my ear.'

He glanced over his shoulder and saw elderly Widow Baker hovering outside. Getting up stiffly, he said, 'Mary will pay you back for the harm she has caused you.'

Sloan stood. 'She has. She's done what I asked. My only reason in telling you is so that you understand what I mean about Stormy Nixon. She couldn't have stirred up trouble if it wasn't already a problem. And I have your word that this will be kept between the three of us.' He jerked his head once toward the door. 'Be seeing ya.'

Cody tipped his hat to Widow Baker, but strode to his truck feeling as if he was going to be ill. His little ladybug, punch-drunk and throwing rocks. Crossing highways and running away. When had everything started changing – and why hadn't he noticed?

It occurred to him, though he didn't like it a bit,

that maybe it was damn fortunate that Stormy Nixon had blown into town. Otherwise, who knew where Mary might have run to?

Zach and Annie gazed at Mary, who looked down at her shoes. They were her parents, but they had no idea what she was going through. She barely had any friends, and to make matters worse, her mom was having a baby. It would be too humiliating for her mother to come pick her up at school holding a baby carrier.

What if her mother carried the baby like a papoose? Mary cringed inside. Sometimes women used those sack things to carry their baby. She closed her eyes and wished to be anywhere but here. If her mother used one of those awful baby carriers, her friends were going to start up with the Indian jokes again. Mary didn't think she could bear it.

'Do you understand how much you frightened us?' Her mother stared at her. Zach rubbed her mom's back in comforting circles.

'Yeah.' She did, but she wouldn't have had to try to run away if they knew what she was going through.

'I don't think you do understand!' Annie stood, stalking about the kitchen.

Mary knew she should be sorry for upsetting her mother; she was a little sorry for that. 'I do understand, Mom! But you just treat me like such a baby! I've tried and tried to tell you, but you just don't listen!'

'Tell us again. We want to work this out.'

Zach sounded reasonable, but Mary knew whose side he was on. After all, her mother was carrying *his* child, his very own flesh and blood. Well, she'd been here first. 'I need to do things for myself. I want to stay out later with my friends. I don't want to wear pink ribbons to school. I want to try out for that part in Stormy's movie!'

'We're just not sure, honey.' Annie's eyes filled with worry. 'I was all for you trying out at first, but I didn't know it was a horror movie –'

'I know. I know. And you're afraid there will be blood.' Mary couldn't believe how dumb they thought she was. 'Mom, I wouldn't be afraid of red paint! I mean, how much of a baby do you think I am?'

'Mary.' Zach reached out to put a hand on her shoulder. 'When I first met you, do you remember your mother cut her finger making dinner?'

'Yeah.' Mary didn't want to think about that.

'Well, I wasn't around when your father . . . died, but you were, and it was very frightening for you. We know you're not a child any more, but some things are always scary to people, even to adults. And I remember how afraid you were when your mother cut her finger. You thought she was going to die like your father did.' He squeezed her hand as he squeezed her mother's shoulders, so that the three of them formed a circle. 'We still just want to protect you a little bit.'

'I know, Zach, but I want to grow up. If I get scared, then I'll have to deal with it myself, and that's the choice I want to make.'

'Well. We'll think about it some more.' Annie took a deep breath and stepped away from the two of them. 'For now, however, you made a poor choice in deciding to run away in the night and cross a dangerous highway. I'm going to ground you until next week, when you go to stay with Grandma and Uncle Cody.' She gave her daughter a stare that was heavy and serious. 'Mary, I'm counting on you not to give Uncle Cody any trouble.'

'See! You're talking to me like a baby again!'

'Well,' Annie snapped, 'when you act like one, I have to treat you like one.' She strode from the room.

Mary's jaw dropped. Zach slowly turned away and walked over to get something out of the refrigerator. She let out a sigh of disgust and left the house, making extra-sure she slammed the door on her way out. There was nothing to do around this old place but feed the fish in the pond, unless they'd grounded her from doing *that*, too. All her friends were probably at the cow-catch this afternoon, trying to catch cows by the tail to see who would win the college scholarship money. Lots of the girls were trying out to be Miss Desperado, the queen of the county fair. Of course, she couldn't do any of that stuff, because her mother didn't have time to take her into town.

And Mary wouldn't win anyway because nobody liked her, and nobody would vote for her.

Cody unloaded several calves for the cow-catch, unconsciously keeping an eye out for Stormy to turn up at the festivities. No doubt she'd never seen a cow-catch and would find all the teenagers running around trying to tie a rope around the nose of a bawling, frightened calf to drag it over to the judge a hilarious sight. Of course, she thought a swim in the pool at two a.m. was great fun. If he had Stormy pegged right, she'd either jump into the ring and have a hand at catching a calf herself, or she'd give him grief for letting the poor little critters be treated that way. Danged female. Turning her nose up at the way folks in Desperado ran their business.

Turning her nose up at the way *he* did business. 'Go on,' he told a calf, giving it a tiny slap to send it running into a stall.

Annie's truck pulled into a parking space and he rose to see where she was headed.

'Cody!'

He waved her over. 'Hey, Annie.'

She walked up beside him and glanced at his truck. 'Are you finished, or can I help?'

'Nope. I'm all done.' He looked her over from her jeans, which still fit snug, up to her glowing complexion. 'Feeling all right?'

'The morning sickness is bothering me in the worst way, but it passes. Sometimes.' She looked away for a second, then turned back. 'I'm going to talk to Stormy.'

'Why are you telling me?' He made himself sound gruff, but his stomach tightened at hearing her name.

'Because I thought you'd want to know.'

He straightened and gave her his most disinterested look. 'Reckon whoever wants to talk to her can. That's what she's here for.'

Annie sat down on a concrete block. 'I was awfully hard on her last night.'

Propping his boot on the bottom of a metal rail, he said, 'I'm sure she wouldn't be in the business she's in if she wasn't used to a little tough talk.'

'I thought you said her job wasn't hard.' She shot him a teasing smile.

'Get back on your subject, Annie Aguillar Rayez.'

'I'm going to accept her offer. She can film *The Devil's Sun* on my land.'

Cody's boot slid off the rail. 'Why?'

'Because . . . well, because. I just think it'll be all right.'

'All right? Isn't there a difference between something being all right, and something you really want to do? I know very well you don't care anymore about a movie, particularly a horror movie, than I do.'

'No. I don't. I don't even have cable on my TV. I'm too busy to watch TV or go to movies, but Mary's hit a bad patch, and I think this movie

thing might . . .' She stared at the calves he'd
penned. 'Might make her feel part of something.'

'Does it have to be on your property to do that?'

'No. But there aren't any other alternatives, for
one thing, and this way I can at least be on the set
every day and keep my eye on her.'

'And if she doesn't get the part? Then you're
stuck with a bunch of city folk tearing up your
land.'

'I have a funny feeling Mary will get a part of
some kind. She's danged determined about this.'
Annie gave him a wry smile. 'Stormy has made a
huge impression on her.'

'Yeah, well.' Crazy purple-haired woman had
made an impression on a lot of folks, it seemed.
Right now, she was off running around with Wrong-
Way Higgins – and Cody'd never seen a man look
more smitten than that one. 'Don't know if it's a
good impression. Hey, what about your restaurant?
How are you going to have time to run a restaurant
and be on a movie set all the time and have a baby?'

Annie shook her head. 'My permit's been turned
down.'

'*What*?'

'The reason wasn't very clear. Zach's going to
look into it. Something about there being a lack of
money in the city coffers to fix the street in front of
my restaurant site. And no money to fix the power
lines around it. And it wasn't a fire-safe location.
There were a ton of reasons.' She looked at him
sadly.

'By damn there were.' He smelled an ugly rat in this mess. Zach could check into the legal aspects of the situation if he liked, but Cody knew that to find a rat, he needed to go straight to the source of the nest – the mayor's wooden bench.

'Maybe it's for the best. I should be spending time with my daughter right now. I think she's worried about how the new baby is going to affect her.'

'Yeah, she's worrying about herself a lot these days.' Cody took her arm and led her toward the exit. 'I don't think Stormy's come back yet, but you can leave a message at the desk for her to call you.'

'Keeping an eye on her, are you, Cody?' Annie's voice turned teasing again. He could feel the tips of his ears turn red.

'No,' he lied. 'Just wasn't sure if her heading out with Wrong-Way was a good idea or not.'

'I see.' She reached up and tugged at his braid. 'You know, Cody, it wouldn't hurt you any to take a girl out every once in a while.'

'It would hurt me to take that one out. Go on.' He opened the door of her truck so she could get in.

Annie grinned at him. 'I sure do appreciate you looking out for Mary last night. I've instructed her not to give you even a whisper of trouble while we're gone.'

'Hmm.' After talking to Sloan, he wasn't sure what he'd gotten himself into. 'Are you sure you've

79

thought this situation over? About the movie set?'

The smile slipped from her face. 'I've thought about it, Cody. I don't like it. I don't like a lot of things lately, but if it will help my little girl, how can I say no?'

He pondered that as she drove away. Something was wrong with the whole scenario, but at the moment he couldn't figure out what was bothering him. Teenager or not, he wasn't completely sure that what Mary needed wasn't a whipping. If he caught her throwing rocks at horses, a whipping would be the minimum he'd recommend to Annie.

Tate's truck pulled past him, and he nodded Cody's way. The grin on Tate's face made him grit his teeth. He couldn't see Stormy, but no doubt that grin told the story. Tate had gotten what he wanted.

Annie was too late. Mary wasn't going to get her movie.

And Cody wouldn't have to look at Stormy Nixon any more. The thought should have been a relief, but the pain in his gut said otherwise.

Five minutes later, he saw Annie's truck and flagged her down. 'Catch her?'

'No, She wasn't in. I left a message.'

'Thought I saw her come in a bit ago with Tate.'

'You sure are noticing her comings and goings.'

'Well, I wouldn't except that darn Tate was wearing a grin the size of a quarter-moon.'

'I see. Well, anyway, I've got to get on home. I've grounded Mary and Zach's watching her, so no doubt he's ready for a break.' She smiled and waved as she put the truck in gear. 'Maybe you oughta take Stormy to the calf-catch tonight, Cody,' she called as she drove off.

'Maybe I ought not.' He grabbed his gear and took it out to throw in the back of his truck. Thirty minutes later, he saw Tate leaving the vicinity at a faster speed than when he'd come into town. Maybe Stormy'd stuck the spurs to his backside.

'Naw. He's just hurrying off to tell the Shiloh bunch they got themselves a deal.' Still, he wandered around the square, all the while glancing through the crowd for Stormy.

After the calf-catch, she still hadn't put in an appearance. Twenty teenagers were grinning and wearing cow manure and straw as they proudly accepted their prizes, but Stormy wasn't there to pick on him about the poor little calves being dragged by their tails. He was sure he would've gotten an earful.

No doubt she had an appointment with some other city mayor, as she'd said she was on an urgent deadline to find a location – if she and Tate hadn't come to terms. However, she just might be sitting in her room, feeling lonely. That would be no way to treat a visitor to their town.

Cody set his hat on his head and decided it was his duty to pay a call on Miss Stormy Nixon.

CHAPTER 6

Stormy didn't answer his knock on her hotel room door. Nor had she answered when he'd rung her room. But, dang it, her rental car was in the parking lot. He'd glanced at the pool but she wasn't there. 'Stormy?' he called. 'It's Cody.'

He heard rustling inside. She opened the door a crack. 'Oh, lord, Cody. I thought Tate had come back.'

His stomach curdled at Stormy's flushed face. If Tate had done anything to her, he'd put a hurt on him he wouldn't forget. 'Are you all right?'

She barely nodded. Her hair was disheveled, her upper lip perspiring a bit. And by golly, for a woman with skin she so proudly called alabaster, she was damn white right now.

Pushing her hair back with trembling fingers, she said, 'Actually, I'm dying. But there's nothing you can do about it.'

'My God, Stormy! Let me in.' He was afraid she was going to faint.

'No, Cody. Please. I just want to be alone. Oh, no!'

She slammed the door. He heard another door inside her room slam shut. The bathroom. Pushing his hat back on his head, he frowned. Not that he considered Stormy attractive, but she certainly hadn't looked right. Something was dead wrong.

A second later, he heard a moan. Briefly considering his options – he could go away or he could risk taking one of those high-heeled shoes of hers in the head if she flung it at him – he decided to make sure she was all right. He barely opened the door, which she had neglected to lock, and poked his head around it.

'Stormy?' he whispered, thinking maybe she'd gone to sleep. Like a horizontal line she lay across the bed, unmoving.

Very slowly, she turned her head to squint at him out of eyes that suffered. 'I don't want you to see me like this,' she said on a breath.

'Jeez. If you're sick, Stormy, let's not worry about me seeing you. What the hell's wrong with you?'

'I don't know.' She closed her eyes.

He took that to mean she wasn't in any condition to bean him with a shoe. A very bad sign. Closing the door behind him, he strode to the bed and stared down at her. 'Can I get you a glass of water? Aspirin?' He didn't know what was ailing her, which made him feel helpless. It was hard to see her feeling so poorly.

She started to shake her head, but suddenly jackknifed to a standing position and raced to the bathroom. He could hear her being violently ill on the other side of the door.

'Damnation,' he said to himself. What could be making her so ill?

A second later, she only made it back to the bed because he leapt to his feet and helped her the rest of the way.

'Cody, I've never been this sick,' she said on a groan. 'I don't know what's wrong with me.'

He helped her lie down. Without speaking, he got a cool washcloth and laid it on her forehead. 'Close your eyes,' he instructed. Quickly, he tried to organize the thoughts swirling in his mind. Mary had thrown up from drinking mint liquor. He didn't smell liquor on Stormy.

Annie had said the morning sickness made her throw up in the worst way. Stormy was tossing her crackers mighty bad.

What if she was pregnant?

He closed his eyes.

It was the fortieth time she'd thrown up, Stormy was certain. There was nothing left in her stomach, and worse, Cody Aguillar was witness to the depth of her misery. She wanted desperately for him to go away, yet she hung on to him like a lifeline.

Oh, my God. I'm going to die.

She must have spoken out loud because Cody said, 'Not if I've got anything to say about it.'

If she could have managed a smile, she would have. As it was, she tried not to move.

'Stormy, you've got to help me out here. If I know why you're sick, I can maybe figure out what to do for you.'

She didn't care.

'Are you pregnant?'

Rolling her head his way, she did her best to glare at him through pain-glazed eyes. 'No.'

'I know you haven't been drinking.'

'No.' She didn't think even booze could make someone this ill.

'Stormy, I think I should take you to a doctor. You're mighty ill for not knowing why. What if you've got appendicitis?'

'No.' She heard him sigh deeply as he shifted his weight from where he sat on the bed.

'Were you sick in Shiloh?'

'No.' It was almost the best she could manage. 'We ate lunch, then Mayor Higgins took me to talk to some folks, then we came back. I started feeling ill then –'

She barely made it to the bathroom in time for another round. To her mortification, she felt Cody standing behind her, grasping her hair up off of her neck. 'There's nothing left inside me,' she gasped.

'You've thrown up enough for ten people just since I've been here. Can you stand?'

She shook her head. He lifted her under the arms. 'Stormy, if you ate in Shiloh, that's probably what's wrong with you.'

'Why?'

85

'They . . . some of those eateries aren't owned by the most hygienic folks you'll ever meet.'

'It's the town of honest people.'

'Yeah.' She heard his snort. 'That doesn't mean spit, for one thing, and it sure as hell doesn't mean they should be operating restaurants. Somebody's paying off the health inspector big time.'

It no longer interested her that there was an ongoing feud between the two cities. Right now, she wanted to die. 'My stomach hurts.'

'It should. Stormy, you have two choices. You can let me take you to the hospital, or I'll take you to my place.'

'No.' She collapsed on the bed.

'You're not listening. That wasn't a choice. I'm seriously concerned about you dehydrating – or worse. It's either the hospital, or I take you to my mother.'

'Is she a doctor?'

'God, no. Better.'

'I'm not dressed for visiting.'

'For crying out loud, Trouble. Shut your mouth and hang on.'

She heard him moving some things around her room. Dazed, she wondered what he was doing, then stifled a gasp as he swooped her up off the bed into his strong arms. He was warm and solid and being in his arms was comforting. After a second, she relaxed against his chest. I'm safe, she thought as she released herself into his keeping. He won't let anything happen to me.

It was the only time in her life she could remember feeling so important, so treasured.

So protected.

'You have never brought a woman home before.' His mother, Carmen Aguillar, came to join him in the den.

'She's sick.' It was all the answer he wanted to give.

'Very. Maybe she needs *el médico*.'

'*No es necessario*.' He shrugged. 'You know as much as any doctor. And she said no hospital, so I had no choice. What do I know? Maybe she has no insurance. Maybe she's afraid of doctors or needles.'

Carmen looked at him thoughtfully. 'The nausea seems to have left her. She is asleep, fortunately.'

'I'm going to call the health inspector in Shiloh. They need to do something about the food services.'

'She does not believe she is sick from the food. Your friend says lots of people were in the restaurant eating.' She went into the kitchen and got herself a glass of tea before coming to sit on a sofa. 'Of course, I told her that maybe it is a little bit like Mexico. Those who live there don't get sick. Those who come to visit might.'

'A health inspector needs to clean that place out. There's something wrong when people get that ill from eating the food. Zach has a cast-iron stomach, and the only time he ate in Shiloh, he was that ill.' He scratched his head, unwilling to remind his mother of the night he'd kept her pretty busy taking care of him, too. 'I just don't believe it's a coincidence.'

'I know.' Carmen nodded. 'So, this is the Stormy that Mary told me about.'

'Yes. She's made a huge impression on Mary.' He leaned back into the sofa. *She's made an impression on a lot of people.*

'She's pretty.'

Cody nodded. 'That's what everyone seems to think.'

'And you?'

How could he explain that he found the woman attractive in a way even he didn't understand, but no, she most definitely was not beautiful? 'She's fine.'

His mother snorted. 'You bring her home. You like her.'

'I would like her not to die while she's in Desperado.'

There was silence between them for a few moments before his mother spoke again. 'Annie has been married for seven years now.'

'And I'm glad.' It was true. Cody got along with Zach, and he liked seeing Annie and Mary so happy. Well, Mary had been happy, until recently.

'You thought you needed to take care of Annie. Now, you're taking care of this woman.'

'Oh, no.' He shook his head adamantly. 'Not the same thing at all.'

'Why not?' Carmen's eyes were inscrutable.

'Because . . . there isn't any taking care of Stormy. She reminds me of a hummingbird that flits around and can't stay still. She's always into something. I couldn't take care of her if I wanted to.'

'You are.'

'No, *we* are.' How to explain this to his mother, who was heading down the completely wrong path on this subject? 'Mary is my brother's daughter, and my goddaughter, and therefore my own. I would have married Annie to take care of my brother's family, which is my own. Stormy Nixon is not my family, and I don't need to be responsible for her.' There. He was very proud of how well he'd stated that. It should wipe out whatever strange notions his mother was having about him and Stormy.

She sighed heavily. 'But you made her problem your own.'

'Not for long.' It was one thing to help a woman who was ill, another to think of her in a permanent sense the way he thought of Annie. He and Stormy had opposite lifestyles: they lived in two states, had opinions at odds with each other. They didn't think highly of one another's livelihood.

But that didn't mean he would let her dehydrate in a hotel room in Desperado where she had no friends or family. That was no way to treat a lady, or anyone else for that matter. He got to his feet. 'I'm going to check on her.'

His mother nodded and turned the TV on. He headed down the hall, bracing himself to talk to the woman in the guest bedroom.

But Stormy was still sound asleep. He was glad to see it. With her eyes closed, she appeared defenseless. Dark eyelashes lay against her porcelain cheeks. He missed looking at her eyes; it was how he knew her. Snapping fire or immensely curious, her light, violet-gray eyes spoke everything her mouth might say, only more.

Reaching out, he gently pushed her hair off her face. For an instant, she opened her eyes and gazed at him. Her lips curled at the edges in the barest of smiles. 'Thank you, Cowboy.'

Something tightened inside his chest as she closed her eyes again. He couldn't stop staring at her. The momentary connection that had flashed between them was hot and alive and sent tingles all over his scalp.

'Sleep,' he murmured, before backing out of the room. 'I'll be close by if you need anything.'

But she didn't open her eyes again. He felt empty and somewhat disappointed. It was crazy. The woman was a pain in the butt.

For some reason, an errant part of his mind was ignoring the pain.

It had to be afternoon of the next day, Stormy decided as she watched the sun send beams of light across the navy bedspread covering her. She felt depleted and still exhausted, but better than she'd felt yesterday – except for the utter embarrassment she was suffering. Spending several hours throwing up in front of a man with a demeanor like a rock made her close her eyes tightly. Cody acted as if her being sick was no big deal, but it was not the way a woman wanted a man to see her. With any luck, he'd be out on the ranch today doing whatever ranchers did and she could call a taxi to take her back to the Stagecoach Inn. She was not letting him see her like this. Straggly, limp hair stuck to her head, and her eyeballs felt as if tiny insects had rooted tunnels through them. If she could make it to the bathroom, she was going to take a warm shower.

As soon as she made it out of bed to stand on very shaky legs, Cody knocked briefly and popped his head around the door. 'How are you feeling?'

She shrieked and fell back into bed, burrowing into the covers and flinging them up over her head. 'Go away!'

'Ah. You must be feeling better.' His boots stopped at the side of the bed.

'Please, Cody, go away. I don't want anyone to see me looking like this.'

'I saw you a lot worse yesterday. Besides, I'm going to help you shower.'

'The hell you are!' Under the covers, Stormy cringed, her fingernails tight around the sheet edges in case he tried to jerk them off of her the way he had the bedspread once before.

He chuckled. 'I'm kidding. Why don't you eat before you try to get cleaned up?'

'The last thing I want is food.'

'How about some soda water?'

If she said yes, he'd be gone long enough for her to dart into the bathroom and lock the door. 'That sounds enticing,' she said sweetly.

'Be right back.' His boots left the side of the bed. She heard him walk down the hall.

Swiftly, she tossed the covers off, leapt from the bed and sprinted to the bathroom. She locked the door and sank on to the bathtub edge. Mission accomplished.

'I've set your water on the nightstand,' Cody called.

'Thank you.' She managed a grin for the way she'd outmaneuvered him.

'Be careful you don't try to move around too much too fast.'

'I won't. Go away now.' She waited, but he didn't reply. Obviously, he'd done as she asked. Sighing, she pulled off the huge T-shirt Carmen Aguillar had helped her put on last night. Thank heaven Cody had brought her here. She couldn't have borne going to the hospital. Mrs Aguillar was cut from the same cloth as her son, which in a way was comforting. No surprises. Just warm, solid comfort.

Her toothbrush and hairbrush were in the bathroom. She remembered Cody moving around her hotel room before lifting her into his arms. She should feel like he'd overstepped himself, she supposed, but truthfully, she was terribly glad to have some of her things. She brushed her teeth, feeling as if she was honestly on the mend.

She stepped into the shower, washing her hair first. Then she pushed the drain stopper down and let the tub fill with warm water because her legs were still too weak to stand for long. It was wonderful to be clean again. She felt cozy and comfortable in this house, and somehow part of a family. Briefly, she let her mind stray to her own parents.

Flower children of the sixties. Constant traveling with a basement band. As a baby, she'd slept in dresser drawers and the back of numerous rickety vans. She'd had an assortment of 'uncles' and 'aunts', all smiling at her sheepishly before they went back into her parents' bedrooms. Free love. Baggies of marijuana, needles, unclean smells. Home was where the heart was. Her home had only been herself out of necessity. Self-reliance kept her sane while she watched cartoons on old TVs in rooms disturbed by flickering strobe lights.

She shuddered, sitting upright in the tub. Thank heaven Cody hadn't taken her to a hospital. She never wanted to be in one again. Hospitals, sanitariums – soul-suckers. The one trap she'd desperately sought to avoid – being a useless drop-out like her parents – had nearly closed its steel metal teeth on her when she'd become addicted to prescription drugs. That time, she'd fought her way out of the hellhole. But if Cody had taken her to the hospital and they'd given her anything for pain, she might have started needing again – and the hard, clutching fingers of panic would grip her. She might not overcome it again.

'Stormy! Are you all right?' Banging erupted on the door, jerking her out of the past. Her heart beat wildly.

'I'm fine!'

'Well . . . you've been in there for thirty minutes. Not that I mind, but I was getting worried.'

'Don't break the door in, Cowboy. I'm coming out.'

She let the water out and dried herself off. Quivers hit her legs as she slipped on a robe Carmen had lent her. 'Oh, my gosh,' she muttered, pulling open the door. 'I feel like a brand-new kitten.'

He scooped her up, placing her gently on the bed. 'See? You should have let me help you. But you're a stubborn woman.'

'Buzz off,' she forced herself to whisper.

He loomed over her, chuckling. 'I brought you some plain toast. Maybe that will help.'

Struggling to sit up, she took a nibble. 'I don't know if I can do this, though I appreciate the effort.'

'Try. And Ma's going to make you some broth for lunch.'

Sighing, she moved her hair off her shoulders and concentrated on the triangle of toast.

'Here. Let me get that out of your way.'

He reached to grasp her hair in his hands.

94

Stormy opened her mouth to protest.

'Be still. It's too wet for you to be comfortable.' He strode from the room before coming back with a blow dryer.

'Cody,' she protested weakly, but he'd already plugged it in and pointed it her way. In a few minutes, her hair was dry.

'Here.' He pulled her hair into a fast braid, sending shivers all over her body that had nothing to do with her feeble state. 'That should make you more comfortable.'

'Thanks,' she muttered, not certain if she liked the big man braiding her hair. 'I look like you now, I guess.'

'No.' He shook his head at her, his expression thoughtful. 'You don't.'

She didn't know what to say to that, and the look in his eyes was one she hadn't seen before. He shouldn't have touched her; they shouldn't be alone in this room together. There was too much heat and it wasn't left over from the blow-dryer. He moved his hand to smooth her hair and tingles raced all across her skin.

'Where's your mother?' she whispered, hoping Carmen was just down the hall. Cody's eyes were focused on her in an expression she recognized as male hunger. She knew he wouldn't take advantage of her weakened state in his house – but was that what she wanted?

'Gone to the market for a few things,' he replied in a husky voice.

'I see.' Her eyes lowered under his intense scrutiny as she cast around for a topic they could discuss that would disarm the emotions she felt building inside. 'Have you always lived together?'

'Since my father died, yes. My mother talked about getting a place of her own, but then my brother died some years back. She doesn't talk about getting a place of her own any more.' He wouldn't release her gaze. 'She is older now. I think she's happy sticking close to home.'

'I . . . understand,' Stormy said on a whisper. *Because you make me feel safe and secure, except at this moment.* 'Don't you have some . . . cows to feed or something?'

'Are you trying to get rid of me?'

He didn't quite smile, but she thought he was amused. 'Not exactly. I might fall asleep, though.' She put the toast back on the plate and moved it to the nightstand to emphasize her intentions.

'Go to sleep, then.' He backed away from the bed. 'Rest well.'

A second later, he was gone. Irritably, Stormy stared at the door he'd closed behind him. How in the heck was she supposed to sleep well – when it had suddenly occurred to her that, if it felt wonderful just for Cody to hold her, how much more wonderful would it be if he made love to her?

CHAPTER 7

Two minutes later, Mary came into the bedroom. 'Stormy? Are you awake?'

Stormy forced herself to sit up although the after-effects from the nausea still made her weak. 'Barely. Come on in.'

'Uncle Cody says you went to eat in Shiloh. He says you got sick.' Mary's eyes were wide as she stared at her. 'I hope you're feeling better.'

'In a manner of speaking.' Muscles ached in her body where she hadn't known she could ache. Her throat was sore. Even her back hurt. 'If you're going to warn me not to eat there any more, don't worry. I wouldn't if I was starving.'

Mary shook her head, puzzled. 'I don't know why the food there is so bad. Uncle Cody says it's because the people are liars and cheats.'

'Can liars and cheats survive salmonella?' Stormy asked wryly.

'He says it doesn't affect them because they have no conscience, and therefore must lack stomach. No, he calls it gut. They lack gut.'

'Hm.' Stormy wasn't surprised by Cody's theory. He had made it clear that he didn't like Wrong-Way, but apparently, feeling strongly against Shiloh and its mayor didn't make him more disposed to giving her the deal she wanted. His land – off limits. She sighed, knowing it wasn't going to happen. Cody was never going to bend. 'Oh, my gosh. I've got to call my manager. Mary, is there a phone I can use?'

'Yeah. Let me get it for you.'

Stormy expected a portable to be brought to her room, but Mary dragged an old black phone from across the hall, its long cord pulling taut on the carpet. 'Thanks,' she said.

'I'll leave so you can talk.'

'Thanks,' Stormy said again, her mind now on the call she had to make. Pulling a calling card from her purse, she dialed the number.

'Jonathan. It's Stormy.'

'Where have you been? I've called your hotel room five thousand times, luv!'

'Sorry. I got sick, and a friend brought me to his house.'

'Oh, really. How nice of him. Love is the best medicine and all that.'

'Hardly.' Stormy injected ice into her tone. 'It was either come here with his mother so she could look after me, or go to the hospital.'

'You sound all better now.'

His patronizing tone grated her nerves. 'I am. I think I've decided on Shiloh, Texas for the shoot.

The mayor is anxious for us to come there; the land looks good. Not as great as here, but I can't get these folks to budge.'

'Oh, Stormy, luv.' Jonathan hesitated a moment. 'I've got some bad news.'

Sinking hit her stomach with a green-tinged wave. 'What?'

'Well, when we couldn't find you – I mean, it had been a couple of days – the folks with the bankrolls were afraid there was a problem.'

'You assumed I was taking some side trips into the pharmacy.'

'You knew we had a deadline, you knew we stood to lose some big stars, Stormy! So when we didn't hear from you and couldn't reach you, they called in Rhonda Harlow. There was nothing I could do.'

'Then I'm . . .' The sinking sensation turned into a sinkhole.

'Fired. I'm so sorry, luv. But what could I do? My hands were tied.'

'A position I'm sure you enjoyed very much,' she snapped, hanging up the phone. 'Damn it!' What in the heck was she going to do now? She had no job, no prospect of another one, and a new black mark on her record. She'd failed on her last chance.

Slowly, she pulled her hair out of the braid, letting it wave around her shoulders. It was time to get dressed, go back to the Stagecoach, and say goodbye to Desperado. There was nothing else she could do.

'Stormy? Are you off the phone?' Mary peeked around the door again.

'Yes.' She watched as the teenager came into her room. 'Where's your uncle?'

'Riding fence. He'll be back this afternoon.' Mary's eyes looked longingly toward a flowered bag which sat in a chair, on top of some clothes. 'Is that your make-up?'

Stormy's eyes widened. Obviously, Cody had made a trip to her hotel room to get her a change of clothes and her cosmetic bag. 'It seems to be.'

She got up to look at what he'd brought her. How thoughtful. This was the last thing she'd ever expected from the stoic rancher.

'Can I try on some of your make-up?'

'Sure,' Stormy said sadly, as she took the clothes into the bathroom so she could change. 'Help yourself.' *I'm kinda going to miss him, now that I have to leave.* Even as the words strayed across her mind, she realized how ridiculous the longing was.

But she'd never met anyone like him.

Fifteen minutes later, Cody knocked on the door, striding in as soon as he saw Mary in Stormy's room. 'What in the hell do you have on your face?' he demanded. *An Indian wouldn't wear that much paint going into war.*

'Stormy's make-up. Don't you think I'm pretty?' Mary's lip wobbled.

He forced himself to slow down and take a deep

breath. Obviously, Mary thought she'd made an improvement in her looks. It was important that he remember she was in a struggling phase of her life. 'Ah, it looks nice, ladybug,' he lied through his teeth, 'though I must admit I like you better with, um, just a little less on. I do like to see my pretty girl's face.'

Mary appeared unconvinced. 'You sound kind of smooth, like Wrong-Way Higgins.'

'Well, I –' He faltered at her perception.

'Uncle Cody,' she said sternly, with her hands on her hips, 'you can't fault other people for fibbing if you're going to do it. And you can't get on to me for it, either.'

'Hold on a minute, ladybug. There's fibbing, and then there's fibbing.'

Stormy walked out of the bathroom, and his breath left him. She was tousled and sexily elegant all at the same time. Why did he have to find himself drawn to her when it was as futile as a moth beating helplessly against a light?

'No, there is not two different kinds of fibbing,' she said, joining into the debate. 'There are no varying levels of lying. Tell her the truth, Cody.'

He sighed. 'I don't like you wearing so much make-up. You look like you're going to be in a horror movie.'

The instant he said it, he damn sure wished he hadn't.

'I'm going to be an actress when I grow up,' his niece replied dreamily, turning back to the mirror.

101

'This is all your fault,' he growled at Stormy. 'Did you tell her she could get in your goo?'

'Yes.' Stormy sashayed to the bed, dressed in the clothes he'd brought her and looking totally refreshed. He'd been at a loss to choose something out of her closet for her, finally settling on a loose dress that had enough material for a circus big top. Unfortunately, when she put it on, somehow a bow here and a tie there made the damn thing float on her body like gentle hands. He stared at her toes, which were small and delicate and had burgundy toenail polish on them. 'You look much better,' he managed. 'Nice, actually.'

'Is that the truth?' She shot him a daring look.

'Yes, it was,' he ground out. 'Can you take a compliment without making a federal case out of it?'

'Testy today, I see,' she murmured.

'Testy most days,' Mary inserted. She leaned close to a mirror, examining her handiwork.

Stormy zipped her handbag closed. 'I hate to leave, but I must, Cody. I'm going to call a taxi, if you'll tell me exactly where I am.'

'A taxi? I can take you back to the hotel.'

'I think I've put you out enough.' She smiled, feeling tired all of sudden. 'I appreciate you taking care of me – saving my life, probably. But the taxi can wait while I pay my hotel bill and grab my things, and then take me on to the airport.'

'Airport?' Cody and Mary both stared at her.

'Yes. As of yesterday, my lodgings are no longer

102

being paid for. So, I'm off, as much as I've enjoyed my stay here.'

'What about the movie?' Mary demanded.

Yeah. What about it? Cody thought belligerently, knowing the answer. Wrong-Way had worked the deal he wanted and now Stormy was off, leaving as breezily as she'd come.

'Well, I suppose *I* must be truthful now.'

A little of the stiffness went out of Stormy; Cody thought she looked defeated.

'I got fired,' she said.

'Fired! How?' Cody asked.

'I had a deadline I needed to meet. What day is it, anyway?'

'Monday. Why?' How could she have gotten fired? If he had a movie company, Stormy would be his emissary of choice. She was popular with folks she met, she stuck to her job without being pushy. He almost admired her.

'I missed my deadline. I needed a set location by Friday, and I guess I've been here that long. I should have called to let them know I was getting close to something on Friday, but it just flew out of my mind when I got ill.'

Hell, yeah. Everything had been flying out her very rapidly that day. Dismay filled him. 'Uh – did you happen to pick up your messages at the desk on Friday?'

'No.' She looked at him curiously. 'Have you been going through my messages?'

'No! Why would I do such a thing?'

'I don't know.' She gestured to her clothes. 'You seem to have helped yourself to my room and my stuff.'

'Oh, for crying out loud. Be sure you skip the gratitude and get right to the complaint department.' He glared at her, but he could feel his expression softening at her teasing smile.

'Can we get back to my messages?'

'Annie said she left you one on Friday,' he said begrudgingly.

'Oh? What did it say?'

'I have no idea.'

'I do.' Mary glanced up from the mirror. 'Mom's going to let you film your movie on her land.' Her expression was hopeful. 'You still can, can't you?'

Stormy stared at Cody, her eyes asking for confirmation of Mary's words. He nodded abruptly.

'Oh, no,' she murmured.

'You can't?' Mary asked.

'I'm afraid it's out of my hands.' Stormy looked at the little girl unhappily.

'You mean, I won't get to audition for the movie?'

'I don't know what will happen now.' Stormy shook her head. 'I'm sorry, Mary.'

The teenager looked down for a few seconds, before putting Stormy's make-up back in its case. Stormy held Cody's gaze.

'I'm sorry you lost your job, Stormy,' Mary said softly. 'I'm going to miss you.'

Cody watched Stormy's gaze instantly flick to Mary. 'I'm going to miss you, too,' she said, and instantly, he realized that Stormy had gotten attached to his ladybug. In a way, he wasn't surprised. They both seemed so fragile, so vulnerable. A lump settled in his throat. It didn't seem right that Stormy would leave Desperado. But if she'd gotten fired, she'd gotten fired. Why did he find her leaving surprisingly hard to look forward to?

'Of course, Annie is welcome to talk to the new location scout. I can give her the phone number of the studio and she can call her.'

Cody blinked as Stormy turned all-business. 'I'll pass it on.'

'Fine. Well, I should call that taxi now.'

'I'll take you to the hotel,' he said gruffly. 'At least save you that cab fare.'

'Thank you.' She gave him a slight smile.

'Ladybug, you stay here with Grandma. I'll be back shortly,' Cody instructed.

'I will.' She got up to hug Stormy. 'Thank you for treating me like a grown-up,' she whispered, but Cody heard. Did he not do the same?

Stormy picked up her handbag and walked into the front of the hall, noticing how long it was. Cody had carried her all this way. It seemed like she'd been here a lifetime – and somehow, she hated to leave.

Carmen stood as Stormy walked into the living room. 'Thank you for taking care of me, Mrs Aguillar.'

105

'Please call me Carmen. I am glad you are feeling better.'

'I do. I'm sure I'd be in the hospital if it wasn't for you.'

'Bah. They don't make decent food in the hospital. They don't let a person sleep. I'm glad Cody brought you here.' The wiry little old lady reached out to take her hand in hers. 'You come back any time.'

Of course she wouldn't, no matter how right it felt to be here. 'Thank you,' she said simply.

'Be back in a bit, Ma.' Cody took Stormy's things from her and she followed him outside. He opened the door for her and she got in the truck, wincing as the door slammed shut. It sounded so final. Cody started the truck, and sadly, she watched the ranch land go by outside her window.

For just a while, she had belonged somewhere.

'Here we are.' Cody parked the truck and got out. Stormy waited, fully capable of opening the door, but knowing he expected to do it. She decided she appreciated his brand of caring.

'You don't have to walk me up,' she said hurriedly, when it became obvious he was going to carry her things up to her room for her.

'I'm taking you to the airport.' His face held no indication that he'd give on this matter.

'But I haven't arranged for my flight back yet.' She reached for the most likely deterring tactic she could think of. 'It might take me a while.'

'I can wait.'

She shrugged, leading him into the Stagecoach. Ornery cowboy. His code of honor bordered on machismo. Still, she couldn't help thinking how nice it was that this handsome man would go out of his way for her. He'd do it for anyone, if he thought it necessary, her conscience reminded her.

Maybe, she argued, but I can enjoy it while it lasts.

He strolled to the window, looking down at the ground. 'Take your time.'

'I – okay.' She couldn't think how to dial the airport, she couldn't remember what airline she'd flown in to Texas on. All that was in her mind was Cody and how big and strong he looked silhouetted against the sun-filled window. 'Wouldn't you prefer to wait in the lobby?' She honestly couldn't think with him in the room.

'I'm fine. Unless you'd rather I did.'

'No, no,' she said hastily. Too hastily. 'I just can't find the phone book –'

He reached to grab it from the nightstand. Handing it to her, he said, 'Why do you need it?'

'I'm not sure,' she murmured. 'I know the 1–800 number for the airline by heart.'

Slowly, he put the phone book away, his eyes never leaving hers. She felt breathless at the sudden purposeful look he wore as he moved close to her. 'I'm not making much sense, am I?'

'No. You talk too much, anyway.' He slid his hands along her arms. 'I'm getting used to it.

107

Think I'll miss it when you're gone.'

'Oh, my gosh,' she whispered, hardly daring to believe it when he lowered his lips to touch hers. Closing her eyes, she reveled in the feel of his firm mouth seeking, exploring. Finding. She moved her hands up his strong back, feeling muscles ripple through the material. And he smelled so good, like man and soap and strength. At this moment, she didn't feel like saying another word.

All she could do was enjoy what he was doing to her. He traced along her jawline with his thumb, then down over her shoulders with both hands until he reached her waist. She moaned when he circled her waist almost completely. He moved his hands up to her ribcage to just under her breasts. Her breath caught as she waited to see if he would go farther.

She wasn't disappointed. Gently, he smoothed her breasts into his hands. Her knees went weak; her eyes teared up with desire she had never before felt. 'Cody,' she whispered.

'What?' he asked huskily.

'Don't stop.'

She felt his fingers brush across her nipples, which hardened instantly. Moisture heated between her legs. Daring herself to do it, she moved her hands down into the small of his back, then along the top of his buttocks. Something inside her jumped in amazement at how wonderful a man could feel. She'd known this man was well-built, but he felt better than she could have imagined.

Wanting to know more, she pulled out his shirttail and ran her hands up his bare back.

He responded by kissing her neck. She leaned her head back so he would give her more of the wonderful sensation. He did, pressing big hands around her bottom and cupping her to him as he kissed her. Hot strength at the center of his legs pressed against her, and Stormy's eyes flew open. Was a man supposed to feel that way? Big and hot and . . . dangerous?

Suddenly, she pulled away, worried that she might have gone too far.

'What's wrong?' he asked. His arms refused to completely release her. Awkwardly, she laid her head against his chest, hearing his heart thunder inside.

'Nothing,' she whispered. 'It's wonderful.' *I wish it weren't.*

He rubbed her back in gentle circles. 'Maybe I shouldn't have done that.'

'I'm so glad you did.' She drew a deep, shuddering breath. 'It's just that it's hard to have you kiss me like that and then put me on an airplane.'

He was quiet for a moment. 'I hadn't planned on kissing you. I really had no call to do that, but if you don't mind, I'm glad you let me.'

She smiled sadly against his chest. 'Well. I should call the airline.' Reluctantly, she backed out of his arms, unable to meet his gaze. She reached for the phone, dialed the airline, and made a reservation. That done, she busied herself packing, uncomfortable with Cody watching.

'Guess if I hadn't been so stubborn about you filming on my land, you wouldn't have lost your job.'

'Oh.' Stormy barely glanced at him. 'Don't worry about it. This happens sometimes.'

'Not a very secure job.'

'No. It's not.' Nothing in her life was secure, but having grown up on the edges of the entertainment industry with her traveling parents, it had been the obvious choice for her to turn to. 'I'll get another job.'

'Will you be okay until you do?'

He meant money-wise and Stormy could feel her cheeks pinken. 'I'll be fine.' She wasn't about to confess her love of shopping; the fact that shopping was the one vice she couldn't give up now. It comforted her when she was down, and her credit card balances spoke of the fact that she was down more times than up. *I haven't bought a single thing since I've been in Desperado*, she realized, amazed. *Not even souvenirs.*

The telephone rang, startling both of them. Stormy snatched if off the receiver.

'Hello?'

'Stormy, it's Jonathan.'

'Jonathan. Hello.'

Cody bit the inside of his mouth at the sound of another man's name on Stormy's lips. *Of course she had a boyfriend waiting for her return. I kissed her*, he reminded himself; *she had not made the* first move. If anything, he'd been poaching. So now he knew to keep his hands and his mouth where they belonged – and his heart firmly encased in steel.

'Oh? I can't imagine,' he heard Stormy say drily. 'It depends on what you have to say, Jonathan.'

Cody stared out the window, opening it to let a dry breeze come in. He hated to hear her playing it cool with another man. On the other hand, it would help him to put her on that airplane and say goodbye without feeling pain. *It wasn't going to bother me, anyway.*

'Well, I'm not a bargain basement movie scout you can just hire and fire because the upper rent ones aren't available. And I've already made my plane reservations. You just caught me as I was going out the door.' She glanced at Cody guiltily and shrugged. He grinned at her fibbing and told himself he was going to give her hell about it on the drive to the airport.

'I don't like this. It's hot as hell here, and I've been throwing up a bad omelet for two days, and there's very few folks in this area of Texas that I find agreeable.' She turned away so she wouldn't have to look at the raised eyebrows Cody sent her way.

'Well, I'll do it, but only because at one time I considered you a friend. Don't jerk me around again,' she snapped, slamming down the phone.

Cody clapped his hands together as if he'd just enjoyed a one-act play. 'Very well acted.'

'Oh, hush. I have to keep Jonathan on his toes or he thinks he owns me. He considers himself my father most of the time, and sometimes I have to remind him that I like his kind, gentle side better than his parental side.' Stormy shrugged. 'I'm staying here another week.'

'You got your job back?' Cody's stomach tightened; his heart did a strange jump in his chest.

'Well, apparently Rhonda wasn't available as fast as they wanted her. Because I was on to something in Texas, I'm supposed to see if I can get a deal closed quick. He's going to make some calls and let the people involved know that they're getting close to having a location.'

'I see.' He narrowed his gaze on her. 'Congratulations.'

'It's always nice to have a job.' Her eyes widened at him. 'You don't sound very happy.'

He shook his head. He didn't know what he was.

Hell, yeah, he did. Staring at Stormy's delicate purple eyebrows perched over purple-gray eyes, he realized he wouldn't have kissed her – wouldn't have gotten near her – if he hadn't been counting on taking her to the airport and getting her out of his life.

He knew exactly what he was.

Scared.

CHAPTER 8

Stormy recognized regret when she saw it – and right now, it was written all over Cody's face. Swiftly, she tried to sort out what had turned his mood sour so fast. There was only one answer, of course. It was because of the kiss.

He'd thought she was leaving, and had acted on the moment. Now she was staying and he didn't quite know what he was going to do about it. She supposed he was concerned that she might expect him to continue taking care of her the way he had been.

Well, she knew how to ease his mind. 'Thank heavens Shiloh is eager to have us there.' Purposefully, she opened the door. 'I'd better call Mayor Higgins and let him know I think we can work a deal due to his very gracious offer. I'm sure I'll be seeing you around, Cody.' She offered him her sweetest smile. 'Thank you so much for bringing me back to the hotel.'

His jaw dropped. 'You're going to take your movie deal to Wrong-Way?'

'Of course.' She shrugged nonchalantly. 'He's got the land. I need a fast deal. It all works out.'

'You're going to accept his deal without talking to Annie first?'

Oops. She'd forgotten about that. 'Well, I haven't looked at her message yet. I forgot to get them on the way up.' Of course she had. Losing her job had made any messages in her box pretty much moot.

Cody's taking her things up to her room had swept any thought of messages clean from her brain.

Irate, he pointed toward the hall. 'Well, your messages are in your box. I assure you there's one from her in there.'

'Well . . .' How could she tell him that it was better for everyone if she was in Shiloh? 'I think what I saw in Shiloh suited our needs exactly.'

'He made you sick and you're going to do a deal with him? Terrific.'

'Tate didn't exactly make me sick. I didn't know not to eat in Shiloh, which you could have told me just as well.'

'I warned you about him, but you didn't listen. Of course, now you're going clean contrary to what you should be doing, which is making a deal with Annie.' He snorted, jamming his hat on his head. 'Loyalty is obviously not a strong suit in the entertainment industry. Give my regards to Cruise.'

He poked his head back around the door. 'And I think that if you're doing business with Shiloh,

114

Desperado shouldn't be picking up your hotel tab.'

'They weren't in the first place,' she snapped. 'My company takes care of that. Desperado hasn't paid for so much as a soda for me so far. Annie's hospitality is about all I've seen.' It wasn't exactly true. Cody and his mother had taken good care of her. But that hadn't been business.

It had been the beginning of something which hadn't had a chance. She kept her chin high as she returned Cody's stare.

Without a word, he stomped out of her room. She listened for the sound of his boots on the stairs, which she heard moving faster than she would have liked. Down, down, down, her heart sinking with every step.

If Stormy didn't have a loyal bone in her body, by golly, he did. Cody headed off to find two codgers sitting on their park bench in front of the post office, which gave them a front-row seat into everybody's business.

Sure enough, Curvy and Pick sat on the bench, damn their interfering hides. Cody got out of his truck and went over to take a seat on the bench.

'Howdy, Cody,' they said at once.

'How's the cow business?' Curvy asked.

'Be a hell of a lot better if Annie was going to be opening her restaurant,' he replied, going straight to the point.

Pick and Curvy instantly glanced at each other. Right on the money, Cody told himself.

'Too bad about that,' Pick said.

'Too bad you had to stick your noses in where it didn't belong.' Cody leveled them with a stare.

'What do you mean?' Curvy asked innocently.

'I mean that everything was going along fine until you heard that Annie wasn't of a mind to have that movie made on her land. Suddenly, a host of problems the likes of which I've never heard are discovered, which impede her opening her restaurant. Shame on both of you.' He refused to release them from his glare.

'Now, Cody, business is business. We might as well give that spot to someone whose business will bring in more money for Desperado. Starting up a restaurant is a dicey business. Could be it'd go over well, could be it'd bomb. There's more security in letting the Michaels brothers expand their funeral home into that space. They're wanting to get into the casket business big-time, as folks from several cities around know they can get the best deal from them.'

'Yeah. Death is always profitable. Of course, then you have a funeral home and its services the highlight of the creek, instead of Annie's restaurant where tourists could eat after a day browsing in the Mom and Pop shops.' He paused for a moment. 'Well, it doesn't matter now. Stormy Nixon is taking her movie to Shiloh.'

'What!' Curvy and Pick exclaimed.

'Yes. She's decided Shiloh better suits her needs. But,' he said, standing to brush off his jeans, 'that's business.'

116

'Now we'll be a casket and a potty stop,' Pick commented.

'Cody, you gotta do something,' Curvy said.

'What could I do, Mayor?'

'I don't know! Talk to that cantankerous woman. Change her mind.'

'Annie's not cantankerous,' he said smoothly.

'I'm talking 'bout Stormy!' Curvy cried.

'Well, I'm talking about Annie, a woman who's lived here all her life and done good things for this town.'

'Now, Cody.' Curvy backed up a pace. 'Let's not compare these two sichy-ations.'

'These days, I've been thinking a lot about loyalty.' Cody put one boot up on the bench beside the codgers. 'If you won't do right by Annie, who's done so much for Desperado, why should I expect any better?' He held up a hand to ward off Curvy's sputtering. 'I bring my cows in for cow patty bingo and for the calf-catch. I've been known to give my money to worthwhile projects in this town. Occasionally, I've even been known to sponsor charity events. Ma spends days cooking for every special event Desperado has.' He slowed down for emphasis. 'But maybe one day I need something from this town. Maybe all I'll hear is no, Cody, we've got better business over here.'

'All right! Annie can have her restaurant!' Curvy cried.

'Thank you, Mayor. Can I have your *word* on that, or do I need it in writing?'

They'd collected a couple of eavesdroppers by now, and Curvy was eager to retain his self-respect. 'I think the Mayor's word is as good as stone.'

'I hope so. I'd hate to have to use one on you.' Cody slid his boot off the bench and began walking away.

'Well?'

'Well, what?' he asked, throwing a glance behind him.

'Are you going to change that Nixon woman's mind or not?'

He got into his truck. 'Nope. That's up to the good mayor of Desperado to take care of.' He nodded at the bent-over little man. 'It's been a pleasure doing business with you, Mayor.'

Actually, Cody thought as he drove away, he wasn't sure he could change Stormy's mind. Moreover, he didn't think he wanted to. The less time Trouble spent in his town was likely for the best.

Unfortunately, he'd kissed her. And as long as his mind kept returning to how her lips felt under his, he was destined to suffer.

His suffering intensified when he walked through the door of his own home. Mary and Carmen sat in the kitchen, trying to act as though nothing had happened.

Something had. Mary's long black hair was now the color of old carrots.

118

'What in the hell have you done now?' He strode over and lifted Mary's hair to run it through his hand. 'It looks like something got sick real bad in your hair.'

Mary started to cry. Cody shifted on his feet, wondering if he hadn't been sensitive to a situation that required it.

'I just wanted to look like Stormy!' Mary cried.

'Stormy's hair doesn't look like this. It's purple, not orange.' He was totally confused.

'She wanted it to be as beautiful as Stormy's,' his mother explained. 'So she tried dying it herself.'

'Is there anything we can do to fix it?' He held his breath, hoping his mother wouldn't say it had to grow out on its own. 'Your mother's not going to be too happy having to look at you like that.' And she did it under my roof. That'll give Annie confidence in my abilities to watch over Mary while they're having their second honeymoon.

'She'll have to go to the beauty salon.'

'Okay.' He sighed heavily. 'Hop in the truck, ladybug. I'll run you over to Hera's. Will you call Hera, Ma, and tell her we're on the way for an emergency appointment?'

Twenty minutes later, Hera shook her head dolefully at Cody.

'This is a mess. I can try to get it back to black, but I just don't know.'

'I want to look like Stormy,' Mary said stubbornly.

119

'Who is this Stormy?' Hera asked.

'The movie scout who's in Desperado. I went swimming with her at the Stagecoach.' Mary was proud of herself.

'Well, I gotta know what color her hair is if I'm gonna make you look like her.' Hera took a long drag on a cigarette as she considered Mary's hair.

'Dark red,' Mary said, while Cody replied, 'Purple.'

'Ya'll gotta make up your mind.' Hera pointed toward a phone. 'Cody, call Stormy and ask what color rinse her beautician uses on her hair.'

'Call and ask her *what*? No way. Mary, you call her.'

'Okay. I want to ask her if it hurts to have ears pierced with three earrings, too.'

'Never mind!' Cody snatched the phone away. 'I'll talk to her.' He rang the desk at the Stagecoach, all the while glaring at his niece. His whole body warmed at the sound of Stormy's voice.

'Didn't expect to hear from you, Cody.'

What an irritating woman. Most beat around the bush and wouldn't say anything more than, 'Oh, Cody, I'm so glad you called,' or something else polite. *She* had to stick the knife in and give it a twist.

'Gotta question I have to ask you,' he said abruptly.

'Okay.'

'We're at the beauty salon and Hera wants to know something.' He faltered, wondering if there were social rules against inquiring into the color of a woman's hair.

'Well, the braid is somewhat archaic, but I like it on you. It makes you look like a throwback to another generation, but that goes along with your personality,' she told him. 'Rock stars wear braids to achieve a certain macho look. On you, it comes across as archaic. But almost a fashion statement.'

'What in the *hell* are you going on about?' Everyone in the beauty salon turned to stare at him.

'You said you were at the beauty salon and your beautician wanted to know something.'

'Listen, Stormy,' he growled, turned his back to the audience and cupping the mouthpiece with his hand so not a word reached interested ears, 'I'm not at the beauty parlor for a day out with the girls, okay? I'm here because my niece decided she wanted to look like you and turned her hair the color of a baby's spit after it's been eating carrots.'

'Oh, dear. But my hair isn't orange.'

'That's the point of this phone call. Hera wants to know what color rinse you use on your hair.' He was completely out of patience with the whole matter, and anxious to get out of this beauty parlor. Something about all the faces with curlers around them was particularly hard on his eyes.

'Let me talk to Mary.'

'What for?'

'So I can explain it to her,' she snapped.

'Fine.' He handed the phone to his niece, thinking it was probably better this way. Talking to Stormy wasn't helpful if he was trying to forget her. And her sassy mouth, with those wonderful, clinging lips.

'Maple. Stormy says a rinse called Maple is put on her hair,' Mary announced to the room at large. 'But she says that, for me to audition for the part, I definitely need to go back to the color my hair was – only have it cut into a pixie style.'

'I can't believe it.' Something inside Cody snapped as he looked at the eighteen inches of his niece's once-beautiful hair. Everything – absolutely everything – had changed since Stormy Nixon had come to town with her nutso way of life. 'You are not cutting off your hair to try out for some stupid part you probably won't get. And it's being filmed in Shiloh, so why would you even consider such a crazy notion?'

'Somebody will drive me over there so that I can try out.' She looked up at him with pleading eyes. 'Won't you, Uncle?'

'Oh, for the love of –' He glared at her. 'Please don't cut your hair off. If you get the part and you still want to, then fine. But don't do it until then, okay?'

'Okay.'

'Hera. How long does Mary need to be here for that rinse thing you're going to do?'

'I need about an hour and a half to work on her.' Hera put out her cigarette and put gnarled hands into Mary's hair. 'Maybe two, so I can trim the ends and shape it up. It's pretty rough.'

He pointed a finger at his niece. 'Don't you dare leave this salon.'

'I won't, Uncle Cody. Where are you going?'

He shook his head at her. 'Call me on my cellphone when you're done, Mary, and I'll pick you up.'

Mary watched as her uncle left the salon. 'He's going to see Stormy,' she told the room at large.

'Does he like her?' Hera asked. 'Be kinda strange if Cody fell for a woman.'

'It's a real unusual situation,' Mary replied. 'They argue like mad half the time, 'cause Stormy's always in Uncle's face about something. Funny thing about it is, he never really seems all that mad at her.'

'Ah,' all the women in the parlor said. Knowing looks were passed around the room.

'Maybe three hours. It may take me three hours to fix your hair, Mary,' Hera murmured with a grin. 'Grab a magazine and sit over there while I finish Ula's hair.'

Cody dialed Stormy's room from the lobby phone. When she answered, he said, 'Stormy, I'm downstairs. I need to talk to you.'

'If you're in the lobby, does that mean you want to talk face to face?'

He could feel his blood begin to simmer at her teasing tone. 'Yes, I would.'

She sighed, and the sound was reluctant. 'Are you going to yell at me?'

123

'Might.'

'You'd better come up, then. I don't want half the country hearing you bellow like a wild moose.'

'I – wild moose? How would you know what one sounds like?'

'I don't. I have a vivid imagination, though, and I'm sure that's a very good comparison to what you'll sound like when you're chewing my ear off.'

'It's your vivid imagination I want to talk to you about.'

'Ooh, I'm intrigued. Come on up.'

His jaw dropped at what almost sounded like a blatant sexual tone in her voice. The phone clicked off in his ear. Cody took the stairs two at a time. He rapped on the door, and Stormy promptly opened it.

'Take a chair over there. It's set up all nice and comfy for maximum venting of whatever's got you hot and bothered.'

He eyed the chair, ignoring it. 'How could you suggest to Mary that she cut her hair off?' he nearly shouted.

'Well, to make her look authentic for the part.' Stormy put her hands on her hips. 'It worked for Vivien Leigh when she wanted the part of Scarlet O'Hara in *Gone With The Wind*. She dressed up like a –'

'I am not interested in movie roles, past or present! I believe you know that is not one of my top priorities, and I want you to stop putting wild thoughts in Mary's head.'

124

Stormy crossed her arms. 'I have not put one single wild idea in her head, and I resent you saying so.'

'She wants her hair to look like yours!' Stormy's hair was curled softly around her face in a fluffy cloud. Cody was momentarily distracted by how lustrous it looked. She actually looked very beautiful herself. When had *that* happened?

'Thank you for the compliment. I've always heard that imitation was the sincerest form of flattery.' She smiled, pleased.

Cody realized she just wasn't getting it. 'Stormy, she's going to ask you if it hurt to get three holes in your ear.'

'Oh, at her age, that's not a very good idea,' she said quite seriously. 'Although she can probably just ask *you* about ear piercing.'

'I just have one hole. I don't know anything about three!'

'Well, I shouldn't think it makes a whole lot of difference. Tell her I said she should wait until she's older. That's what I would tell my daughter – and my son.'

'No boy of mine would ever have three holes in his ears.' Cody sent her a look of total disapproval.

'Well, most parents would say that about one hole. Does your mother ever complain that her son wears an earring?'

'I wish you wouldn't get on my back and get me off my subject, woman! Do you know that no matter what subject we're on, we never stay on

125

it for more than five seconds? It's like you have no concentration.'

'Me?' Stormy stepped forward and punched his chest lightly with one finger. 'I'm not the one who went from hairdos to earrings! You did.'

He considered that for a moment. 'It's just that you get me so twisted up.'

'You get yourself all twisted up.' She shook her head at him. 'Don't try to blame me for your shortcomings.'

There was nothing he could say to a woman who was so certain she was right about everything. 'I reckon you'll be heading down to Shiloh tonight.' It was a straw he clung to. Life would slow down considerably when this woman was out of his town.

'No. I'm staying here.'

'For how long?'

'Until the week is out.'

'But you're going to do a deal in Shiloh!' He felt his bravado shrinking. Surely he wasn't going to have to hear about Stormy, think about Stormy, dream about Stormy, for another whole week . . .

'I like it better here. Why would I go stay in a town where the food is poisonous?' She looked at him as if he wasn't all right in the head. 'It's only twenty minutes away, and I know how to drive, Cody.' She took a deep breath. 'But it isn't a problem, anyway. I returned Annie's message, and she and I are close to an agreement. She just wants some more information on what all will be involved with the movie, as far as using her land is concerned.'

Cody dropped into the chair Stormy had first offered him. He mulled the situation over rapidly. Annie wanted her restaurant, which would keep her very busy. She was also pregnant and sapped from morning sickness. Strangers coming and going all the time, making noise and dropping trash would be a strain on her. Mary was quite a handful right now, too. She claimed Annie didn't spend any time with her any more. A movie was a lot for Annie to take on at this time in her life. But she was dead-set on doing this for Mary. Annie would also give her right arm to do anything that was good for Desperado.

He would do anything for Annie. 'No,' he said slowly, 'I don't think you should do that. Answer me one question.' He raised his eyes to hers. 'Why Desperado?'

'Well, it had to be Texas. They wanted flat land for filming. They also wanted weather that would be relatively dry and warm most of the time. It had to be an area with the lots of space. I came this way, and I fell in love.' She looked at him with an expression in her eyes that touched him. 'I simply like this area, this town, these people. It feels like something I haven't had before.'

He nodded slowly. 'It's a good place.'

'I know.'

They stared at each other for what seemed like a long time. Finally, Cody said, 'I'll let you use my land.'

'You will?' Stormy's eyes sparkled with excitement.

'Yeah. I must be crazy, but I will.'

'Oh, this is wonderful! I can't believe it! This is –'

'No, it's not,' he interrupted. 'It's not going to be wonderful. You've turned my life inside out, you've got my niece thinking hare-brained stuff, you've got respectable people acting like yo-yos. I don't know how one little hundred-pound female's got a bunch of folks acting like they lost all the sense they were born with.'

'None of that's true.' She gave him a hurt look.

He ignored it. 'It is true. Everything was calm, like a river. Now it's like a meteor landed in the water and shot everything out in different directions.'

'You don't sound like you like me very much.' She gazed at him sadly. 'Why are you going to let us use your land?'

'Because I love Annie. Because I love Mary. And they both want it. But it has nothing to do with you.' He felt cruel, and obviously his words were, because Stormy flinched.

'Fine, Cowboy.' She turned her back to him, presenting him with another very nice view. 'I'll have the papers sent to your house, and I'll tell Annie you and I came to terms.'

'That's just fine, Trouble,' he said, adopting her attitude. 'But you have to promise me you won't put any more weird stuff into Mary's head.'

She shrugged. 'I'll stay as much out of all of

your ways as possible. We shouldn't even have to see each other.'

He wasn't sure that was exactly what he'd wanted. But now that he'd drawn such a stern, uncompromising line with her, he'd have to go with it. 'I'm sure that's for the best.'

'I'm sure it is.'

Her slender back stayed firmly turned toward him. He'd hurt her, and he knew it. He just didn't know how to undo it. They weren't resolving this the way they should be, with both feeling like something good was happening for everybody.

'Shouldn't we shake on this or something? Isn't that how business deals are usually conducted?' he asked.

She didn't reply for a moment. Then she said, 'Nothing about this is completely business, and you and I both know it.'

His jaw sagged. It was true. He felt a little silly for trying to pretend that it was, just so he could stay in her company for another couple of seconds under the guise of business. It was irritating that she wasn't fooled by his bluff, and had bald-faced called him on it without so much as an ounce of bashfulness. Grimacing, he opened the door, glanced at her back one more time, and left.

CHAPTER 9

Stormy knew she had to call Annie after Cody left, even though she really wanted to sit down and think about why the cowboy made her so mad she could feel herself sizzling in his presence. Forcing her mind off him, she dialed the number.

'I want to let you know that Cody was just by here,' she said when Annie answered the phone. 'He really felt strongly that it would be best for everyone if the movie was made at his place. I hope that's all right with you.'

'Well, yes. I'm a little surprised he changed his mind. That's not like him.'

Stormy could imagine it wasn't. 'I don't know why he did, actually. It was a complete surprise. He came to my room awful mad, but then, he stays that way with me.'

'Oh, Stormy. Don't let Cody worry you. He's . . . got a lot on his mind.'

That was putting it mildly. She wondered if Annie knew that Cody had made a trip to the beauty salon to get his niece's hair dyed back the color it should have been. She decided it was a topic best not mentioned.

'Stormy, I have a favor to ask of you.'

She liked Annie. Although she couldn't imagine what the favor was, she would do what she could for this woman. 'How can I help you?'

A moment passed before Annie spoke again, and Stormy briefly wondered if she was uncomfortable.

'Zach and I are leaving on a trip this weekend. A second honeymoon.'

'I know. I'm so happy for you,' Stormy murmured.

'Cody and his mother are going to keep an eye on Mary while we're gone.'

'I've just been the recipient of their hospitality myself.'

Annie laughed. 'I heard. Well, I would worry a little less if Mary could spend some time with you. Carmen is a wonderful mother-in-law. We've stayed close, even through her son's . . . my husband's, death. And Cody, gosh, I can't say enough about Cody. He's great with Mary.' She paused a second. 'But right now I know my daughter needs more. She needs a friend, someone she can trust. She looks up to you, Stormy. You've been such a good influence on her.'

Stormy nearly fell out of the chair she was sitting in. If Cody could hear what Annie had just said, he would swear she'd lost her mind. 'I don't think –'

'Oh, yes, you are. Mary's a completely different

person since you've been to town.'

'Ah – yeah.' She was sitting in a beauty salon with orange hair. Completely different, thanks to Stormy.

'She didn't have siblings. She's worried about how this baby will displace her. The truth is, I think she enjoys talking to you. She's going to tell you things she wouldn't feel comfortable telling Zach or me. Or Cody.'

'I don't know –'

'It's a lot to think about, I know. But I see my shy little daughter coming out of her shell, and I know it's because of this movie project, and because you think she would be right for a part in it. Teenagers like to know that they've got something special. Of course, to us, Mary is special. But her school friends are hard on her, and now she has something in her life that's all hers. Am I making sense?'

'Yes.' Annie was replaying everything Stormy had experienced in her teen years. Unfortunately, Cody would never see that she might be beneficial for Mary. 'I just don't think I'm the person you're looking for.'

'I know it's a lot to ask. In fact, I don't even have the right to ask. You're here on business, and as a business woman, I know how much there is to do. But just spending an afternoon with you, or having lunch with you, would mean so much to Mary. Of course, I certainly understand if you're not comfortable with the idea.'

132

Stormy swallowed hard. She thought about Mary crossing the highway in the darkness. She remembered how much the girl had appreciated spending the night with her. Mary loved to go through Stormy's cosmetics. Was it so very much to do for the awkward teenager, when Stormy wasn't even going to be here much longer? Not too long ago, it had been Stormy who'd had no one to turn to.

It was going to get her in scalding hot water with Cody. But she took a deep breath and said, 'It's so easy for kids to get bored in the summer, anyway. Why don't you let Mary stay with me for a day or so? She can swim in the pool, and listen to me make business calls. Not very exciting, but at least she'll be in a different place for a couple of days. Maybe that will help.'

'Oh, thank you, Stormy! I just knew you would understand.' Annie took a breath. 'I'll tell you a secret. Everyone thinks I'm so strong, such a rock. I don't know any other way than to stand on my own two feet. But I love my daughter, more than I can ever say. And if it's not me she needs right now, if it's someone who sees her in a new light, then I'm not going to let my pride stand in the way of what she needs.'

She paused, and Stormy hesitated, not quite sure what to say.

'I can't thank you enough for this. I'll call Cody on his cellphone right now.'

Annie hung up, and Stormy stared at the receiver in shock. Cody had just left her hotel room about five minutes ago, practically breathing fire. When he found out what she'd done before the color had even finished setting on Mary's hair, he was going to have a fit.

It would be best not to sit here like an unmoving target. She knew exactly what Cody would do when he got Annie's call in his truck. He'd ricochet back in sixty seconds or less to give her a good lecture.

She needed to be ready to step out the door the instant he arrived, with the excuse that she had a very important appointment and didn't have any time to talk to him. If she hurried, she might make it to the parking lot before he got to the hotel. Quickly, she brushed her hair, her teeth, and ran a lipstick over her lips. She grabbed her purse, and flung the door open.

Cody stood outside, his hand raised to knock. 'Going somewhere?'

'Yes, I was. I am. I have an appointment.'

'You'll have to be a few minutes late. I want to talk to you.'

Her heart thundered in her chest. He was so large, his expression so forbidding, and she knew he was extremely displeased with her right now. 'This isn't a good time –'

He strode into the room. She shook her head at him. 'I'm sorry. I really am leaving –'

Cody shut the door, all the while looking into her eyes. Without saying a word, he reached into

134

his pocket and drew out a nail much too large to ever be used for hanging pictures.

'Good thing I was riding fence this morning,' he said. 'This is to make sure you and I come to an agreement.'

Before her astonished gaze, he pulled off a boot and hammered the nail into the door. 'You're not leaving, and I'm not going, until we figure out how you can possibly stay in Desperado another week and not turn my life into a soap opera.'

'I have no idea what you mean.'

'You darn well do. I no sooner leave here than Annie calls to tell me that Mary's staying with you for a few days. Was I not just in this room telling you that you're a bad influence on the child? Did you mention to her mother that, because of you, Mary has fluorescent hair?'

'No,' she said a bit weakly. 'I didn't want to get Mary in trouble.'

'You didn't want Annie thinking badly of you!' he thundered. 'You're not about to do anything that might jeopardize your movie deal!'

'Well, I am,' she shot back. 'Obviously, I've upset you, and you're the one I made the deal with. So that doesn't wash.' Angrily, she crossed her arms over her chest. 'Either you take that nail out of the door, or I call the desk.'

'No, you won't. It's just as much for your peace of mind as mine that we figure out a way to get along for the period of time you'll be running in and out of Desperado. Because I have no hope that just because you say you're only staying another week, it will really happen.'

In the movie industry, who knew? Jonathan had mentioned something to her about flying back to Desperado later to work as an assistant to the director, if she managed to work this deal out. It was a job, and though she and Jonathan fought constantly, he did try to look out for her employment-wise.

'I don't know myself.'

'That's my point. I don't think I've gotten a solid day's work done since you've been here. You've got to stop meddling in my business – and my family. Mary has no reason to be here with you.'

'On the contrary,' Stormy snapped, her feelings hurt, 'Annie seems to think I'm a good influence on Mary.'

'Of course she does! She doesn't know about the hair and the three earrings she's decided she wants!' Cody glared at her.

'That's not the point and you know it! You know what I think?' Stormy drew herself up to match his glare. 'I think you're jealous. Of me. I think you're flustered because you know that Mary likes me.'

He frowned at her. 'There's nothing about you at all that I find remotely flustering.'

Stormy stared at Cody, thoroughly put out. The big man was going to jump from point to point and refuse to admit she wasn't the problem. He thought it was all right to lock her in her room

136

so they could talk, but that wasn't what he wanted at all. He just wanted to blame her for things that weren't all her fault. Yes, the hair-dying incident could be laid uncomfortably at her door, but Mary's problems had started long before Stormy came to Desperado. And Crazy Cody was used to scaring people off, relying on his nickname to give himself some bluster.

Well, she wasn't fooled.

'Cody, I'm asking you one last time to remove that nail,' she said quietly. 'Or you'll force me to do something drastic.'

'I find everything about you drastic. I'm past the shock stage, little woman.' He shook his head in the negative. 'But all I want, all I'm asking for is for you to quit – *what are you doing?*'

She knew how to stop his pointless arguing, his constant harping and posturing. Stormy reached under her shirt, pulled off her red satin bra, and tossed it at him.

His jaw dropped. 'Stormy –'

Obviously, more ammunition was required to win a retreat from him. Her hand reached into her silky pants.

Cody felt his heart going wild in his chest. What was the woman up to? He heard snap! snap! and a dainty piece of red lace and satin landed on his boots.

'Maybe you and I should get to the real issue,' she said softly.

She was torturing him! The tiny woman with

the big mouth was determined to win at any cost, the she-devil! He felt sweat running down his brow. It would be best if he called 'Surrender!' and left with his pride if nothing else.

Her white blouse hit the floor. Cody stood riveted. The fight or flee instinct seared him. Either he could throw this woman to the bed and ravish her, or he could run out the door. But that would give her the upper hand, and the satisfaction of knowing she held all the winning cards.

He had never been a coward. Cody stood fast, although her round breasts with russet-tipped nipples definitely had his complete attention. Surely, she didn't intend to go any further with this game.

She reached for the drawstring of her floral pants, her fingers hovering there. Something inside him snapped, and he reached to give the drawstring a good tug. The pants fell to the floor.

Stormy Nixon was a true red-head in every sense of the word.

She was also as beautiful as a goddess. His mouth dried up; his body reacted instantly.

He had to have her.

Stormy faltered at the hunger that flared in Cody's eyes. For a second, she wondered if she'd pushed her luck too far. Something had taken over her, urging her to bring their relationship to the point that all the arguing was merely camouflaging. She wanted him, and he wanted her. He bent to take her in his arms, sweeping her up and over to the bed.

With eager fingers, she helped him get his clothes off. Quickly. He stared at her with purposeful eyes, and Stormy gloried in his obvious desire for her. She drew him into the bed with her and sighed when his body met hers. When he kissed her lips, her neck, her breasts, it was all she could not to cry with relief.

'I have a condom in my wallet that's so old I'm not sure it hasn't rotted,' he said, his voice taut with need.

Stormy's eyes widened at the unexpected message in his words. 'Here's hoping for the best,' she said as he reached for it.

It didn't appear to have suffered ill effects from age. Stormy's breath caught as she helped him put it on, touching his body in places she'd always wondered about. Her experience with men and stable relationships was non-existent. Were all men so strong, so well-built? Or was it just her lover who had a rock-hard body that was thrilling to touch? Gasping in a small breath of air, she felt his tongue run along her lips, before he took her mouth completely. His hand smoothed along her back, clasping him to her tightly. There was a part of her body that desperately wanted his touch, and he found that, too, before he joined himself to her. Stormy cried out, unable to comprehend that a man and a woman could feel this way together.

He stared down at her. 'Are you all right? Did I hurt you?'

'No,' she whispered. The pain was worth the pleasure. 'Don't stop.'

It was fire and ice; dark, hard-marble body riding her smooth, alabaster one. Black hair flung over strong-muscled shoulders that held her pressed against his chest tightly. He groaned, sending a thrill through her and urging her to move faster against him. They were so different, yet this loving felt so right. She knew it in her heart. Suddenly, she felt passion filling inside her, sweeping her along and carrying her over the edge of a waterfall of delight. Crying out in astonishment, she heard Cody's hoarse answer as he found the same pleasure.

She pulled his face to hers so that she could kiss him, and as they melded together, Stormy found the place she'd always dreamed of. She found security. Something far more exciting than anything she ever found on her shopping trips, her endless forays to find things to fill her life.

She found complete heaven.

Cody lay still, his face buried in Stormy's hair, which smelled tantalizing and wonderful. His mind raced. What in the hell had he just done? He'd made love to an oddly named, unusual-looking woman with whom he had nothing in common. How could this fair-skinned woman whose world revolved around glamour and make-believe make him feel like a king in her arms?

This could go no further than it had. There would be no magic triumph over the matters that separated them in their future. Cody kissed Stormy one more time, lingering over her lips, before pulling gently away. It felt like leaving half of himself behind.

Then he saw the tiny spots of blood on the white hotel sheet. Unwelcome perception hit him like a lightning bolt.

'You were a virgin!' he exclaimed hoarsely.

She cocked her head at him, her hair spread over the pillow. 'Yes.'

Shock put cold fingers around his heart. He fought off the emotional trap. 'How did that happen?'

'What do you mean? Are there no thirty-year-old virgins in Desperado?' She eyed him curiously.

'Maybe, but I doubt there's an abundance in Hollywood.'

Bristling, Stormy said, 'You act like I have a social deficiency.'

'No.' He sat up wearily on the side of the bed. 'I just wish you'd told me.'

'So you wouldn't have made love to me? Do you regret it?'

He ran a light finger along her leg, mesmerized by the softness of her skin. 'Yes.' What in the heck was he going to do with the gift of her virginity? He certainly didn't deserve it. 'I didn't have the right to . . .'

141

'I see. You weren't looking for any kind of commitment and taking my virginity implies one.' Stormy pushed his hand away. 'Oops. Guess you'd better interview your next bedmate.'

Knocking at the door made both of them jump.

'Stormy?' Mary called.

She rattled the doorknob. For one second, Stormy blessed the nail that Cody had banged into the wood.

After a disastrously long moment, they heard Mary's footsteps in the hall as she left.

'Oh, my gosh!' Stormy whispered frantically. 'We nearly got caught! I'm supposed to be a good example for –' She caught Cody's glare on her. 'Oh, don't say a word. You're the one with the handyman urges.'

She pulled on her clothes. Cody had his on. They faced each other awkwardly.

'I hope you'll think about what I said,' he told her. 'Mary needs guidance, not wildness.'

'Oh, and it's guidance she's getting from her uncle. I hope you'll think about what an overbearing boor you are.'

His lips pressed flat. He reached up to jerk the long, flat-headed nail from the wood. It wouldn't budge.

'Wait,' Stormy said, catching his arm. 'Did you come up to my room to ravish me?'

'No way. I assure you it was the last thing on my mind. I was prepared to lock you in here until I talked sense into you where my niece is concerned.'

'I see,' Stormy said coldly.

He tried again to pull the nail out. It stayed firmly embedded.

'I may need something to get this out,' he said, his expression turning sheepish.

'What if there'd been a fire?' Stormy demanded. The old hotel was nearly completely wooden, with a paddle wheel out front on the creek side. She wondered if the antiquated place even had sprinklers.

'I'd have thrown you out the window,' he replied nonchalantly.

'Nude, I suppose.'

'You want to give these country bumpkins a show so badly. Well, you would have. We could have called it a preview to *The Devil's Sun*.' He reached up again, and jerked with all his might. The nail came loose, bringing a piece of wood with it.

Thoroughly incensed, Stormy opened the second-story window. 'Get out.'

'I am.'

He went toward the door, but Stormy started to scream. Rushing to clap his hand over her mouth, he stared down at her in shock. 'Do you want everyone in the hotel to know I'm in here?'

'I'm giving you the same consideration you would have given me. Out!' She pointed to the window.

'I'm not going out the window.'

'Yes, you are, or I scream the place down. You

143

should thank me for not pushing you out.'

'I could break my leg,' he warned her. 'This is not the way to get what you want from me.'

'Out!'

'I was only kidding about tossing you out the window –'

She started to scream again. Cody held his hands up. 'Okay! Okay!' Lord, what a mouth this tiny woman had on her!

Watching her closely as he edged toward the window, he eyed the courtyard. There was no one out there, and plenty of soft grass for him to land on. Cursing Stormy and how she'd managed to turn the tables on him again – and knowing very well he was getting what he deserved for his smart-alecky attitude when he should have been tender and sensitive – he went out on to the ledge, hanging by his hands to drop the few feet to the ground.

'We'll need a stuntman for the movie,' she called after him. 'Maybe you should audition!' As if it were a wedding bouquet, she tossed his cowboy hat out of the window.

He snatched it from the air, then stalked off. How could a lady so petite, so vixenish, have had him groaning with desire just a half-hour ago?

Now he was back to the beginning, wanting to wrap his hands around her little white throat.

He had the funny feeling that would get him no place but back into her bed – which was where he really wanted to go. He just couldn't allow it to happen again. The woman was draining all the

144

common sense out of him. If he wasn't careful, he'd end up cockeyed and irrational, just like her.

Mary watched her uncle leave the Stagecoach courtyard, dusting off his jeans as he strode away. Stunned, she realized he came from the vicinity of Stormy's window. Suspicion and hurt bloomed in her mind. Going upstairs, she knocked on Stormy's door.

Stormy opened the door, her expression odd and guilty.

'I came by earlier,' Mary said.

'I must not have heard you knock.'

Mary looked at Stormy's nervous eyes and flushed face. Her heart sank. Stormy wasn't just her friend. She was also Uncle Cody's friend. She suspected Stormy was important to Uncle Cody in a way Mary never could be, if he was jumping out of windows.

She lowered her eyes, thinking that maybe she couldn't even trust Stormy.

'Do you want to sit down for a while, Mary, and watch TV?'

She shook her head. 'No, thanks. I think I'll walk back to the hair salon and wait for Uncle Cody like I was supposed to in the first place. I knew he had an errand to run, and I – I wanted to come by and show you my hair.'

'It looks nice,' Stormy said, 'I can't tell any difference.'

'That's what Hera said. She worked at it awful

hard. Said if my Mom says yes, she'll put a Maple rinse on it like yours.'

'Oh, Mary. I've got Maple on my hair just so it won't be the color of one of your uncle's red cows. It makes the color one I can live with. If I had hair like yours, I would never put dye on it.'

Mary gazed at her. Stormy's hair was the color of a deep-heated jewel. It made her glamorous. Obviously, Uncle thought so, too, despite him always saying her hair was purple. Mary backed away from the door, seeing the rumpled sheets on the bed. A nail lay on the floor, the kind she'd seen Uncle use to nail fences and gates with, and barn doors. Stormy wouldn't have a nail like that. Uncle had been here, and Stormy didn't want her to know.

'I'll talk to you later,' she said slowly. 'I gotta go.'

'Okay.'

Stormy nodded as if she understood, but suddenly, Mary wondered if the woman had ever understood anything, or just pretended to like her because of Uncle. Sadly, she went down the hall and outside.

But she didn't feel like going back to Hera's to wait for her uncle. Instead, she headed for the bus station.

CHAPTER 10

Stormy made a calling out of being a happy person. She had to. Otherwise, with the way she'd grown up, she would have spent way too much time being depressed and withdrawn. A lot like Mary.

Right now Stormy couldn't hang on to the happy mission. She hadn't expected a proclamation of love from Cody, but it hurt that he had been so apparently repulsed by her virginity. More men than she cared to think about had wanted to get her into bed. No man had been right for her.

So she had waited to feel something special before sharing herself. Her parents might have believed in free love, but she did not. No, she had not wanted Cody to be grateful for the fact that there had been no man before him. But she had hoped he would think their lovemaking was more than just a spare few moments in the sheets. It was worse that he expected her to be easy, or to be 'Hollywood', whatever the heck that meant, and had been disappointed when he'd discovered she wasn't.

Hypocrite. The fact that the condom they'd used had held together at all was astonishing. Barely any lettering had been on the foil. That cowboy had spent a few years keeping that packet warm as it stayed hidden in the wallet in his jeans back pocket. Cody wasn't any more into easy sex than she was. How dared he act as if she should be an experienced woman?

He'd said he regretted making love with her. Maybe she should regret it, too. After all, it hadn't made anything better between them. Their business relationship would undoubtedly suffer because of what they'd done.

Mary was suffering, too. Stormy had seen it in her face. Maybe the teenager didn't know exactly that Stormy and Cody had made love, but something was wrong. She'd seen Mary's nervous glance toward the unmade bed.

Everything had gone awry. Clammy fingers of sadness gripped her. She fought for the positive side of the matter, the silver lining in the cloud, but she couldn't quite get there. All she felt was lost. Alone.

But although she knew she should feel regretful about their lovemaking, she didn't.

'You can be proud of yourself,' Cody said, heaving himself into a chair in Sloan's office. 'Between you and the two old codgers, you finally got me to do something I didn't want to do.'

'Hm.' Sloan steepled his fingers. 'Go to church?'

'Don't start.' Cody sent him a grim frown. 'The movie will be on my ranch. Hopefully so far away I won't even know it's there.'

'Really?' Sloan perked up considerably. 'The rough way you were treating the movie scout, I'd heard she was taking her business to Shiloh.'

'Well, you could have only heard that from Curvy and Pick. They've been thinking up schemes, Mary's been after me . . . I tell you, it's been hell. Even Annie's thrown herself in with Stormy's lot.'

'Well, that's great news for Desperado!' Sloan jumped to his feet. 'We can use this publicity for next summer's tourist flyers. Even a billboard, so that everybody who's passing us by to get to San Antonio and the beach resorts will want to stop here!' He rubbed his hands with glee.

The disgruntled expression on Cody's face made him quit. 'What's the problem?' He slid back into his chair.

'Nothing.'

'Then what's your chin dripping into your coffee mug for?'

'It's not.' Cody gave him a wave-off.

'Is it the scout? I heard you two don't hit it off too good.'

'No, it's not the scout.' For once, the gossips were wrong. He and Stormy hit it off way too good. 'It *is* the scout. But I don't know what's bugging me about her.'

'Maybe it's doing a deal with a woman.' At

149

Cody's derisive snort, Sloan said, 'You know how it is around here. It's usually men doing the talking, the dealing. We slap each other on the back and shake hands, and we're happy. With a woman, it's different all the way around.'

Yeah. He hadn't slapped Stormy on the back. He'd slept with her. *Jumping Jehoshaphat*. 'Sloan, I gotta get going.' He rose to his feet, and his cellular phone rang.

'Excuse me,' he said to the sheriff. 'Hello?'

'Cody? It's Annie.'

'Hey, Annie.' Talk about a woman having trouble doing business. After her husband had died, nobody'd wanted to do business with her. She was a woman, and a widow, and she'd all but lost her farm that drought-stricken summer six years ago. Zach had pretty much been her life-line.

'Have you seen Mary?' Her voice held a small note of worry. 'Your mom said you took her into town.'

'I dropped her off at the beauty salon. When I went to pick her up, they said she'd walked over to a friend's house. I'll yell at her for that in due time. I'm waiting for her to call me, because she knows I'm bringing her over to your place.'

'Oh. Why was she at the beauty parlor?'

'Uh –' Cody realized there was no reason not to tell her, except that she was probably going to be mad at her daughter, and maybe him. 'She dyed her hair orange. I took her to Hera's to get it fixed.'

Cody pointed at Sloan as he laughed out loud. Annie giggled, too.

'What's so funny?' he demanded. 'I didn't think it was funny at all.'

'I did that when I was a girl. I wanted so badly to be a platinum blonde.'

'A platinum blonde?' Cody couldn't believe his ears.

'Oh, lord,' Sloan groaned.

'Yes. I turned my hair green, though. Did Hera fix it?' Annie asked.

'I'm sure. I haven't seen Mary yet. I'm sitting in Sloan's office shooting the breeze.'

'Okay. Well, I want her to come home soon. I've got some good news for her.' Annie paused, pleased. 'Stormy called and told me that you're going to let them do the movie shoot over at your place.'

'Yeah.' He was in no way enthusiastic about it.

'I hope you've checked into all the details,' she said, her voice teasing. 'Particularly about the explosion they're planning to set off.'

Well, hell. An explosion or two on the furthest end of his twenty-five hundred acres wasn't going to hurt anything, especially if he had time to move his steers to the opposite end.

'Mary doesn't know she's going to get to stay with Stormy for a few days. Don't tell her, okay? I want to surprise her.'

He couldn't see what was so dang exciting about staying with Stormy. Instantly, he thought of a few

151

things he'd like to do if he could stay with Stormy for a few days. 'I won't say a word,' he promised irritably.

'Well, bring her home as soon as you two hook up, okay? Tell Sloan hi.' Annie hung up.

Cody turned the phone off and laid it on the desk. 'Annie says she hopes you end up with a platinum blonde one day.'

'She did not,' Sloan said, chuckling. 'She knows women and the law do not get along.'

'You're just plain not interested in getting tied down.' Cody crossed his arms. 'That'd be the same for you as roasting in hell. Well, I'm wishing a platinum blonde on you.'

Sloan laughed as if there were no tomorrow. 'I think misery wants company! You want me to be as bent out of shape as you are! You've fallen for that crazy scout, haven't you?'

'No.' Cody's denial was flat.

The sheriff slammed his palm against the desk as he roared with laughter. 'Stormy Nixon. Stormy Nixon! That little bitty woman's roped her a big ol' cigar-store Indian. Ha!'

Sloan's mirth dug at Cody's pride. He got to his feet and pointed one meaningful finger at the sheriff. 'A platinum blonde. Who can't cook and who thinks a church is just for getting married.'

'Uh-uh, friend. This is misery you have to suffer all by yourself.' Sloan wiped his eyes. 'Your phone, Cody. Don't forget your phone. It gets expensive using quarters to call women.'

Glaring, Cody stepped back in the room. In the space he left in front of the door, Curvy and Pick came in.

'Figured sumpin' more had to be going on in here than on the bench,' Curvy said. 'It's too hot for folks to be out right now.' He squinted at Cody. 'Saw your niece at the bus station. She going on a trip?'

'*What*?' Fear shot into Cody's stomach like a thrown rock.

'I said, we saw Mary go into the bus station. Is she –?'

'Damn it!' Cody hurried out the door.

'Hang on, I'll go with you,' Sloan said, jumping up to follow. 'You boys answer the phone,' he called back to Curvy and Pick.

The two elderly men looked at each other. Curvy slid into Sloan's seat. Pick took the one Cody had vacated.

'I told ya,' Pick stated.

'You did.' Curvy nodded agreeably.

'That bus pulled out already,' Pick said.

'Yep. Don't matter. Cody and Sloan'll run it down.' He rummaged around in the sheriff's desk. 'Look at the size of this hunting knife,' he murmured. Out of curiosity, he picked at the bottom drawer lock, which he'd never seen open. 'It sure is a heavy knife. Wonder who he confiscated it from – well, would you look at that?' The lock popped and he slid the drawer open easily. 'I always thought picking drawer locks was something they did in

153

movies to make you scared of what might pop out.'

Curvy reached into the bottom drawer and felt around. 'Nothing in here. Wait a minute.'

His fingers grasped cold metal. He held up a picture frame. 'Would you look at that?' he asked Pick, though he didn't have to, because Pick was craning to see.

It was a wedding photo of a young Sloan and a woman. They were both smiling as if they'd found Paradise. He didn't have the grim lines of worry on his face that he carried now, and she was a delightfully perky blonde with straight teeth and breasts that caught Curvy's attention. 'Didn't know Sloan was a breast man.'

'Reckon I didn't, either.'

'I don't know her.' Curvy scratched his head.

'I didn't know he'd been married.' Pick sat back in his chair and pulled out his matchbook to use on his teeth.

'She's a cute little thing.'

Pick shrugged. 'Probably ugly as green goat cheese now.'

'What makes you say that?'

'Dunno. He didn't stay married to her. She must notta been worth much.'

Curvy frowned, sliding the picture back into the drawer and locking it. He put the hunting knife back where he'd found it. 'He never told us.'

'Even the sheriff's allowed to have a secret,' Pick reminded him. 'We have plenty of our own. Besides, one bad marriage is enough. Wouldn't want to talk about it, and I sure as hell wouldn't want to do it again.'

'That's a fine excuse for Sloan, but it leaves Cody in the cold. He's just too stubborn to let anyone into his life in the first place.'

'He woulda let Annie.' Pick met Curvy's eyes. There was no need to say more about that.

Curvy chose another subject. 'Wonder if they've caught Mary by now?'

'I don't know.' Pick rolled his eyes. 'I sure feel sorry for the driver of that bus.'

'I know. Cody's probably going to ride up on it like all hell's-a-popping.'

'He should stick to ranching.'

'Damn right. 'Cause he's striking out with that spicy redhead *and* his niece.'

They laughed themselves into hiccups on that one.

'Dig around in the sheriff's desk some more,' Pick instructed. 'We might as well entertain ourselves until they get back.'

Anger and panic brewed inside Cody. Pain he'd never felt before pierced his chest as he came up on the end-of-the-line bus stop. 'Hope I made it.'

'Hope you did, too.' Sloan jumped out of the passenger side and strode after Cody.

They'd asked at the Desperado bus station for information. Yes, a girl, who'd told them she was nineteen, had bought a bus ticket two hours ago. One way non-stop to Austin. Fear had taken on new meaning for Cody as he'd torn off in his truck after the bus.

Every moment he kept hoping his phone would ring to tell him Mary was somewhere else. That this had all been a mistake.

He was seriously becoming afraid that, in order to keep an eye on his niece while her folks were gone, he'd have to let Sloan lock her up in the jail.

'I'm looking for my niece,' he said to the man at the Austin ticket counter. 'She's tallish, young, has black hair.'

'I see a lot of people,' the ticket agent replied, disinterested. 'Don't know that I saw anyone by that description.'

Sloan stepped up to the desk. 'Maybe the bus line would be interested if I told them the child we're looking for is thirteen? And shouldn't have been sold a ticket in the first place?' His badge glinted on his chest.

'I'd like to help you, I really would,' the man said hurriedly. 'But I swear, I see a lot of people – is that her?' He pointed toward the middle of the station.

A young girl with long black hair went inside the ladies' room.

'Thanks,' Cody said. He strode to wait outside the door, with Sloan behind him.

Ten minutes later he was tapping his boot. 'What in the devil is she doing in there?'

'I don't know, but I'm not going in.' Sloan

shook his head. 'Not even for you.'

A second later, Cody straightened as the young girl came out. She was dressed in a short, flowery skirt, and little white sandals. Her hair was piled up on her head. With a happy cry, she ran into the arms of a boy dressed in a military uniform.

Cody's jaw dropped. 'We've been standing out here waiting on the wrong kid.'

'She doesn't look much like a kid to me,' Sloan said with a grin. 'They're married.'

The terminal emptied out. There were no other buses being loaded. Cody and Sloan looked at each other.

'She didn't buy a ticket under her name. She couldn't have had a whole lot of money on her,' Cody said, more to himself than to Sloan. 'You don't suppose –'

'Pick and Curvy sent us on a wild-goose chase?' Sloan stared at him. 'No way. Serious charges are involved for lying to an officer of the law. I can think of several ways of torturing them. For one, I'd fine them for loitering and take away their bench.'

'Still, it doesn't make sense.' Cody's heart sank. 'I hate to make this call, but now I have to.' He dialed Annie's number.

'It's Cody,' he said, when she answered. 'I hate to say this, but I have no idea where Mary is.'

'I thought she was getting her hair dyed.'

She had been. But Cody knew very well she'd

slipped away from the shop because she'd knocked at Stormy's door while he'd been in there. He couldn't tell Annie that.

'We missed connections somewhere.'

'Call over to Stormy's,' she suggested.

'I'm in Austin.' He was glad of the excuse. 'Maybe you'd better.' He didn't want to call Stormy today.

'Austin! Why are you in Austin?'

He sighed heavily. 'Pick and Curvy thought they'd seen her in the bus station. It wasn't her, though. Now I'm two hours away from Desperado, so you'll have to hunt her up. I'm sorry, Annie.'

'This is absolutely preposterous!' Annie's voice turned agitated. 'I'll call your mother and put her on the look-out, and Stormy.'

She hung up. Cody turned his phone off.

'She isn't very happy with me,' he told Sloan.

'Didn't reckon so.'

They walked toward Cody's truck. 'Can't figure that young'un out,' he confided.

'She's having a tough time.' Sloan slammed the passenger side door as he got in.

'*I'm* having a tough time.' He started the engine, his hand hovering over the keys. 'I'm more convinced than ever that I wasn't meant to have children. Being an uncle is hard enough.'

He felt the sympathy in Sloan's gaze, but it really didn't help much. Wherever the heck Mary was, he had lost her.

With a silent prayer that she was all right, he headed toward Desperado.

Two hours later, Stormy sat quietly with Carmen Aguillar and Annie, and a downtrodden Mary. Annie had called, asking her to come to the Aguillar house. She had gone to the ranch, believing the movie would be discussed.

To her great chagrin, she had discovered that Mary had left her hotel and wandered around Desperado for a few hours. Cody had run off on a wild-goose chase from which he had not yet returned. Annie was frantic, and when she'd found Mary, all hell had broken loose.

Annie's proposition to Stormy upon her arrival startled her. The three women had a long talk, with Mary crying a lot. They had come to an agreement.

Stormy had hoped Annie would tell Cody about her idea before he got home. That way he'd be forewarned as to the way his sister-in-law felt. Unfortunately, Annie had waited until he walked in to tell him what was on her mind.

That moment was now. Stormy's hands trembled as she heard his boots in the foyer. When he saw her, he instantly halted.

'What's going on?' he demanded.

The question might have been taken as a greeting of sorts, except that he was looking directly at her. His expression was not one of pleased surprise. She forced herself to look away from him. Why did he have to make her heart beat faster?

159

'We will go outside for a while.' Carmen got to her feet. 'Come on, Mary, honey.'

Mary followed her grandmother outside, with a shamefaced look at her uncle.

'What's going on is that something went very wrong this afternoon,' Annie stated once they'd left. 'I realize Mary is a handful, but I would think, between you and Carmen, she would at least be somewhat under control.' She took a deep breath. 'Cody, I'm really starting to worry about Zach and me continuing with our honeymoon plans this weekend.'

'We'll be able to handle it.' He was nowhere near as confident as he sounded. The little scamp had just burned up a tank of his gas and his patience. 'We must have had a miscommunication of sorts today. That's all.'

'How does a miscommunication get you to Austin, and my daughter sitting in a bus station?'

'She really was in the station?' He couldn't believe he'd missed her.

'Yes. She said she wandered around and thought for a while, and then got hot. So she went to sit in the bus terminal. At which point, I'm assuming, you were well on your way to Austin.'

He slid a look at Stormy. She was staring at her hands, obviously embarrassed. He couldn't figure out why she was here, unless Annie had called her in on the search. 'I don't know what had Mary so upset.'

Stormy slid a silver ring back and forth on her

160

finger, refusing to look at him.

'I don't know what had her so upset, either. She won't tell me,' Annie said. 'What I do know is that I can't leave for a honeymoon with the situation as it is. I would cancel it right here and now, except that we've already paid for the plane fare and the vacation package to Bermuda.'

'No! Ma and I can hold the fort down.' *If I have to tie my niece to the saddle in front of me.* 'You deserve some time alone with Zach, Annie. Your life's fixing to be turned upside down by that baby.'

She took a deep breath. 'I really want to take this trip. I hope you understand when I tell you that, although I love you and trust you and your mother both, I do think Mary is acting out of loneliness and displacement. I want her to have someone she can talk to. Look up to. Someone else to keep an eye on her.'

Cody waited for the punch line. Maybe Annie wanted them to hire a nanny for a week. That might work – if the nanny came with the ability to mind-read.

'Your mother and I have discussed this and we are in complete agreement. Quite generously, we feel, Stormy has agreed to spend the last week of her stay in Desperado here.'

'Here?' he repeated, wondering what was different about that. She'd always been there.

'In this house. With Mary. Sort of as a companion. This is very kind of Stormy, because I know

161

she's a busy woman. I feel quite fortunate. I know you'll be relieved as well.'

Stormy wouldn't look at him. Cody felt buzzing in his ears. Relieved? Hell, no. He wasn't relieved. That woman had him jumping out of windows. She was a menace.

She'd given him her virginity. It had destroyed his peace of mind.

She would be staying in his house.

It just might kill him.

CHAPTER 11

Stormy watched the skin stretch tight across Cody's cheekbones. He wasn't happy to hear Annie's news. She herself wondered if staying here was a good idea. The idea of accepting the invitation had drawn her immediately. She loved this house, the sense of warmth and love its strong walls contained. She'd lived in the back of vans and slept on bean bags through most of her childhood and teen years while her parents stayed on the road. Shag carpet, swinging beads and peace sign posters had been the mementoes of her constantly changing life.

She wanted *this*. Her eyes swept the room, taking in the tidy living room. The spray of flowers on the table. The aroma of cookies wafting in from the kitchen. Just for the rest of this short week, she could be part of a real home.

Cody glared at her as if everything he'd heard was her fault. She blushed and looked out through a lace-curtained window, then forced herself to meet his angry glare.

If the truth were to be known, she wouldn't mind having a little more of him, either.

'Why does *she* have to be the magic bullet?' he demanded, jabbing a finger Stormy's way.

Annie shrugged. 'Mary is doing her best to emulate Stormy. The hair dye incident proves that Stormy has influence over my child. I think she's good for Mary.' She gave Cody a narrow look. 'Can you think of someone better?'

He made an obvious effort to think of someone, but as he shot a resentful glance her way, Stormy knew he couldn't think of a soul. *Great. He can't think of anybody better, but he wants me here like he wants saddle-sores.* She wondered now why women slept with men, if marriage wasn't in the offing. Oh, yeah. It had felt great. Heavenly. But the wonderful, body-melting sensations weren't worth the dislike in Cody's eyes. Making love with him had put them on the edges of an ever-widening chasm. His rejection hurt her in places she'd never dreamed she could be hurt.

'I can't think of anyone. But Annie, we barely know Stormy.' His face colored instantly. 'I mean, to bring her into our family life, I –'

He caught Stormy's eyes with his gaze. Her heart dropped as her eyelashes swept down to cover her dismay. *He* knew her. And he was desperate not to have her around.

'Well, Cody.' Annie sighed, sinking into a chair. 'Maybe this isn't the best idea after all. I wasn't aware you'd have such doubts about it. Perhaps

I'm being selfish. I know I am.' She rolled her shoulders. Stormy felt sorry that Annie was feeling the tension in the room; it was like crackling electrical wires. 'It's always been my dream to go to Bermuda. I've worked hard to get my salsa business going, and on the plans for the restaurant. Now is the only chance Zach and I will get to have time alone together, because after the baby's born, things'll get busier. With this latest stunt of Mary's, your mother is worried about being at home with her so much during the day when you're out doing chores.' She sighed heavily. 'But perhaps this isn't the best solution.'

'It's fine,' Cody suddenly growled. 'It's only until the weekend. We can last that long.'

He glared at Stormy as if to say that every waking moment would be torture, but he would make this sacrifice for Annie. Stormy stood, staring down his unwelcoming expression. 'I'll see you in a few days. Annie, I'm sure we'll talk before you leave.'

She refused to say goodbye to Cody, that big, feeling-sorry-for-himself oaf. All he cared about was how much she was going to put him out. He didn't care about the inconvenience to her schedule, or even his niece's distress. All he wanted was to jump from square to square like a checkerboard piece and avoid her. Fine. She could find plenty to do with Mary that didn't involve being on this property all day. At night, she would barricade herself in her room with a book. Their paths need never cross.

She marched from the room, her head held high – and her heart breaking.

Annie put her hands on her hips. Her eyes flashed blue fire. 'Cody Aguillar, I have never heard you be so rude in my entire life. *What is your problem*?'

'I don't have one.' He threw himself into a chair. 'I just happen to think that woman is the source of a lot of the problems we've been having with Mary.'

'How do you figure that?' Her eyes narrowed on him.

He shook his head. 'We wouldn't have had the orange-hair incident and the ride into Austin if Stormy had never blown into Desperado.' *And into my life, like gale-force winds.*

'It's not going to work,' she said softly. 'You can't put the blame on Stormy. We had problems before, Cody, and they're not her fault. It's easier, I know, to feel that way. God knows, I've wished a hundred, a thousand times, that Carlos hadn't gotten on that tractor that day. I'm sorry you had an argument with your brother.' Her voice dropped lower as her eyes pleaded with him.

She laid her hand on his arm. 'I'm sorry Carlos went off in a moment of anger. I know it's something that has haunted you ever since.' She took a deep breath. 'I'm sorrier that he died. I wish with all of my heart that Mary had not seen her father that way.'

Cody drew her into his arms, holding this

166

woman who was his sister in so many ways.

'But I wish more that you could forget,' Annie whispered against his chest. 'Maybe not forget. But at least move on. You can't hold yourself away from everyone just because . . . just because you're afraid to care deeply again.'

He bit the inside of his jaw as he clenched it. His heart felt like heavy stone in his chest. He understood what Annie was saying. It was something he knew deep in his heart. But he couldn't get past the guilt and the fear that ate at him most of the time. Today, his heart had nearly shrunk to the size of a piece of gravel as he'd chased Mary to Austin. Something had gone wrong in his relationship with his niece, the child who Cody had sworn on his brother's grave to take care of as if she was his own. But Mary was suffering her own hell and it was all coming back to haunt them. Closing his eyes wearily, he knew he was part of the problem. He couldn't be strict with her at all, the way she needed sometimes. The fear of losing her, too, was great inside him. Annie was right. He was part of the problems Mary was having.

He just didn't want Stormy to be the solution.

'Is there something I should know about Stormy that you're not telling me?' Annie asked, slowly pulling away to sit in a chair. She watched him with suddenly curious eyes.

'No. It's going to be fine, Annie. You know I'm just uncomfortable around people sometimes.' It was a straw, and he grasped at it.

167

'You seem more uncomfortable with Stormy than most. Is there something I'm missing here?'

A smile hovered at the edge of her lips. He shook his head, anxious to keep his secret hidden. 'Nope.'

Annie got to her feet. 'Well. For a moment there, I wondered if there was something going on between the two of you.' She shrugged, smiling. 'I haven't seen you this out of sorts about a woman before.'

'I'll admit we don't get along very well.'

'That's not exactly how Carmen put it. Your mother says you spent more time in Stormy's bedroom when she was sick than you did on your land.'

'She was afraid to be alone.' He headed into the kitchen to show that this conversation had gone far enough.

'It's a good thing Carmen is here to be a chaperon for Stormy. We wouldn't want there to be any gossip about Stormy and you in town.'

'A chaperon! That woman isn't worried about her reputation –' He halted immediately. Stormy had been a virgin, a fact he couldn't forget nor take lightly. She was a good woman, as much as he'd Hollywood-stereotyped her. She deserved to be treated as respectfully as a woman who wore white dresses buttoned up to her neck and sat in church seven days a week. 'I hadn't thought about that.' He dumped ice in a glass and scowled.

'Well, now you have,' Annie said brightly. 'Of course, it doesn't slip my attention that you're not

168

insisting that there isn't a reason for gossip concerning you and Stormy. That there's nothing going on between the two of you . . .'

Cody stared at his sister-in-law, realizing he'd been maneuvered into a trap. He started to say something to her, make a stinging reply of denial, but her eyes were laughing at him. He shrugged as if it didn't matter.

'Maybe Mary's not the only one who's taken a liking to Stormy,' she said softly as she patted him on the shoulder.

'I haven't!' he denied. 'Don't look at me. I don't like her, like that. She doesn't affect me one way or the other.'

'I meant me,' she said smoothly, with a grin as big as Texas, 'but now that you've mentioned yourself, I wonder if you're trying just a little bit too hard to act as if you don't like her. Relax, Cody,' she said, as she left the kitchen, 'Stormy's not a rattlesnake that requires special handling. She won't bite you.'

He closed his eyes. For a snakebite, there was antivenom.

For what Stormy was doing to him, there was no antidote.

Mary stayed with Stormy in town the few days she'd been promised, and Cody didn't go near the Stagecoach. He spent a lot of time thinking. He and Annie had come to an agreement. If Mary created a ruckus while her folks were gone, he was going to take her to task. Punish her if need be. Though this went firmly against his grain, he knew that he could no longer allow Mary to manipulate him. If situations arose during the time Annie and Zach were gone that were serious, Mary was going into counseling upon their return.

He hated that idea. But it was true that he'd allowed Mary to work him like a cow dog. He hadn't done a whole lot to curb her wildness, preferring to sit squarely in the role of favored uncle. While he wasn't crazy about Stormy Nixon, at least she'd kept Mary's attention off rock-throwing and on matters more typical of her age, such as wanting to be beautiful.

So, either peace and quiet existed at his ranch while her folks were gone, or Mary was getting the reining-in she deserved. Cody sighed, wishing they were past the weekend already. He knew Stormy had her return plane ticket set for Sunday. Annie would be back, and Stormy would be gone. His life could return to normal.

The biggest, most important rule of all while Stormy was in his house was that, while he treated her courteously and with the respect she deserved, no way was he ending up in her bed. No matter how much she enticed him. No matter if it killed him, he was not falling into that woman's arms again. She was destructive to his lifestyle and his brain; he hadn't stopped thinking about her since her arrival in Desperado. Now he had an itch. It kept him awake at night, and kept him company in the saddle. His body craved that woman. His mind was fascinated by her. His heart ran scared from her.

She turned his entire being inside out.

From the window, he watched her pull the thing she called a suitcase from the car. Her flowered carpetbag looped over her arm, and a mashed, vagabond-style hat covered her hair.

The hair on the back of his neck electrified as she walked toward the house. Four days. It was only four days.

Temptation, thy name is woman.

He went out to help her carry her things.

'I'm glad you're going to stay with us, Stormy.' Mary's eyes filled with happiness. 'It's going to be so much fun!'

If you like constant friction, Stormy thought. Cody had taken her suitcase inside, which she hadn't expected. Usually, he acted as if he might catch a disease if he touched her. Except for the time they'd made love. He hadn't had any problem touching her then. Afterwards, of course, had been a different story. Then he'd been afraid of getting caught by Mary – and by me. Cody definitely didn't want anything that remotely felt like commitment – and her virginity had certainly run him off.

She watched his wide back as he walked inside the house. 'I'm glad I'm staying here, too,' she told Mary. 'It will be fun.'

171

'Stormy,' Mary suddenly said, 'you did mean what we talked about? About Uncle, I mean?'

Stormy stared down into the teenager's eyes. During their two-day stay together at the Stagecoach, she and Mary had a lot of heart-to-hearts. One thing that had come out was that Mary feared Stormy just liked her because of her Uncle Cody. Stormy had taken great pains to assure Mary that the two were totally separate. She felt affection for Mary. She felt something else about Cody. Hurt, mainly, but she hadn't said that to Mary.

'I promise, it's just going to be me and you for the next four days,' she told Mary. 'Maybe we'll get your grandma one day and all of us can go shopping.'

'Oh, good. I'd like a hat like yours,' Mary said happily.

'We'll see how it suits you. We need to find you your own style, Mary. What looks right on me might not look as pretty on you as something else might.'

She walked inside the house, noting instantly the fresh spray of flowers on the table. Taking a deep breath, Stormy forced herself to relax. *This is what you wanted. You get to be in a real home for four days.* Nothing else mattered. She had worked hard on this project, and now she was going to enjoy a small vacation of her own. Annie dreamed of going to Bermuda, but Stormy . . . nothing so exotic for me, she thought. This is my dream.

'Supper!' Carmen called into the living room.

'Stormy, don't stand there like you're a visitor. Come on in and join the family.' She waved a welcoming hand her way.

Stormy didn't look at Cody as she stepped into the yellow and white painted kitchen. It was like walking into heaven – and if there was a devil standing guard in the dining room, well, she wouldn't pay him any mind at all.

They had supper at the oval formal table in the dining room. Cody didn't look at her much, and Stormy purposely avoided looking his way. She talked to Carmen and Mary about anything she wanted, and when they asked her questions, Stormy basked in their obvious interest in her life. Family time around a real dinner table. She wanted the night never to end, even if Cody didn't say a word. He didn't have to. The sun set low in the distance and she helped Carmen do the dishes. Afterwards, she and Mary walked through some fields. It was this land which had brought her here. The open land that would be used for the filming was farther away, but this ground under her feet had drawn her to this ranch. This place. It was giving her something she'd always wanted – for now.

'Are you having fun, Stormy?' Mary asked.

'You have no idea how much I'm enjoying myself,' she told her. Glancing toward the house, she could see two cigars glowing on the porch as Cody and his mother savored a late-night smoke after supper. That suited her. She just wanted to walk and listen to the country sounds and dream.

'I don't know why you like it so much,' Mary said, her face wondering. 'I get bored out here by myself.'

She smiled. 'I know. But I've never had this. It's all new to me. Being in LA seems typical to me, but you'd probably like it a lot because it would be different.'

'I suppose.' Mary jumped up onto the wood fence and hooked her feet over a lower rail. 'I'm not bored when you're around.'

'I know. It's fun to get to know new people.'

'I hope I meet lots of people when the movie comes.'

'You will.' Stormy listened to the sound of birds Cody had briefly tried to teach her, so that she could distinguish between mockingbirds and mourning doves. He hadn't appeared to like his role of teacher much.

'Will you be here then?' Mary asked.

'I'm not sure yet. I've been offered a job doing something different on the set, but I like being a location scout. I like going new places.' It might not be the best idea to spend too much time in Desperado. She'd see how a few weeks away from Cody affected her perspective, but she suspected her emotions would still be raw where he was concerned.

The two cigar lights went out, and the front door shut loudly.

'Grandma goes to bed early,' Mary explained. 'I usually like to stay up and watch a late movie, but tonight I'm tired. Will you mind if I disappear on you?'

'No, I'll feel like part of the family.' Stormy smiled. 'I'm going to walk for a while, then come in myself.'

' 'Night, then. See you in the morning.'

'We'll go shopping.' She waved goodbye and then turned to gaze into the paddock. Closing her eyes, she tried to let her other senses work. Manure, grass, night wind smells. A steer shook his horns. Stormy took a deep breath and let all of the moment work its magic on her. She adored this place. The peace was intoxicating. *Peace, brother,* she heard her father say. Peace wasn't in pot plants, psychedelic drugs and soul-disturbing music.

It was right here, under a majestic Texas sky.

Cody watched the woman from his position on the porch. She appeared lost in a world of her own. He couldn't imagine what she found so interesting in a paddock full of cow chips and knee-high grass, but it had her riveted. Maybe she was lonely. Maybe she hadn't really wanted to be here. He hardened his heart against those thoughts. She and Annie had gotten attached to one another in some sisterly fashion he couldn't fathom. She and Mary had gotten together like ticks on dogs' backs. If she was feeling out of place now, that was her problem.

175

Stormy had wanted to be here. So now she was. He wasn't going to go running out there and make sure she was all right.

He wanted to. He wanted to so much he knew it was a bad idea. It was only her first night here. He'd vowed to get through the next four days without compounding the mistake he'd made once. That meant he had to avoid tripping over her at every loose moment. One like this one here, which called to him to go see what was rolling around in her tizzy little brain. With the darkness and the quiet they'd get to talking – and maybe more. No, best he head back inside and not worry about a woman who claimed she could handle herself.

'Cody, ask Stormy if she wants some Key lime pie for dessert!' Ma called from the kitchen. 'I tried a new recipe I found in *Southern Living* magazine just for her.'

Key lime pie? What the hell for? he wondered. There was no need to go out of their way for Stormy's sake. Why couldn't they eat what they were used to, such as a quick bowl of ice-cream before bed? He preferred not to think about how Key lime pie would taste on Stormy's lips. Stomping out the door, he realized the scout had wandered about half a mile down the fence line. A frown fixed on his face. No good shouting. He'd have to go after her, or risk appearing rude by hollering.

He caught up with her, calling to her when he was about fifty feet away. 'Stormy!'

'Yes?' She turned to face him.

'Ma wants to know if you want some Key lime pie. She made it special for you.'

'Oh. How nice of her!'

He could see the pleasure on Stormy's face even in the darkness. It irritated him. 'You shouldn't be walking out here so late without a light,' he said gruffly. 'You might come upon a snake.'

'I see snakes all the time when it's full light and I'm in a crowded room. Sometimes they just can't be avoided.'

An uncomfortable thought crossed his mind. What was she referring to? 'I don't quite get your drift.'

'Never mind.' Stormy took off walking toward the house.

'Hang on a minute,' he said, catching her by the arm and gently turning her around. 'You're not implying that I'm a snake, are you?'

She shrugged. 'If the skin fits, wear it.'

'Now, look, Stormy. If you're going to stay in my house for four days, we're going to have to get along.' He meant there to be no nonsense on this point.

'You're right. I apologize. I shouldn't have taken advantage of an opportunity to take a cheap shot. Especially as you've been a wonderful host for the six hours I've been here.' She turned again and headed away.

'Stormy, we should talk.' He caught up with her and turned her around to face him. 'We should talk about what happened.'

177

She stared up at him with eyes that were round and captivating and hurt. Cody swallowed hard. 'Or maybe not,' he murmured, sliding his hand up to frame her face with his hands.

This is such a bad idea, he thought as he lowered his lips to hers. He moved close against her so that they melded together. Such a bad idea, but it feels so good.

CHAPTER 12

Stormy pulled away instantly. 'I think I'll go try some of your mom's pie.'

He kept her from turning away. 'Wait a minute. I know something's bothering you. I'd like to fix it.'

'By kissing me?' She gave him an assessing look. 'I think that adds to the problem.'

Cody lowered his head, knowing she was right. 'Okay. In fact, I apologize for the way I treated you the other day. I behaved like a jerk.'

'It's over and done.' She rubbed her hands over her arms. 'But just in case you think that I'm staying here because I want to be near you, I want to make it clear that I'm doing this for Annie, because she asked me to. I'm doing it for Mary, because she needs a friend. And I'm doing it for me, because . . . well, I've got my own reasons.' Her eyes never strayed from his. 'But they have nothing to do with you.'

'All right,' he said carefully. 'I'll keep that in mind.'

'Please do,' she replied softly. 'We knew what

we were doing when we made love, Cody. We knew there was no future involved. Staying in your home doesn't mean I want to have a convenient, ongoing bedtime relationship. Once was enough for me.'

He grimaced. 'That isn't what I want, either. Will you tell me one thing, though? Will you tell me *why* you did it?'

'Why I let you be my first, you mean?' Stormy looked away. 'I don't know, quite honestly. But I do know it wasn't a good idea.' She turned to walk off into the night, calling over her shoulder, 'I'd relax if I were you, Cody. You're looking real hard for the trap I set out, but there wasn't one.'

The dry grass crackled softly under her footsteps as she walked away. Cody closed his eyes. He couldn't believe he'd kissed her. He couldn't believe she had rejected him. His brain wasn't working right, because he knew better than to touch that woman. Stormy was right. There was no future between them.

Four days and three nights stretched like an eternity before him. He couldn't sit at the table every night with her, and wake up every morning to her in his house without going mad. There were some things a man had to do, and there were some things he just couldn't do.

He couldn't stay here.

Sloan glanced at Cody as they finished artificially inseminating the triple-registered, black and white spotted Arabian mare. 'One down, four to go.'

Cody grunted. 'Good.' He was bunking at Sloan's for the next two days, run out of his own house like a frightened dog. Thank goodness he'd promised Sloan his help with the mares. The timing was right, because it gave him a good excuse for avoiding Stormy. On the last night of her stay, he'd go home ever so casually and shake her hand. The next morning he'd wave as she drove off in her rental car – and say goodbye to the passel of trouble from California.

'Wanna get some grub?' Sloan asked.

'No.' Shaking his head, Cody said, 'I'm going to grab some water.'

'I've never seen you eat so little. Something the matter?' Sloan went behind a wooden partition in the barn and rummaged through some equipment.

'Nope.' And that was all Cody intended to say on the subject, even to his friend.

'When's the scout leaving?'

He shrugged and swigged water. 'Saturday night's her last night. Then she's back to La-La Land.'

'You ever been to California?' Sloan squinted over at him.

'Nope. And I ain't going. I don't like beaches; can't stand sand getting into everything. I can get dirty right here at home. Palm trees and earthquakes leave me cold, too.' Cody sighed, wiping his face with a rag. 'Can't see any reason to go someplace like that.'

181

'Where would you go, if you ever took a vacation?'

'Why the hell would I?' Cody couldn't imagine it. He hadn't taken a break from the ranch in years.

'Annie and Zach are,' Sloan pointed out.

'Yeah, but they're looking for some romance before the baby. I don't need romance.'

'Hmm.' Sloan strode to the back of the barn and looked to make sure the next horse had been readied for insemination. 'Romance has its good points. Women have their good points. I just can't remember any myself.'

'That's why you and I are friends.' Cody held the horse still while Sloan went to work. 'You understand about a man needing his space.'

He heard a grunt. From the other side of the spotted mare, Sloan glanced at Cody. 'Seems to me, though, that there's a difference between space you have to have and space you're just hanging on to out of habit. I heard you'd been spending plenty of time with that red-haired gal.'

'It's all business, Sloan. Just like this is business.' Cody slapped at a bothersome horse fly.

'Oh, well. I heard plane fare out to California is high as a cat's back anyway,' Sloan commiserated.

Cody eyed him sharply. 'Montana. Wyoming. If I went on vacation, those would be the places I would choose. Something tells me California is not my cup of joe. But I'm not going anywhere.'

'I'm going to the French Riviera one day.' Sloan

grinned at him. 'I want to sit on the beach and look at the girls without their bikini tops.'

'You'd waste money just to sit around and look at breasts?'

'Damn right.' Sloan stood, too, and thumped Cody on the back. 'I like beautiful things. I heard France has got plenty of beautiful things.'

Sloan walked back into the barn to retrieve some equipment, but Cody sank down on to a wood block, keeping his eyes on the mares. Staying in his home was a woman with a set of breasts which were quite attractive. Stormy was built like a man's dream come true. It made him shift uncomfortably just to think about it. The day was hot, and the sun beamed down on him like yellow fire, and suddenly Cody thought about being with Stormy again. The clinical act he and Sloan were performing on these horses had to be done, but there had been nothing clinical about getting inside Stormy Nixon.

Just when Stormy had become used to Cody's absence in the house, and finally relaxed enough to enjoy herself, he came back. This was especially annoying, despite the fact that it was his house. She and Mary and Carmen had enjoyed themselves thoroughly the three days Cody had been gone. They'd shopped, they'd stuffed themselves with delicious food, they'd picnicked in a hot field under an ancient live oak tree. Carmen and Mary had treated her like a beloved sister whose visits were cherished. Never in her life had Stormy been so happy.

Then he came back, destroying the girls-only feeling the women had delighted in. Instantly, all the other emotions came flooding back to Stormy, as she met Cody's dark brown eyes for a fast peek. He was darker from the sun, and looked rough and sexy in worn jeans and a faded western shirt. His jet-black braid enhanced his swarthy features. Stormy swallowed as desire and wistfulness hit her all at once.

'Mary behave for you?' he asked, as she dried dishes in the kitchen.

'We didn't have any trouble at all. In fact, we girls just kicked up our heels and had a great time.' She wouldn't look at him, though he picked up a cup towel and started drying alongside her.

'Guess you'll be glad to get back home tomorrow.'

Home was a small apartment with a huge rent bill every month. Big deal. Stormy shrugged. 'I'm happy wherever I am.'

'You don't have friends or family anxiously waiting for you to get back?'

She laid the towel over her shoulder and shot him a questioning look. 'I have a job, and acquaintances. I have a boss who tries to take care of me.'

'No family?'

Stormy turned her back to Cody. 'Not in the usual sense. My folks aren't into family quality time. We don't see each other much.'

'No boyfriend?'

Slowly, she turned back around. 'Why are you asking?'

He loomed large as he stood beside her in the small kitchen. She couldn't help noticing how wide his shoulders were – those same shoulders she'd clutched in the throes of sexual awakening.

'I don't know why I'm asking. It's not any of my business,' he said. 'I guess I want to know.'

Her heart skidded inside her chest. He knew she wasn't serious about anyone if he'd been her only lover. It had to be a male-territorial thing on his mind. Either he wanted to know that she had a boyfriend so that he could forget about her more easily – or he wanted to know that she didn't so that he could satisfy himself that he'd marked her as his appropriately.

'I don't think it really matters,' she said smoothly, tossing the cup towel on to the drain-board. 'I'm going to sit out on the porch with your mother for a while, and then I'm going to bed. I doubt I'll see you in the morning, as I have a very early flight. However, thank you for your hospitality. I have enjoyed my stay here with your family.'

She neatly side-stepped him and left the kitchen. 'Oh, and by the way,' she said, poking her head back into the room just in time to see the struggle on his face, 'I talked to Jonathan today. He says he'll be in contact with you soon about paperwork and details for the movie.'

185

Swiftly, she made good her exit. She had to. They'd been heading into dangerous waters. For a moment, it had felt cozy. The two of them, sharing a task and making conversation – but he had run off for three days. His retreat had been okay with her, but she didn't want him thinking that just because it was her last night in Desperado, he had to be nice to her.

She joined Carmen on the porch, taking a seat on the wooden step and shaking her head at the offer of a cigar. 'Where did Mary run off to?'

'She's in her room talking on the phone to one of her friends. Here lately she's had more kids calling the house.' Carmen took a long drag. 'Guess it didn't take long for them to find out she had an honest-to-goodness Hollywood person staying with her.'

'Oh, for heaven's sake.' Stormy laughed. 'What I like about staying with you is that nobody in your family treats me like that. It's just a job, you know. Not particularly more glamorous or wonderful than anything else.'

'You meet famous people.' Carmen's eyes watched her.

'Yes, but famous people are the same as everyone else, basically. It's just as much fun to meet the folks in Desperado. I've had a great time.'

'You are a good girl, Stormy.' Carmen nodded. 'You have your head on straight.'

'I hope so.'

They sat comfortably for a long time without

saying much. One of the things that made her feel so much a part of the family was that Carmen didn't seem to think she had to entertain her every moment. If Carmen didn't have anything to say, she didn't say it.

'You got your sights set on my boy?'

The question coming out of nowhere startled Stormy. 'I'm not sure,' she said softly. 'I can't see any way for it to work out, so I'd have to say no, I don't.'

'Hmmph.' The cigar tip glowed bright in the darkness. 'Don't reckon I'd be much of a mother-in-law.'

Stormy wanted to say that she suited her, but since it was never going to happen, she didn't think she should comment on it.

'My son likes you.'

'Oh, no, Carmen. He says I'm too flamboyant to be real.'

The tip of the cigar glowed again. 'Cody is not going to fall easy, girl. He had no father growing up, and then he lost his brother. I am old.' She rocked back in the chair. 'He appears strong, but he is afraid of losing someone else.'

'Everybody's afraid of that.' She filled her world with surface interactions because it was all she'd ever known. But deep inside, she didn't want to be abandoned again.

'Yes. But he is using it as an excuse. You just go on being yourself and you will get him. He wouldn't be interested in a namby-pamby woman.'

187

'I don't know. We battle an awful lot. And I'm leaving tomorrow. I think it's for the best.'

They were silent for a long time. Stormy could hear night noises in the dark that she never heard in California. Rustling air, a frog somewhere, a cow's moo in the distance.

'Where are you from, gal?'

'LA.'

'I mean, where are your people from?' Carmen asked.

'Oh. A hippie commune,' Stormy replied, highly embarrassed. How much she'd like to say she came from a small town like Desperado, and a house like this one, with a family who cared about each other!

'Then you will recognize the expression, make love, not war.' Carmen got up and went inside the house, apparently through dispensing wisdom.

Stormy stared after her, astonished. *Make love, not war.* Was she actually suggesting Stormy should fall in love with her son? Make love with him? That was not the way into Cody's heart, as she'd painfully learned after the one afternoon they'd spent together.

Cody came out onto the porch and settled next to her. She could feel warmth radiating from him even as she felt her whole body came alive. A star twinkled brightly in the midnight sky. *I want him,* she told the heavens.

But she couldn't have him. 'I've already shared a cigar with your mom, so I'm going to turn in,' she said, getting up to make her escape just as he'd made his three days ago.

'Don't leave yet,' he said, reaching to tug lightly on the hem of her denim skirt. 'Please.'

She gazed down into his eyes. 'Why not?'

'I can't let you go back to California without knowing that we've ended this as good as we possibly can.'

She didn't want it to end. Cold chills tickled Stormy's stomach. 'I'm fine, Cody. Don't worry any more about it.'

'I am. I haven't been fair to you since the beginning. It's not right to let you leave without telling you the truth.'

Reluctantly, she sat down next to him. 'If it will make you feel better.'

He locked his fingers together and stared out into the distance. 'I guess you wouldn't be surprised to hear that I've never met anyone like you.'

'You told me I remind you of a soap opera character,' Stormy said mildly, 'but I've got to tell you, some of your friends have me beat for drama. Pick and Curvy come to mind quite quickly.'

He chuckled. 'Well, they do make up their stories as they go along.' For a moment he sat thinking. Then he said, 'What I really meant is that I've never met a woman like you.'

'I know you're counting your blessings about that.'

'I don't know how I feel anymore. When I met

you, I got bent out of shape, I'll admit. As time went on, you unexpectedly slid into my life more and more. I'm a bachelor and want to stay that way.' He shot her a how-are-you-taking-all-this look. 'But I can't deny that I'll never forget you.'

Stormy's lips parted. That was the last thing she'd expected Mr. Macho cowboy to say. 'I won't forget you, either,' she said slowly, deciding to play it careful, 'nor any of the rest of your family.'

He shook his head. 'No. I mean, you've gotten to me in some way I never expected. Don't get me wrong.' He hesitated for a second. 'I still think you're way out there. I still think you may have some loose wires in your brain. It's goes without saying that, for the long haul, you and I definitely would not make it.'

That hurt. Stormy lowered her lashes to hide the pain she knew would show in her eyes. 'I didn't come out here with man-hunting on my mind.'

'I know that,' he said huskily. 'What I'm trying to say, and not doing it very well, is that something happened between us that neither of us was looking for. Maybe didn't even want. But it happened, and it kind of pushed me off my boots. Woman, you've made me crazy.'

She raised her eyes to meet his. 'You've made me crazy, too,' she whispered.

'I think I'm kinda glad about that.'

And before either of them could think it through, their lips met, touching off desire that rivaled those earthquakes in California.

190

'I can't help wanting you,' he groaned. He didn't know how else to put it, but he hoped she wouldn't take his meaning wrong.

'I feel the same.'

Her lips were soft and sweet under his, and Cody thought he just might explode. She snuggled up to his chest, allowing him to wrap his arms around her, and sighed with what sounded like passion. Gosh, he hoped that was what had her sighing. He didn't want to be the only one way out on this limb.

'I tried too hard to stay away from you,' he murmured in her hair.

'Cody, shh. Don't say another word. Just love me,' Stormy told him.

The lights were all off inside the house. They were safe to step inside and give release to what they both wanted. 'Are you sure?' he asked.

'Yes.' Her eyes glimmered in the darkness. 'Hurry.'

They sneaked inside the house quietly, making certain the screen door didn't slam. Gently, he took her by the hand into his bedroom and closed the door behind them.

'So this is your cave,' she said.

'Yeah.' He drew her to him for a long kiss.

Her fingers went to the buttons on his shirt. He tensed as she undid them, and moved his shirt away from his chest. Her lips touched him here, and there, and she touched him in his heart. He edged her over to the bed and leaned her back into it.

'I like taking off your clothes.' He pulled off her blouse, and then her denim skirt, revealing panties and a sweet pink bra – and adorably puckered nipples. 'I like everything about your body.'

She giggled, and he heard the nervousness. Forcibly, he recalled that she had been a virgin, and that he'd been none too gentle with her. No wonder she sounded nervous. This time, he would go slowly.

She worked his shirt off, and then his jeans. His boxers followed that. She stared at his naked thighs, mesmerized by the large, hard muscles. Jet hair sprinkled along the ridges, emphasizing his strength.

'What are you staring at?' he asked huskily.

He startled Stormy into speaking the truth. 'I've never seen anyone as beautiful as you are. You are like a finely carved master statue.'

He didn't move, his body struck into instant awareness. 'You are a strange woman.'

She nodded slowly, her eyes caught on his. 'You are a crazy man.'

Crazy for her. He rolled, catching her underneath him. 'So crazy to want you as bad as I do.'

Stormy could feel Cody's readiness at the inside of her thighs. 'Come on,' she said softly.

'I have to get some protection.'

'No,' she pleaded, holding her to him. 'Don't leave me now.'

He fought with the desire to do as she asked. 'I have to,' he said, kissing her on the tip of her nose

192

as he reached to the nightstand. 'If I got you pregnant, we would have an ugly baby.'

She laughed, even as he struggled with the foil packet. 'Is that one as old as the other one you had?'

'Damn it, yes. It's from the same box. If you were staying longer, I'd make a trip to the store, but as it is, we'll just have to hope this one stays together, too.'

He was beside her again quickly. Before he touched her again, he stared down into her eyes. 'I'll be gentle this time.'

'I know you will.' It was the last worry on her mind. His fingers were stroking her, teasing her to wild readiness, and she wanted him like nothing else. 'Cody?'

'Yes?' He waited, not wanting to push her if she had reservations.

'Ugly because of you – or me?'

'You.' He buried himself inside her, nuzzling his face in her burgundy hair with a feeling of relief that was almost painful. She had started to giggle at his answer, but the sound ended on a gasp of pleasure at his entry. 'The townspeople might throw rocks at it,' he murmured.

She beat on his back, wrapping her legs around him tightly. 'Cody Aguillar, you're a chicken.'

He lifted his head. 'I haven't been accused of that before.'

'Everyone is too afraid of you to say it.'

Inside her he moved faster, craving the feel of

193

her body against his. 'But not you.' He took her lips with his, tasting her, holding her close so that he felt her orgasm building and felt her surprised squeal against his mouth. 'You're not afraid of me,' he whispered harshly, reeling as his own release came upon him like strong waves. He fell into her waiting arms.

I'm afraid of you.

They went to sleep, still intertwined. Some time in the night, Stormy had to get up. As gently as possibly, she moved the big rancher off of her and grabbed a tissue to clean herself with. Her lips parted in dismay.

This condom had not passed the test of time.

CHAPTER 13

Three months later – October

'What will it hurt you to go back?' Sun Nixon arranged several pots of herbs on a shelf, barely sparing a glance for her daughter. 'A job is a job. You like traveling. Go.'

Stormy pursed her lips. It would hurt her to go to Desperado. There were reasons it was best she stay in California.

'I don't seem to crave traveling as much any more.' Stormy walked through the small greenhouse. 'I want to settle down, get a more stable job.'

This had been on her mind a lot lately. She had to make some changes in her life. Soon.

'Is that the right way to treat Jonathan?' Moon Nixon glanced up from tightening guitar strings to give her a stern eyeing. 'I'm lucky to have such good friends in the business, and you're lucky that they keep you employed.'

Despite your bout with pills. Her father hadn't

195

said it, but she knew he was thinking it. That brought another thought searing into her mind.

'I'm pregnant.'

Sun and Moon stared at their only child in dismay. 'Pregnant?' Sun repeated.

'Are you getting married?' Moon demanded.

'Yes to the first question, and no to the second.' Stormy shook her head at them. 'Don't act so shocked. You both had revolving doors on your bedrooms most of my childhood.'

'Well, yes, but we knew how to use birth control,' Sun informed her. 'Even in the heyday of the sixties, we were careful about those things.'

So free-spiritedness had flown out the window now that they had turned fifty years old. Stormy shrugged. 'I didn't know I was going to need birth control pills.'

'Why not?' her mother demanded. 'If you engage in sexual activity, you need precaution.'

'Well, up until my trip to Desperado, keeping my knees together had been a sufficient form of birth control.' Stormy sighed, going over to plop down in a round sofa. What little furniture was in this shabby house in the California mountains retained the late sixties-early seventies look.

'Are you saying that you were a virgin until the age of thirty?' Sun stared at her daughter in astonishment.

Stormy wondered why conversations in her family always had to be so open. At some point, there should have been limits to what

196

was discussed with Mom, what could be aired with Dad, and what constituted private matters. 'Sex in the nineties can kill you. Free love died some time back. Yes, I was a virgin.'

Sun started to weep. 'That means you finally fell in love. Why aren't you getting married?'

'Neither one of us is interested.'

Moon sighed and put away his guitar. 'I don't understand this new generation. It's all divorce and lack of commitment.'

'Oh, no,' Stormy groaned. 'I can't believe I'm hearing this.' Perplexed, she stared at the parents who had named her Virginia Caroline Nixon, but then crumbled under their hip pretensions and nicknamed her Stormy. Her mother said giving birth to her on the coldest, windiest night of the year had helped. Otherwise, they would have named her Star, so their family would have been complete. Sun, Moon, and Star. She sighed. 'Listen, I don't think we're going to get anywhere with this discussion. Mom, could you just tell me what to do about morning sickness?'

'Oh, dear.' Her mother grabbed a tissue to wipe her eyes. 'Yoga. You need to meditate, dear. You must get rid of the inner turmoil inside you which is causing your morning sickness.'

'Oh, for crying out loud, Sun,' her father complained, 'give her the name of your herbalist and spare her that meditation crap.'

Stormy got to her feet and went to give each of her parents a kiss. 'I'll figure it out myself. Thanks for your help.'

She went to the front door, but her mother called after her.

'If you lost your virginity in Texas, hon, maybe you'll find peace if you go back. You should consider Jonathan's offer carefully.'

'Thanks, Mom. I'll call you if I do.' Stormy closed the door on her parents' home and left, shaking her head. They didn't understand. Making love didn't necessarily mean marriage any more now than it had during her parents' generation. Falling in love still hurt, though. What Cody felt for her was complicated, but he certainly had stressed he didn't want marriage, never mind children.

Getting into her car, she opened the ash tray and pulled out a set of hinged snake teeth she'd swiped from Cody's dresser when she left. He'd been lying in bed asleep. It had been three o'clock in the morning. She'd discovered the problem with the condom and, quickly calculating her cycle, realized she might be at a fertile time. All she wanted to do was escape. There was no way she could say goodbye to Cody easily, and thinking about it left her sleepless. She'd packed her stuff, grabbed the teeth, taken a last lingering look at the big slumbering rancher, and made a director's cut on that scene in her life.

She had found peace in Desperado once, but there would only be pain there now.

'Heard from Stormy?' Sloan asked.

'Hell, no. Why would I?' Cody wished everybody he laid eyes on wouldn't ask him that. He was damn tired of answering the question. What had that woman done while she was in this town to make folks wonder about her so much?

Lots of things. He shifted uneasily in the chair in Sloan's office. 'Do you mind not asking me that constantly?'

'Sorry, pal. Just thought that since the movie crew had landed, you mighta heard.' Sloan eyed him easily.

'Don't expect to,' he said curtly. 'She never said she was coming back.'

'Well, then. Guess you won't mind going out on a double date Saturday night with some twins from Shiloh.'

'Hell, yes, I would mind!' Cody stared his friend down, wondering if he'd lost his sanity. 'The only twins over there are Wrong-Way's sisters, and I wouldn't have contact with anything of his.'

'You got nothing better to do.'

'I've always got something better to do than go out on a date with women I don't want to talk to. It's a poor reason to put dress jeans on. I can't stand trying to make small talk. It makes my scalp itch.'

'Nah. That's 'cause your braid's too tight. Come on, Cody. Let's relax, have some fun, let your hair down.'

'Nope.' Cody got to his feet. 'You're a laugh a minute today, but I never went out with women much before Stormy came around, and I see no reason to change my way of doing things now. Nice try, though, friend.'

'What?' Sloan put on an innocent expression. 'What do you mean?'

'I'm well aware that you think I'm mooning after that loony movie scout. Three months without her being around ought to have convinced you that I'm not suffering any heartbreak.'

'Yeah, right,' Sloan mumbled into his coffee mug. 'You're like a stallion that's been gelded. Sore and confused.'

Cody shook his head. 'Not true. If I'm sore, it's from getting my steers down to the State Fair for auction.'

Sloan sighed. 'Well, if I can't talk you into double-dating, and I can't talk you into getting off that ranch of yours, you better get out of my office and let me do some work.'

Cody didn't move. Sloan reached over and socked his arm. 'There's the door.'

'I know where the door is,' he muttered. 'I'm just taking my time getting there.'

'You've got no energy since that woman left, Cody. We sure did enjoy watching her torture you. But now,' he shook his head at him, 'you're kind of boring.'

'Thanks, friend. I'm out of here.'

Cody left, highly disgruntled. He tried hard not

200

to think about Stormy, but with small planes coming and going as they dropped off equipment and a movie star or two, and the occasional stretch limo that pulled through Desperado, it was impossible not to think of her. All this was her fault. She'd brought this disarray into his town, and damn near up to his door. She'd made mush out of his brain.

Damn, but he was glad she was gone. It was nice not being angry, or horny. Angry *and* horny. Always at the high end of the emotional spectrum with her. Shoot. He hadn't been energized with her in his life – he'd been full of adrenalin. With fall in the air and the recent touches of winter's crispness, it was time to think about slowing down and getting ready for the long grey months ahead.

Yawning, he slid on to Curvy's and Pick's bench, glancing around. They weren't anywhere to be seen, which was probably a good thing. Lately, they'd found a new haunt down at the movie set, a place he had completely avoided. His land might be momentarily full of stars and costumes, but he wasn't going to be drawn into what had everyone's attention around here.

The shops along the creek had changed, putting their focus on quaintness that might draw the eye of big city folk searching for that kind of nostalgia. Annie's restaurant was progressing, as was the size of her belly. She'd mentioned that her morning sickness had passed and that was a good thing. Briefly, he wondered if he could stand being made an uncle again. Mary had darn near given him coronary distress.

Of course, Stormy seemed to have straightened out Mary's confusion. Somehow, the movie scout had pulled strings to get Mary a very small part, one that didn't include guts and gore. Grudgingly, he admitted that Stormy's choice was very appropriate for his niece. And she didn't have to cut one inch off that wonderful black hair of hers that he adored.

That didn't make him feel a whole lot better, though. That peculiar woman had never once called him. Not once! He should have at least rated a call from the lady, a pretension that she liked him enough to give him her phone number, and that he would want it. He didn't, and would never call her back, of course. But she could have called, damn it. Especially after sneaking out like a thief in the night. No goodbye, no nothing. And she'd taken the snake teeth off his dresser. No matter that there were five other sets laying right next it – she'd thought he wouldn't notice. He had. It was a helluva souvenir to take home – most women would want a picture to remember a man by – but then, he'd never come close to figuring Stormy out.

He sighed and got to his feet. Maybe he'd mosey on home and see what Ma was up to.

Maybe Stormy had called while he was out, to mention that she had his teeth.

He drove home slowly, parking in the drive. On

the porch were several suitcases, his mother's old ones. Puzzled, Cody got out to see what she was up to.

'Ma?' he yelled inside the house.

'I'm so glad you're here,' she said, bustling out of the kitchen. She had on her best Sunday dress and comfortable shoes. 'I need you to drop me off at the bus station.'

'What for?'

'I am going to stay with my sister for a while.' She eyed him sorrowfully. 'I might move out that way with her.'

'Why?' he demanded incredulously.

She gave him a sorrowful gaze. 'It is like a funeral around here, Cody. It's depressing. I am not going to spend the last years of my life under a black cloud.'

He lowered his brows at her. 'This isn't going to work, Ma.'

'What isn't?' She reached to grasp the handle of a suitcase and headed toward the truck.

'Pretending you're going off because I'm in a bad mood. I know you liked Stormy, and Sloan liked her, and everybody did, but she wasn't the woman for me.'

'It does not make any difference to me.' She tossed the suitcases into the truck bed. 'Get the rest of them, son,' she called, getting inside.

'Jeez.' He got the rest of her luggage and loaded them up, then got into the truck with her. 'Don't do this, Ma.'

'I have to. I'm an old woman. I am going to die living with you.' She had her hands clutched around the handle of a white wicker purse he would swear she'd never before used. Church dress and fancy purse. Cody frowned. All this for a simple ride on a bus.

'You haven't died yet, and we've lived together since Pa died.'

'Yes. And I liked it. But you're grumpy, and moody, and I can't stand it. I know you work hard, but it is difficult looking at your sour face every night.'

'Sour face!' If that didn't beat all. 'You . . . don't go like this.'

'It's time you were on your own, anyway. It is not right for a bachelor to live with his *madre* forever. The local women worry that I'll breathe fire on them if they come around my boy.'

'I hope you do,' he muttered. 'Ma, I know this is about Stormy. But she just wasn't the right one.'

'It is not about Stormy. It is about you. You can not forget about her, and you are as much fun as a squirt of lemon in the eye. Start the truck. I am going.'

Cody mashed his lips together and nodded jerkily. 'If that's what you want.' He started the truck.

'I said I did.' She looked resolutely forward.

He let her off at the bus station, making sure she had enough money on her. 'Are you sure you want to do this? I can turn around and take you home

204

right now.'

'Quit pecking at me, son. I'm still in my right mind, ya know. Don't fiddle at me like I cannot take care of myself.' She gave him a fast, dry kiss on the cheek. 'It is time I saw something outside of my own back yard anyway.'

And then she was gone, hurrying on to a bus in her flower-printed dress and white wicker purse. Cody sighed as the bus rolled off. Getting back into his truck, he went home. The house was dark. Ma had left something on the stove for him, but he didn't feel like eating. Throwing himself into a chair, Cody slumped his face into his hand. He had never felt so tired, so run down.

So lonely.

'Ain't nobody seen Cody in a week or better,' Pick said in a stage whisper to Curry. 'A few folks have heard him playing his guitar, though, and decided to stay the hell off his property. Danged Spanish music's got everybody looking around for ghosts.'

Curvy scratched his head. 'It's just him out there now. Guess he's lonely. He doesn't have as much to keep him busy as we do.'

'Reckon we ought to pay him a visit?'

Curvy stared at him. 'I'd like to stay in one piece a while longer, thanks.'

'Aw, he wouldn't do more than bark at us. He's done that plenty of times.'

'What the heck would we say to him?'

Pick shook his head, stumped.

Curvy glanced toward the movie set where Mary was rehearsing her part. 'We could tell him that Mary wants him to watch her do her stuff.'

Pick brightened. 'That's a thought. Hey! We could call him and tell him that! Safer that way.'

Curvy nodded. 'I think so. He's still a little angry that we told him Mary had left on a bus.'

'We thought she had! We were trying to be helpful.' Pick felt crushed just looking back on that incident.

'Got a quarter?'

Pick checked his pockets. 'Nope.'

They were silent for a few minutes.

'Well, heck. I didn't really want to call him anyway.' Curvy glanced around. 'If he's run his ma off, he sure isn't going to take it easy on us.'

Pick squinted into the sun, gauging to see when it might go down. 'You know, Cody oughta just call her.'

They had no need to mention who.

Curvy shook his head. 'He won't.'

Pick sat up straight. 'We could do it. Kind of make up for the little bus problem we had.'

That earned him a probing stare from his friend. 'And say what? That Cody wants her to come back? That he's roaming around on his land like a living phantom and folks won't go near him? Oh, boy, that'll bring her running.'

'We could tell her Cody's sick. Maybe even terminal,' Pick said dramatically, warming to his subject.

'No, friend. We made ourselves a New Year's resolution that we were going to cease meddling.'

'Yeah, but that was in preparation for next year's New Year. We've got more'n two months to go,' Pick reminded him.

'I don't know.' Curvy rubbed his stubbled chin doubtfully. 'This time, he might have Sloan lock us up in his jail or something worse.'

'Look at it this way.' Pick rubbed his hands and leaned close. 'We make an anonymous call. We tell Stormy that Cody has wasted away to a bone for missing her –'

'Nope.' Curvy interrupted him, waving his hands. 'I'm not messing in anyone's love interests.'

'All right.' Pick sat back, defeated. Almost immune to the sight now, he watched a black limo pull in front of the wooden kegs they were perched on. A leggy redhead got out. Pick focused on her legs, almost falling off his chair when he realized who it was. 'Did you see that?' he demanded excitedly.

'See what?' Curvy swiveled his neck, craning from side to side.

'See that woman! The one in the mini-dress! I almost missed who it was because of the dress! Stormy Nixon's come to town, and she's wearing a dress!'

'If that don't beat all,' Curvy mused. 'Are you sure? I never saw one on her before.'

'Me, neither. And this one was short enough to get the hairs up on the back of Cody's neck.' Pick clapped his hands gleefully. 'We don't have to call. No doubt they've already made plans. See, everything always works out. We'll just sit back and watch the fireworks.'

Curvy slapped his buddy on the back. 'Good eye, old friend. It's bound to wake up around here now.'

'Yep. If she can't bring Cody outta his lair, nothing will.' Pick grinned broadly. He hadn't gotten a good look at Stormy, but what he'd had was good. She was tinier and prettier than ever. Feminine. Delicate.

Just right to brand a mean-eyed and foul-tempered rancher who needed taming.

Mary ran to hug Stormy. 'What are you doing here?'

'I'm only in for the day. I'm supposed to deliver some papers, and look over some extras.' Stormy's eyes drank in the thin, dark-haired girl. 'You look wonderful. How's the part?'

'I'm having a blast,' Mary said happily. 'Everything's changed since you came, Stormy. I'm so glad you're back.'

'Just for today,' she reminded her. 'You get back to rehearsal,' she said with a guilty look toward the director. 'I've got to do some things.' She gave her a last hug and headed toward a makeshift office.

If time had healed Mary, Stormy could be grateful for her time in Desperado. The teenager

208

seemed like a new person. Stormy's heart lifted in gratitude. She couldn't take any credit for the transition, but it certainly was nice.

Now to get on to the job at hand. Jonathan had sent her by special plane to spot-check a few things, and then she was off again. This was their agreement. She hadn't wanted to come; he'd claimed he could trust no one but her. She didn't want to be here any longer than possible. Certainly not long enough to run into Cody.

Unhappily, she rubbed her barely swollen stomach. The nausea had passed, thank heaven. She was sore in places, but mostly glad about the baby. Her mother had stressed that she should tell the father, but Stormy just couldn't. Three months apart hadn't made her feel any better about their relationship. She might think about him all the time; might know she'd lost her heart to him. But she knew that she was not the woman he would fall in love with. He would not welcome a bond between them, particularly a child. Her lifestyle was not his way; California would never suit him. They had too much that would keep them apart.

She hated to think of what he would say if he knew she was carrying his child. Quickly, she got to work, determined that, the sooner she left Texas, the better for everyone.

Particularly me, she sadly told the baby growing inside her. I want to give you a home. I don't want you to grow up feeling you're not wanted. I want you.

Cody would offer to marry her. Cody would shoulder the burden of his offspring, just as he shouldered Annie, Mary, and his mother. Sometimes even the needs of Desperado. He was a good man, and he would do the 'right' thing.

For a woman who desperately craved to be wanted and needed, being an obligation would break her heart.

CHAPTER 14

'Stormy! Hang on a sec!' Tate Wrong-Way Higgins jogged to catch up with her. 'Long time, no see!'

And a sight for sore eyes. He'd been hoping for a chance like this. Desperado might have gotten the movie, but he was flat determined to get the girl. The baby doll dress teasing the middle of her thighs made his throat dry enough that his voice hit a high note when he'd called out to her. He hoped she hadn't noticed.

'Hello, Tate.' She offered him a warm smile. 'It has been a while.'

'You're purtier than ever,' he told her, quite sincerely. For the longest, Hera at the beauty salon had kept her eye on him. But he wasn't interested in the big-boned Hera. Any woman who could probably wrestle him down wasn't for him. No, sir. He admired Stormy's long legs under the flippy, short white dress and sighed to himself. He was deeply interested in *that*.

'Well, thank you, Tate. I didn't expect to see

you in Desperado.' She kept smiling.

Tate hoped that meant she'd keep talking to him a while longer. 'I keep my eye on what everyone's doing around here. Besides, it's fun watching a movie get made.'

'I'm sorry that Shiloh didn't turn out to be quite what we wanted.' Her expression was sincere.

He waved off her apology. 'No matter. Maybe we'll get the sequel when they make it. I just know they will. It's going to be great.'

'Thanks.' Her smile turned rueful. 'I hate to rush, but I really –'

'Now I was going to tell you that you oughta let me take you out to dinner.' He put the broadest smile on his face so she'd accept.

'I'm flying back out tonight. I'm sorry, Tate.'

She did appear to regret that they couldn't get together, and hope soared inside him. 'Well, maybe you could give me your business card so that I can call you on a movie idea I've got.'

'Um – sure.' She handed him one and he took it like a drowning man.

'Hot dang, Miss Stormy.' He tipped his hat and backed away slowly, as if he were afraid she'd snatch the card back. 'I'll call you some time.'

'Okay. Bye, Tate. It was nice seeing you again.'

She walked inside an office, and he sighed to himself happily. Stormy Nixon was the woman of his dreams. About ten yards away, he saw Hera walking around, viewing the set. Obviously she was on her lunch break. He snuck off in the

212

opposite direction before she could see him. Hera had specific ideas where he was concerned, and he didn't want her pointing her sharp scissors his way. Just because every once in a while he went by and gave her a little pleasure, it didn't mean he was going to marry her. She'd hinted last Christmas about an engagement ring, but he'd gotten off with a pretty pin. He hadn't mentioned the stones were cubic zirconia, of course, and while Hera had seemed a little disappointed with the pin, she had thanked him for it the way he liked to be thanked.

It wouldn't do for her to catch him with another woman's phone number. That would get him kicked out of her bed for a while, which would be inconvenient. Worse, she might try to drag him into that tiny white clapboard church she attended. On Sunday, anybody who walked past it could hear the Baptist preacher shouting hell and damnation to any sinner within earshot. Tate always scurried past as quickly as possible. He wasn't about to enter those double doors with Hera Gonzalez.

No way. Not while he had a chance with Stormy Nixon. He gazed at her card with supreme delight.

For her, he'd be willing to move to California – and make a trip to the altar.

'Uh-oh. That piece of cow turd Wrong-Way's talking to Stormy,' Curvy said. 'You best get on the horn fast with Cody and let him know she's here.'

'No way. We got in big trouble for messing in his business last time. Ain't gonna have him chew my head off again.' Pick was adamant about this. 'We already agreed.'

'Yeah, but that was before she showed up here! We don't have to call and make up nothing! We just have to let Cody know she's here!'

'I'm sure she called him,' Pick stated laconically.

'I'm sure she didn't if Wrong-Way's over there poaching. Just look at him.' Curvy's eyes bugged with disgust. 'I think we should call Cody.'

'He does appear to be finagling,' Pick agreed as Tate took something from Stormy. 'Maybe you better call up to the ranch.'

'Uh, maybe *you* better,' Curvy negotiated. 'I'm still deaf from him yelling at us last time.'

'Flip for it.'

'Oh, heavens to Betsy.' Curvy went and borrowed a quarter from Hera Gonzalez, returning a minute later. 'Call it.'

'Heads.' Pick sat up stiff as a bone, watching as the quarter landed in the dirt. 'It's heads! You gotta call!' he cried triumphantly. 'And you best hurry too, because she's going inside. Who knows how he'll find her if he don't come on?'

'All right.' Curvy picked up the quarter and ungraciously stumped off toward the pay-phone. *Trust Pick to get me into this*, he thought grumpily. 'Cody,' he said when the answering machine switched on, 'it's Curvy. And Pick,' he added as a safety precaution. 'We just saw Stormy on the movie set and wondered if she'd had a chance to call you yet and let you know she's around. That's all now. Bye.' He hung up and headed back over to the wooden keg. 'He wasn't home.'

'Just your luck,' Pick grumbled. 'What a waste of a quarter, which you gotta pay back.'

'Hey!' Curvy stiffened at this unexpected attack. 'It's not my fault if he's not at home!'

'I didn't say it was.' Pick glared at him and mopped his brow. 'I just mentioned that your luck always seems to be bad.'

'It isn't!' Curvy was affronted by his friend's sudden change in mood. 'Let's not forget who got elected mayor around here, and who didn't!'

Pick jumped to his feet. 'That's a down and dirty thing to say! A fair-minded opponent wouldn't gloat in his victory over his best friend!'

'Hmmph.' Curvy moved his wooden stool a few inches away from Pick's.

Pick responded by moving a few feet in the opposite direction.

Curvy swiftly pulled his stool a few yards away.

Pick hauled his wooden keg to the complete opposite side of the set, sat down on it, and turned his back to his friend.

Curvy's jaw dropped. How dared he! 'Hmmph!' he said to himself, but the sound didn't bear much strength. He'd been friends for so long with Pick, gotten so used to his tooth-picking, that he wouldn't be able to look at a toothpick without feeling out of place. Sadly, he turned his gaze toward Mary, who was saying her lines with a tall, dark stand-in Curvy had never seen. Suspiciously, he wondered if the stand-in looked none too clean, and perhaps even a bit shifty. After they finished practising, the gophery-looking fella walked Mary over to get a drink, gently touching her back as he handed her a cup. Curvy watched in alarm. He wasn't at all sure if Cody shouldn't be told that his niece was being eyeballed by such a disreputable-looking character.

Unfortunately, the one man he could worry and fret over the situation with had just turned his back on him.

About seven o'clock in the evening, Cody made it into town. He was dirty and hot, but Curvy's message had perked his spirits up in a way they hadn't been in days. Weeks. He'd decided to head on down to this section of his land and see if he could locate Stormy. Maybe he could talk her into going out to dinner with him. On her previous visit, he hadn't had the chance to take her out the way a lady should be treated. He'd like to do that once before she returned to California.

There was a lot more that he'd like to do with her, of course, but one didn't stoop to such things when the lady in question wasn't a girlfriend in any sense of the word. With this many months separating them, he couldn't ask her to hop in the sack with him, no matter how tempting holding her again would be. But he could take her out to dinner and spend the evening listening to her cheerful laughter.

Actually, he looked forward to that. He'd shower and shave and put on his best dress blue jeans and boots.

Out of the corner of his eye, a black limo slid past. Cody barely paid it any attention. He was only interested in finding Stormy.

'Uh-oh,' he muttered. The codgers were seated at opposite ends of the movie set. Both appeared wilted by the day's heat – and maybe flared tempers. 'What's going on, boys?'

'Nothing!' Curvy stated loudly, staring at Pick's back.

Pick shrugged, refusing to take the bait. Cody sighed. 'I got your message, Curvy. Do you happen to know where Stormy is? I'd like to say howdy to her.'

'Ah –' Curvy stared up at him in dismay. He glanced at his friend's back as if for assistance. 'She just left in that limo, Cody. She's heading back to California.'

Cody's stomach felt as if it dove into his boots. 'Did she say that?'

'Yep.' Curvy nodded. 'She sure did. She also said to tell ya hi.'

'I see.' Disappointment whistled through him, sharp and well-defined. 'Well, guess I'll head back up to the house. Thanks for calling, Curvy.'

'You're welcome.'

He glanced over at the other codger. 'Thanks, Pick.'

'Sorry you didn't catch her, Cody,' Pick called. He kept his back turned decisively toward Curvy.

Cody sighed and walked toward his truck. He supposed he should ask what had derailed the codgers for the moment, but his heart ached too much. He couldn't believe Stormy Nixon had set foot on his ranch without trying to hunt him up. Whether he wanted to admit it to himself or not, their relationship was obviously over.

Stormy gasped as Cody walked past the limousine.

'Is everything all right, ma'am?' the chauffeur asked.

'Fine.' She whipped around to peer out the back window after Cody. He looked strong and sturdy, and wonderfully sexy. There was dirt on the back of his jeans and his boots were worn and dirty, but she didn't care. Cody Aguillar looked like a miracle to her. 'There's your daddy, baby,' she said, rubbing her stomach.

'Pardon me, ma'am?'

'I'm just talking to myself,' she called to the chauffeur, turning back to watch Cody. He moved with purpose and long-legged grace, and Stormy couldn't help thinking there was no more fabulous man on earth. Maybe she should have called him to let him know she was in Desperado. Since she wasn't showing yet, it would have been safe enough. But she would definitely have gotten misty. She seemed to cry at anything these days, which the doctor told her was hormones. Her mother recommended transcendental meditation. Actually, Stormy suspected her recent bouts of teariness had more to do with pining for a certain rancher. Watching him hungrily as the limo left him behind, Stormy suddenly wondered if he'd come looking for her. Mary surely had not called him to mention Stormy's presence. Pick and Curvy might have, though. Hopefully they wouldn't do something like that. After all, she and Cody hadn't exactly advertised their relationship.

No, she thought, turning back around in her seat, he hadn't been coming to see her. Mary was rehearsing and no doubt her proud uncle wanted to watch. It was ridiculous for Stormy to imagine – hope – that he'd hotfoot it down to the set to see her. Touching the snake teeth she'd had made into an exquisite silver collar necklace on her return to California, she closed her eyes and let the tears slide down her cheeks.

'Yes, Cody. I talked to Stormy,' Annie replied to his carefully casually worded question.

She turned to him as he sat with a soda in front of him that he couldn't drink if he had to. Though her kitchen was nearly a second home to him, Cody felt awkward.

'She called to see how I was progressing with my

pregnancy, and we chatted about morning sickness and things like that. Why?'

'Just curious.' He glanced at her stomach. 'You are feeling okay, aren't you?'

'Yes.' Annie laughed. 'Everything seems to have calmed down this fall. Mary's a changed child, and the nausea passed. I feel positively blossoming.'

She looked it, too. Cody was happy for all of them. 'Glad to hear it,' he said, jamming his hat onto his head. 'Guess I'll head back to the house.' He walked outside the house disconsolately.

'Uncle Cody!' Mary called, running to meet him at his truck.

'Hey, ladybug. How's my film star?'

'Oh, Uncle Cody.' She gave him a peck on the cheek. 'I'm not a star. But I'm having lots of fun.'

'And you're getting your homework done, too?' He gave her a stern look.

'Yes,' she said, laughing as if she didn't have a care in the world. 'I think I'm going to have all A's this first session.'

'I hope so.' A stray thought struck him and he paused before getting into his truck. 'Did you get to see Stormy?'

'Oh, yes!' Her eyes gleamed with happiness. 'She said I looked so pretty, and then she came out and talked to me again and gave me a hug before she left. I just love her, Uncle Cody.'

His niece's eyes shone with a light-hearted delight he'd never seen before. Cody nodded to himself. If Stormy had made this many good changes in Desperado, then so be it. He couldn't be angry with a woman who'd meant so much to so many people.

'Didn't you see her, Uncle Cody?' Mary's eyes gazed at him curiously, almost worriedly.

'Nope. Missed her. I was out in the fields all day.' Briskly, he got into the truck. 'Probably catch her next time. Love ya, ladybug.' He started the engine and drove away, his heart crushed by the knowledge that apparently Stormy had made time for everyone in Desperado that she had ever talked to.

Except him.

Mary watched her uncle leave in dismay. He looked old suddenly, and somehow worn. Well, maybe not old exactly, but certainly tuckered out. The strangest expression had come over his face when she'd told him that Stormy had hugged her goodbye. Mary swallowed, remembering that, once upon a time, she had thought Stormy only liked her because of Uncle Cody. She'd even thought that she couldn't trust Stormy if she was going to be best friends with her uncle. Mary had been so frightened of being left out, like she was sometimes at school.

Well, not so much any more. Now that she was in a movie, she had more friends than ever. She got invited to all kinds of parties where even the parents asked her lots of questions that made her feel important. Like, how did you get the part, and do you know anyone I could call to see if there might be a part for my kid? Yes, she had lots of friends now.

Sadly, she looked at her feet. Of course, Stormy had done her best to help Mary out. All her new-found friends she owed to Stormy.

But poor Uncle hadn't gotten to see Stormy. And he hadn't looked very happy about it. Sadness filled Mary's heart. Stormy could have called Uncle if she'd wanted to. And Stormy could have made an appointment to see him, if she'd wanted to.

Suddenly, Mary knew why Uncle looked so lost. He had wanted to see Stormy. But Stormy, for some reason, hadn't made time for him. She'd made time for Mary, though.

Once that would have made Mary feel like a princess. Now she just felt sorry for Uncle. All her life her uncle had been there for her. She'd always been his ladybug. Even when she was mean and bad, her uncle loved her. Any time she needed him he rushed to her side for whatever he could do to help.

She felt small and selfish for being jealous of him before. She was going to have a new baby in the house to love and care for, but Uncle was all alone in his big, empty ranch house. Mary sank on to the top step of the porch and put her face in her hands. *Poor Uncle Cody*. He liked Stormy too. He needed her friendship.

But there was nothing Mary could do to help

him. Though he had ridden in like a handsome knight to rescue her many times, she couldn't do that for him. She couldn't make Stormy like him if she didn't.

Sloan allowed three days to pass after he'd heard Stormy'd been in town. When he still hadn't heard word one from the stoic rancher, he decided it was time to put in a surprise appearance. A do-drop-in of sorts, to surreptitiously check up on the ol'desperado.

He was in a shed skinning rattlesnakes. Sloan sighed and took a seat on a busted chair. 'You've been out of sight lately.'

'Yeah.' Cody didn't look up, but he nodded. Sloan scratched at his chin and looked his buddy over. Maybe eight or ten pounds of weight loss, which could be blamed on Carmen being gone, but he thought there was more to it than that. Cody was a damn fine cook. He could rustle up his own grub.

Weight loss and a taciturn expression could point to a rancher suffering the pangs of love.

He leaned back and examined his hat. 'Heard from Stormy?'

'No. Hadn't figured I would.'

'Heard she was in town,' Sloan probed.

Cody shrugged. 'Free country.'

'It is that.' He thought for a few moments. 'Ever considered calling her?'

'Not really. Don't have her number.'

'Well, hell, Cody! Call information, for the love of Sam!' Surely the big man didn't expect him to fall for such a weenie excuse. If that was the only reason he hadn't gotten in contact with Stormy, then he didn't really want to.

'I did. She's unlisted.'

'Oh.' Sloan thought that over for a second. 'Did you try calling that studio?'

'Yeah. They put me on hold for about twenty minutes, so I called back. Then they put me on hold for another twenty minutes, and I gave up. Either they don't know who she is, or she doesn't work there, or they have the most screwed-up phone system in California. Must be all those earthquakes scrambling people's brains.'

Sloan pushed out his lips thoughtfully. 'Do Mary or Annie have her phone number?'

'Don't think so. She said she'd write them, but never has, best as I can tell.'

'Well, you just might have to waltz down to the film shoot and ask some nosy questions. If you have to, ask Pick and Curvy to ferret it out for you.'

Cody looked up. 'Are the codgers speaking to each other yet?'

'No. As far as they're concerned, they're not even in the same county together.'

Cody sighed. 'I may have to do something about that.'

'You got troubles enough of your own. Besides, how do you get two old men to talk to each other when they plainly don't want to?'

'There are ways.' He finished up and washed his hands. 'Do you know that crazy woman stole a set of snake teeth off my dresser?'

'Er –' Sloan hesitated. 'Dresser, as in your bedroom?'

A flush spread up his buddy's neck. 'Only one I've got.'

Well, *now* they were getting somewhere. Being a sheriff had taught him to listen to everything a person said to catch the nuances, and he'd just caught him a helluva nuance. 'You never said you'd –'

'I don't have to.' Cody glared at him. 'That's between me and the lady. All you're supposed to focus on is that she stole my teeth.'

'Jeez. Some women want wedding rings. Trust Stormy to be unique.' He crossed his arms on a sigh. 'Well, you're going to have to hire Curvy and Pick to do your dirty work, then. She feels something for you if she took your teeth, and you're going to have to hunt her up this time. You're going to have to get off this damn ranch and get your hide to California if you want her, earthquakes and airplanes and all. I know it scares you outta your gourd, but you're going to have to do it.'

'I'm not scared,' Cody growled at him. 'I'm not chasing after a female who's not interested in me, and who's not cut out to be a part of my life anyway. Think about it. Can you really imagine that upside-down woman being happy on a ranch?'

'Nope.' Sloan shook his head.

'Well, then.'

'She'd be happy on your ranch, though, and that's what you gotta get through your thick skull.' Sloan ambled out of the shed. 'When you quit being a chicken-skinned coward, you might get up the gumption to ask around down at the set. Somebody knows some way you can get ahold of her.'

'Thanks, pal. Don't forget to leave your business card for the next time I need advice from Dr Lovelorn,' Cody grumbled.

Sloan shrugged it off and headed to his truck. It was up to Cody to figure out whether Stormy was just a minor storm in his blood he could wait out until it passed – or a raging, twisting tornado with an aftermath he might not ever get over.

Jonathan sighed as he sent another glance toward Stormy's stomach. 'What are you going to do about it?'

'I'm not doing anything yet.' She walked to a window and stared out at the freeway below. 'The baby seems kind of happy to be doing its own thing.'

'You didn't want to tell the cowboy?'

She shook her head. 'It didn't feel like the right thing to do. He wasn't that wild about me.'

'Hm. Wild enough to get you pregnant.'

'As I said, he tried to be very conscientious about that. He's very concerned about becoming a father.' Stormy laughed softly. 'He's got a little niece that keeps him turned inside out, and quite frankly, he sees himself as too lucky to be staying a bachelor.'

'Oh, gawd. One of those self-proclaimed forever single men.' Jonathan yawned. 'Well, no doubt a baby would throw a kink into his life.' He considered her long and thoughtfully. 'Stormy, we should just get married.'

She frowned at him. 'I don't think I heard you right.'

'Yeah, you did. It would solve this problem for you. And it wouldn't change my life in any way. But you'd have a name for your baby.'

Stormy stared at the man who had known her father for years, the man who kept her employed when no one else wanted to give her a job. Jonathan was a handsome, older man, near the same age as her father. He'd been involved in a long-running affair with a woman who was never going to divorce her husband. The situation suited everyone involved. She knew what direction his thoughts were taking. They would get married, he would continue to see his lady-love, and she would have the security of a large, well-tended house and the finances to care for her child. In time, her heart would heal, and she would be free to pursue other relationships if she chose.

Stormy sighed. 'It's a sweet offer, Jonathan. I appreciate it. I'll have to think about it.'

'We could do it quickly. A few papers would need to be drawn up, but otherwise, it's basically a trip to Las Vegas.' He smiled at her benevolently.

She lowered her eyes and went to sit down. All the energy was slowly draining out of her. 'You're a good man, Jonathan.' *Of course, I wouldn't want my baby growing up the way I did, with its best clothes coming from thrift shops and being afraid to buy an occasional new toy in case I lost my job.*

But she wasn't in love with Jonathan. And in all the years she'd spent sleeping on shag carpets and bean bags and playing with other misfit love children, she'd wanted an Ozzie and Harriet existence for herself. Shoot, she'd settle for Lucy and Ricky Ricardo, if it meant that she and the man she loved stayed under one roof and raised a family – together.

'I don't know, Jonathan,' she murmured. 'I'm still trying to get over the shock of being pregnant.'

'Well.' He shot her a paternal glance. 'Take your time. The offer's open. In the meantime, you and I need to fly to Texas to do some sorting out. Apparently, the locals are giving the director a bit of a fit.' He grinned at her. 'I'm not sure it's their fault, either. This director is very difficult to deal with, as you know, and I believe he's putting some noses out of joint. We'll fly in there and take care of some things,' he said hurriedly, when she started to interrupt, 'and leave the next morning.'

She got to her feet. 'I'm too old for you to try to work this out for me, Jonathan.'

'I'm not! Honest!' He put a hand over his chest.

Stormy shook her head. 'You can do this by yourself.'

'No. You're the one who charmed the locals. They respond to you. I've heard this from more than one person. We go together.'

She pursed her lips, giving him a narrow-eyed stare. 'I think you're making this up out of some good-hearted intention.'

'Trust me, I'm far too busy. We need to do lunch with this director and try to gently break it to him that he's got to take it easy with this batch of folks. In New York, we wouldn't have this problem.' He sniffed disdainfully. 'These country people apparently don't like to be yelled at, and Cronich sounds like a bullhorn when he's getting on someone's case.'

'Oh, no,' Stormy murmured, wondering if Mary had been on the receiving end of any directorial angst. 'Okay. But a quick trip, and that's all. And I do lunch with a director and some soft shoe about the problems and then you bring me home. Understood?'

'Completely.' Jonathan nodded, his silver hair gleaming in the light. 'And your secret is safe with me.'

CHAPTER 15

Rain finally came to Desperado, despite the weatherman's prediction that the heat would continue without a break. The storm was vicious, throwing sheets of water against Cody's face and blowing his clothes tight against his body as he got out of his truck near the movie set. With jagged lightning in the sky, he didn't like the look of this particular storm. Though he was sure his niece wouldn't appreciate his concern, he'd decided to pick her up and take her to his house until it passed.

The movie folks themselves were on their own, however. They had trailers and other shelter. He grunted, pushing against the rain until he found a door to the set and went in. Mary sat, apparently unworried, talking to a few of the more minor stars.

'Hey, Uncle Cody,' she called.

He nodded at the folks sitting around her. 'Hey, ladybug. Want to come up to the house for a snack?'

A slight frown creased her face as she came over to hug him. 'Uncle Cody,' she whispered, 'did you come to see me, or Stormy?'

He leaned back and peered down at her. 'What do you mean?' he asked in the same whisper.

'She's here.' Mary glanced around them. 'I don't see her now, but she was here this morning. She spent the night in Austin last night'

'Hm.' Cody couldn't begin to put a name to the emotions that raced through his brain at the thought of Stormy being back. 'Well, I came to take you home with me, but I also have a bone to pick with her.' He thought for a moment. 'I don't like the feel of this storm. I'm going to take you up to the house, and I'll pick that bone with Stormy later.' It still rankled that she hadn't spent the proverbial dime to call him on her previous trip through.

'Why do I have to go home?'

'Just for now, while filming's basically stopped. I'll bring you back later, I promise, as soon as it passes.'

'What about Stormy? If it's not safe for me, it's not safe for her,' she said with an authoritative tone.

He scratched under his collar. 'I can't take everybody home with me, ladybug. You're my only concern.'

She eyed with him with an I-don't-believe-you look. 'I don't think so, Uncle Cody,' she said in a sing-song voice.

Sighing heavily, he said, 'I haven't seen Stormy in months, hon. What would I say? Come home with me, because you'll be safer at my house?'

Mary brightened. 'Hey, that would probably win her over.'

'I don't want to win her over to anything,' he said gruffly. 'Now look here, don't go meddling. This is adult –'

'Stormy!' Mary cried with delight. 'Come over here!'

Cody's gut clenched so hard he couldn't breathe. Sure enough, there was the woman who never got out of his dreams long enough to let him sleep the unbroken sleep of the peaceful man. Stormy walked toward him, her lustrous hair all cut off into a snappy pixie style, her wide lips hesitantly smiling under beautiful expressive eyes – and her belly sticking out four inches in front of her. Cody gulped, his eyes riveted to the mound moving toward him, emphasized by a short white dress with cap sleeves. 'Oh, lord,' he said under his breath.

'Hello, Cody,' she said, her voice soft.

His eyes snapped back up to hers. 'Hi,' he managed on a rasp.

'Come on, Stormy.' Mary took her by the hand. 'Uncle Cody's going to take us up to his house. He says he doesn't like this storm, and his house is the only place he feels we'll be safe enough.'

She grabbed Stormy's hand and herded her toward the door. Caught off guard, Cody barely jerked the door open in time for them to precede him. Without umbrellas, they ran to his truck and piled in.

'I've never seen rain like this!' Stormy said from the seat next to Cody.

The three of them had room to sit across the front seat of the truck, but Cody and Stormy were pressed elbow-to-elbow. He could smell her perfume, could see the almost shy look in her lovely gray eyes. Swallowing hard, his heart going a mile a minute, he switched on the engine and got the windshield wipers going. Water slashed to the left and then to the right with each motion of the wipers, but all Cody could think of was that Stormy had never looked better. Water beaded on the tip of her little ski nose, and he reached up to gently wipe it off.

She smiled self-consciously. 'I bet I don't even have any mascara left. It's probably running down my face.'

He hadn't gotten past her haunting eyes to notice. Damn, but he'd missed this woman! Dry-throated, he said, 'You look fine,' and fixed his gaze to the windshield. Fiercely concentrating on the road that was quickly turning to mud, he headed the truck toward the house.

Mary, scallywag that she was for getting him into this mess – and he knew she'd done it on purpose – hadn't said a word. Very uncharacteristic. His knuckles clenched around the steering wheel as he guided the truck over ruts and bumps in deference to the baby obviously growing inside Stormy, Cody wondered how to handle this very embarrassing matchmaking of his niece's. Stormy might have been a virgin when he'd met her, but obviously she hadn't waited long in finding another lover once she returned to her natural habitat. A large, sparkling engagement ring on her left hand burned a hole in his peripheral vision. He gulped, telling himself that Mary no doubt meant well, but she'd gotten him stuck in a vise-grip of a problem.

What was he doing with this pregnant woman in his truck? He hadn't wanted to fall in love. His life was simple, and it needed to stay that way. Anger flared inside him, along with overwhelming fear and gnawing rejection.

In the beginning, Stormy had wanted his land for her movie project. Against his better judgement telling him not to, he'd agreed. Maybe even then he'd been falling for her. Certainly, he'd been under her spell. But if her stomach and that ring were any consideration, all she'd wanted was his land for her movie anyway.

He was the fool for stepping into the trap of wishing there could be more.

At the house, he parked the truck and eyed the heavy rain. 'I could get an umbrella, but I don't think it'd make much difference.'

'I think we'd be better off running for it.' Stormy met his gaze, and they both looked away at the same split-second.

'You're going to ruin your shoes,' he said gruffly. On her feet were delicate white high-heeled sandals, which would never survive the mud. No doubt she'd twist her ankle trying to run and he didn't want that to happen.

With that teasing smile of hers, she slipped off her sandals. 'I'll just leave them in your truck for safekeeping.'

A muscle worked spasmodically near his Adam's apple as he looked at her bare feet and smooth white legs. His gaze slid up to the skirt hem, which ended at mid-thigh.

'You'd better carry her, Uncle Cody.' Mary leaned up to look past Stormy at him. 'If she slips in the mud, she might hurt her baby.'

He quickly checked Stormy's reaction to Mary's suggestion, glancing just as fast at her stomach. *There can't be a baby in there!* his mind shouted. Only six months ago he'd been loving her body. How could she have turned to someone else so fast?

He felt like a fool.

'He doesn't have to carry me,' Stormy said swiftly. 'I'm perfectly capable of walking.'

'No. Mary's right.' He steeled himself for the feel of her as he opened the truck door and scooped her into his arms. 'Mary, wait here. I'll be right back for you.'

He lifted Stormy out and kicked the door shut behind him with his boot heel. She put her head against his chest so that she nestled under his chin. Torrents of rain slashed against them, but Cody

235

didn't care. The feel of Stormy tucked protectively into his arms was heaven. He walked up the porch steps and gently deposited her in front of the door. Unlocking it, he said, 'I expect you remember where the bathroom is. Grab a towel to dry off with.'

And then, because he couldn't bear the look in her eyes, the look that said *thank you*, and, worse, acknowledged the attraction still burning as hot as ever between them, Cody turned to get his niece out of the truck.

Mary bounded up on to the porch.

'I thought I told you to wait.' He eyed her bare feet, and the flat tennis shoes dangling from her hand.

'I know. But there's no point in you having to come out after me. I can take care of myself.' She gave him a mischievous grin.

'You might have slipped and hurt yourself,' he said gruffly.

'Yeah, but I'm not pregnant. I'd only have hurt my bottom.' She ran past him into the house.

'Damn well better never be pregnant until you're married,' he grumbled under his breath. He hoped Stormy realized she needed to set a good example for his niece. None of this glamour puss, Hollywood fast life for Mary. Stormy might be unmarried and expecting a baby, but in his home he frowned upon it. He hoped Stormy realized that on this subject, Hollywood and Desperado, Texas might as well be different continents. This getting pregnant and maybe-we-will, maybe-we-won't-make-it-to-the-altar stuff was unacceptable.

She walked out of the bathroom toward him, carrying a towel. He clean missed her intention to dry him off because he was staring at how the white dress molded to her stomach. Gosh, she looked big right there. And her breasts were fuller, too. Lots fuller. He felt desire beginning to build inside him. Pregnancy definitely agreed with her.

Soft hands pressed a towel against his head, rubbing lightly. Helplessly, he stared down the smooth expanse of her arm, through the armhole of her dress where he could see a white lacy bra. He'd never known this woman to wear a white bra before. But the white looked clean and enticing, just like the jiggle of her breasts as she moved around him.

Electrified, he allowed her to rub the water off his neck. The cotton was soft, yet somehow scratchy, and her fingers were firm as she plied the towel.

Cody closed his eyes as she patted his hair down, her fingernails crisply pecking at his skin. What in the heck was he going to do with this woman? He had never gotten over her.

'Where's your mother?' Stormy asked. 'I thought she'd meet us at the door.'

'Ma moved out.' The spell broken for him, Cody moved away. Without meeting Stormy's eyes, he sat down and reached to pull a boot off.

'Moved out? Can I ask why?'

'You can. I doubt I have a good answer.' He doubted he had a good answer to anything. Stormy was wearing the snake teeth she'd stolen from him, in a gaudy, earth-mother kind of necklace that suited her. Why? It didn't imply any kind of commitment, or longing for him, not if she was wearing an engagement ring. 'She felt like she was keeping me from settling down.' He glanced up at her. 'Why don't you have Mary grab you something of Ma's to wear so you can dry out?'

'Okay.'

She moved past him, her white legs slick with dampness. Cody pulled his gaze away and tossed his boots on to the fireplace ledge to dry. Thunder boomed, rattling the windows of the house, and lightning cracked so near that the hair on the back of his neck stood up. He couldn't see his truck from the window for the water blowing sideways against the house. There was a big storm churning his stomach, too.

Going into the kitchen, he filled a pot with water. 'Want some tea?' he yelled.

'Yes, please.' Stormy joined him in the kitchen, looking much more relaxed and less sinful in a flowered housecoat of his mother's. Cody felt himself relaxing just a bit. Her stomach was less visible under a flowing robe. Now maybe he could get through this storm without staring at her body every second.

'Cody,' she said softly, putting her hand on his

forearm. He stiffened, instantly attentive to the texture and feel of her skin. 'I think you and I should talk.'

Why did women always want to talk when there was nothing to say? He sure as hell didn't want to hear anything that might make him feel worse than he did. They were stuck here in this house for the afternoon, and he had a feeling the less he heard, the happier he'd be. Lord, he did not want to hear about how it had been love at first sight between her and her intended.

'I've never had a whole lot to say.' He moved away from her hand and leaned against the wall while he waited for the water to heat. She fixed him with a wary look.

'That might be true in most cases, but where I was concerned, you always seemed to have plenty to say.'

'Maybe. But you want to talk, and you want me to listen. And I guess what I'm trying to get across is that I'm not in a listening mood.' He crossed his wet-sleeved arms and set a stubborn expression on his face.

She looked down at her bare feet for an instant before meeting his gaze again. 'Just listen for a minute, okay?'

'All right.' He didn't want to, and he had a feeling it would be more than a minute. But maybe she had something good to tell him, something he wanted to hear.

Like, *I couldn't get you out of my mind.*

'I'm getting married,' she told him softly.

Okay. Good. All she wants is congratulations and chat time can be over. 'So I noticed. I know you're happy.'

She glanced away for a second. 'I think it will all work out for the best.'

'Good. Mary! You want some tea?'

'No, thanks, Uncle Cody. I'm going to take a nap,' she hollered back up the hall.

'Teenagers. They can sleep through anything.' He got up and paced the kitchen, glancing out the front windows. 'I heard on the radio a couple of tornadoes had been sighted east of here. Hope they stay east of here.'

'Do you have tornadoes often?' Stormy came to stand at his side.

'Not much. We've been way too dry this summer and I guess all hell's going to break loose today. Unfortunately, we'll get the water so fast it'll all run off. I'd have preferred a gentle, soaking rain.' He glanced down at her, trying to think of anything to discuss that would keep them off the painful subject of her marriage. 'How'd you get the name Stormy?'

'My parents named me Virginia Caroline, to counter the counter-culture movement they were involved in.' Stormy's lips turned up in a rueful smile. 'They were going to give me the commune name of Star, but the night I was born was the stormiest, coldest night of the year, and it wasn't a far leap for them to call me Stormy.'

240

'Virginia?' Cody couldn't reconcile the prim name to the woman who had a temper on her that could match his.

'You can stick with my nickname,' she said, smiling up at him. 'I'm not the Virginia type.'

His gaze swooped to her mid-section. Her stomach pushed slightly against the belted area of the robe. Swallowing tightly, he shook his head and looked away. 'Don't know what type you are, Stormy.' *Not my type, which I knew in the beginning*.

'Well, better Stormy than Star, too,' she said with airy cheerfulness. 'Wouldn't want folks to think I was the type who always dreamed of being a star.'

'What do you dream of?' He slowly turned his head to look into her eyes.

'Oh . . . the same thing every other woman dreams of. A house. A good husband. Security. Babies to spoil.'

He grunted. 'Looks like you're batting a thousand. Everything you ever wished for seems to be coming true. I'm happy for you.'

'Are you?' She cocked her head and held his gaze.

'Yeah.' He sighed heavily. 'I won't say that seeing you again doesn't stir up feelings. I remember how good making love to you felt. But we knew what we were doing. We knew there wasn't a future for us.' Unable to meet her eyes, he stared at the rain-stricken landscape outside. 'I guess everything works out as it's meant to.' Part of him felt sorry for himself, lonely. He was alone. She was going to have a family.

Damn it. 'Stormy, I don't want you to think that what we did together didn't mean anything to me. It did. You're special to me in a way I haven't let anybody else be.' The memory of it made him suck in a tight breath that never got past his ribcage. How much longer could he keep up this pretense of not wanting her? 'You deserve someone who can give you all the things you want. Me, I don't want kids. I've raised Mary as best as I can, and sometimes, I think I'm winning that battle, but most of the time, I'm sure I'm losing it. I'm real sorry to see you go, and to know that we –'

'Shut up, Cody,' Stormy said suddenly, pulling his lips down to hers. 'Just shut up and kiss me.'

If she had to listen to him saying how happy he was for her any longer, she'd probably beat him over the head with a pan. She didn't want him to be happy for her. She wanted him to want her and love her and need her, and if he was going to stand there and congratulate her, then he was wasting breath when he could be kissing her.

His lips came down readily against hers, touching and tasting and probing. Winding her arms around his neck, she leaned into him, cherishing the feel of his hard, soaked body against hers. 'You should change your clothes,' she murmured, knowing even as she said it that she wanted to take them off for him.

A groan escaped him, and he reached inside the robe to hold her at the waist. His fingers slipped over her stomach, feeling his way along. Fearful that he would be repulsed and stop kissing her, Stormy twined her fingers at the nape of his neck and prepared to refuse to let go if he tried to escape. 'I've missed you,' she murmured against his mouth.

'Coulda fooled me. I heard you made a separate trip to town and didn't so much as pick up the phone to call.' He pulled back for a second to stare into her eyes, but made no move to draw away.

'I was afraid to.'

'Why?' Dark eyes searched hers.

She thought about where his hands were placed on her waistline and encouraged herself to tell him. *Just tell him.* He would probably offer to marry her. Responsibility was his strong suit. It had been that way for his mother. For Annie. For Mary. It could be that way for her. It *would* be that way for her.

That was not the way she wanted Cody Aguillar.

'I . . . don't know why I was afraid. It was hard to convince myself that you wanted to hear from me.' Her eyes lowered for just a second. 'I worried that you might say you were glad I called, but that you were too busy, or something.'

'No.' He shook his head ever so slightly, but didn't release her gaze. 'I would never be too busy for you,' he said huskily. Then his mouth slashed down against hers, again and again, and it was all

Stormy could do to hang on and not beg him to take her to his bed.

'Cody?'

'Hmm?' He broke away and looked down at her. 'What's wrong? Have I hurt you?'

She shook her head. 'What's that smell?'

He looked around. 'Oh, shit!' He jumped over to the stove and switched the stove burner off.

Stormy stared into the pan. All the water had boiled out, leaving a filmy smoky residue. 'Oops.'

Running a hand through his hair, he sighed. 'Still want tea?'

'No, thanks.' She had lost her thirst for tea. The coziness of the kitchen haunted her. How she wished she could be here with Cody, just the two of them, making a home –

The kitchen phone rang suddenly. Cody snatched it from the wall. 'Hello?' After a second, he said, 'Yeah, she's here.'

He handed the phone to her. She took it in surprise. 'Hello?'

'Stormy, we've got a flight to catch, dear,' Jonathan said.

'How'd you know where I was?'

'Believe me, it wasn't that hard to figure out.' He chuckled. 'But since the storm's passed, I think I'll point the limo that way, if the timing's convenient.'

'The storm has passed?' She glanced out the window. While it was still raining, the worst seemed to have passed.

244

'We only had one trailer blow over. No one was hurt, which was lucky.'

'It was,' Stormy murmured, feeling Cody's eyes on her. He must be wondering what man was calling her at his house. 'Yes. Do come on up here and get me. I'll be ready.'

'Fine.'

He hung up and Stormy glanced at Cody. 'I've got a flight to catch.'

'And he's on the way to pick you up?' Cody watched her intently.

'Yes.' She slipped past him into the hall and hurried into the bedroom to pull her clothes on. Fortunately, the dress had mostly dried out. Quickly, she fluffed her hair.

'You'll need these,' Cody said, walking into the bedroom with the sandals that had been in his truck.

'Oh. Thank you.' She couldn't meet his eyes. They had needed to talk, but they hadn't gotten nearly enough talked about.

'Was that the man you're marrying?'

Stormy nodded, unable to meet his gaze. 'Yes. Jonathan.'

'He knew you were here?'

'I imagine someone on the set probably saw us leave and told him.' She went to move past him, but he caught her as she tried to squeeze past.

'He doesn't mind you being here?'

'No,' she said breathlessly. 'Jonathan and I have an understanding.'

Cody stared at her for a minute. 'That's big in California, isn't it? Understandings?'

She shook her head at him. 'I don't know what you mean.' She did know what he meant, and it stung. He was drawing a reference to an understanding that wasn't a committed marriage. A Hollywood relationship. Not the kind of monogamous relationship he would expect. Demand.

'It wouldn't have worked between us,' he murmured. 'We're too different.'

'You're probably right.' She couldn't help the tears that sprang into her eyes and tried to get past him again so that he wouldn't see them, but he wouldn't release her.

With one finger, he touched her necklace. 'You took something from me.'

Her lips parted. *If you only knew . . .*

'I've got the other end of that rattler if you're partial to snakes,' he said. 'The tail makes a pretty rattle.'

She shook her head. Outside, a horn honked. 'Maybe I'll get it another time,' she gasped, taking his hands from her arms and hurrying down the hall. She wanted to say goodbye to Mary but the teenager had said she was going to nap. If she took a second longer, she wasn't going to be able to keep her secret. The truth was pressing against her conscience, threatening to burst from her lips.

I took a lot more from you. With one last desperate glance over her shoulder, she said, 'Goodbye, Cody.' And then she hurried out the door.

Jonathan took a long look at Cody before tossing his hand in a casual wave. Patting Stormy's leg, he asked, 'Have a nice visit?'

'Oh, Jonathan,' Stormy snapped. 'Don't pick at me.'

'I don't mean to.' He glanced out the window as the limo slid past the grim rancher still standing, legs braced, on the porch. 'He looks a lot like that Indian in *The Last Of The Mohicans*. The one who ended up getting stabbed and falling over the cliff.'

'Jonathan, I'm not in the mood to discuss story-lines or actors, or anything to do with Hollywood right now.' She burst into tears.

'There, there,' Jonathan said, pulling her close to him. 'If it's any consolation, he didn't look very happy that you were leaving.'

'He didn't?'

'No.' Jonathan pulled out a handkerchief and offered it to her. 'Did you tell him?'

'No. It . . . I couldn't.'

'Well, that's good. I was afraid you were upset because you'd told him and then he refused to marry you. And then I'd have to beat him up for being so insensitive to my favorite girl.'

That made her smile just for a second. Poor Jonathan was at least twenty years older than Cody, and in nowhere the same shape. 'I love you, Jonathan.'

'I know. I love you, too.' He squeezed her close.

'I'll tell him after the wedding,' Stormy said suddenly. 'That way he'll know he has a child, and he won't feel obligated to marry me.'

'I'm going to be a dead man,' Jonathan groaned. 'Can you tell him after I've gone to Cannes next year?'

Stormy sniffled. 'He doesn't want children, Jonathan. He's not going to want the child. You're safe.'

'Hm.' Jonathan sighed and settled back in the seat. Stormy stared out the window, watching the road go past, taking her away from the only man she'd ever wanted.

Cody folded his arms, staring after the limo. That woman was a lunatic. She kissed him like there was no tomorrow and then went off like Cinderella in a coach. It was a backwards fairytale. He was the villain, the troll. A past-his-prime prince had just rescued her from him. Cody sighed, digging his fingers into the back of his neck. There was nothing he could do about it. She was engaged; she was having a baby. She was happy.

He was a bachelor; there was no one to bother him. He'd always been a loner, and he'd been a fool to try to fit a loony purple-haired woman into his life. It was that simple. Everything had worked out just the way it should have. They'd both gotten what they wanted. The End.

It was just a damn good thing he'd been extra-careful about birth control or he might have wound up playing the prince role in happily-ever-after land.

'Uncle Cody,' said Mary, as she came out on to the porch, 'where's Stormy?'

'Gone back where she belongs.' He swiped at her hair playfully to take the harsh edge off his words.

'Oh. What did you two of you decide?'

An uncomfortable grumble worked through his stomach. 'About what?'

'About me going to California to try out for some auditions? Stormy said she was going to talk to Mom and Zach and you about it.'

He ground his teeth so hard they hurt. 'She did not mention that,' he gritted out, feeling the blessedly cussed stubborn anger that he always felt about Stormy rising to the surface. It ran off all the other pitiful feelings he'd been suffering. 'Maybe she called your mother. But don't drag me into that one, because I vote no.'

Absolutely not. Uh-uh. No way did he think his ladybug was old enough to go out to California with a woman who was pregnant and not married. Cody stomped inside the house, glad for the new-found fury. Annie was a sensible woman. She would refuse this latest ludicrous idea of Stormy's.

But if he ever got his hands on Stormy's phone number, he was going to give that woman a piece of his mind.

CHAPTER 16

Life as Cody had known it was over. Everyone around him had gone insane. The storm had left the movie people in a bit of an uproar, but he didn't really care about that. Mary had finished most of her part, but she still hung around the set after school, star-gazing. She'd been real quiet with him, and he suspected he'd been too hard on her about going to California. The codgers still weren't speaking with each other. It was as if the storm had blown their wooden kegs further apart. And he hadn't seen Sloan in an age, which worried him. Late autumn in Desperado was turning into a strange season of confusion and restlessness. He could feel it in his steers. He could feel it in himself.

'Sloan!' he called as he walked inside the sheriff's office. The sheriff was nowhere to be seen, which was irritating because they'd specifically planned to meet this morning at this time to discuss hauling livestock over from a ranch that was selling off. Frowning, he threw himself into a chair to wait.

Suddenly, he recognized the smell of liquor. Something pungent, obviously a strong brew. Leaning up, Cody sniffed the air again. 'Whew!' he exhaled on a short breath. He got up to look at Sloan's desk, since that was the direction the smell was strongest. His eye was caught by the liquor bottle tucked in the bottom drawer, sticking out, uncapped.

'Uh-oh,' he said, striding from the room. Sloan wasn't in the men's room, nor was he loitering in the hall. Growing more worried by the second, Cody went through the hall to lock-up.

Sure enough, Sloan lay on a cell bed, snoring comfortably. Alcohol reeked to the rafters. In his hand, a picture frame was tucked up against his chest. 'Jeez,' Cody muttered, pulling the frame from Sloan's unresponsive hand. The wedding picture brought a grimace to his face. Woman trouble. He might have known.

'Get up, damn it,' he told Sloan, briskly slapping him on each cheek. 'You need a shower something bad.' Sloan didn't move, so Cody tucked the frame between his stomach and jeans, and leaned to haul Sloan off the bed. 'You're like a bag of lead, my friend.'

'Hey, *amigo*. Whash happenin'?' Sloan asked with a stupid, sleepy-eyed grin.

'Not much, except I may die from fumes. Don't talk until I get you into the shower.' He helped Sloan down the hall into a cement shower area and shoved him inside, turning cold water on him full-blast.

'Yi-yi-yi!' Sloan cried, trying to leap out.

Cody pushed him back under the water mercilessly.

'You crazy cigar-store Indian! Let me out 'fore I hurt you! I'll 'rrest you for this.' Drippy hair fell into his eyes, making his threats sound absurd.

Cody grunted at him. 'Sober up, my friend. Then I'll let you out.'

'I'm sober! I'm sober, you son of a bitch!'

'Wash your mouth out while you're in there. It has bad words in it.'

'Aguillar, if you don't turn off that water, I'm beating the skin off of you.'

He shook his head. At least now Sloan seemed fighting mad instead of falling down drunk. Switching off the water, he tossed a torn towel his way.

'You sorry-ass —'

Cody reached for the water. Sloan held up his hands in surrender.

'I suppose you want my thanks,' he grumbled.

'No. I want you to pull yourself together so we can discuss business.' Cody turned his back and walked from the room. 'Hope you have dry clothes.'

'In my truck.' Sloan came out, muttering under his breath.

'You know that if Widow Baker had seen you like that, you would have never lived it down.'

'I know,' Sloan said under his breath. 'I should thank you. But I was enjoying a private party when you crashed it.'

'Have anything to do with her?' Cody pulled the

252

frame from his jeans and handed it to Sloan.

'Nope. It doesn't,' Sloan snapped, tossing it into a drawer and locking it.

'Sure it does.' Cody took the chair he'd sat in before. 'Women are usually the reason a man tries to pickle his organs, though it's a bad reason to do it. A woman isn't worth that kind of damage to your body. But if it's not her, maybe you went on a bender because you're an alcoholic. I don't know.'

'I'm not.' Sloan shot him a nasty look. 'It's my anniversary, okay? I'd like to celebrate my anniversary in peace, if you don't mind.'

'That was celebrating? Remind me not to get married.' Cody stared at the ceiling, telling himself not to think about Stormy and her engagement ring and elderly husband-to-be.

'Nobody has to remind you because you're dead-set against it. Some of us made it down the aisle, okay, and lived to regret it. I'm over it.'

'Ah, yeah?' He moved his gaze to his fingers so he wouldn't look at Sloan. 'You never told me.'

'It's none of your business.'

'True.' Cody nodded. 'Care to celebrate the day you got married with some breakfast now? We've got work to discuss.'

'I would.' Sloan jammed his hat on his head. 'But for your information, I wasn't celebrating my wedding day. I was celebrating the day I got divorced, eight years ago today. Not that it's any of your business.' He stomped past Cody. 'I'm going to get my clothes out of my truck.'

'Fine. Fine and dandy.' Cody remained where he was. Dang, but if he was celebrating his divorce by drinking himself into a stupor, he must not have been the one who'd wanted out of the marriage. Cody bit at a hangnail, considering how a tough guy like Sloan could allow himself to get so riled over a female. Of course, the woman in the picture had been attractive, but that wasn't a good excuse.

He must have really loved her. Cody worked that over for a moment. Some raw part of his emotions warned him that he'd better examine his own glass house before he threw rocks, although his first reaction was that he would never let himself get to the point where Sloan had been. A woman wasn't worth it.

Stormy is, his mind insisted. Though his heart didn't want to listen, didn't want to fall into the prison of loving someone, he knew it was true.

'Damn it!' he heard Sloan shout. 'Cut that out!'

Cody shot to his feet, striding outside. A throng had gathered, cheering and clapping over something. He elbowed his way through the crowd and groaned. Wrong-Way and Hera were having an all-out, fighting-mad bout over something. Sloan stood in the middle of the two combatants, trying to keep them separated.

'You lying piece of horse dung!' Hera screamed, reaching around the sheriff for a good grip on Tate's shirt.

Beyond reason, she shoved Sloan out of the way with her free hand and grabbed Tate for a round of jerking and pulling. Tate's head snapped around as if it was on a rubber band, and buttons popped off his shirt like popcorn to lay in the dirt.

'You're under arrest,' Sloan said, trying to come to his feet. Still off-center from the effects of the alcohol, he couldn't stand as quickly as he wanted, and ended up taking the brunt of Tate's body as big Hera whirled the hapless cowboy in a circle.

Cody leapt forward and pulled the sheriff out of the dog-fight before he could get stomped on. 'You're gonna get yourself killed doing that,' he warned him. 'Maybe we ought to stay out of this one.'

'But she's manhandling him. As an officer of the law, I'm obliged to make certain that she doesn't beat him to death. There's assault and battery to consider here, Cody!'

He nodded, picking up Sloan's hat which had fallen into the dirt. 'Yeah. But don't let your bad feelings about women get you heated up too quickly.'

'I'm not! This has nothing to do with my . . . celebration.'

'Well, then, just stay out of it for a second. You know very well Tate's a sidewinder. Give Hera a chance to sort him out.' Cody leaned back against the courthouse wall and watched as the skinny cowboy took a roll in the dirt. On the sidelines, Curvy and Pick watched with great enthusiasm. Tate let out a yelp as Hera sat on him, bouncing up and down for good measure.

'Have any idea what this is all about?' Sloan glanced at Cody.

'She might have realized he has no intention of marrying her.' Personally, Cody felt sorry for Hera. Tate had been leading her up the garden path for a long time, with absolutely no inclination to make an honest woman of her. Men who didn't make an honest woman out of a woman they bedded, especially more than once, deserved –

Whoa, Cody told himself. *Hang on here. You knew you weren't going to marry Stormy. You had no business taking her to bed, and you sure didn't have a right to her virginity.*

'All right, Hera,' he called, moving forward swiftly. 'Let Wrong-Way up.'

'He's led me in the wrong direction for the last time!' She threw pieces of paper she'd torn in half into the dirt. 'Either he heads to the courthouse right now to get the marriage license, or I stomp him.' She bounced on him again for emphasis.

'You're crushing my spine, Hera!' Wrong-Way glanced toward Cody and Sloan for assistance. 'Get this woman off of me!'

Wrong-Way wasn't a friend of his. He wasn't doing him any favors. Cody shook his head, and reached down to swipe the two pieces of white paper from the ground. 'Stormy Nixon,' he read. Her company name and several phone numbers were on the card. Blind anger and sudden jealousy roared through him. 'How did you get your paws on this, Tate?'

256

'Stormy gave it to me.' The cowboy tried to wriggle out from underneath Hera without success.

Cody glared down at the slightly built, flailing man. 'Why would she give you this?'

'She said I could call her.'

'You call her and you ain't ever calling on me again,' Hera stated. She kept her ample bottom on Wrong-Way like a boulder-sized paperweight.

Cody himself wanted a turn at Tate. How in the hell had that weasel charmed Stormy's personal phone numbers out of her, when she hadn't so much as given him her work number, for crying out loud? He'd had to pry that out of the movie set people, and even then, he hadn't been able to get in contact with her. Frowning, he remembered that Stormy had tried, the very first time she'd come to his house, to give him a white card like this one. He'd shoved it back in the ridiculous carpetbag she carried, not wanting anything to do with her.

He damn sure didn't want Tate having anything to do with her.

'Careful,' Sloan murmured next to him. 'Remember. You're the one who said that a woman wasn't worth it. But I see blood in your eye, *amigo*.'

Very casually, very deliberately, Cody slid the halves of the business card into his jeans pocket. 'Wrong-Way, it looks like you have two choices. It's either the courthouse for a wedding license, or hell for eternal damnation. Look at it this way. With Hera, you spend one day a week in church wishing you didn't have to be there. In hell, you spend every day wishing you weren't there.'

The gathered crowd grew silent, waiting expectantly for the pinned cowboy's answer. Cody couldn't help feeling sorry for a man who was being forced to do something he didn't want to do. Lord only knew he hadn't enjoyed jumping out of Stormy's window. The guy deserved this humiliation, though, for cheating on Hera. Tate liked availing himself of a good woman's charms, then not following through on his promises.

I never made Stormy any promises, Cody comforted himself. Still, he enjoyed watching the cowboy suffer for even thinking he had a chance with Stormy. *Stormy's a free woman.* And he was a free man. They were both satisfied with their situation.

'I'll go!' Wrong-Way suddenly shouted. 'I'll get a marriage license!'

The crowd burst into applause. Mayor Curvy did a little jig with his thin, crooked body. 'Our two towns will be united at last!' he cried jubilantly.

Pick clapped his hands together gleefully, reaching out to Curvy to take his arm. Without hesitation Curvy set his arm around Pick's, and they continued the jig together.

Hera got up off her groom, lifting him to his feet and dusting him off quite proprietorially. Then she gave him a great, smacking kiss which took up half his cheek, much to the delight of the onlookers.

Sloan slapped Cody on the back as they walked

over to shake Tate's hand. 'You did two good deeds today. You rescued me and Tate. And Pick and Curvy forgot all their turmoil in the excitement.'

He refused to reply to that. There had been no rescuing of anyone, as far as Cody was concerned. Just some things that had needed to be straightened out. They shook hands with the cowboy and kissed his intended bride, then headed toward Cody's truck.

'My clothes have dried out,' Sloan said. 'Don't need to change after all.'

'Good. You've slowed me down enough for one day.' Cody started the truck and pulled away, his thoughts busy.

After a few minutes, Sloan said, 'Hey, Cody, what are you going to do with that business card Hera found on Tate?'

Cody shrugged as if he could hardly remember taking it. In truth, it was burning a hole in his jeans pocket. 'I have a bone to pick with her.'

'You're going to call her?'

He nodded curtly. Most definitely he was going to call her and explain to her that Mary wasn't setting foot in California for auditions of any kind. He'd warned Stormy before about putting weird ideas in the teenager's head. Annie and Zach would set Mary on the right track about this matter.

He would straighten Stormy out once and for all, just as he'd straightened out these other matters this morning.

259

His cellphone rang in the truck. Cody switched it on. 'Hello?'

'Cody? It's Annie.'

'What's happening?' He smiled at the sound of her voice.

'I have a favor to ask of you.'

'Another one?' A slight smile curved his lips.

'I know it's a lot to ask of you. We've been calling on you a lot lately. But this is a big one.'

'Shoot.' He glanced at Sloan, his eyebrows raised in benevolent patience.

'I wonder if, now that you've gotten past the auction, you have time to take Mary out to California.'

His jaw dropped.

'It's so much to ask, I know, but Cody, Mary has simply blossomed since this movie came to town. I know you've seen it. Maybe she's found her calling. I don't know. Certainly it isn't what I would have chosen for her. But you remember how painfully shy and unhappy she was. All that's gone now. She's happy, excited, enthusiastic. The way a teenager should be.' Annie's voice turned pleading. 'I hate to ask, I really do. I wouldn't, if it didn't mean so much. And I would do it myself, but I'm in no condition to take her right now. Oh, Cody, do you think there's any way you could?'

Cody finally gained his voice. 'Have you lost your mind? I can't think of anything worse than allowing Mary to run around with Stormy Nixon.'

'Why, Cody? She's been so good for her.'

'She's pregnant! And not married! What kind of example is that for a young, impressionable girl?' He stopped the truck before he had a wreck. His hands were shaking. How in the hell would he fly out to California? Airplanes. Earthquakes. Stormy. Hell, no. It would be flying into the face of everything he secretly feared. Of course, a man such as he didn't have fears. Wasn't supposed to.

I can't go to California.

'Is it yours?' Annie cut into his thoughts.

His insides felt queasy. 'Hell, no. She's engaged to some fellow she's dragging around like a toy dog.'

'Oh.' Annie hesitated for a moment. 'I'm sorry.'

'Don't be.' His tone was brisk, signaling that he wasn't.

'Okay,' she said reluctantly. 'Stormy's business is not mine, Cody. All I know is what she's done for my daughter. Maybe if you think about it for a while, you can see your way clear to go. If not, I'll understand.'

Her voice said she'd be very disappointed. Cody blew out a breath, a deep release of emotion that didn't come near to venting the agony in his soul. 'I'm sorry, Annie. I don't need time to think about it. I can't go to California. Nothing about the idea feels right to me. It's just another one of Stormy's impulsive gestures. I'm sorry, but I have to say no.'

'All right.' She, too, sighed. 'Maybe you're right.'

The line clicked off. He turned the phone off, feeling terrible. 'Damn,' he muttered.

261

'Family trouble?'

'Yeah.' He jerked his head in a curt nod. 'As usual, it can be laid at Stormy's door. She wants Mary to go to California. Annie wants me to take her.'

Sloan began whistling, which irritated the hell out of Cody. 'You're going to ride in the truck bed if you keep that up,' he muttered.

'Yep. California, here he comes,' he sang.

'I'm not going. I'm out of good deeds.' Cody eased the truck back out into the traffic. 'Rest assured, there is nothing that could make me go.'

Mary sat outside the movie set, waiting for her mother and Zach to pick her up. They'd only been gone an hour – long enough for her to finish filming the last bit of her part. She was sad about that. So much about the movie had brought new excitement into her life. Uncle Cody had been so wrong to worry about her being in the movie. She hadn't been afraid of anything.

Unfortunately, yesterday her mother had told her that Uncle Cody wouldn't take her to California to audition for upcoming parts that Stormy thought had promise for her, and which could be worked around her school schedule. Uncle didn't think she was old enough. Tears sprang into her eyes. No matter how much she'd grown up in the last few months, Uncle just couldn't see that she wasn't a baby any more.

The stand-in from somewhere in Texas – she

couldn't remember where – ambled over to take a seat next to her. 'How are you, Mary?'

She knew his name was Sam, and that was about all. It didn't matter, though. Sam listened to her. He didn't think she was a baby. Since the moment work had begun on the project, he'd been kind to her. Mary knew she could confide in him, and he would make her feel better.

Not like Uncle, whom she loved, but who just didn't understand her. 'I'm fine,' she sighed dramatically.

'You don't sound fine.' He gave her an attentive look, which made her feel important.

'It's just that I have this chance to go to California, but I can't.' She raised her eyebrows at him and shrugged as if it didn't matter, but he would know it did.

'Why can't you?'

'My uncle doesn't want me to. He doesn't think I'm ready yet.'

'Well, now.' Sam reached out and gently stroked her back. 'I think you're ready, Mary. I sure do.'

CHAPTER 17

Cody never dialed the number on Stormy's business card. It didn't seem right. She was marrying someone else. He couldn't see himself calling up a woman who had proclaimed her love to someone else.

When he caught himself picking up a whisky bottle for a generous pour, he remembered Sloan's tortured face and the picture he kept hidden in his desk. Cody put the whisky bottle back in the cabinet, untouched. In no way was he in as bad a shape as Sloan.

The phone rang, and he leaped to jerk it off the cradle, glad for something to do. 'Yeah?'

'Hera's over at my house breathing fire,' Sloan told him. 'Wants to know where her groom has disappeared to.'

Cody's eyebrows shot up. 'I'm not hiding him over here.'

'I don't think she's worried about that. She thinks he may have gone to California to visit Stormy.'

Nausea curled in Cody's gut. If Wrong-Way had done that, he'd kill him. He'd kill him for being that much of a sniveling coward to say he'd marry Hera and then run off to another woman. Of course, he'd get a few licks in on principle. How in the hell could Tate do something Cody wouldn't do? 'If you're wanting my humble opinion, I don't think he's there.'

He heard Hera's voice instructing Sloan in the background. 'She says she knows you've got Stormy's business card. Maybe you better give us the number where she can be reached, so we can ask her. That might simplify matters.' Sloan was silent for a moment, while Hera's voice raged in the background. ' 'Course, Hera says she ain't particular as to who calls her to find out if he's there. She says maybe you oughta call Stormy, Cody.'

Something tingled inside him, making his stomach tighten and pitch with excitement that didn't feel good. 'No can do, friend. I didn't even keep the card,' he lied, staring at it as it lay in two pieces on top of the trash where he'd tossed it. 'Truthfully, I think Hera better search elsewhere for Tate. Stormy's engaged to be married and would show that loser – I mean, her prospective bridegroom – to the door.'

'I thought you said you had a bone to pick with her,' Sloan said in a low voice.

'I did, but I decided it was in everybody's best interest not to.'

265

'Did you chicken out?'

'Hell, no,' Cody retorted. 'Just think I oughta stay out of the woman's life when she's hooking up with another man.'

'Well.' Sloan didn't reply for a moment. 'Once the "I do"s are said, you're a casualty. Just a reader of the Advice to the Lovelorn column.'

'Guess so.' Cody wasn't going to get drawn into that. 'Tell Hera if I see Wrong-Way, I'll rope him for her.'

Sloan conveyed the message, but the phone line couldn't disguise the crack of the front door as it slammed shut.

'She's pretty put out with Tate,' Sloan said.

'I don't know what she sees in that skinny, handle-bar-mustached *vaquero*.' If he was Hera, he'd be looking in more profitable fields. He didn't think Tate was ever going to do more than give lip-service to his intentions. If she found him to drag him to the altar, Cody thought it'd be a miracle.

'You don't think he went to California?'

'Naw. He's hiding out. Going to lie low until Hera gets over wanting to marry him.'

'He'd better never show his face around here again. Hera won't take well to being scorned. She'll flatten him.'

It didn't feel good to be scorned. Even though Stormy hadn't really scorned him, Cody could sympathize with Hera's feelings. What the hell did Stormy see in that old dude-in-a-suit who'd been with her? His insides ran tight and prickly as barbed wire. 'I don't care what happens to Tate. I've gotta go.'

'Be seeing ya,' Sloan said cheerfully. 'I'm gonna hang around here for a while. Ain't got anything pressing on *my* mind like you do, such as whether some sidewinder's gotten the guts up to visit the woman I love.'

' 'Course, since you're still celebrating your divorce, you don't really give a damn who's sleeping with the woman you love,' Cody snarled, goaded. He threw the phone down and exhaled a few choice curse words. He cared. He really did. He hurt so much he ached in places he hadn't hurt before. But a man could only go where he was wanted. If Tate had gone to California, he would only succeed in making a fool of himself. Cody wasn't about to do the same.

Throwing himself into a recliner on a wave of self-righteous pity, Cody tried to get his mind on his work. Absently, he wondered how his mother was doing. She certainly hadn't bothered to send a shout his way. He'd heard from her once, a casual, brief call that set a record for world's shortest conversation between two people who loved each other.

And Tate had gone missing. How could a man his age jump from irresponsible action to gutless action and wake up to look at himself in the mirror every morning?

Sighing, he got up and roamed through the house once aimlessly. It was too quiet, too

267

empty. Ma had been right. When had it gotten so damn depressing around here? When had his life gotten so out of whack?

Since Stormy hit my porch. He hated to admit that to himself. Sometime he'd become an empty, dried-out husk. 'No wonder Ma bailed out on me.' The realization pained him deeply. Fortunately, he still had Mary. Maybe he'd call over to Annie's and invite himself to dinner so he could see the only person left alive who cared about him at all.

Swiftly, he rang Annie's number. 'Hey, Annie,' he said, feeling immensely better now that he had a voice on the phone that was familiar and friendly. 'Got enough for an extra mouth tonight?'

'Sure, Cody. If you don't mind me trying one more time to convince you to take Mary to California.'

He'd forgotten about that. 'I'm sure I can fend you off if the cooking's good. What time is dinner?'

'In twenty,' she told him, 'so you'd best hurry if you want it hot.'

'I'll be there.' Hanging up, he stopped in front of the hall mirror to run a careless hand over his hair before slapping on his hat. He grabbed his truck keys and strode out the door, hurrying to his truck.

In the house, the phone rang and rang before the answering machine clicked on. There was shuffling in the background, then the caller's phone slammed down before anyone could speak.

Twenty minutes later, Cody arrived at Annie's house, hungry and ready to slide into the comfort zone of family. 'Where's Mary?' he asked, after shaking Zach's hand and kissing Annie on the cheek.

Annie turned to him. 'Is she not with you?' She glanced past him to his truck.

'No.' He shook his head. 'If I'd known she was still at the set, I could have picked her up on the way.'

'She should have been finished hours ago. She said she was going to walk up to your house and drag you over here for dinner.' Annie frowned and Zach looked up from where he was going over papers. 'Didn't she call you?'

'No.' Cody rubbed his chin, thinking. 'And I've been home a bit today. There was no message, either.'

'That's strange.' Worry leapt into Annie's eyes.

'I'll drive over and get her,' Zach offered, standing.

'No.' Cody held up his hand. 'I'll run back out. You two sit down and eat some dinner. We'll be back before the beans can cool off.' He tried to sound calm, but his heart was jumping in his chest. Why hadn't he thought to check at the set? He'd been so full of misery and self-pity ever since he'd seen Stormy with her elderly fiancé that he'd quit thinking right.

'I've got a number for the set director I can call,' Annie said, digging through some papers. She punched some numbers into the phone, her eyes holding Zach's in maternal worry. Cody envied the connection they shared, a soul-uniting that didn't require words for reinforcement. 'No one's answering.'

'Never mind. It'll only take me twenty minutes to run over there.' He reached for his hat and went to the door.

'She said the filming would only take an hour to wrap up, then she'd walk to your house,' Annie said, her voice disbelieving, as if she couldn't accept that it had been five hours since she'd spoken to her daughter.

'Maybe there's a cast party, or she got hung up talking to some friends. I've got my cell phone if she calls you.' He didn't waste any more words, heading to his truck, trying to ignore the sick feeling in his stomach. Mary didn't have many friends. She'd been known to take off before.

He had refused to take her to California. His niece was well-acquainted with the location of the bus station. 'Surely to God,' he muttered under his breath as his fired the truck engine to life. Surely the lure of La-La Land and its starry glitter hadn't proven irresistible to the child he loved more than his own life. The image of Mary alone on a cross-country bus filled him with sickening dread.

When he reached the set ten minutes later, breaking a sound barrier for speed, he found it closed up and empty. Even Pick and Curvy had vacated their stools. He drove up to his house, in case Mary had let herself in. No one was there, and there was no message on the recorder.

His stomach clenched in a tight fist of apprehension, Cody decided to check with the codgers. They sat on their wooden bench outside the post office, keenly watching the comings and goings of the townsfolk.

'What's happening, Pick? Curvy?' he asked, using nonchalance to cover his fear.

'Nothing. Slow today,' Curvy replied.

'Seen Mary?'

'Nope.' Pick stuck a toothpick in his mouth in a side space where a tooth was missing. 'She finished up early this morning with her part, then the set closed up after that. We've been sitting here since then.'

'I see.' He slid a glance toward the bus station. It loomed large and ugly with its grey colors and the smell of exhaust. He thought he might throw up if Mary had left town – and she might have. It'd be best if he checked the outgoing schedules to see if any buses had been heading west. Casually, he said, 'Guess I'll mosey on.'

'Looking for yer niece again?' Curvy demanded, his eyes lit by the first excitement he'd had all day.

'Yeah.' Cody nodded curtly, not wanting to start any gossip about Mary running off again.

'She ain't been over there,' Curvy told him, jerking his head toward the bus station. 'We'd have seen her.'

Relief filled Cody for an instant, before *Where the hell could she have gotten to?* ran through his mind.

'Thanks.' He reached under his hat to scratch at his head. 'If you see her, tell her supper's waiting. I want her to call my cell phone.' Patting his pocket, he reassured himself he still had it. Damn it! Where could the scamp have headed off to?

'Want us to help you look for her?' Pick asked.

'Nah. She's probably gone over to a friend's. Just let me know if you see her.' He backed up with a brief wave and jogged toward his truck. *Mary, where are you?*

In a trailer on a rarely used area of Cody's land, Mary watched Sam with terrified eyes. Why had she believed him when he'd told her how grown-up she was? He'd appeared to treat her like an adult just so she would trust him – and she had. Mary's fearful gaze roamed over the disgusting things Sam had in the trailer. Ropes, which looked like good lasso rope. Lots of gloves. Of course, he was a stand-in stuntman for the film project, and supposedly a regular cowboy the rest of the time – or at least he'd said. Now she didn't know what to believe.

What she did know was that she was hungry. She was thirsty, and tired, and he wouldn't let her leave the trailer. He just sat there staring at her with empty jet eyes. Every time she said her folks would be worried about her, he just shook his head. Mary knew Sam wasn't afraid that they'd find her. Everybody on the set had gone into town to celebrate wrapping up the project and do some last shopping for souvenirs before they started packing up. It could be days before anyone thought to look back here for her.

What was he going to do to her? Mary watched, paralyzed, as Sam got to his feet and walked toward her. He slowly ran his hands through her long dark hair and she closed her eyes, wishing with all her might that Uncle Cody would come busting through the door to rescue her. *Please, Uncle Cody! Hurry!*

Perplexed, Cody tapped his fingers on the counter in his kitchen. Knowing she would have called if she'd heard from Mary, nevertheless, he rang the house. 'Any word?' he demanded when Annie answered.

'No! Cody, I'm really uneasy about his. I have the strangest feeling that something's wrong.'

Annie panicking wouldn't be good for the baby she carried inside her. 'Let Zach and me do the worrying,' he instructed gruffly. 'I'll find her.'

'Should you call Sloan?'

'I may go ahead and do that. I'll call you shortly.' He hung up and called the sheriff to alert him to the situation.

'You don't really think she's gone to California, do you?' Sloan asked.

'No,' he said slowly, 'she hadn't been to the bus

station.' She'd hitchhiked over to see Stormy at the hotel once, though, and he couldn't put that out of his mind. 'Most likely Mary didn't have enough money on her to buy a ticket to California.'

'There's that,' Sloan agreed. 'Don't think she'd be at a friend's house without calling her mom.'

'No. Not these days.'

'Well, some of the cast are in town. I'll go check around and see if anybody's seen her.'

'Thanks.' Cody hung up, unable to put off the one notion that bothered him more than anything. One way or the other, she might have decided to get to California on her own. Racked by indecision, he pulled the two pieces of white paper from the top of the trash and stared at them. There was no way around it. He was going to have to call Stormy; his mind wouldn't rest until he did.

Resolutely, he dialed, his heart thundering as he waited.

'Hello?'

His insides went to jelly at the sound of her voice.

'Stormy? It's Cody.'

'Cody!'

'Got a minute?' He hated to think that he'd interrupted anything she and her elderly fiancé might be up to.

'Yes, I do. Is everything all right?'

'It's fine.' No, it wasn't. 'Lost track of Mary, though.'

'Oh. I'm sorry to hear that. Why are you calling me?'

He thought Stormy's voice was a bit cool, somewhat remote. Pressing his palm against the side of the counter so hard it hurt, he tried not to think about how good it was to hear her voice on the other end of the line. He had really wanted to talk to her. 'I don't know. A hunch. You got her all excited with that flighty idea of going to California.'

'And you thought I was hiding her out here?' Stormy's voice had turned to ice.

'Not hiding her. Thought you mighta heard from her.'

'No. I haven't. Better check closer to home.'

'I have. The set's closed up and she's not in town, that Pick and Curvy have seen. And they see about everything.'

'I can't help you, Cody,' Stormy said, her voice reluctant and strangely aloof, 'but I can tell you that Mary isn't on her way out here. I wouldn't encourage her to leave home, anyway, and would call her mother immediately. For that matter, I'd bring her back on an airplane myself. But what makes me mad is that you think Mary would do something so thoughtless, Cody.'

He straightened, taking his palm away from the counter. He didn't need the pain to keep him from focusing on Stormy now; she'd just sent a barb out that had his complete attention. 'What do you mean? She's run to you before.'

'But she's changed, Cody! I'm sorry you haven't noticed. Mary isn't the depressed, withdrawn little girl I met when I first came to Desperado. She's happy, effervescent, shining with hope and discovery of talent that's all hers. That's why I invited her out to California. Not to get under your skin,' she said sarcastically, 'but to give her a chance to succeed. She's quite special on the screen, not that you probably ever had time – or interest – to find out for yourself.'

'I went around when I could.' He felt very defensive about this.

'Fine. And what did you notice, when you could?' she demanded.

'That she seemed to be having fun.'

'Okay. Did that clue you in to anything? Like maybe, Mary being happy was a far cry from how she was a couple of months ago?'

'No,' he said slowly, hearing the anger in Stormy's voice more than anything.

'Of course you didn't! To you, it was child's play, Mary amusing herself. You were tolerant while she had her fun, weren't you, Cody? Did you ever stop to think that she might really have a natural talent for acting?'

'No.' He was reluctant to admit it. Sounding like an ass wasn't pleasant, and that was what Stormy was painting him to look like.

Stormy sighed heavily. 'Look. You didn't take me seriously when you met me. Basically, you thought I was a flighty woman with a squirrelly occupation you didn't deem important, or worthwhile, because it wasn't what you were used to. You did the same thing to Mary, overlooking the shine that came over that child because she'd finally found something that made her feel good about herself, gave her something to work for.'

He hung his head, trying to see this new angle. 'Maybe.'

'Okay.' She sighed again, this time as if she were drawing in patience. 'Mary isn't here, Cody, because she wouldn't have run away again. She's not unhappy. The last time I saw her, I had tears in my eyes for how much she'd changed. Grown up. I'm so proud of her. You need to be, too.'

Rubbing underneath his chin, he said, 'I am. You're right. She was going in a direction with this acting thing I wasn't comfortable with. I didn't pay it much attention.' Actually, he'd paid Mary's new-found excitement damn little attention, waiting it out until the set closed up shop and moved off his land. He'd been counting the days until the project was finished. Obviously, he should have been paying attention to a lot of other things. 'So. Got any suggestions as to where she's off to?'

'Without being there, no. You didn't have any fights or arguments?'

'No. I mean, I wouldn't bring her to California, but I think . . . we didn't fight about it. I just said no.'

'I see.' Silence on the line seemed to reveal Stormy's feelings of what she would likely call his pigheadedness. 'Then I would call the sheriff and his deputies and every other soul in the town to look for her because if she's been gone long enough for you to phone me thinking she was coming this way, then something's wrong.'

Cold fear snaked into his stomach. 'You really think so?'

'I damn well think you'd better get off this phone and start hunting for her right there in your own backyard!' she shouted impatiently, uncharacteristic for Stormy. 'Do you always need a neon sign, Cody, to tell you when you're wrong?'

His concentration had shattered. Stormy had convinced him beyond words that he'd been on the wrong track. 'I'll call you when I find her.'

'I'll be waiting.' A second later, she said, 'Hurry, Cody. I don't like the feel of this at all. She could just be at a friend's, but I think she would have called if she could have. The director said she'd been on time for every single shoot.'

Slamming the phone down, he ran to his truck to head back into town.

When Sam picked up the scissors, Mary screamed.

'If you do that again, I'm going to bind your mouth,' he said quietly. 'I don't want to tape those pretty lips. I won't be able to see them. So sit still and let me do my work.'

Gently, he grabbed a hank of her hair, slowly cutting it so that the sh-sh sound electrified Mary's fear. Carefully, he put the handful of shorn hair into a bowl. Picking up another handful, he cut that, too, all the while exhaling soft, excited breaths of air against Mary's newly exposed neck.

She closed her eyes and prayed.

CHAPTER 18

Sloan met Cody as he roared on to the set lot. 'Heard anything?'

'No. Called Stormy. She hasn't heard from her.' He got out of the truck and slammed the door. The blast of sound startled some sparrows from the roof a nearby trailer.

'I don't like this.' Sloan's gaze narrowed as it roved, searching the set beyond Cody.

'I sure as hell don't.' The squabble of static from the radio in Sloan's car tensed his fear.

'Just to satisfy myself, I drove down to the orchard where I'd caught Mary and her buddies drinking and throwing rocks. I didn't expect to find her, but . . .' His voice trailed off.

Where the hell could she be? 'Last we know, she was here while they wrapped up.' Cody shifted, his boots grinding on the gravel beneath his feet. 'The codgers hadn't seen her in town.'

'Nobody in the crew remembered her joining the party going into town, either.'

Cody grunted. 'Nice to know they were keeping

such a close eye on her.'

'Actually, they were. Said she'd been talking to some guy named Sam. Apparently, the two of them hung around together between takes.'

'Great. Where the hell do we find Sam?'

'Well, they weren't exactly sure. He's a stand-in, supposedly from somewhere in North Texas. They thought he might have gone on back home since they didn't need him anymore.'

'Take me to the damn director. I want to know more than Mary was talking to some man who might have gone home with my niece!' Cody erupted.

'Yeah. I don't like that myself. Let me call my guys and have them track down the director. You start searching the trailers.'

'What for?'

'Maybe she fell asleep in somebody's trailer. Maybe her and this Sam fellow are holed up in one having a Coke.'

'I'll kill him.' Cody strode toward the trailer area.

'I know you will,' Sloan called after him. 'I may help you. But keep your head cool, Cody, until we find her. Hell, she could be at the library studying.'

'Not without calling her mother,' Cody retorted over his shoulder. Stormy said Mary had changed. She thought Mary had outgrown her selfish, childish tendencies.

This time, he was going with Stormy's theory. Some sixth sense was telling him that, wacky as she was, Stormy knew Mary better than any of them did lately.

Long trails of black hair lay gleaming silkily across an ugly table in the trailer. Sam had put some of it in a bowl, where it shone under a dull light. Tears seeped from Mary's eyes. 'Don't cut any more,' she begged. She couldn't bear for those sharp scissors to be so close to her neck. Cold steel touched against her nape every time Sam cut more off. What did he mean to do to her? She was so frightened she was afraid she was going to pee in her pants.

'Sh,' he said in a comforting tone. 'I'm almost finished.'

With a snip, he put one last length on the table. Mary's hand flew up to feel the harsh edges of what was left of her hair. He'd cut it to just below her ears.

'Don't cry,' he whispered, wiping her tears away with gentle fingers. 'I love your hair. I'll take such good care of it.' He moved her hands away from her neck and touched her bare skin before moving to feel the ragged pieces of his handiwork. 'You're so soft,' he told her, moving close, his obsidian eyes locking on her mouth.

Horrified, Mary tensed as Sam put his lips against hers in a wet, clammy kiss. His fingers moved to undo the buttons on her blouse. She pushed him away, but he clasped her hands to his chest.

'Am I going to have to tie you up? It won't be any fun if I do. You won't enjoy it near as much,' he assured her, his dark eyes solemn. Little drops of sweat ran along the edges of his thin blond hair. His gaze held hers as he put her hand to the crotch of his jeans. 'I want you to feel me.'

Mary screamed, pushing against Sam with all her might. Kicking out, she kept shrieking. Dizzy stars leapt into her eyes when he slapped her across the face, but Mary grabbed wildly for the scissors. 'Get away from me!' she yelled, crying. Holding up the sharp blades, she watched him. 'Stay back!' If he came closer, she'd stab him. There would be blood, lots of it, but she had to steel herself against that. *Blood is red, blood is red* she thought crazily. *My father bled so much.* She held the scissors higher, tensing her hand with determination.

Sam backed away, watching her nervously. Mary knew that if she went for the trailer door, he'd pounce on her in a flash. She had to deflect his attention long enough to make her escape. Her eyes lit on Sam's treasured piles of her hair. Striking out hard with one hand, she flung the bowl to the floor. The gleaming lengths on the table also scattered, drifting downward.

'Oh, no!' Desperately, he reached for the bowl, but she kicked it with all her might. It struck him in the face and Mary jumped for the trailer door, screaming.

Just like magic, it jerked out of her hands. Uncle Cody stood outside like a wrathful avenging angel.

'Uncle Cody!' she cried, falling into his arms.

'What the hell happened?' His eyes sought the doughy man who still clutched Mary's hair in his hands. Rapidly, he touched the short ends of it at the nape of her neck. 'Are you all right?'

'Yes.' She burst into tears and dropped the scissors.

'Mary, go sit in Sloan's cruiser.'

'But Uncle Cody –'

'Now.' His tone offered no compromise as he stared at the man who'd harmed Mary. All Cody could see was Mary's beautiful hair laying in straggling pieces on the drifter's shirt; his eyes wouldn't allow him to focus on anything else except the petrified expression on his face.

Mary ran off. Cody reached into the trailer and bunched the man's dirty-smelling shirt in his hands to jerk him in a sniveling heap to the ground.

'Sloan! Sheriff McCallister!' Mary cried, sprinting toward the cruiser. 'Hurry! You've got to stop Uncle Cody!'

Sloan stared at her. Self-consciously, Mary reached up to touch the shorn locks as she gasped for breath.

'Stop him from what?'

'Killing Sam! Oh, please, Sloan, hurry!'

'Are you all right?' he demanded, his gaze roving from her head to her toes, not missing the undone buttons at the top of her blouse.

'I'm fine!' She tugged at his arm, but Sloan

merely took her hand to walk her around to the passenger side of his car. 'Don't you care that Uncle Cody is going to hurt him?'

He was silent as he helped her get in. 'There's an unopened soda in that bag right there,' he finally said. Without answering her question, he radioed that she'd been found and instructed someone to call her parents. Mary's heart pounded like a raging waterfall in her chest.

'Are you sure you're all right?' he asked. 'Did he hurt you anywhere?'

'No.' Mary shook violently, her teeth beginning to chatter. Sam might have, though, if she hadn't managed to get away. If Uncle Cody hadn't come to her rescue. She had trusted Sam. Hiccuping, she started crying hysterically.

'I thought so.' Sloan tucked her head up under his chin and patted her back in gentle circles. 'You're safe now. Your mom and Zach will be here in just a minute, and then you can go home.'

Mary cried and cried, unashamed that the tears wouldn't stop coming and her body couldn't stop shaking. After it felt like all the tears had run out of her, she took a steadying breath. 'Don't you think you'd better go check on Uncle Cody?'

He sighed, shaking his head. 'Nope. I never interrupt him while he's working. He's got a mean temper on him.'

'Poor Sam,' Mary said.

'Nah. Don't waste any time feeling sorry for him. Cody won't kill him, but the bastard won't be riding for a while. Hope he's got good health insurance. Here's your folks.'

Mary jumped out of the cruiser and ran toward her mother and Zach, toward the enveloping arms that she knew now she would never be too grown-up to need.

'Shit. That's not a pretty sight.' Sloan eyed the unconscious drifter. 'Damn it to hell. Good thing I radioed for an ambulance.' He locked handcuffs around the bloody pulps of Sam's wrists. 'I sure don't want him in my cruiser.'

'How's Mary?' Cody rubbed his knuckles, not sparing a glance for his handiwork.

'I got the impression she was glad to see you.' Sloan thumped him on the back and gave him a shove. 'Go on. I'll clean up your mess and then meet you up at your house for a beer. I need one. Lord, what a mess.' He peered inside the trailer. The sight of Mary's hair laying like fallen strands of black silk turned his stomach. 'You're a lucky bastard,' he said to the man on the ground. 'You don't know it, but you oughta be waking up in hell.'

Glancing at Cody, he saw the big man walking away. His broad back was stiff, and Sloan watched him reach up with bloodied fingers to touch the length of his black braid. On the ground, the silver scissors lay, glinting in the dimming twilight. Sloan sighed and shook his head at the nearly unconscious man on the ground. 'Pervert,' he said, before heading back to the cruiser to get an evidence bag and a pair of gloves.

Cody, Annie, and Zach all stood around Annie's truck hugging Mary. The family scene brought tears to his eyes, but it was the sight of Mary standing on tiptoe to kiss her uncle goodbye before she left that put a boulder in his throat. Zach and Annie drove off with their daughter, and Cody got in his truck to drive up his land to his house.

He had the strangest feeling that Cody would never be the same again.

His buddy looked aged, Sloan thought, watching Cody down a glass of whisky thirty minutes later. He'd showered and put in a call to Annie to check on Mary, but there was nothing peaceful about his expression. He looked haunted. 'Care to share what's on your mind?'

Cody shook his head. He poured himself another glass.

Sloan nodded, crossing his boots and making himself more comfortable in the chair. Staring into the fireplace, he realized that soon a fire would be crackling in there. Winter's chill would seep into the air, and the cattle would start eating a bit more. Annie's baby would be born, and Cody would be an uncle again.

'I've been wrong about a lot of things.' Cody stared into his whisky as he spoke.

'Been telling you that for years,' Sloan agreed,

injecting fake cheerfulness into his tone.

It didn't bring the desired crusty response he'd hoped for. Cody merely nodded. Sloan set his drink down. His friend was taking this whole incident a damn sight harder than he was letting on. 'Well, just because you've been wrong is no reason to let it eat ya, Cody. Hell, the President's wrong most of the time, and look at his approval rating.'

He shook his head and didn't reply.

'Well, heck,' Sloan tried again. 'What's wrong with being wrong? It ain't gonna kill you, or anybody else. It's not preferable, of course, but it's not you know . . . like you're Tate Higgins or anything. He's been wrong from the day he was born. It's something in his brain. But you're okay, Cody. Don't take this so hard.'

For a moment he was afraid his words were falling on deaf ears. Then Cody said, 'Tate ran out on Hera.'

'Well, sure he did, 'cause he's a sonavabitch. That's not a newsflash, not even to Hera.'

'I ran out on Stormy.' Cody almost couldn't bear to think of it. The realization pained him. But he had. He'd basically told her how the relationship was going to run. His way or no way. Why had she given him her virginity?

How could she be pregnant with another man's child?

Do you always need a neon sign, Cody, to tell you when you're wrong? Why would she tell him she

288

was pregnant with *his* child when she knew he wouldn't leave his ranch, wasn't interested in commitment, wouldn't marry *her* any more than Wrong-Way was going to marry Hera?

He'd been careful about using condoms. There was always the possibility that he had exceptionally determined sperm that didn't intend to let a little bit of latex stop them from getting where they wanted to go.

He bit the inside of his jaw. Or maybe he wanted to go to California and was too damn stubborn to admit it. *He* just might be a father, not that elderly city slick who didn't look as if he had any sperm left in him. The idea of being a father was strangely frightening after today's incident with Mary being kidnapped. For a man who regularly shot and skinned rattlesnakes, he oughtn't be afraid of fatherhood. The terrified look in Mary's eyes and the ugly uneven cuts of her hair symbolized her loss of innocence. His heart shattered inside him as he held off the tears he wanted to weep for her. She had been forced to grow up today, and she had faced it better than he had.

The knowledge that he might be a father scared the hell out of him. Yet he was more afraid of not knowing the truth. Something had been left unsaid between him and Stormy. No matter how much it twisted his guts into a knot, he had to go have a talk with that little purple-haired gal.

He got to his feet.

'Where're you going?'

289

'California.' Cody put the whisky bottle away.

'California! Thought you said all that was out there was earthquakes and brain-scrambled hippies!' Sloan sat up, surprised into wearing a highly amused grin.

'I don't need a neon sign to tell me when I might possibly be wrong,' Cody informed him grumpily. 'You've been itching to see me get my ass on a plane. So find the door, Sloan. I gotta pack.'

CHAPTER 19

Stormy had been on a maximum buying spree. She sat in a taxi with Jonathan, surrounded by packages and overflowing bags, thinking that all the baby things and maternity clothes she'd bought ought to make her feel happy. That was the purpose, wasn't it? To feel happy about the baby, and feel happy with her life?

Searing the plastic edges of her credit card with purchases hadn't made her happy. Thinking about Cody took the edge off of any excitement she might be feeling. It was so purposeless to hurt this bad. Even in her wildest dreams, she couldn't make herself imagine any angle where she and Cody could intersect their lifestyles to form a future. For the sake of the baby, they could most likely work something out, an arrangement that would be cold and formal. Not the loving warmth she knew Cody was capable of, and that she wanted from him.

I want him to want me.

'Jonathan,' she said suddenly, 'I have to tell you something.'

'What, luv?'

He put his hand on her shoulder, but it was the purely platonic gesture it had always been. Jonathan didn't mind giving her his name for the sake of her child – and for the sake of the friendship he'd had for years with her parents – but that protection wasn't the answer, any more than all her purchases.

'I'm not going to marry you,' she said, her eyelashes lifting so that she could meet his gaze. 'It's sweet of you to be willing to help me out, but it's probably the worst thing I could do to both of us.'

He removed his hand. 'Are you sure? If you're worried about me getting into your personal affairs, you needn't, you know. We don't even have to live on the same premises.'

'I know,' she said hurriedly. 'You've been very understanding about this whole matter.' *You people in Hollywood are big on understandings.* Cody's voice haunted her. She didn't know what she was going to do, hadn't planned to end the pretense of a married life with Jonathan, but nothing felt right and it all had to change. The prospect of raising her child alone was scary, but she could do it. She'd basically raised herself, and she'd turned out fine. For many years, Annie Rayez had raised Mary by herself after her husband's death. Stormy wasn't going to marry Jonathan just so she wouldn't have to be a parent by herself. It was time to quit relying on support systems, be they pharmaceutical or emotional.

'I'm taking back all this stuff I bought,' she said resolutely.

'Why?' Jonathan gave her a sidelong glance.

'I shouldn't have bought it. I can't afford all of it, anyway.' It wasn't only that, but she could get by with a couple of the maternity dresses and about half of the baby layette she'd bought. The rest had been to fill a gap in her emotions that couldn't be filled with material things.

'Well, you can't take it back now,' Jonathan told her as the taxi pulled up in front of her apartment building. 'Crocodile Dundee has come to the city.'

'What are you talking about?' But even as she said it, she saw Cody lounging in the doorway. The door man was eyeing him warily, and Stormy smiled, seeing exactly what the doorman saw. Cody was a big man, and though his posture was relaxed as he leaned against the wall, his gaze was alert, watching everything. He had on jeans that hugged his body and snakeskin boots that looked like he wore them only to church. A black hat with some kind of tooth tucked into the rawhide braid around the crown rode low on his head. His ebony braid, peppered with a few grey strands, emphasized a square-jawed, determined face. His arms were crossed over his chest, and Stormy watched several women try to catch his eye as they went past. He barely smiled at them. Stormy watched the women drinking him up as if he were some kind of movie star with novelty sex

293

appeal, and her heart sped up like mad.

'Lady, you getting out or not?' the cab driver demanded.

'I'm getting out,' she replied, not aware that she'd already opened the door.

Jonathan got out, too, and handed her as many of the packages as she could carry. The rest he set on the sidewalk. 'I'd offer to carry those up, but I think you're going to have all the help you need.'

'Thanks, Jonathan.'

He leaned down to give her a kiss, with Cody's gaze simmering on them. 'I'll call to check on you later.'

'Okay,' she said breathlessly, only barely aware the taxi pulled away from the curb. 'Hi, Cody,' she said, walking toward him. Her mouth felt frozen, her face muscles tight. What could she say to this man that wouldn't sound utterly foolish?

'Hi.'

He came forward to stand near her but didn't touch her. His gaze swept down to her belly and Stormy felt a flush run all over her that had nothing to do with the Los Angeles heat or her pregnancy.

'I'm surprised to see you here,' she said.

'I'm surprised to be here.'

'Oh?' Stormy looked around. 'Did you bring Mary for the auditions?' she asked, trying her best to sound nonchalant.

'No.' His gaze was focused on her. 'I thought about bringing her. Sometimes, it was the best excuse I could think of to get out here. But then I realized you and I need to have a little time to talk. If you don't mind, and if your fiancé won't mind.'

'No, he won't,' she replied swiftly, completely forgetting to tell him that she was no longer engaged. 'Come on up. I'm dying to hear what the subject of this conversation is if it couldn't be handled over the phone.'

He leaned down to pick up the packages, shaking his head at her when she tried to take some from him. 'No. You convince that doorman I'm not here to do anyone bodily harm, and I'll manage the rest.'

Quickly, she told the doorman that Cody was her guest. The doorman frowned at Cody, and Cody glowered back, and Stormy tried not to smile at all the macho posturing.

'Come on. It's a good thing I returned when I did. The two of you might have engaged in fisticuffs,' she said wryly, digging out her key.

Cody didn't say anything. Stormy hurried to press the elevator button, and they stepped inside. The elevator whooshed to the sixth floor a whole lot faster than she would have liked. The thought of having Cody in her little apartment made her hands tremble as she put the key in the lock. She felt like stuck film in a film projector, with images jumping crazily all over the screen.

'Home, sweet home,' she said, pushing the door open so he could pass her.

'I got it.' He propped the door with his boot and waited for her to move past him. She did, but her belly and all the packages he was holding made it a tight squeeze. 'Let me take some of those,' she said to save face. 'I'll put them away.'

She worried that he might ask what was in the bags, but he didn't, saving her from bringing up the need for baby necessaries. 'Can I get you anything?' she asked, unable to look at him.

'Didn't come all the way west to share a soda with you, Stormy,' he said, coming to stand in front of her. He caught her chin with his hand and forced her to meet his gaze. 'Are we having a baby?'

'Yes,' she murmured, swallowing in a suddenly dry throat. There was no point in denying it.

'I thought so.' He let out a tense breath and released her chin, moving away to sit heavily in the nearest chair.

She sat opposite, knotting her fingers. He seemed overwhelmed. She felt the same way. This man and she had created a human being. The knowledge that their lives were locked together in this way for all time hit her. 'I'm sorry. I should have told you sooner.'

He rested his hand against his cheek, scratching at his temple.

'Well, I thought about it,' she said hurriedly, 'but there never seemed to be a right time.'

He eyed her dispassionately.

'I didn't know how to tell you.' She pleaded with

her eyes for him to understand. 'I was . . . afraid of how you'd feel. About me. About us . . . having a baby.'

He nodded once, as if he completely related to the words she was babbling. Stunned, Stormy realized he was at a loss. 'Are you okay?'

'Yeah. I'm trying to decide what to do.'

'About what?' She hoped he wasn't angry, though she knew he had a right to be. But do? There wasn't anything for him to do. He was the father, not a participant at this point. Maybe never a participant.

'I'm either going to wring your neck or holler out loud that I'm going to be a father. I'm afraid that doorman's got security listening outside the door, so maybe I won't yell. Wringing your neck would be a quieter operation.'

'I won't let you wring my neck, Cody.' Stormy waved him off with a dismissive hand. 'I understand you being upset but what's done is done. There's nothing to do except wait until the baby comes.'

'Anger suits my mood right now; waiting doesn't.' He stared at her. 'Why shouldn't I give you the yelling you deserve?'

'It's a waste of time,' she said, faking an airiness she didn't feel. 'Just because we've developed this unexpected hitch is no reason to get all uptight.'

'You're not marrying that elderly man you drag around like a security blanket,' he stated.

'What?' she repeated, outraged.

'He's not raising my child. Shoot, I doubt he's even got enough breath left in him to pitch baseballs to my son.'

'Baseballs?' Disbelief swept Stormy. Of all the reactions she'd expected from Cody, this wasn't one she had envisioned. 'Jonathan would be a good father.' She ought to know. He'd certainly kept a paternal eye on her through the many stages of her creative parents' up and down career.

'I understand that you and he have a relationship, but he's not going to be a father to my son.'

Hot fury whipped from out of nowhere. She jumped to her feet, pointing at her stomach for emphasis. 'This might be a girl, not that you'll allow your chauvinistic brain to consider your having anything in you but requisite male chromosomes. Heavens! Since it's your child, I might give birth to a donkey!' Setting her hands on her hips, she glared at him. 'You can quit criticizing Jonathan, too. He's been unfailingly supportive.'

'I'm not interested in that.' Cody stood, too, meeting her furious gaze with some righteous heat of his own. 'Let's stick to the problem at hand. If you're going to marry an old man and have an "understanding" marriage –' he repeated the term she knew he despised '– and if you intend to continue living like a flake, then I think in the interest of all parties, the child is better off living with me in Texas where he can grow up like a man.'

Stormy sucked in a breath. 'How dare you!'

'We need to come to some terms, and if I'm not as supportive and understanding as you'd like, I'm sorry. I'm just the way I am. I say things the way I see them. One time, that was a quality I admired about you.' He stared at her, regret in his eyes. 'You mighta sounded like a wacko, but at least you were an honest wacko. Now, you're living such a big lie I wonder if I ever knew you.'

'What in the hell do you mean "big lie"? ' Her neck stiff with anger, Stormy refused to release his dark, angry gaze.

'You don't love that man. You're going to have an "arrangement".'

'What's it to you?' Stormy snapped.

'It's a lot. Your whole way of life is something I don't want my son growing up around.'

'Well, I beg your pardon! You didn't seem to mind –'

Knocking at the door halted the abuse she was about to heap on him. Promising with her eyes that she wasn't finished with him yet, Stormy opened the door. Her heart sank. 'Hello, Mother, Father. Please come in.'

'We decided to drop by and get you to go to dinner with us. We want you to be sure you're eating right for the –' Her mother caught sight of Cody and her voice trailed off awkwardly. She walked past Stormy into the room, burnt-orange hair crimped into a frizzy ball and three-inch yellow peace signs swinging from her ears. Her father wore his best clothes, Stormy had to admit, even if the jeans were more than ragged and the sandals worn down to the thinness of paper.

'Mom, Dad, I'd like you to meet Cody Aguillar,' she said, pointing to the black-eyed man staring at her folks. 'Cody, these are my parents, Sun and Moon Nixon.'

Slowly, he swept the hat from his head, nodding. He put his hand out for her father to shake. 'Nice to meet you.' They echoed his greeting, but he wasn't paying attention. His eyes had shot back to hers and it was all too clear what he was thinking. *What a bunch of fruitcakes. These nuts aren't going to get the chance to turn my son into a fruit.*

'You must be the father of Stormy's baby,' Sun said without preamble.

'Mother, why don't you sit down?' Stormy asked hurriedly. 'Father, can I get you something to drink?'

They ignored her, frozen into an uneasy moment with Cody.

'Stormy confirmed my suspicions about that a few moments ago,' he replied.

Sun nodded, walking over to sit down. 'We tried to get her to tell you at once.'

'We did. But she wouldn't listen to us.'

Moon went to sit beside his wife as if they were the same teenagers who'd fallen in love during their hippie days. Cody propped himself into a round, flowered chintz chair that didn't quite accept his body.

'We tried to explain to her how important it was

300

for children to have strong parental influences in their lives, but Stormy has always gone the opposite direction of anything we tell her.'

'What?' Stormy stared at her parents, shocked. 'When did you two turn into model June and Ward Cleaver types?'

'We always were,' Sun admonished her lightly. 'You had the most normal childhood of any kid in any family we ever traveled with.'

'I'm sorry.' Stormy stepped forward so that she was speaking directly to Cody. 'They've been breathing too much fresh California mountain air. Never did we have a normal lifestyle in any definition "normal" can be stretched to include.'

'Maybe it wasn't your average suburban home,' Moon agreed, 'but we stayed married. It's better for children to have a home where the parents live together.'

'Even when they're sleeping with other people?' Stormy nearly shouted. 'Have you two gone off your health-store medication? Don't even try to pretend that you were apple pie parents!'

'We weren't.' Sun shook her head, smiling at Cody. 'Stormy was never an apple pie child, either.'

'I believe you,' he said sincerely. His gaze flashed to Stormy, for one moment lighting on her ankle bracelet, or maybe the tiny tattoo she had on her bare ankle, she wasn't sure which. No doubt he'd rather have a woman who wore boots all the time, she thought sourly. Then she thought about

Annie, who'd treated her like part of the family. Annie had boots on every time she'd seen her. She shouldn't have let such a bitter, narrow-minded thought get in her head. Stormy took a deep breath, putting a hand on her stomach to soothe herself and any turmoil she might be causing the baby.

'I wasn't an apple pie kid myself,' Cody said conversationally. Suddenly, he had everyone's attention riveted on him, waiting for him to elaborate. He swallowed hard, feeling stupid, the kind of rattled stupid he'd felt when a bull gave him a good thump into a barn wall. His brain whirled with everything he'd heard in the last forty minutes. Stormy's parents stared at him as if he were some unique animal in a zoo. He held his hat in his hand, pressing the edges of it between his fingers for something to do, then realized what he was doing and stuck it under his chair. 'I was never as good at school . . . as my brother was,' he said softly. 'I . . .' He broke off, thinking about Carlos and how he'd died, and suddenly, Cody knew he'd spent all his life in a shell. A secure, somewhat narrow-minded shell of things familiar and not intimidating. He'd never been on the hot seat with anybody's parents before. Any home he'd been in to see a girl, the family had known him for ages, and his parents, too. This was different. He didn't know the Nixon way of life, but they didn't know the Aguillar way of life either. And it was kind of hard to explain to a woman with orange

302

hair and a man who looked like a cave dweller that his intentions toward their daughter were honorable, in some ways.

He owed them that respect. This woman with her searching gray-purple eyes like Stormy's, and this man with a worn road for a face and eyes that looked permanently strobe-lit, were Stormy's parents. He had gotten their daughter pregnant. No matter how disgusted he might be with Stormy right now, he was going to sit here and let her parents examine him until they'd gotten it out of their systems. 'I was the wild child, the spoiled younger brother.'

'His nickname in Desperado is Crazy Cody,' Stormy supplied helpfully.

He gave her a pointed stare-down for her help.

'Crazy Cody?' Sun repeated, looking like she might break into tears any second.

'Ah . . . yeah.' Cody scratched the back of his neck uncomfortably. 'I don't know how I got that handle.'

'He lies. He revels in the respect being crazy gets him.' Stormy brought out a tray. 'Here's some spring water, Cody. Try it. It tastes a lot better than that murky stuff Desperado calls water. They pull it out of a lake and it always tastes like dirt,' she informed her parents.

'It does not!' Cody sat straight. He'd been drinking that water all his life and it was just fine.

'Oh, it does.' Stormy shook her head as she squeezed some lemon into a glass. 'You don't notice it, but I called the water company, just to inquire. I thought maybe the lake had gone dry, and the city didn't realize they were pumping up the last little drops of their supply. Well, the water man said they were having a hot summer and the lake was warm but they'd pour more chemicals into it. Chemicals!' She shook her head at her parents.

Startled, they stared at Cody for confirmation. 'You better drink all the spring water you can while you're here,' Moon told him. 'This is as fresh and pure as it gets.'

Cody took a tentative drink. 'Tastes like water,' he pronounced.

'That's right!' Stormy looked so proud. 'Water, not dirt! You see? You can tell the difference.'

He couldn't, but the Nixons all seemed so pleased with their spring water he wasn't about to bust their collective bubble.

'We should take Cody out to dinner, Moon.' Sun turned to look at her husband, peace signs all a-sway. 'Don't you think so?'

Cody realized he was being treated as a son-in-law prospect. That really wasn't a good idea. He and Stormy hadn't even had a chance to air anything out between them. An evening spent with her parents probably didn't bode well for his bachelorhood. Heck, their daughter was carrying his child. No doubt they expected his ring on her finger before the night was over. He swallowed, feeling distinctly cornered. 'That's all right. You don't have to do that, but I sure do appreciate it.'

Moon snapped his fingers, catching Cody's attention in a sudden way. The man had long fingernails. Obviously, he had never done much riding or roping.

'Sushi. We should take Cody to a sushi bar!' Moon suggested.

'What a wonderful idea!' Sun beamed at Cody. 'Have you ever had sushi?'

Stormy waited for his reply with a sarcastic smile, knowing full well he was a meat and potatoes man.

'Is sushi that raw fish stuff?'

'Oh, yes, quite delicious,' Sun told him.

He could maybe eat some fish. 'Will they cook it for me?'

'I . . . don't think so.' Sun looked at her husband, obviously perplexed as to why anybody would want their dinner cooked.

'Well, maybe they've got a steak or something.' Cody had pretty well resigned himself to this adventure with the Nixon crew from outer – *No, they aren't weird. Just a . . . little out of the ordinary. Like Stormy*. His gaze caressed her belly. She might be out of the ordinary, but she looked fabulously sexy in spite of it.

'Steak?' Sun repeated. 'Stormy's a vegetarian.' She sent her daughter a questioning look that said, *what were you doing in bed with a man who eats red meat*? 'In fact, Moon and I never touch red meat. Or any meat except fish. The muscle meats aren't

305

healthy for you,' she said, obviously trying, by the smile on her face, to be informative and helpful.

'Cody raises cattle for a living,' Stormy murmured.

The awkward silence in the room burned Cody's ears.

'Oh,' Sun said awkwardly. 'You *raise* cattle.'

Those disgusting muscled creatures, she might as well have said. 'And eat them, too,' he said smoothly, because they were all feeling so awkward he felt like an absurd remark would take the tension to extra-tight. 'Truth is, I don't waste my time listening to rock-'n'-roll music. It's the equivalent of jelly for your brain. Much healthier to stick to classical music, or country and western.'

Of course he knew that Stormy's parents were rock-'n'-roll junkies. He crossed his arms over his chest, seeing clearly the startled, wondering glance Sun sent her only child. The deck was cut, the cards reshuffled. Teams were chosen. In his mind, they were on one side, and he was the unpicked player. Odd man out. The different, undesirable one.

'Take me to a restaurant where they cook the food and I'll buy your dinner,' he said to restart the game.

'Cool,' Moon said, jumping to his worn-sandaled feet. 'We'll take you up on that.'

'Good.' Cody put on his black hat with the tooth in the leather hatband and held the door open for Stormy and her diminutive, eccentric parents. As

306

she passed by him, his eyes promised that, after this interesting side trip, the two of them were going to hash out their differences and come to a compromise.

'Nice going, Cowboy,' she murmured. 'You've obviously met a lot of girls' parents.'

'I have yours eating out of my hand.' He gave her a slight whack on the behind, making her jump and shoot him a warning glare. 'I didn't come out here to eat raw fish and drink untreated water, Trouble.'

'Take a walk on the wild side, Cody,' she said, raising her brows at him as he slipped his arm through hers, escort-style.

'Obviously I did more than walk on the wild side when I met you. Lucky for you I'm so damn easy to get along with. And your parents are wondering how a flake like their daughter managed to meet such a great guy.'

'Cody, they're tripping harder right now than they ever did on any plant form they smoked.' She patted his arm as it lay linked through hers. 'I think it'll be good for you to have such a positive experience in California. You might decide traveling is a lot of fun.'

'I don't think you're going to make a convert out of me,' he whispered in her ear as the sushi restaurant loomed in sight. 'Eating uncooked food can give you salmonella, which you traveled to Shiloh to discover for yourself.'

'I'm not trying to make a convert out of you.'

She poked him when he opened the door for her parents. 'None of us is going to change our ways.'

'A thick, juicy steak would be very healthy for my baby,' he said hopefully. 'Protein for his brain development.'

Stormy laughed out loud. 'Peanut butter will do the same thing. Come on, Cowboy. The fish is fresh from the ocean.'

She was wearing another man's ring, a real rock, Cody noted sharply as he followed her to a table. He might not be able to stomach raw fish, but he'd damn sure do that before he'd allow his child to be raised by another man. If he and Stormy didn't agree on another thing tonight, they were going to meet at the pass on that.

'I'll have your biggest, rawest fish,' he told the waitress. 'And some untreated water.' He gave Stormy a sporting smile.

'It's not going to work,' Stormy warned him. 'I'm not fooled a bit.'

'I'm not trying to fool you. But if I can try a little of your way, you ought be willing to try a little bit of my way.'

'Such as?' she asked brightly, her parents and the waiter eagerly listening.

'You order a steak. I'm not leaving my baby's intellectual and physical development up to peanut butter with a fairy on the label.'

'Do I look unhealthy to you?' she demanded.

'No, you look fine. It's my child whose nutrition shouldn't suffer.'

She blew out a breath and ran her fingers through her short hair as she thought through his request.

'If I can compromise, you can, too.'

'Fine!' She glowered at him. 'I'll have the biggest, bloodiest slab of dead cow you've got.'

'A small one will do. See how agreeable I am?' Cody smiled at her and patted her on the back.

'You're deliberately trying to make me ill!' Stormy snapped.

'I could say the same,' he reminded her.

She didn't reply.

'See how easy this is?' Sun asked happily from the opposite side of the table. 'Peace is easy to achieve when one allows it to come into one's life.'

Cody stared at Stormy. Her chin pointed at him belligerently. He'd allowed her into his life. Peace had definitely not come with Stormy.

Stormy stared at Cody. He'd battled her since the day he'd first closed the door on her proposition for setting the movie on his land. Ornery, overly stubborn male with more testosterone than was healthy for any of his species. Peace wasn't something she'd experienced from meeting him, Crazy Cody.

And now he was fixated on the baby she carried. Stormy drew a deep, unsettled breath. There wasn't likely to be peace at all between them any time soon – especially after she told him that she intended to file for full custody of their child.

CHAPTER 20

'That was interesting.'

Cody closed the door behind them as they walked into Stormy's apartment. Sun and Moon had left for parts unknown right after dinner, which had actually turned out to be somewhat interesting. Stormy thought that her parents were fascinated by the big man, and he by them.

It had been kind of fun to watch them, three characters in a script trying to learn their parts.

'I've got an early call in the morning.' Stormy turned to face Cody. 'As much as I know you want to talk, I can't miss work. So, can we be fast?'

'Not really.' He gave her a thorough staring. 'We have a lot of things to hammer out.'

'How long are you staying?' Stormy sank into a chair, trying to maintain a stern façade, and not sure how long she was going to be able to keep herself from succumbing to the temptation of Cody in her apartment. 'I imagine you're flying back out tomorrow?' she asked hopefully.

He shook his head at her as if she were a naughty

child. 'Bought a one-way ticket. Since you can be hard to work sometimes, I figured I'd probably save money if I didn't have to change reservations a hundred times.'

'Very funny.' Stormy brushed her hair back and considered him. 'Pick the topic, then, as long as you're out by ten. My alarm clock is set for four o'clock.'

'Okay.' He drew his middle finger down the bridge of his nose, deep in thought. 'I don't like living so far apart. It's going to be hard for the child.'

'You're right. Can't move Texas on the map, though. Next topic?'

'Stormy, I feel like you've got me on a timer. Do you mind just sorting through this with me and coming to a reasonable solution?'

Slight anger rose inside her. 'If you don't mind me pointing this out, I have everything sorted, Cody.'

'So if I hadn't figured out you were carrying my child, you were prepared to plow full steam through raising it without telling me? Without including me?'

'Last I checked, you weren't interested in being included,' she stated, trying to keep the impatience from her voice. 'You plainly said on more than one occasion that you didn't want to be a father.'

'That was before I became one!' He furrowed his brows.

'I would have told you eventually,' she allowed.

'But I don't want to talk about that. Frankly, I'm a little put out that you think you can rush in here and solve everything for me and then buy a return ticket, Cody.'

'You need solving!'

'In what way? I think I'm doing just fine without your help!'

They stared at each other, each refusing to budge.

'For starters, if you're going to marry that white-skinned old man, I don't think he's going to live past the wedding night.'

'That's none of your business!' Stormy was outraged.

'It is. Contrary to what you and your folks keep trying to tell me, I don't think California's all that healthy. He certainly doesn't appear to be in too good a shape. I'm worried how that will affect my child.'

'First of all,' Stormy ground out, 'I am not marrying Jonathan. We had just called it off when you showed up uninvited.'

He brightened. 'Now you're showing some sense. Nothing good can come of marrying a man who's got snow on the roof and no heat in his wiring.'

'Cody!' Stormy leapt to her feet. 'Let's get to the crux of our problem, okay?'

'Fine by me.' He gave her a brisk nod.

He wasn't going to like what she had to say. But it was time to get it out in the open once and for all.

'You have always enjoyed criticizing my livelihood, and where I come from.'

'I don't –'

'You do. You call it living in La-la Land, which I know is a common enough term, but you seem to think it fully applies to me.' She took a deep breath and held his eyes steadfastly. 'I happen to think you're living in the Land of Denial. You think everything can be overcome one way or the other, if you're just stubborn enough. You'll eat raw fish, and I'll eat red meat. Well, now we're having a baby, and what you refuse to see is that you and I are going to have a damn difficult time doing anything but driving each other mad over this situation. There is no half and half where a child is concerned. I don't want there to be.' She paused before her next words. 'I'm going to file for full custodial rights.'

'Now, wait a minute –'

'No.' She turned her back on him, her heart breaking. 'I'm not going to have this child screwed up, growing up caught between California and Texas. I'm not going to have it shuttled around with no stable home base, the way I was.' Whirling to face him, she said, 'And I'm not going to have this baby torn between you and me. I'll do anything to make certain it has a fully secure childhood.'

'Even if that means giving me no rights?' Cody couldn't believe what he was hearing.

'You'll be welcome to visit. I may let the child visit you in the summer. I know you're a very fit guardian because I've seen what you do for Mary. But we're not doing a split custody arrangement where the child grows up neither here nor there. This nor that.' She began to cry. 'I want my child to be secure, and never in doubt of its importance in my life.'

'I do, too.' Cody stepped close to hold her, but she moved away, avoiding him.

'So you agree?'

'Hell, no. I don't agree.' He sighed heavily and strode to stare out a window at the Los Angeles traffic. 'But I don't have an alternative to suggest. I can tell you I don't see what's so healthy about growing up in a smog-choked environment. There must be a million people here, all crawling over each other like ants. No room to run and play. To stretch out.'

'I know it seems strange to you,' Stormy said, wiping her eyes, 'but this is a fine place to live. The issue isn't the best place to grow up. The issue is growing up as securely as possible. And I don't think that can happen if there's a question of allegiance. The child will think it's either you or me. California or Texas. And I think that's a horrible thing to do to a child.'

'So is being without a father.'

'Lots of children have only one parent, or neither parent, and turn out just fine.'

'Yeah, but the odds are better if there are two parents, Stormy. Surely even you can't argue with that.'

'What do you mean, even I can't argue with that?' She heard condescension in his tone and it made her madder.

'Beyond all the peace, love, and spring water, there are some things you can't argue with. A whole family is one of them. You had one, so surely you can see that.'

Had she been better off because she'd had two parents, selfishly inconsiderate of her childhood as they'd been? 'I don't know,' she murmured miserably.

'Well, *I* didn't have the benefit of a father,' he stated, his voice hard and bitter. 'He died when I was very young. My older brother, Carlos, became my whole lifeline, my connection to what a father might be. He married Annie and for a little while, Mary had the best father anyone could have. My brother –' his voice broke, tearing at Stormy's heart '– my brother died a death so horrible we're all still affected by his loss. Can you not even tell what it's like to not have a father from Mary's behavior? Zach is great and Mary loves him, but there's no doubting that her childhood was scarred by her father's death.'

He stared at her, his dark eyes damp with furious regret and memories. 'I had no one but my mother, and while I love her, we were both damn lonely. And damn left out. So do not talk to me about how good it will be for my baby not to know me. I will never, never agree with you. I will never, never let you do that.'

'I'm sorry,' she said, weeping tears she couldn't control. 'I'm sorry, Cody. I only think of how I grew up and what I want to be different for my child.'

'I know.' Now he did pull her close and Stormy went gratefully into the warm, hard shelter of his arms. 'I think the same way. I don't think it's a bad thing. We just need to work out the inherent differences with this problem and go from there. That's why I'm here.' He framed her face with his hands, brushing her tears away gently. 'We're going to disagree a lot, but in the end, we can probably work through it.'

'I don't know how,' she sniffled miserably.

'I don't either. I don't think too good on an empty stomach.'

'We just ate!' Stormy stared up at him, enjoying the feel of his strong fingers touching her face.

'You just ate. I pretended to eat.'

'That's sneaky!' Stormy couldn't believe she'd eaten red meat, while he'd sat on his side of the table innocently acting as if he was eating his sushi.

'I do not eat slimy things, woman,' he said huskily. 'There are some things a man cannot compromise on.'

'You told my parents it was delicious!' She stared up into his eyes, allowing herself to hope that he would kiss her.

'I said it was very well prepared. It's bad manners to offend your host and hostess. Even in the country, we learn manners.' Gently, he

316

lowered his lips to hers. She didn't move, merely closed her eyes on a sigh of desire. '*You* are delicious,' he murmured against her mouth. 'You are soft and smell good and feel so good you drive me wild.'

He pulled her up tight against him and kissed her until she had no breath. Then he nuzzled his face into the curve of her neck, as if telling her how much he needed her. Red-hot fire and want rushed through Stormy.

'You already were wild,' she said, trying to hang on to her sanity so that she wouldn't give into the sensual craving flooding her senses. 'Crazy.'

'That was just a nickname. But I'm loco for you and all I can think of is how much I want you.'

'I want you, too,' she whispered, turning her head so that he would kiss her again. 'I want you to make love to me.'

He unzipped her dress. Cool air rushed against her back, peaking her already sensitive nipples. Slowly, he slid it from her shoulders and dropped it to the floor. Hesitantly, she reached out to unbutton his shirt. 'Guess we won't have to use a condom this time.' She gave him a very shy glance.

He ran his hands down her shoulders and over her shoulder blades to unsnap her bra. 'It doesn't seem to have done us much good,' he agreed. Gently, he drew her bra off and dropped it to the floor, too. He stood staring at her for a moment, before gently picking her up in his arms. She

317

nestled against his chest. 'I have to tell you, I'm kind of scared of being a father.'

'I'm a little afraid of being a mother,' she admitted.

'Let me take you in here so I can see the little fellow.' He carried her into the bedroom.

'Little person,' she gently corrected. 'Most likely my femaleness will triumph over your maleness and we'll have a little lady. In fact, I'm positive of it.'

He laid her on the bed and sat beside her, putting one hand over her stomach. 'Do you know you're having a girl and you're not telling me?'

'No.' She ran a teasing finger along the edges of his lips. 'I'm giving you a hard time. You seemed damned determined to have a boy.'

'I don't really care what it is.'

'I didn't think so. With you, everything is naturally phrased in the masculine sense.' She gave him a seductive smile. 'Do you remember when you told me that we'd have an ugly baby? That the townspeople would throw rocks at it?'

He nodded.

'Did you mean it? Do you really think that?'

'Yeah. But I'll love it anyway, poor little thing.' Stroking his hand around the bulge where the baby lay nestled inside Stormy, Cody then moved his hands inside her panties. He smoothed his hands over her buttocks, squeezing lightly, before drawing the lacy thong slowly down her legs. 'The last time I saw you, you had no stomach.'

318

'I've gotten fat since then.'

'No.' He lowered his head to kiss her stomach. 'You've gotten more beautiful. You were so thin, I didn't know how you could stay alive.' He pressed kisses from her navel to where the top of her panties had been. 'I like growing my baby inside you.'

'Let me take your clothes off.' If she had to wait much longer to hold Cody to her, she was going to fly apart. She busied herself scooching his jeans down, and he helped her. Then she pulled him into her arms, sighing at the sensation of being close to him.

'I won't hurt you, will I?'

'No.' She smiled reassuringly, then gasped as he suckled on her nipples. 'Oh, Cody.'

'Say it again.'

'Oh, Cody,' she murmured, pulling his head hard against her. 'Oh, Cody!' she cried as he entered her. She rocked against him, feeling tears pour down her cheeks at the wonderful sensations overwhelming her. All she could do was wrap herself around him and hold on tight, before a rollercoaster tugging enveloped her. 'Don't stop,' she moaned. 'Oh, don't stop!'

He didn't until she went over the edge, then he followed, a hoarse cry escaping him. Stormy held him tightly to her, running her hands lightly over his sweat-soaked back.

Please tell me you love me, she thought. *Please say we're going to do more than work this out.*

319

Cody buried his face in Stormy's soft, fragrant, distinctly purple hair. His heart thundered in his chest as he tried not to crush her petite body underneath him. *She drives me mad*, he thought. It felt great to be inside her without any barrier between them. He was going to build up a lot of air mileage flying to see this woman and his child. Could they make a future based on frequent flyer miles and long distance calls?

The odds were against it. Cody rolled off of Stormy gently, his whole brain confused as he tried to think his way through the aftermath of their sexual attraction. *I could ask her to marry me, but she'd say no. What would she do in Desperado?*

'Ever think of moving to Texas?' he asked.

'No.' She rolled her head to look at him. 'Although the sex is good enough to make me give it a second thought.'

Sloan had been wrong. Stormy didn't want to live on his ranch. So much for that idea. 'You're an unconventional woman.'

'I'm sorry. Am I supposed to follow you around, hoping that if I do it long enough, you'll ask me to marry you one day?'

'Most women would,' he said grumpily. 'Of course, you're not like most women.'

'That's in my favor, right?'

'At this moment, no. You're damn hard to pin down.'

'You have no room to talk. You're not like most men I know, either.'

320

'I'm scared by the one I've seen you with. I damn sure hope I'm not like him.'

'Jonathan is a very nice man. He offered to marry me.'

'So?' He kept his eyes trained on hers, scowling. 'I do all the work and he gets to marry you and take the credit?'

Stormy laughed out loud. 'Making love to me is work?'

'No. Getting you pregnant through a condom. That took superhuman strength and sperm.' Cody actually didn't feel like making light of the situation anymore. 'I'm offering to marry you.'

She propped herself up on one elbow, which made her breasts tilt in a manner he found most attractive. 'Are you?'

He swallowed hard. 'Yes. I think I will.'

'Will what?'

'Ask you to marry me.' His whole being shrank under her soft expression. He hadn't intended to do that, had he? Yes, he had. He was no Wrong-Way Higgins, to leave a woman stranded after availing himself of her body.

'Are you doing this just because of Jonathan?'

He swallowed. Definitely he didn't want the old geezer putting his hands on his woman – or his child. 'No.'

'You don't seem very . . . anxious.' She eyed him, a worried look in her eyes.

'I am anxious. I don't know how else we're going to solve this, do you?'

'We don't have to get married just because . . .' She drifted off, realizing what she was saying. She wanted him to ask her so bad that she was putting words into his mouth. She wanted him. He wanted to do the right thing. He had never once said he was in love with her.

And that was what she had said all along that she would not do. Make the mistake of marrying because of the baby. There were too many other obstacles in the way to compound the problem by tying him to her with holy matrimony. It would never work out. Marriage was a momentary stop-gap to make them feel like they were working out their differences. Compromising.

But over time it would turn into a yoke holding them together. The child would suffer. They both wanted to do the right thing for their baby.

It was not right to say yes, no matter how badly she wanted to.

'I love you,' she said.

'I love you, too.'

'I know you do.' Like a friend. Somewhat like anybody else he rushed in to take care of, whether it was his mother, or Mary, or asking Annie to marry him after Carlos died. She didn't want to be a responsibility. She wanted him to be in love with her. She lay her head down on his shoulder and wrapped her leg over his. 'I don't know what I want.'

'I didn't think so.' He wound his fingers into her hair and held her face against his cheek, wondering what he was going to do with this movie scout who was holding his future in the cradle of her belly.

Outside the bedroom, the telephone rang. The answering machine clicked on. 'Stormy, this is Jonathan. Good news. The head honchos decided you did such a good job with the film location in Texas that they want to give you a promotion and a blockbuster film to scout a location for, possibly China or Africa. Lotta, lotta bucks involved with this one, luv. Give me a call . . . when Crocodile Dundee rides out of the big city.'

CHAPTER 21

'Africa!' Cody hollered. 'Have you lost your mind?'

Stormy glanced at him, startled. Beautiful gray-mist morning eyes watched him warily as she moved to sit at the small breakfast table. One bare, sexy foot wrapped around the chair rung as she considered him.

'No, I haven't lost my mind. Why would going to Africa and China constitute me losing my mind?' She bit into a piece of toast before reaching for a pad on which she began scribbling notes.

'Hey.' He went over and sat at the table too, putting his hand over hers to stop her writing for a moment. 'You wouldn't actually do that, would you?'

Her brows lifted. 'Why would I actually not consider going?'

'Because you're pregnant!'

'Oh. That.' Stormy lifted his hand off of hers and continued writing. 'I would only make a preliminary trip to each location right now. Filming isn't slated for two years. After the baby is born, I could get into the project big-time.'

His jaw dropped, his stomach curdling with dread. Stormy had spent probably six months shuttling back and forth between California and Desperado while she smoothed the path for the movie deal. She could be gone for a long time – with his child. Obviously, no reasons lodged themselves under that devilish purple hair of hers of why she shouldn't leave the country for uncivilized places. Damn it! He'd already asked her to marry him. That was his only trump card to keep her from going, and she hadn't been interested in his offer.

For the first time, Cody recognized the woman sitting across the white table from him as a person with her own plan in life. One that damn well might not include him if he didn't play it straight with her. His heart began drum-like palpitations in his chest. 'Stormy, I really don't like the idea of you going to China or Africa,' he said slowly.

She looked up from the notes she was eagerly writing. 'I know. You didn't like the idea of California, either.' Nodding, her face held understanding. 'You've never been out of Texas, have you?'

'Well, once my boy scout troop crossed over the river into Arkansas, but that was at the end of the water where it was only about an inch difference between the two states.'

'You see? My parents dragged me from one end

of the country to the other for gigs. So living out of a suitcase and waking up in new places doesn't bother me. In fact, I find it invigorates my life.' She sighed, shaking her head as she patted her stomach. 'I thought I was ready to quit traveling for a while, but this is too big a deal for me to turn down. And I want my baby to have the benefit of being well-traveled. Male or female, I think it's good for a child to be broad-minded and aware of the world.'

'I know you do.' Cody bit the inside of his jaw. 'Maybe you could leave the baby with me after it's born? Don't you think that would be healthier? I mean, in China he's definitely going to eat a lot of sushi, and . . .' He trailed off, not even able to take in the notion of being separated from his child for months at a time.

'Sushi is Japanese, not Chinese. Well, maybe it would be better while the child is an infant,' Stormy conceded. 'We could agree on that. It's just that later on, I would want my child to have the benefit of traveling, especially on the studio's tab. It would be silly to pass up such opportunities.'

Cody drummed his fingers on the table. 'I guess it would.' Hell, he didn't even know what he was saying anymore. It seemed sillier to him to fly off to far-away places where millions of people crowded into strange places and ate strange food. He kept drumming. 'I don't think I've ever seen a Chinese person up close.'

326

'You're kidding.' Stormy dropped her pencil.

'Well, there aren't any in Desperado,' he said defensively. 'Is it my fault if they haven't moved to that neck of the woods?'

'No,' she said slowly, 'but guess what you're having for dinner tonight, then?'

'Chinese food?' he guessed.

'I think you'd better, and not at some trendy restaurant that happens to serve specialties like last night. There's a whole other world out there you've been missing out on.'

His brain was fried. Not only did he feel ignorant, but his sweet little lover was turning into a travel guide right before his very eyes. 'Do you have to go to China and Africa?' he asked, somewhat pleading. 'I know it sounds chauvinistic, but I'd feel a whole lot more comfortable if you'd settle down a bit.'

She came to sit in his lap, which unsettled him even more because she wore no underwear underneath the silky wrapper. 'I have to do this, Cody. I want to.'

'I know.' He was developing a massive hard-on.

'Let me tell you why this is important.' She held his face between her cool, delicate hands. 'I got addicted to prescription pills. It was a bad time in my life. I wish it had never happened, but I was lucky enough to get a second chance in this industry.'

His hard-on died. 'Addicted?' What exactly was an addiction to prescription pills?

'Addicted.' She nodded at him, her eyes very serious. 'As in, spent time drying out, imagining bugs in my hair and hooks in my skin. Shaking like a maracca.' Her chest heaved as she breathed deeply. 'It's why I wouldn't let you take me to a hospital. I just can't face the smells right now, the sterility. I'm too afraid to take anything other than maybe an aspirin. I don't ever want to fall into that hell again.'

He didn't know what to say. He'd never met anyone who was addicted to anything before. No, that wasn't true. Sloan was probably pushing the limit on alcoholism, though neither of them discussed it. But pills? It sounded so Hollywood. 'Don't you think you'd be better of coming to live in Desperado, Stormy? Maybe there's some bad influences out here in LA you should stay away from.'

She lightly tapped his head at his temple. 'You can take the pills out of the addict, Cody, but you can't take the addict out of the addiction. It's always with me, no matter where I am. I could get pills just as easily in Desperado.'

'I would keep an eye on you.'

'Yes, and you'd drive me nuts. What you are not hearing me say is that I overcame it on my own. But at that time, I was given a second chance at a job I love. If it hadn't been for Jonathan, I would never have worked in this industry again. I don't know what I'd be doing.'

'How come you let him take care of you but you won't let me?'

With a light finger, she smoothed the furrows out of his brow. 'He isn't going to be taking care of me. I realized that was what I would be doing if I married him. And he doesn't take care of me where my job is concerned. Obviously by being given this promotion, the studio thinks I'm good at what I do. I earned that, Cody. I earned it all by myself.' She looked into his eyes. 'Which is why it's so important for me to do this next project.'

He put his forehead against his tightly curled palm.

'If you tried to work in an office, would you be happy?' she asked.

'Hell, no.' But he didn't look up.

'Then can you try to relate to my feelings?'

'I'm trying.' After a moment, he looked at her. 'You know, I think when I came out here I believed that this was going to be easy. I thought we could solve this situation. I would ask you to marry me, you would say yes, and we'd live happily ever after.'

'In Desperado.'

'Yes. That's where my livelihood is.'

'I know. And my livelihood is here. But I do have down time, when I can come stay at your ranch with our child.'

He took his forehead off his palm. 'I'm really struggling with the idea of having a bi-state parental agreement, but I guess . . . there's no other way, is there?'

'I don't see it,' she said softly. 'The only thing

329

that we have in common is our baby.'

'Our baby,' he murmured. 'He's going to be so screwed up.'

'*She's* going to be just fine.' Stormy kissed him along his hairline and tugged at his braid. 'She'll have her mother's gift for adaptability.'

'But he's going to want to live on a ranch and raise steers like his father does!' Cody insisted. 'He's going to want a horse of his own, and to enter Future Farmers of America events with his live-stock. Then what'll we do?'

'I don't know.' Stormy sneaked a hand into his boxer shorts. 'It's safer in California, though, Cody. No rattlesnakes in this part of LA.'

'Hmmph.' Desire tautened the lower part of his anatomy. 'I've been meaning to talk to you about those snake teeth of mine you filched.'

'Come on back to my bed. You can talk while I do something more interesting with my mouth.'

He followed her into the bedroom where early west coast sunshine touched everything with bright light, and dove under the covers with the woman he couldn't get out of his system.

Couldn't live with her. Couldn't live without her.

An hour later, he opened his eyes, instantly rolling his head to glance at Stormy on the pillow next to him. She gazed at him through tangled burgundy hair, her lips smiling at him.

Dang but he loved waking up to this woman.

330

He rolled over to nuzzle against her neck. 'I want you again.'

She giggled huskily and ran her hand along his back. 'I like your direct approach.'

Nibbling at her ear, he said, 'I've almost gotten used to yours.'

She laughed again. 'You have not. Name one thing you like about anything to do with me. Besides my body, because that's too easy and I won't accept a cop-out.'

'I like your parents.' He trailed kisses down her neck to her shoulder.

Shaking her head with a wry smile, she stopped his descent, knowing where he'd be kissing next. 'You do not. But I give you a passing grade for trying, even if I don't believe it was an honest answer.'

'I do. Really.' One hand found the smooth rise of her rear. The soft velvet of her skin felt like heaven to his rough hands. 'They're pretty typical parents.'

'They would die to hear you say that. They've worked so hard to cultivate eccentricity.'

'Well, they are working from a natural base of it. But overall, they're just normal parents. Your mother reminded me of my mother.'

Stormy laughed out loud. 'How do you figure?'

He tucked his hand around her waist and slid her up next to him. 'She wants the best for you. She wants you to be happy, same as my mom.'

'Carmen isn't suffering from a personality warp, though.'

331

'Yeah. She is. She's off on some junket to Alaska right now. Suddenly, she doesn't want to live where she's lived all her life. She stayed with her sister for a while, then joined a tour going through Alaska. Who knows where she'll go after that?'

Stormy gazed up over her shoulder at him. 'Experiencing some new things is healthy for a person.'

'Maybe your parents would like to visit my ranch, then.' He gave her an evil grin. 'We don't have many long-haired hippie types in Desperado, but maybe they could start a trend.'

'I'd want Hera to try to fix my mother's hair, that's for certain. She must have dyed it with carrot juice or something. Bozo Orange.'

'Aw, now.' He snuggled under her ear to kiss her. 'She probably thinks your purple hair is extreme. I know I did when I met you.'

'Did you? You didn't find me attractive?'

'Well, not in the . . . um, usual sense of the word. You made me mad. You argued with me.' He bunched her hair up in his hand so he could kiss the back of her neck. 'Nothing's changed, has it?'

'Nothing except that I've fallen in love with you,' she whispered.

'I love you, too,' he repeated the words he'd said earlier. 'Why won't you marry me?'

'Because you're not in love with me. It's like you just said, you weren't attracted to me when you first met me. And nothing's changed.'

'Now, wait a minute! That is not what I said!' Cody pulled back. 'You're putting words in my mouth.'

She sat up and reached for a robe. 'But it's true, Cody. You're not in love with me. You want to marry me because of the baby. We're a responsibility.'

'I still love you,' he said stubbornly, reaching for his jeans.

'Yes, but you wouldn't be here if you hadn't thought I was pregnant. You wouldn't ask me to marry you if I wasn't having our baby.' She stared at him. 'Would you?'

'Well –' He stared at her, hung up like a sheet twisted in a clothesline. 'That's not the case, so I don't see the need to worry about it.'

'I do.' She rose from the bed. 'I'm not your dream come true, Cody. It terrifies me to think that you'll marry me because you're doing what you've always done, take care of people since your daddy died. But you might meet the woman of your dreams one day, and there I'd be. Tying you down.'

'I don't understand your brain. You want to talk about what-ifs. I want to act on what is. Let's not dwell on what might have been.'

'I don't think I can,' she said sadly. 'My parents got married because of me. They weren't ready for a child, and I was always in their way. I don't want to be in your way.' She looked at him, her eyes haunted. 'I don't know if it's a good idea to marry a renegade.'

Cody stared at her. 'Me? I'm an easy-going, always-been-in-one-place-all-my-life country boy. You're the renegade.'

'No, I'm not. I just want a normal life for my child.' She turned her back and walked through to the dining area.

'You don't even know what normal is,' he said, following her. 'If you're defining normal as average, you're not average.'

'All I know is that I'm in love with you. And you're not in love with me. It doesn't bode well for a future together.'

He shook his head at her. 'You're making this as complicated as one of Pick and Curvy's melodramas. We're having a child together. It's irrelevant how I felt about you when I met you.'

'It's relevant how you feel now. And you're not in love with me, are you, Cody?' Slowly, she forced herself to slide her gaze up to look at him.

'I'm here, aren't I?'

'Yes.' She was going to have to be satisfied with that, Stormy knew. He couldn't say what she wanted him to say because he didn't know what she wanted to hear. 'You're here.'

'Come back to Texas with me until you have to leave for China.' He slipped his arms around her. 'I need to get back to work. If you come back to Texas, you can help me vaccinate livestock.'

'Mm. Sounds like fun.' Stormy closed her eyes.

334

'We can talk some more about this being in love stuff. I've heard Hera and the ladies talk about Oprah. I know how important it is to thrash around about emotional stuff.'

She laughed. 'I'm not thrashing.'

'You are. You're trying to make a perfectly simple situation hard.'

Smacking him on the arm, she moved away. 'There's nothing simple about what's getting hard on you right now. And since that's what got us into this problem in the first place, I'm going to go take a shower.'

'Hey, wait a minute.' He caught her by the hand. 'This isn't a problem where I'm concerned. Why is it a problem?'

'Well, it is, Cody. We're going to have a baby with only one resident parent at a time, unless one of us gives up our home and our job as we know it.'

'Can't you work out of Desperado? I've got room for you to have an office in the house.'

'I could,' she said uncertainly.

'Maybe I'm not the only one who doesn't like to be uprooted.' He gave her a measuring look.

'I don't. I've been honest about that. I travel well because we never settled down, but I like having a home to return to. It's good for me to be close to the action.'

'Yeah.' He nodded. 'I know. Same with me.'

'So one of us has got to give. And you can't be away from your cattle six months of the year.'

That was true. 'No. But I still say we can work

335

this out. Let's shower.' He pulled her toward the bathroom, forcing a reluctant smile from her. 'And then I want to see what's in all those shopping bags you brought home. I never knew a woman who likes to shop as much as you do.'

'That's because there are no department stores in Desperado,' she said, allowing him to drag her.

'There are. There's the K-Mart, and the Dollar Store.' He jerked the robe off of her and lifted her under the running water with him. 'You've probably bought all you need for a while, anyway. Come back and help me vaccinate cattle until you have to leave the country.'

'All right,' Stormy said. She reached to lather him in some strategic places, and Cody forgot about cattle and department stores and not being in love.

An hour later, Stormy and Cody were dressed and sitting on the sofa gazing out the window of her apartment. She'd been quiet for the last few minutes and idly he got up to look down at the street from the balcony. Sliding the door open, he saw signs of bustling activity: People walking, cars crowding the street. He turned to Stormy with a grin, which faded quickly. She was pale and not smiling.

'What's wrong?'

'Nothing.' She shook her head limply. 'My stomach aches a little.'

Instantly, he came to sit at her side. 'I told you

336

nothing good could come of eating raw fish. You probably made yourself sick.'

'Oh, Cody.' She gave him a wan smile. 'Would you mind if I went and laid down for a second?'

'Absolutely not.' He helped her to her feet. 'Is there anything I can do?'

'No, but thanks. I'm sure I'll feel better after I lie down for a while.'

'I'll sit out here and let you rest.' He felt guilty that he'd been in bed with her as often as possible. Watching her go into the bedroom and close the door, Cody frowned. Maybe they'd made love more than was healthy for a pregnant woman, even though Stormy wasn't near her due date.

'Cody!'

He dashed into the bedroom. 'What?'

Stormy's frightened voice came from the direction of the bathroom. 'I think . . . I think I'm bleeding.'

CHAPTER 22

Cody rushed Stormy to a hospital, fear choking the breath out of him. She looked so white and strained as she clutched her middle. He prayed silently, desperately, words running around in his mind like an endless train. He helped her into the emergency room.

'My wi – I mean, my girlfriend's bleeding,' he stated urgently to the nurse at the desk. 'We're afraid something might be wrong with the baby.'

'How far along is she?' The sour-faced nurse glanced over the desk at Stormy.

'About six months.' He wished the woman would just take Stormy back so she could see a doctor. 'Maybe seven.' For his life, he couldn't remember.

'Seven,' Stormy said on a moan.

'Fill out this form, and this one, and sign down here.'

Cody stared at the clipboard he was given. His son's life could be in danger. He leaned over the desk. 'She's bleeding! She needs to see a doctor.

338

There's two lives at stake here, hers and the baby's. If I have to, I'll go back and –'

'Sir!' the nurse snapped. 'I understand the urgency. I will take her back, and you can sit and fill out the paperwork for her. That's how this ER works.'

'Fine.' His gaze flicked to Stormy. Her arms were crossed tight against her mid-section. 'Please hurry.'

The nurse's face softened a bit. 'I could go faster without these delays,' she said sternly, but not nearly as much as before.

He was left alone with the papers and his foreboding. Stormy hated hospitals with a passion. Wouldn't go near one.

Hadn't made a whimper of protest when he'd said he was bringing her here. She had to be awfully frightened for the baby's sake. He sat down heavily in a vinyl chair and closed his eyes. And prayed.

Two hours later, the doctor came out to get him, his face sad and sympathetic. 'Your girlfriend had a miscarriage, Mr Aguillar.'

A cold fist of denial hit Cody. 'Can't you do anything?'

'We tried.' The doctor shook his head. 'Unfortunately, you and Miss Nixon have different Rh factors in your blood. Had her gynaecologist known of this, no doubt an injection of rhogam would have been advised. She should have been fine with this first pregnancy, but the fact that she'd had a blood transfusion at one point in her life complicated the situation.'

Cody's brain tried to hang onto what he was hearing. 'I don't understand all the medical terminology. Is Stormy going to be okay?'

'She'll be fine. We've given her something so she'll sleep. She's quite distraught because she had to go through an actual labor process.'

'You gave her something so she'd sleep?' Cody's eyes glinted hard at the doctor. 'Did she know that?'

'She was aware we were giving her medication. Is there a problem?' The physician eyed Cody cautiously. 'She didn't indicate one.'

'I'm not sure,' Cody murmured. 'Are you positive she's going to lose the baby?' He couldn't accept that the child was gone. He would never hold his baby. His heart tore apart with agonizing denial and crushing disappointment.

The doctor's dark eyes softened with commiseration. 'Miss Nixon had lost a lot of blood, Mr Aguillar. And the fetus was aborting. I'm sorry.' He put a hand on Cody's arm. 'We've given her a rhogam shot so that future pregnancies . . .' He trailed off at the look of anguish Code sent him. 'Why don't you go home and try to get some rest? Miss Nixon was almost asleep when I came out here to talk to you.'

'No. I need to see her.' Cody headed toward the double doors of the emergency room, not waiting for the doctor to advise him differently.

340

'The last door on the left,' the doctor instructed.

Cody went in the room, his heart clenching at the sight of Stormy's pale face. She turned toward him, her face drawn, her eyes sleepy.

'Cody,' she said weakly.

'I'm here.' He grasped her hand and hung on.

'I lost the baby.'

Her mist-violet eyes stared up at him in frantic despair. He hated the helplessness that trapped him. He could do nothing to help her – and he would have given anything to be able to. 'I know.' He patted her hand which clutched tight to his other wrist. 'I'm so sorry, Stormy.'

'No. I'm sorry.' Tears began streaking down her cheeks. 'It's all my fault.'

'Shh. No, Stormy. It's nobody's fault.'

'It is my fault. The baby knew I was afraid of it.'

'Every new parent experiences that same feeling, I'm sure. It's normal. I was scared, too. But the baby knew you would love it, honey.'

She shook her head, wiping at tears that couldn't stop. 'It didn't want to come to a mother who wouldn't appreciate it. I was trying, but I . . . I didn't know how. I think the baby knew I wasn't doing everything I could to make it healthy.'

'Stormy –' Cody began, to try to check the flow of her frantic words.

'I told my obstetrician we had compatible blood types.'

Chills prickled along the back of Cody's neck. 'Why?'

'I assumed we did!' She was crying so hard now that Cody handed her a tissue with one hand and pulled a chair over with his boot so he could sit next to her. 'I'm O +. It never occurred to me that you'd be in the minority of the population with a negative factor. And we weren't together enough . . .'

She held her hands up to her eyes, rubbing them with the tissue.

'Oh, no,' Cody murmured. She hadn't wanted him to know about the baby, so she'd made an assumption on something that had jeopardized her pregnancy. It had been a hell of a gamble. 'I'm A –,' he said pointlessly, since the information couldn't help them now.

Her head lolled back against the flat hospital pillow. 'I'm so tired,' she whispered. 'I feel so old.'

He leaned over to kiss her temple. 'Your system's shocked, Stormy. You're overwhelmed. You're going to be tired for a while. And the doctor gave you a sedative.'

'A sedative?' She opened her eyes briefly to stare at him. 'No wonder I feel so heavy. I feel so . . .'

Her voice trailed off. Cody realized she'd fallen asleep. He reached to hold her hand, gently rubbing her skin with his fingers. A tear gathered in one eye and then the other, finally working down his cheeks. He wouldn't have allowed himself to cry in front of Stormy. She needed his strength today. But he couldn't help feeling sorry for her and for himself. They'd lost a child. He'd looked forward to holding the baby. Once he'd learned of the pregnancy, anticipation had begun building inside him. He'd daydreamed about being out working, daydreamed about teaching his work to his child, about buying first boots and a hat for his baby.

Cody pressed a palm against his eyes to try to stop the flow. He had wanted this baby very much. It didn't matter that he hadn't thought he was ready to be a father. He'd wanted the child Stormy had been growing inside her.

Come back, baby, his mind cried. Absolute grief and heartache tore through him as he stared at Stormy's transclucent skin, her very still features. There wouldn't be another one, he knew suddenly. This baby was the emotional glue that had bonded them together. She was going to some faraway place, and he would head back to the ranch alone. There would be no happy ending.

'Stormy,' he murmured, though he knew she couldn't hear, 'we should have taken better care of each other.'

When Stormy awoke, grogginess kept her from fully opening her eyes. The weighed-down sensation didn't stop her from remembering she'd lost her baby. *Oh, no*, she thought, fresh tears welling up behind her eyes. *Why didn't I do this right? Why didn't I just tell Cody in the beginning? I'd still have my baby. I'd still have Cody.*

The pressure of his hand on hers told her he was still beside her. She refused to allow her eyes to open and see the remorse that would be on his face. The cadence of his voice had changed when she told him that she'd assured the doctor their Rh factors were the same. Louder than a thunderclap, she'd heard the horror in his voice. He hadn't said an accusatory word, but she knew. Flaky, wacky, loony were words that came to mind. She'd heard the same tone when she'd told him the truth about the baby. Irresponsible.

Maybe it was true. Certainly she had never dreamed of the consequences or she would have told Cody immediately about the baby. But people had been having babies for hundreds of years! What had they done before rhogam had been invented? How could she possibly have known of this problem?

Remorse forced her to keep her eyes closed. She couldn't bear to see him. She pretended she was asleep and hoped he would go away. Cody had offered to marry her because of the baby.

The baby was gone, and she was pretty certain the marriage proposal was, too. She'd killed the only link between them.

In his voice, she'd heard the death of his love for her. She wanted to cry for that, too. It was all so sad. It was so sad that she had done something so dumb. She had nobody to blame but herself for losing everything she'd wanted.

'I think you'd better come to the hospital,' Cody told Sun over the phone. 'Stormy doesn't seem to be responding the way the doctor thinks she should. I don't know if it's the medication they gave her, or depression. But maybe having her mother would help.' Someone who knows her better than me, he was forced to add silently. The vibrant woman he'd known was only a pale remnant of herself. She wouldn't look at him. When she opened her eyes, she merely looked out the hospital room window. Her once-vibrant hair lay limply on the pillow, no longer alight with shine and fire. Without her saying it, he knew she was avoiding him. She didn't want him there any longer. The baby had brought them together. Its loss was tearing them apart.

'I can come,' Sun said. 'You don't think they'll check her out today at all?'

'No. The doctor is concerned that something else is bothering her. She's just . . . not Stormy.' It was hard to explain, but he felt strongly it had to do with her heart. She'd been so looking forward to the baby. The old fighting spirit had been strong within her, to the point that she'd planned on taking the baby to Africa with her.

She was grieving, and Cody didn't think anything the hospital recommended was going to help her. Health-wise, maybe, but emotionally, Stormy needed to lean on someone.

She seemed damned determined not to lean on him.

'Moon and I will be right down, Cody.' Sun hung up the phone.

Cody stared at the black receiver in his hand and sighed. He glanced over at the sleeping woman in the hospital bed, his eyes automatically shying away from the intravenous tube in her arm. One thing was for certain, the pills they had given Stormy for sleeping seemed to have an adverse affect. Instead of sleeping peacefully, she thrashed and moaned in her sleep. He wondered if she had told them anything of her medical altercation with prescription pills.

Clasping his hands tightly together in fists, Cody decided the next time Stormy awakened, he was going to ask her about that. She hadn't been interested in speaking to him, or much of anybody, but it was high time he got the truth out of her. If she hadn't made the doctor aware of her problem with drugs, then he would, patient-doctor privilege notwithstanding. All the fight had gone out of the woman he knew to be a renegade, a stand-on-her-own lady. What he feared more than anything was that the will to fight an addiction to painkillers might have also gone out of Stormy, as long as she was suffering over the baby she'd lost.

'Mother, you've got to get him to leave!' Stormy said urgently, as soon as Cody went down the hall to get a soda. 'I'm fine! He watches over me like a hawk and it's driving me crazy!'

Sun eyed her, orange-puffed hair aflame. 'He seems to think you need watching.'

'I don't! I'm just sleeping a lot. But it's hard

346

to rest knowing he's here watching my every move!'

'He's worried about you. I should think you'd find that reassuring. Once upon a time, you said you didn't think he cared about you enough to marry you. Now you know he does.'

'You don't understand. I'm a responsibility now. He'll stay here until he knows I've recovered. Cody is a natural-born protector. But . . . I killed his baby with my selfishness.' Stormy sighed deeply, her heart tearing in two. 'I can tell you that it's over between us. He won't tell you that, or me, right now. Not while he's shouldering this burden. But it's over. It goes against a protector's instincts when someone kills something they love.'

'Stormy, aren't you leaving Cody out of this scenario? Shouldn't you ask him how he feels? Give him a chance to say his feelings have changed, if they have?' Sun's pencilled eyebrows soared.

'I can't bear to hear him say he doesn't care, Mom. But he acts different. And that tells me a lot.' She picked at the cheap hospital bedspread, too miserable to explain more.

'Honey, you're a bundle of hormones right now. You don't know what you're hearing. Everything is magnified five hundred per cent after a trauma like this. Please try not to upset yourself.' Sun reached out a comforting hand and smoothed Stormy's hair. 'Put it all on hold for now.'

'I can't. I can't bear for him to stay here any

347

longer.' Agitated, Stormy pushed herself further up on the pillow. 'He came out to California because he'd figured out about the baby. Once I confirmed it was his, he proposed. None of this would have happened if we hadn't used a condom that was past its sell-by date. Trust me, Mother, he wasn't interested in getting tied down and now that the baby is gone, there isn't any reason for him to marry me.'

On the other side of her, Moon scratched his head. 'I think you ought to listen to your mother. She's making sense to me. Why don't you just wait a while, then air all this with Cody? If he wants to make the great escape, he'll tell you.'

'I can't bear waiting for it to happen. It's awful knowing someone feels tied to you! I never wanted to be added to his list of burdens!' Unwanted tears sprang into her eyes. 'Please try to understand how desperate I feel about this. Say something, anything to him, but please get him to go back to Texas!'

'All right.' Moon patted her on the hand. 'Don't get upset like this. Mother and I will tell him something. You go to sleep now.'

'Thank you.' Stormy closed her eyes and allowed her head to fall back onto the pillow. Cody had to leave. She couldn't stand him hanging around to take care of her. He needed to go home and take care of Mary and Annie and his mother. But not her. She didn't need him to take care of her. All she wanted was for him to be in love with her – and she'd killed that dream as surely as she'd killed her baby.

Cody froze outside Stormy's hospital room. 'Say something, anything to him, but please get him to go back to Texas!' he heard her plead. He nearly dropped the soda from his hand. Never would he have guessed she felt like that! His pride burned inside him, even as he tried to rationalize why she might feel that way. She was upset. And he understood that. Maybe after more than forty-eight hours had passed, the shock of the miscarriage would wear off.

But a miscarriage ought to make a woman want her partner's support more. His fingers tightened on the aluminum can. Annie enjoyed Zach being around even more now that she was in the advanced stages of pregnancy. He'd even redesigned one of the smaller bedrooms as an office so that he wouldn't have to be away much.

Maybe that was the crux of the situation. Stormy wasn't pregnant. His eyes burned at the fresh, raw sense of realization. Possibly his presence was keeping her from dealing with the loss the way she might be able to if he left. He closed his eyes briefly, almost too embarrassed to walk into the room. Facing Sun and Moon was going to be awkward as hell now that he knew they were troubled over having to give him his walking papers.

He made up his mind at that moment. Striding

into the hospital room, Cody set the untouched soda down in front of Sun. 'Moon, could I talk to you for a minute? In the hall?'

'Sure.' Moon got to his feet, his sandals squeaking as he walked. 'What's up?' he asked, once they were outside.

'I called and checked my messages while I was in the cafeteria. Something urgent has come up with my ranch. I left a friend of mine watching over my cattle while I was gone, but with the heat and all, a few problems have surfaced. I'm going to fly back this afternoon.'

'Oh, sure, sure.' Moon nodded, his expression serious, as if he knew exactly what kind of problems Cody might be facing on a ranch. 'I understand completely.' His tone was so relieved, Cody had to remind himself that the man was a guitar player, not an actor, and hadn't prepared himself for his impromptu part.

'Is Stormy awake?' He knew she wasn't.

'Oh, no. She just . . . um, dozed off.' Moon's eyes were wide with eagerness.

Cody made himself look indecisive. 'I hate to leave without saying goodbye –'

'Oh, she'll understand.' Moon quickly waved his worries away. 'I'll tell her an emergency cropped up. Trust me, Stormy is an adaptable girl. Don't worry about her. Sun and I will stick close to her, and she'll come through this smelling like a rose.'

Stormy had learned to adapt at her parents' knees, Cody thought grimly. She'd adapted to being pregnant without him. Now obviously, she wanted to adapt to not being pregnant without him. A solo return to her life as it had been.

'Well,' he said, reaching out a hand for Moon to shake, 'thanks for everything.' He didn't know what the hell he was thanking Moon for – letting him off the hook, maybe? 'Keep in touch.'

'We will, I'm sure.' Moon nodded as he released Cody's hand. 'Don't worry about us. We're hanging tough, man.'

Cody backed away after poking his head in one last time to peer at Stormy. Her eyes were closed. She appeared to be sleeping quietly. He couldn't see Sun's face as she watched her daughter, staring down at her while she slept.

Suddenly, Cody felt like an intruder. He nodded at Moon, put his hat on his head, and strode down the hall. No baby, no woman to make his wife. He was an outlaw, riding off into the sunset.

Alone.

An hour later, Stormy opened her eyes. 'Hi,' she said to her parents.

'Hi to you.'

Sun looked so anxious that Stormy frowned. 'Is something the matter?'

'No, dear.' It looked as if Sun forced the worry from her expression. 'How do you feel?'

'Much better.' Surprisingly, she did feel a little stronger. She glanced around the room, looking for Cody's strong, watchful presence.

'Cody had to leave,' Moon said.

'Did you ask him to?' Stormy ignored the sudden shock of dismay she felt at her father's words.

'No. He'd gotten an emergency call from Texas. He had to return.'

'I see.' Stormy closed her eyes, the sweep of energy she'd been experiencing flushing back out of her body. She did see. *Just as I thought I was going to make it over this hill, I feel myself sliding back down.* Tears rushed into her eyes, but she wasn't about to let her parents see.

I just didn't want him to want to leave. I wanted it to be like the time I was sick in Desperado, and though I told him to go, he wouldn't. He stayed with me and cared for me and held me, and that's when I knew I was falling in love.

'Isn't that what you wanted, Stormy?' Sun asked.

'Yes, it is.' She opened her eyes. 'We were only together because of the baby.' Then she burst into full-blown crying she couldn't stop.

Sun and Moon leapt to comfort her, but it wasn't the same as Cody. She wanted him so much, but all the while she'd been spinning the fantasy, she'd known it would come unwound sooner or later.

And when the nurse came in a little while later with something to help her sleep, Stormy took it just so she could forget about everything a little bit longer.

CHAPTER 23

'I don't know, Cody,' Annie said, the next day while they stood around in her kitchen. Her belly was getting bigger every day, to the point where he wondered how comfortable she was, and how much further she could stretch. 'Maybe you came home too soon.'

He sighed, pushing his hat back on his head. It was a relief to unburden his soul to this woman who had known him for so long. 'I didn't know what else I could do. Stormy didn't want me there, and I thought if I left and she could be with her family, she might recover better.'

'I know.' Annie turned to stir something in a pot. 'Well, you can call her in a few days, I guess.'

'I guess.' He wasn't sure what the protocol was at this point. What could he say to a woman who had suffered the loss of her child – their child? She was experiencing so many different emotions and he wasn't sure how he fit into her feelings any more. 'I was all set to marry her.'

'Oh, Cody!' For a moment, Annie's expression

353

was shocked, then she smiled sadly as she threw her arms around his neck. 'Are you going to?' she asked, stepping back to look at him.

'That's the part that has me confused.' He turned a chair so that he could straddle it. 'It all came about because of the baby. She was having my child, so of course I was going to marry her.'

'And now?'

'Well, now there's no child.' He scratched at the back of his neck uncomfortably. 'And since she'd already told me no when she was carrying my child, it makes me kinda think the answer is a flat hell no now that . . .' He broke off his words. It was too hard to say that there was no child.

'I'm so sorry, Cody.' Annie's blue eyes sparkled with compassion and sympathy. 'I wish she'd, I mean, I don't want to sound critical of Stormy, but I do wish she'd talked to you sooner so she would have gotten proper prenatal care.' A heavy sigh escaped her. 'I feel so bad. I'd like to write her, or call her, but I guess now is not the time. There's not much I can say, except that I'm sorry.' She reached out to touch his shoulder. 'I'm sorry for both of you.'

'I know. I am, too.' He touched her hand briefly. 'Thanks.'

Annie stood before him, round and blossoming with her pregnancy, following doctor's orders and resting as she should. He thought about Stormy, heedlessly making up blood types as she went along and planning trips to foreign countries and he felt a sad anger stir within him. She should have known better. But that was the same way he'd felt about her in the beginning. She was headstrong and impulsive. Trying so hard to be independent that she actually caused herself problems by not leaning on anyone else.

He loved her. He wanted her to lean on him.

'Well,' he said conversationally, so the heartache wouldn't be revealed in his voice, 'guess I'll mosey on home.'

'Sure you won't stay for supper? I've got plenty extra.'

He shook his head, his boots loud on the tile floor as he left the kitchen. 'No, thanks. I've bent your ear long enough. Tell Zach 'hi' for me.'

'I will.' Annie walked out on to the porch behind him.

Turning, he suddenly stared at Annie, remembering that he hadn't inquired about his niece. The miscarriage had bothered him so much he'd needed to talk to someone who would listen and understand his sorrow. 'Where's Mary?'

'Over at a friend's house. She missed you while you were gone.'

'She still got the acting bug?'

'A little. Mostly she talks about the new baby sister who's on the way.'

That caught his attention. 'Girl, huh?'

'Yes.' Annie's smile was radiant.

'Well. Bet that did tickle Mary.'

'Yes. She said her uncle would have another little girl to spoil.'

Quick stinging tears jumped into his eyes. 'Sounds good to me.' *But I won't have my own child to spoil, much as I'll love this new niece of mine.*

'You know how much Mary loves her favorite uncle.'

'Only uncle,' he said gruffly, getting into his truck. 'Even though I wouldn't take her to California?'

Annie laughed. 'Mary doesn't hold a grudge. I think she decided she needed to finish out this school year and then she'd hound you again about going.'

He started the engine. 'A lot can happen between now and then. I could change my mind. Could be I don't.' Wiping his chin thoughtfully against his shoulder, he said, 'You know, I just can't see her parading around in Hollywood, wearing a bunch of make-up, and playing make-believe.'

'You just don't want her to.' Annie reached in the window to playfully pull his hat down over his eyes. 'To retain favored uncle status, you may have to be a little more broad-minded.'

Pushing his hat back up, he stared at her belligerently.

'Or maybe not.' Annie shook her head at his stubbornness. 'Cody Aguillar, you can't keep her a child forever.'

'You're her mother. You're supposed to.'

356

'Do you realize I married your brother when I was only a few years older than Mary?' Annie's expression turned serious.

The cold water of forgotten memories washed over him. 'I'd forgotten that,' he whispered. His brother had just finished high school. They'd been a young couple. Carlos had married Annie and immediately started working her farm, trying to bring it around, even though he'd always been more of a student than a sodbuster. As a younger brother, Cody had wondered why his brother, the person he looked up to with admiring, proud eyes, didn't continue with his scholarship to pursue a dream he loved. Instead, he'd turned to making a success out of a dusty, hundred-acre, barely productive farm.

He'd done it because he'd fallen in love with Annie. And Cody knew that Carlos had never looked back on his decision. A tractor might have ended his life, but Cody knew that if his big brother were here today, he would tell him that he would do it all over again the same way. And if Carlos could give him the advice he'd been looking to Annie for, his brother would say that being in love took some changing. Maybe going in a different direction than he'd planned on.

Overhead, the clouds parted and the sun beamed down directly on the front of his truck. Cody ignored the chill-bumps sticking up on his skin. 'Well, I'm not ready to get Mary married off yet,' he replied.

357

'I know you're not. I'm just saying that she's growing up. One day, we're going to have to let her go.'

He nodded briskly and put the truck in reverse. He'd let Stormy go, and he hoped that was the right thing to do. He wasn't sure. 'Have ladybug call me when she gets home.'

'Why?'

'Because I want to tell her that I missed my girl while I was gone. And that maybe, just maybe, but I'm not making any promises – and if she makes good grades all year and doesn't get into any scrapes *and* keeps being such a help to her mom – I might, hear me, *might*, be persuaded to take her to California to have a look-see on some . . . some of those audition things.'

'Oh, Cody.' Annie leaned in the window to give him a quick kiss on the cheek. 'You are a good man.'

'Yeah, well. You'll be busy with the new baby, and – heck. I can't believe I'm actually saying I might willingly take my niece to the land of make-believe.

She laughed. 'This will elevate you to sainthood as far as Mary's concerned.'

'I'm no saint.' He shook his head and began backing the truck down the dirt road. 'But if Mary's got this dream she think she's just got to go after, then I'd better see what I can do to help.' He touched a finger to his hat and drove off quickly, before the tears he felt building at the

358

back of his eyes could spill. It was the least he could do for his brother's child. Carlos had known about dreams, and if his daughter had one, then it was up to Cody to help her. He sighed, his heart bruised and sore, his emotions as dry as an overworked well. He hadn't known he had a dream – until he'd lost his baby.

The price of losing a dream was a pain he didn't want his niece to suffer. She'd already lost enough when her father died.

My brother. I loved my brother more than anything. I didn't know he'd been gone so long. Fresh tears pressured Cody's eyes, though he refused to release them.

And now my own child is gone.

Stormy sat in her dark apartment alone. She'd sent her parents home and pulled the curtains so the sun couldn't bring its light inside. It was almost too much to bear, losing everything at once. And she had no one to blame but herself. She had some pills for anxiety the doctor had given her, with a referral to a psychiatrist he wanted her to see, as well as her regular obstetrician for a follow-up examination. The hospital physician had been seriously concerned about depression overtaking her.

She blinked away tears, then allowed herself to weep unashamedly. There was no one here to see, after all. She was completely on her own now.

She wanted a pill. It would be best to take one,

so that she could sleep. If she was unconscious, she wouldn't have to suffer. She thought about Rip Van Winkle, who'd slept for so many years that when he awakened everything had changed. It was a tantalizing picture. Could she out-sleep the pain? Would she wake up refreshed and full of vitality, instead of feeling this terrifyingly empty sensation that filled every part of her body and made her so tired? So unable to fight?

Maybe a hot bath to soothe her. Or maybe a cool shower to wake her up.

She was too overwhelmed to make a decision. Clutching a tissue, she fell asleep on the sofa, her body curled into a tight ball of misery.

'Stormy! Stormy!'

She forced her eyes open at the sound of Jonathan's voice outside her apartment door. 'Just a minute!' she called. With one hand, she pushed her hair out of her eyes and went to let him in.

'Are you all right?' He took in her disheveled appearance at a glance as he walked inside. 'I've been trying to call you for hours.'

Perplexed, she glanced at the phone. 'I didn't hear the phone ring.' It was in its usual place in the small den.

He checked to see if the ringer was on. 'Maybe I dialed the wrong number.'

Of course he hadn't. Jonathan had known her phone number by memory for years. Stormy nodded at his attempt at an explanation and sat down on the sofa, gesturing for him to take one of the stuffed chairs.

'Well, I just wanted to make sure you're all right.' He stared at her uncomfortably. 'I'm sorry about the baby, Stormy. Your folks told me what happened.'

She shook her head. 'I'm sorry, too. I wish I hadn't been so irresponsible about my pregnancy. I wish I . . .' Her voice trailed off. It wasn't right to say that she wished she'd told Cody from the beginning. 'Hadn't lost the baby,' she finished, and glanced away from Jonathan.

He leaned back in the chair, obviously trying to make himself comfortable when he wasn't. Stormy knew she looked like a mess, but she didn't care. It was too difficult to worry about anything. All she could think about was how much she'd fouled up her life. And how she had lost any chance of Cody loving her by trying so hard to make sure he loved her by the standards she'd set. Her stubbornness had cost them both.

'Where's all that stuff you bought?' Jonathan glanced around the room.

The packages and bags that Cody and she had heaped on the floor were gone. She had not even looked for them because she knew seeing the baby clothes would make her start crying again. Astonished, Stormy got to her feet. 'They were here when I . . . went to the hospital.' She hadn't put anything away, preferring to spend her time with Cody making love. Her heart tightened at the

361

memory of their moments together. It had felt so right being with him.

On the kitchen bar she found a note written in Cody's strong hand. 'Dear Stormy, I took the baby things back to the store and returned them on your credit card. I hope you won't mind, but I didn't want you to have to do it. Cody.'

She glanced over the note at Jonathan, her eyes wide with unshed, sudden tears. She'd never met a man who tried to protect her the way Cody did. Jonathan was a wonderful friend, his love for her fatherly. He didn't have the emotional connection to see inside her heart the way Cody did. For the first time, Stormy became totally aware of his feelings for her. It was true that actions spoke louder than words. Cody might not express his emotions the way she felt she had to hear them, but he'd been strongly committed to her and the baby.

'Nice of him,' Jonathan said.

'It was,' Stormy agreed softly. 'I probably wouldn't have taken anything back. It would have made me miserable to do it. I'm sure that I would have just buried everything in a dark closet and never opened it again.'

'Jeez, Stormy.' Jonathan wiped a hand across his face, his expression worried and sincere. 'I'm damn sorry.'

'I am, too,' she whispered. *Sorry that I'm figuring out what matters most too late.*

* * *

At the sound of a key in the lock that evening, Cody straightened, listening. The sound of feet being wiped on the mat outside reached him, and immediately, he knew who was on the porch. Going to the door, he threw it open. 'Ma.'

'Hello, son. Get my bags, please.'

And that was all she said as she bustled past him. Cody grinned at her retreating back. 'Good to see you, Ma.'

'I know. Get my bags. I think it's going to rain.'

He went outside and scooped up the suitcases beside a waiting taxi cab. 'Do you need to be paid?' he asked the driver.

'Nah. She paid me. I just wanted to make sure she got in safely.' The driver smiled cheerfully at him. 'She's a character.'

'She is that.' His mother would take that as a compliment.

'Couldn't say enough about ya.' He put the cab in reverse. 'Said you was her only child, and she sure was glad of ya, even if you were too stubborn.' The driver waved and took off, leaving Cody standing there with a heavy heart. He was her only child, now. She'd been proud of Carlos, too. Carlos had been so good at everything, a natural. Cody had fought his way over the stumbling blocks of life. It felt good to know his mother was proud of him, even if at one time he'd thought she might have been happier if it had been he who had been taken by death rather than Carlos. Of course, that was a worry that swept the mind of anyone who was left behind. At the time, he had prayed to God to take him instead of Carlos to make his mother happy. He wasn't sure if she could bear losing her husband and her favorite son, to be left with only him for comfort.

As an adult, he knew that fate didn't deal in the business of bargaining chips. Still, in his heart he knew that if he could have done it, he would have given his life for the life of the child Stormy had lost. He would have done that for her.

'Get in out of the rain, son!' Carmen bellowed. 'My suitcases are getting wet!'

But it was him she threw a towel over when he went inside. He hadn't even noticed it had started raining. Nor had he realized his face was wet with tears.

He put the suitcase down and scrubbed himself dry with the towel.

'Anything changed around here?' Carmen demanded, going into the kitchen.

'No.' He could say that much had changed in his life, but he wouldn't be able to tell the story.

'I don't know if me leaving did much good, then.'

'What do you mean?' Cody followed her into the kitchen, eyeing his petite mother curiously.

'Thought you needed me out of the house. Wanted to give you some breathing space to live on your own.' She gave him a frank look with her dark eyes. 'I'm worried that you stay single because I live with you.'

'No.' He shook his head. 'That's not why.'

'Hmmph.' His mother poured him a drink of iced tea. 'What happened to Stormy?'

'She went home.' Sitting down, he kept his gaze away from hers.

'For good?' she demanded.

'Yes.'

'*Por que?*' Her hands were on her hips.

'Because the movie was finished and her home is in California.'

'*Y su corazón?* Her heart? Where is it supposed to live?'

He sighed heavily. 'I don't know, Ma.'

'I know. Me, I know. I told her I would not make a good mother-in-law. She understands this. But she doesn't care. For you, she cares.'

'Ma, how was your trip to Alaska?' he asked to change the subject.

'All the places I saw were beautiful. I have pictures to show you. I want to know why you are sitting on the fence, afraid to get down like a little boy.'

'Ma!' Cody got to his feet. 'I'm not talking about this any more.'

'Hmmph.' Carmen gave him a pensive stare. 'Annie told me about the baby. I'm sorry for you, and for Stormy.'

'Annie told you?' He should have known soft-hearted Annie would have told his mother. She would be worried about him.

'*Si.* So I came home.' Pointing a gnarly finger

365

his way she said, 'I think for once in your life you are very scared.'

He stared at her out of half-closed eyes.

'You were scared when your father died, and when your brother died. I know.' She waved her hand. 'But you are a man now. And you are afraid of loving this woman because you'll have to lose the, the –' she broke off as she struggled for the word '– the outside hardness. No. That is not it. The shell.'

'Okay, Ma.' He walked out of the room.

'You say, okay, Ma, but you don't listen. I know why you don't listen.'

'Why, Ma?' He turned to face her out of respect, not because he wanted to hear what she had to say.

'You don't want to care so much for one person again.' She walked up and hugged him tightly, as she had when he was a child, only now she barely reached his chest. 'Cody, care. Otherwise, you are not living.' She patted his face and moved away. 'You think about what I say.'

'I will,' he promised. She went into the kitchen again, and Cody rubbed at his eyes. His throat felt raw and burning. The taxi driver had summed her up in one word. Carmen was a character. Like Stormy.

'It's good to have you back, Ma,' he suddenly called toward the kitchen, not out of respect or obligation but because he meant it more than anything.

'I know,' she hollered back. 'It is always good to be where the heart is.'

In her darkened apartment, Stormy rolled over and groaned. Eventually, she had to open the blinds. Maybe even turn on the TV. Go for a walk. Never in her life had she been so over-whelmingly tired and depressed. All it seemed she could do was either sit on the bed and cry, or walk out to the living room to sit on the sofa with tears streaming down her cheeks. And sleep. She slept most of the time to keep from thinking about the baby. To keep from thinking about Cody.

Forcing herself to sit up, Stormy pawed her hair back. She took a sip of water from the glass on her nightstand and rearranged the gown she'd been sleeping in for two days. The silence in her room was deafening, the darkness suffocating. As if trained, her hand reached for the small bottle of pills beside the glass of water. Suddenly, she realized it had been at least two days since she'd put anything nourishing in her body. She slept, she cried, and when it got too painful, she washed down a pill.

She was dying. This dark, closed-up apartment had become her shell and she was inside it, shriveling into non-existence. A memory, beckon-ing like a too-intense light beam, flashed its painful presence into her mind. She was sitting cross-legged on the floor in a small room, listening to

367

people walk in the halls outside. Occasionally, they would bring her something to eat. Something to drink. Make certain she didn't have anything she could use to harm herself. They were trying to make her well, but she knew she had to heal herself so that she could get out of there.

Instantly, she knew she was at a crossroads, a defining moment in her life. She had to heal herself, this time for good, or she'd always exist addicted. Which was not living at all.

She would be dead inside. Slowly, she put the pill bottle back on the table and pushed herself out of bed. Throwing open the curtains in her bedroom, she looked down on the busy street below. The cars hurried, the people hurried, but Stormy took a slow, deep breath. 'If I ever have the chance at love again, I am going to allow myself to depend on that person, to lean on them if necessary. I will never again lose someone because I tried to fit their love to what I thought it should be.'

The promise she made to herself brought strength flowing into her soul. It would be hard to give up even a small part of the control she desperately held over her own life, but until she did, she would always be the shy, uncertain child of counter-culture, drug-taking parents. They had changed. She had not.

Now she had to, or she would never be truly well.

That evening, Cody went down to the sheriff's office to find Sloan. He and the codgers were sitting in the dimly lit room playing a three-handed game of hearts.

'Looking for a fourth?' Cody asked.

'Be helpful.' Sloan barely looked up at him as Cody seated himself on an old wooden chair. 'Where the hell have you been?'

'Finding myself in California. Isn't that the popular thing to do?' He didn't want to answer any questions, so he gave a flip answer and hoped that would satisfy his friend.

'Still look lost to me,' Pick said.

'Nah. Not lost,' Curvy argued. 'He looks like his horse walked on him. Something happen out there while you was locating yourself?'

'No.' Cody shook his head and looked at the hand he'd been dealt.

'Well, did you do anything?' Sloan asked. 'Please tell me you at least went surfing or something. Did you at least unwind that braid of yours a little?'

'You guys get off of me,' Cody told them all sincerely. 'I came down here for a little R and R.' He threw down another card, beating the others, and pulled the pile to his side. 'What's been happening in my absence?'

'Not a damn thing as usual.' Sloan pressed his lips together. 'No excitement without you around.'

'Right. I'm always the life of the party.' He pulled in another round of cards. 'Did Wrong-Way ever return?'

'Hell, no. Hera's still on the warpath, too, so I

369

recommend you stay away from her shop. She's liable to do something drastic to anyone who says the *wrong* thing to her. Hahaha.' Sloan looked at Cody's unsmiling face. 'Guess that wasn't very funny.'

'No. It wasn't.' He shook his head.

Sloan sighed deeply. 'I think she's feeling scorned.'

'What does she see in him?' Cody picked up the three cards his beat.

'Who knows?' Pick eyed the growing pile in front of Cody unhappily. 'Who can explain why and when love hits?'

'Not me. I didn't understand it when it hit me and I hope to hell it never does again,' Sloan said.

'How come you're dating those sassy little sisters of Tate's then?' Curvy demanded.

The sheriff shrugged. 'For fun. To have somebody to go out with when I want to see a movie.'

'You can take us. We'll go with ya,' Pick offered.

'Thanks, but I like to look at something pretty after a hard week at the office.' Sloan pulled in a round of cards. 'It's nothing serious, and they know that.'

'Who knows what?' Cody realized he'd missed something in the conversation. His mind had been caught by the mention of movies, which had necessarily made him think of Stormy.

'The twins know it's nothing serious.' Sloan picked up all the cards and reshuffled the deck. 'I take one out one week, and the other the next

370

week. It's a very simplified arrangement.'

'Sounds complicated to me.' Cody looked his friend over steadily.

'Nope. I invited you to come with me on a date with the twins, remember? Well, I knew you weren't ever going to be available, and I wasn't in the mood to pass up pretty women – despite their relationship to Tate – so I happened upon this deal. The women were very supportive of it.' He grinned. 'They like knowing that each of them gets a turn every other Friday night.'

'What do you mean, I wasn't ever going to be available?' Cody glowered at him. Sloan stopped shuffling. Pick and Curvy stared with rapt interest.

'Well, you . . . you know,' Sloan said uncomfortably. 'If you gave up and went out to California, Stormy's got you pretty well tied down.'

Cody bit the inside of his jaw. The three men stared at him.

'We couldn't work things out,' he finally confided to his three friends.

Sloan set the pack of cards down. 'Are you sure?'

'It wasn't meant to be from the start, I guess. We're too far apart. Our lifestyles are too different,' he said heavily.

'There's a child's future to think about,' Pick intoned.

Anguish tore through Cody, but he stared at his fingernails as he said, 'She lost the baby.'

'Ah, hell,' Sloan said. 'I'm sorry, Cody.'

He couldn't say that he was, too, because he was

afraid he'd start crying. Tears stuck at his eyes, blinding him, and finally, he got up and left his friends sitting in the office.

The three men sat silently watching the big man leave.

'Guess I'll mosey outside and make sure he gets to his truck.' Pick got slowly to his feet.

'He'll be fine, mother-hen,' Curvy said, getting to his feet too. He went to the doorway. 'Goodnight, Sloan.' Impatient with Pick's slow gait, he snapped, 'C'mon, slowpoke! What's taking you so long? We'll never catch up to him with you moving like a turtle!'

'I'm coming, I'm coming,' Pick said placidly. He reached out a hand to his friend, who helped him move out of the office and down the hall.

That left Sloan sitting by himself in the near-darkness. He sighed heavily, his heart sad for his friend and his loss. Pursing his lips, he leaned back in the chair for a moment, his hands clasped behind his neck. Losing someone you loved was the hardest thing that could ever happen to a man. Admitting a relationship wasn't going to work out was a sonofabitch. Saying goodbye to it was the pits.

Without wanting to, knowing it was going to hurt, Sloan reached to unlock the bottom drawer of his desk. He pulled out a picture frame, which showed him and his wife smiling, dizzily in love. Damn, but Celia Wintergreen was the most beautiful woman he'd ever laid eyes on. Sweet, sweet.

He knew exactly why Cody was hurting so bad. Unfortunately, he couldn't tell him any way to make it better. It had been so many years since Celia had left.

Yet every day of his life, he still thought about her.

CHAPTER 24

Four weeks later, Cody rode along his fences, noting repairs that needed to be made. A few things had to be done, such as buying hay and other supplies to get the ranch through the winter in good condition. All in all, they had survived another summer pretty well. He felt lucky that he'd been able to stay on the profitable side of the business. Some of the farmers and cattlemen he'd talked to had put up a good struggle, but the heat had simply beat everybody down for a second summer in a row.

Surely, next summer would be better. Hopefully, the winter would be fairly mild as well. Cody eased back in the saddle, realizing that these were the same thoughts he had every year about this time. Only, this year, he felt different. The building anticipation and sense of securing the ranch for the winter was missing. The usual pride in his achievements and the ready-to-fight spirit hadn't come to him. But it was only November. The feeling of just tending to the ranch as a chore and moving through the motions would clear up soon enough, like sunshine breaking through a cloudy day. All the excitement and chaos of having the movie set on his land had been new and different. It was probably natural to feel that life as he'd always known it was routine now.

He pulled the horse around suddenly, deciding that enough was enough. If he was ever going to get past this curious, detached feeling about his life, he had to call Stormy. He had to prove to himself that there was nothing between them. Talking to her would be difficult, but he would face it. Then he could return to normal. The way his life had been before Stormy.

Inside the house, he dialed her number, still remembering it without a hitch. Impatiently, he waited for her to answer, but the number just rang and rang. Suddenly, the line clicked on, and his heart soared.

'Hello?' a male voice said.

Caught off guard, Cody hesitated.

'Hello?' the man demanded.

'This is Cody Aguillar,' he said, 'I'd like to speak to Stormy Nixon if she's available.'

'I'm afraid she's not.'

Cody's insides turned clammy at the terse reply. He knew exactly who the man answering her phone was: the guy who wanted to marry her. Obviously, she wasn't waiting for Cody to call her.

'As much as this is none of my business, I'm going to tell you something,' the man said.

Here it goes, Cody thought. Stormy doesn't want me calling her anymore. 'Shoot,' he said briskly.

'Stormy has left for Africa. She's got some sites she's planning to look over. Tonight, she's staying with her folks so they could take her to the airport. I happen to know that they've gone out to dinner, so you probably can't catch them. But if it were to be of interest to you, her plane is connecting through Dallas some time tomorrow. If you're interested in speaking to her, they might be able to get a message to her.'

Cody listened disbelievingly to the advice he was receiving. 'I'll keep it in mind. Thanks.'

'No problem.'

The phone went dead in his hand. His jaw sagged. Stormy would be in Texas soon. He might be able to get hold of her, if he wanted to. He could hear her voice in Texas, so much closer than California.

Or he could just let her go about her business, relieved that obviously she had recovered just fine without him.

'Hi, Uncle Cody!' Mary cried, running toward him.

'Hey, ladybug!' He swept her up in a giant hug. 'What are you doing over here?'

'Grandma brought me over. She said she needed a night with me since she hadn't seen me in so long.' Mary stared at him solemnly as he set her

376

down. 'She says I've grown up on her.'

'You have.' He nodded, reaching out to ruffle her hair just to assure himself that she was still his little girl. 'It scares me.'

'It shouldn't.' She wrapped her arm about his waist and walked with him up onto the porch where they both sat down. 'Unless you're afraid you're getting old.'

He grinned at her saucy expression, his spirits lifting immediately despite his earlier conversation with Sloan. Mary was the child of his heart. They had their ups and downs, but she would always hold a place in his soul no one else ever could. I see my brother in her, he thought. 'Watch your mouth, young lady. Age doesn't matter except to teenagers, for some reason.'

She laughed at him. 'Don't be so grumpy.' Laying her head on his shoulder, she said, 'I've come to a decision, Uncle Cody.'

'Oh, boy. I can't wait,' he replied, his tone dry.

'Grumpy, grumpy,' she teased. 'What would you say if I told you I've decided I'm not ready to go to California to audition for movies and commercials and stuff?'

'Hallelujah?'

'No, really.'

Seeing her smile and the absolute serenity in her eyes, he shrugged. 'Why'd you change your mind?'

'I don't know.' With the whimsical attitude of a teenager, she flipped her hair airily. 'I'm not ready. I've made a lot of friends at school. My new baby is

arriving soon, and I want to be able to help Mom.'
She gave him a huge kiss on the cheek. 'You'd miss
me if I became a big star.'

'I would.' He meant it.

'So there's always next year. Maybe you can take
me in the summer. If you would.' She gave him a
sidelong look.

'I will.' It was a promise and they both knew it.

'Uncle Cody,' she said suddenly, 'I never had a
chance to tell you thanks about coming to my
rescue after Sam –'

'Don't. Please, ladybug.' He shook his head, his
expression serious, and put his arm around her
shoulders. 'I couldn't bear it if anything ever – let's
not talk about this.' He took a deep breath, unable
to remember how close he could have come to
losing his beloved niece. 'I am proud of your
bravery. You were very level-headed.'

'Thanks.' She tugged at his braid. 'Has Sloan
told you what happened to –'

'Don't say his name,' he said sternly. 'Sloan
didn't mention it.'

'He's in jail down south of here. Apparently, he
was wanted for a bunch of junk and after you
slowed him down and Sloan put him in jail and
ran his records, the police had time to catch up
with him.'

'I'm glad. Change the subject.' He couldn't bear
to think about it any more.

'Well, I love you.'

He glanced down in surprise. 'I love you, too. I

378

always will. You're the best thing that ever happened to me.'

Carmen came out on the porch and sat in a rocker behind them. She lit up a cigar, handing Cody one over his shoulder. 'Thanks, Ma. I've missed having an occasional smoke with you.'

'Can I have one, Uncle Cody?'

'Hell, no.'

She laughed out loud. 'Can I cuss, Uncle Cody?'

'No, you can't cuss or smoke or anything except be my ladybug.'

He lightly pinched her sides to tickle her, and she squealed with delight. Then they sat silently for a while, the three of them enjoying the fall of evening and humming dragonflies and the even circle of a red-tailed hawk over the open land.

Mary sighed, the sound hopeful in the gray dusk. 'You know, Uncle Cody, I don't have to be the only best thing that's ever happened to you.'

'What do you mean?' He took a stick and jabbed at some mud on the edge of his boot heel.

'Well, Stormy loves you as much as I do. I guess I've known you longer, so maybe that's more, but she definitely loves you, too. You know? If you'd promise not to be so ornery with her, she'd probably marry you.'

'It's not that simple, ladybug.'

'You're making it harder than it has to be,' she replied, with all the optimism of youth.

He wasn't sure. 'I don't think it would work out.'

They were silent for a moment.

'You know, this time I'm siding with Mary,' Carmen said. 'I think maybe you ought to give Stormy a chance to tell you no. Some time has passed. Things have changed. You don't know what is in her mind if you don't find out.'

Getting up from the porch, he shook his head and ground the cigar under his boot. 'Ma, don't you think Mary's grown up this fall?'

'I do. I couldn't wait to see her.'

Something told him he had to make tonight a special night, that the time alone they were sharing wouldn't come again for a while. 'We'll go out for a drive and a soda at the drive-through tonight if you two would like.'

'We'd like, Uncle Cody!' Mary cried happily.

'Sounds good.' His mother nodded.

'I'm going in.' He headed to the door before glancing back. 'I'm proud of you, ladybug. Thanks for the talk.'

'You're welcome, Uncle Cody.'

'Be ready in fifteen minutes,' he instructed.

Then he went inside. He pulled out the phone book and glanced through the pages. His heart pounded madly in his chest as he dialed the number.

'Reservations,' a woman said when she answered the phone. 'How can I help you?'

'I want to know if the flight tomorrow that is departing the airport for Africa is still scheduled for tomorrow afternoon.'

380

'I'll check, sir.'

A moment later, she gave him departing information, which he scribbled on a white pad before he thanked her and hung up. At his elbow, a voice spoke.

'You can see elephants at the zoo, Uncle Cody. You don't have to go all the way to Africa,' Mary pointed out, eyeing his scribbling.

'Never you mind, ladybug.' He tucked the paper into his jeans pocket.

'Is Stormy going to Africa?' Mary stared up at him curiously, as did his mother.

'You know, one thing about the two of you being gone, I kind of got used to my privacy,' he grumbled.

His mother nodded, but her eyes were lit with merriment. 'Change can be very good for a man.'

'He hasn't changed much,' Mary commented. 'He's still grouchy as all get out.'

'It's okay,' Carmen said, shooing Mary outside toward the truck. 'His lady seems to like him that way.'

Stormy waited tensely as the passengers filed on to the airplane. Her scalp prickled. For some reason, she was uneasy being on Cody's turf. It made her want to see him. Yet she didn't dare call his house. He had called her a couple of times since she'd lost the baby, but she'd been asleep, allowing the answering machine to take all the calls. She hadn't returned any of his messages, a fact that didn't make her proud. Guilt made her unable to face talking to him. Despair that their relationship could never work out kept her from telling him the words that she knew she should say to him. *I'm sorry. I was wrong.* Emotional cowardice was difficult to overcome.

She glanced up as a man buckled himself into the seat beside her. She stared at Cody in astonishment. 'What are you doing here?'

'Going to Africa. Brought a camera. I'm sure there's a lot I've never seen before.' He looked her over thoroughly, his gaze settling on the necklace at her throat. 'You're wearing my teeth.'

'Yes,' she whispered, hardly daring to believe that he was actually beside her. Her hands trembled; her blood raced like a wild horse's. 'Snake teeth seem to suit my personality. A man I once knew told me I was very unusual.'

'Looks good on you.' His heated gaze told her she was beautiful to him.

Her heart tightened. 'Why are you really doing this?'

'I had a good time in California.' He shrugged at her. 'I'll probably have an even better time in Africa. If you think you'll have time for me.' He leaned over and kissed her.

Gently, she pushed him slightly away. 'You don't even have a passport. You'd never been out of your own backyard before you came to California.'

'Wrong.' He flipped it out to show her proudly.

'I started the paperwork as soon as I got back from California.'

She examined it, half-afraid he was kidding. Wild hope flared inside her that his going meant what she wanted it to mean. 'Cody, there's something I have to tell you.'

'What?' He cocked an eyebrow at her.

With uncertain fingers, she traced the rough fabric of the seat. 'I'm sorry about everything. I was –'

He put his lips on hers, stopping her words. He kissed her long and deeply. 'I'd like to go forward from here,' he said as he pulled away gently from her mouth. 'If you think we can.'

Her heart caught, tightening with sheer happiness. 'I'd like to.'

'Can I get you to marry me, then?'

She wanted to believe, wanted it to work, but she didn't know how. 'I thought we agreed we didn't want a dual–state marriage. That it wouldn't work out.'

'Yeah, well.' Gently, he ran a hand along her cheek, 'Things change.'

'Like what?'

'I leased the ranch to Sloan. Need a new place to set my boots.'

'You did *what*?'

'Sloan needed a bigger spread to breed those spotted horses of his. Figure I can buy a place in California that'll suit me.'

Stormy's lips parted.

'I like it when you do that,' he said, leaning over to take advantage of her open mouth.

'But what about earthquakes and hippies and pollution?' she demanded when she could breath again.

'I'll deal with'em just the same as I did rattle-snakes and droughts and movie scouts that strayed on to my land.'

Tears filled her eyes. 'I can't let you do that.'

'I make my own decisions.'

She smiled through happy tears. 'I know you do. But your ranch is too important to you.'

'*You* are too important to me.' He shrugged and belted her seat belt for her. 'There's a catch, though. Ma wants to come with me. She thinks there'll be future *niños* to care for.' He swallowed down the painful lump in his throat and pressed forward. 'And Mary wants to come out in the summers for acting lessons and such.'

'Oh, my,' she breathed. 'I'd love all of that. Are you absolutely sure about this?'

'I am.' He nodded. 'If you won't mind having my family. Guess it's a package deal, if you take me on.'

'I would be so happy. It would make me feel like . . . I had a real home. My mom will love your mom,' she said decisively. 'They're both so unique.'

He laughed at the sassy grin on her face, the expression he loved more than any other. 'If we decide to change our mind one day and move back,

384

I can always boot Sloan out. Or keep him,' he said on a sudden thought. 'There's plenty of room to build another house and I could use a paying tenant.'

'Can this really be happening to me?' she asked, her gray iris eyes wide-open with dreamy amazement.

He thought he could see a future of happiness shining in her gaze, and it warmed his heart. She made him feel like a king with the power to make her dreams come true. He leaned back in the chair but kept his hand on hers. 'You know, I've always wanted a hacienda-style house.'

'Oh, yes. Yes!' She smiled at him, but then the smile slowly melted away. Her eyes serious, she said, 'I never told you I needed you, Cody. But I do.

'I know you do. You're a helpless female.' But he said it in a teasing manner and held her hand against his chest. 'It means a lot to hear you say it. I love you being your own woman, but I gotta feel like there's something for me to do in our marriage. A part for me to share in.'

'There's lots that we can share. I had many empty places in me that you've helped fill,' she said, meaning it. 'I can't believe you're going to Africa with me.'

He grinned at her, proud that he'd finally put one over on her. 'You never figured me out, Trouble. I may be crazy, but I'm not stupid enough to try to live without the woman I love.

385

I can't keep feeling this twisted up. Guess that means I'm in love with you. Good enough?'

She smiled. 'Yes. I love you, Cowboy.'

'I know. I'm an easy man to love. You, on the other hand, are a difficult woman.'

'I'm easier than you are!' she exclaimed.

'I was hoping you'd say that,' he said, slanting his mouth against hers for another quick kiss. 'We'll debate that one when we get back home.'

'There's no need to debate.' She gave him a wicked grin and grabbed his shirt collar to tug him back for another kiss. 'You win.'

'Mm.' He accepted the kiss she gave him and framed her face with his fingers. 'How shall I celebrate this victory?'

She whispered an idea into his ear and Cody grinned at her before pulling her close. 'Whew! That's a heck of an IOU, woman.' He exhaled on a ragged breath. 'And to think I once wanted to be a bachelor forever.'

'Crazy, huh?' She raised her brows and smiled teasingly.

'There's crazy and then there's crazy.' As the plane moved away from the gate, he held her hand in his. 'Did I ever tell you I used to be afraid of flying?'

She shook her head and squeezed his hand in commiseration. 'No, you didn't. What happened?'

He gazed into her eyes, knowing that all he'd ever needed was this woman in his life for the long haul. 'I came to my senses after I met a special, one-of-a-kind lady.'

'And that was all it took?'

He grinned at her. 'That, and jumping out of a second-story window.'

THE EXCITING NEW NAME IN WOMEN'S FICTION!

PLEASE HELP ME TO HELP YOU!

Dear *Scarlet* Reader,

I have some wonderful news for you this month – we are beginning a super Prize Draw, which means that you ***could win an exclusive sassy Scarlet T-shirt!*** Just fill in your questionnaire and return it to us (see addresses at the end of the questionnaire) before 31 November 1998, and we'll do the rest! If you are lucky enough to be one of the first four names out of the hat each month, we will send you this exclusive prize.

So don't delay – return your form straight away!*

Looking forward to hearing from you,

Sally Cooper

Editor-in-Chief, *Scarlet*

QUESTIONNAIRE

Please tick the appropriate boxes to indicate your answers

1 Where did you get this Scarlet title?
   Bought in supermarket ☐
   Bought at my local bookstore ☐ Bought at chain bookstore ☐
   Bought at book exchange or used bookstore ☐
   Borrowed from a friend ☐
   Other (please indicate) _____

2 Did you enjoy reading it?
   A lot ☐   A little ☐   Not at all ☐

3 What did you particularly like about this book?
   Believable characters ☐   Easy to read ☐
   Good value for money ☐   Enjoyable locations ☐
   Interesting story ☐   Modern setting ☐
   Other _____

4 What did you particularly dislike about this book?
   _____

5 Would you buy another Scarlet book?
   Yes ☐   No ☐

6 What other kinds of book do you enjoy reading?
   Horror ☐   Puzzle books ☐   Historical fiction ☐
   General fiction ☐   Crime/Detective ☐   Cookery ☐
   Other (please indicate) _____

7 Which magazines do you enjoy reading?
   1. _____
   2. _____
   3. _____

And now a little about you –
8 How old are you?
   Under 25 ☐   25–34 ☐   35–44 ☐
   45–54 ☐   55–64 ☐   over 65 ☐

cont.

9 What is your marital status?
Single ☐   Married/living with partner ☐
Widowed ☐   Separated/divorced ☐

10 What is your current occupation?
Employed full-time ☐   Employed part-time ☐
Student ☐   Housewife full-time ☐
Unemployed ☐   Retired ☐

11 Do you have children? If so, how many and how old are they?

_____

_____

12 What is your annual household income?

under $15,000	☐	or	£10,000	☐
$15–25,000	☐	or	£10–20,000	☐
$25–35,000	☐	or	£20–30,000	☐
$35–50,000	☐	or	£30–40,000	☐
over $50,000	☐	or	£40,000	☐

Miss/Mrs/Ms _____

Address _____

_____

_____

Thank you for completing this questionnaire. Now tear it out – put
it in an envelope and send it, before 31 December 1998, to:

Sally Cooper, Editor-in-Chief

USA/Can. address
SCARLET c/o London Bridge
85 River Rock Drive
Suite 202
Buffalo
NY 14207
USA

UK address/No stamp required
SCARLET
FREEPOST LON 3335
LONDON W8 4BR
*Please use block capitals for
address*

DESPER/6/98

Scarlet titles coming next month:

A TEMPORARY ARRANGEMENT   Margaret Callaghan
Businessman Alex Gifford is a fairly unusual parent. He
denies his young son James nothing – except affection.
When Stella starts her nannying job with him, he makes
it clear that this is part of her job! However, he is not
incapable of strong feelings – he wants her and he always
takes what he wants!

SECRETS RISING   Sally Steward
When Rebecca Patterson's parents die in an accident, she
discovers she was adopted. She enlists the help of private
investigator Jake Thornton to help find her biological
parents but he is reluctant, knowing her quest may not
end happily. And soon it becomes clear that someone else
doesn't want Rebecca to find out the truth . . .

**WE ARE PROUD TO ANNOUNCE THE JULY
PUBLICATION OF OUR FIRST _SCARLET_ HARD-
BACK**

DARK DESIRE   Maxine Barry
Determined, angry, clever, sexy and power-packed Haldane
Fox is a man with a mission. Fox plays with fire, but always
wins. Electra is very beautiful but, due to a traumatic past,
has dedicated herself to her career as an orchid grower.
When these two ambitious people meet, something's gotta
give and Electra is determined it won't be her.

JOIN THE CLUB!

Why not join the *Scarlet* Readers' Club – you can have four exciting new reads delivered to your door every other month for only £9.99, plus TWO FREE BOOKS WITH YOUR FIRST MONTH'S ORDER!

Fill in the form below and tick your two first books from those listed:

1. *Never Say Never* by Tina Leonard ☐
2. *The Sins of Sarah* by Anne Styles ☐
3. *Wicked in Silk* by Andrea Young ☐
4. *Wild Lady* by Liz Fielding ☐
5. *Starstruck* by Lianne Conway ☐
6. *This Time Forever* by Vickie Moore ☐
7. *It Takes Two* by Tina Leonard ☐
8. *The Mistress* by Angela Drake ☐
9. *Come Home Forever* by Jan McDaniel ☐
10. *Deception* by Sophie Weston ☐
11. *Fire and Ice* by Maxine Barry ☐
12 *Caribbean Flame* by Maxine Barry ☐

ORDER FORM

SEND NO MONEY NOW. Just complete and send to *SCARLET* READERS' CLUB, FREEPOST, LON 3335, Salisbury SP5 5YW

Yes, I want to join the *SCARLET* READERS' CLUB* and have the convenience of 4 exciting new novels delivered directly to my door every other month! Please send me my first shipment now for the unbelievable price of £9.99, plus my TWO special offer books absolutely free. I understand that I will be invoiced for this shipment and FOUR further *Scarlet* titles at £9.99 (including postage and packing) every other month unless I cancel my order in writing. I am over 18.

Signed ....

Name (IN BLOCK CAPITALS)..

Address (IN BLOCK CAPITALS)..

....

Town... **Post Code**.............................

Phone Number ....

As a result of this offer your name and address may be passed on to other carefully selected companies. If you do not wish this, please tick this box ☐.

*Please note this offer applies to UK only.